The Karma Booth

Jeff Pearce has had an eclectic career as a radio talk show host, a farm reporter (without ever seeing a farm), a ghostwriter for an Indian community newspaper and a journalism teacher in Burma. He has also written several works of historical non-fiction. He can be found on Twitter @jeffpropulsion

The Karma Booth

JEFF PEARCE

HARPER
Voyager

Harper*Voyager*
An imprint of HarperCollins*Publishers* Ltd
1 London Bridge Street
London SE1 9GF

www.harpervoyagerbooks.co.uk

This Paperback Original 2015

First published in Great Britain in ebook format by
Harper*Voyager* 2015

A catalogue record for this book
is available from the British Library

ISBN: 978-0-00-812059-7

Automatically produced by Atomik ePublisher from Easypress

Printed and bound in Great Britain

For Blair Cosgrove. My friend, my brother.

1

They used the word *execute* for Emmett Nickelbaum, and even though he was the first to experience the procedure, no one would ever think of him as a pioneer. Emmett Nickelbaum was the first death row inmate to go. He was to be exterminated, eradicated, expunged.

They had a harder time describing what happened after the execution—and what terminology to use for the new arrival.

Emmett Nickelbaum was a thirty-eight-year-old mechanic. Caucasian, born and raised on the edge of Morningside Heights in New York City, back when it wasn't impossible for a family to rent there, and he stood six foot four and had a build like a massive wall of solid, turn-of-the-century yellow brick. His coworkers at the garage where he worked—not his friends because he had no real friends—called him "The Fridge," as in the old 1950s models with door handles like bank vaults. Nickelbaum had thinning hair and wire-mesh stubble, his disheveled features only adding to the intimidating effect he had on people. An effect he had discovered as a teenager and enjoyed right up to the day of his last crime. When he broke into the Queens home of one of his garage's customers, she didn't stand a chance.

Twenty-four-year-old graphic designer Mary Ash was only five foot one and weighed a mere hundred and ten pounds. Nickelbaum was a mountain in shadow that didn't belong in the topography of her apartment, his huge palm covering her face and whipping her head into the wall with such force that the plaster broke.

The girl's roommate Sita was away for a holiday week visiting relatives in Birmingham, England—a fact police were sure saved her life. Nickelbaum kept Mary Ash prisoner for seventy-two hours, during which time he raped her repeatedly and amputated two of her fingers with an electric turkey carver. It was Fourth of July weekend when Nickelbaum was at his most depraved, and no one heard Mary's scream as the electrician's tape, wet from her feverish terrified sweat and worn from her mouth straining to cry out, at last peeled away. *Please*, Mary Ash cried out. Please, and then please again, please until she died.

Nickelbaum didn't mind at all filling in the details for police when they caught him. He had fantasized about causing Mary Ash pain, and the two police officers were sickened by the fact that under the cheap Formica table holding the Styrofoam coffee cups he had an erection as he described his victim's last moments. There had been brief controversy when Nickelbaum was selected to participate in a college study (for which his family members would be paid), answering questionnaires from psychologists on what made him tick. The study had been canceled after an embarrassing article in the *Times*. Then Emmett Nickelbaum turned up as a candidate for a far more unusual research project that didn't hit the papers and the TV news. Not then. And he would participate whether he liked it or not.

His execution was not formally announced, so there were no placards for or against his demise outside Sullivan Correction Facility in Fallsburg.

The booths. The booths taught Emmett Nickelbaum fear.

For the first time in his life, he understood that his fingers weren't tweezers designed to pincer shrieking, tiny, helpless things begging for their lives. Beads of sweat polished his bare forehead under the receding hairline, and his mouth opened wide. His limbs were flailing in the shackles, because there were *two* booths ahead of him, and that suggested something would be done to him that would make him into something else.

"What is this?" he asked. "What the fuck *is* this?" Again, his bass voice climbed octaves with his terror: "What's going on? You don't need that thing for a lethal injection, man! I just lie on a table, and they gimme a fuckin' needle! Where's the needle—where's the fuckin…? *What is this?*"

Nobody offered him an answer. No one cared particularly about Emmett Nickelbaum's comfort, certainly not whether he left this world at peace with his personal god or sobbing for his mother. His shackles were locked to the rail inside the booth on the left. A note was made that a minor sedative should make the prisoner more controllable during the final transfer, but the use of shackles wouldn't affect the procedure at all. Emmett Nickelbaum would not reappear like a magician's bunny in the second booth on the right.

Some of the witnesses felt an abstract relief that no pain was supposed to be experienced in the final few seconds of life (but no one asked to be *sure* for the sake of the monster forced into the chamber). As Emmett Nickelbaum stared wide-eyed through the blue tinted window of the booth—a dull anti-climactic chamber with a thick index of specially tinted glass—he did, indeed, feel dread.

Faces with spectacles studied him with an impersonal, clinical detachment—the same kind of detachment Nickelbaum gave Mary Ash as he tortured her, as he watched her face run a gamut of expressions of agony. Then a brilliant white light filled the booth, faintly tinged with a bluish hue. No one could mistake it for a beam from Heaven.

Instead, the light seemed to *carve* his body, split it open to show a darkness with pinpoints inside. There were whorls, nebulae; yet even this dazzling view was perverted with flashes of gangrenous skin, flesh made necrotic by whatever technical or divine force scooped him from the inside out. And the smell... The smell was horrible, as if rot had been amplified and sped up on a dial and then served up as a dish from a cold meat locker.

But they were told—

They were told it wasn't supposed to be a painful procedure.

No one said a word, watching from thirty feet away. It was agreed later that the inmate had screamed because of primitive terror, fear of death—not actual physical trauma. There was nothing, of course, to substantiate this assertion. The scientists simply wanted to believe it.

They also thought they would find something. Remains. Granules. Something. They didn't.

It would be a good day when Emmett Nickelbaum left the Earth, but that wasn't the only reason.

The light effect started in the second booth as they were busy examining the first. No one had typed on a keyboard, flicked a switch, turned a knob—done anything at all. No one had adjusted or touched the equipment or even considered it. They had been told to expect "a secondary effect" (whatever that meant), and that the booth on the right-hand side existed to contain this... whatever it was.

The whorls and flashes and peculiar reflections, the fading in and out of skin pigments, went on and on for the fascinated audience, and there was a different odor this time, defying description. Not a stench, thank God. Not a waft of destruction. Nobody dared to interrupt the process, even though none of them had no idea how long it would go on. And when it finished at last, they had company.

The researchers stepped forward even as the nude, pitiful figure backed up against the wall of the booth. A woman. Her head turned with feral, desperate sharpness, the eyes as frightened as those of Nickelbaum, but with the haunted blankness of a wandering refugee. Unwashed brown hair hung in her eyes, and when the girl's hand lifted to touch the glass—

"Sweet Jesus, it's *her*!" yelled one of the researchers. "It's her, it's her! *It's really her!*"

The hand had two small stumps caked with blood. Two missing fingers.

Mary Ash was back among the living.

Doctors rushed forward now, the room filling with rapid conversation addressed to no one specific. Orders and suggestions were all fired at once but only a precious few had the good sense to take action. Get her a gown. Get her a chair. For Christ's sake, doctor, shouldn't we get her to the prison infirmary? Noise from almost everyone except the returning victim herself.

Nickelbaum's execution had involved an experimental method, so it had been thought prudent not to invite members of the Ash family as witnesses. That meant her parents, her older brother who lived in Seattle—all the members of the Ash family—were absent for Mary's return from the dead. Her eyes darted from face to face of these strangers in front of her as she whimpered in shock. Her hands were up in a fetal prayer with her arms close to her body, too afraid even for the modesty of the gown.

"*Bbbbaaabbaaa… Bbbaaa!*"

She could manage nothing else for the next fifteen hours. The prison doctor gave her a sedative that put her to sleep, during which time the researchers and physicians and experts all decided Mary Ash should be transported back to New York City. She would be monitored and kept in protective custody, while her parents would be contacted and trusted to help Mary recover.

No one even knew who should make the announcement or how to announce what had happened. How do you announce a miracle anyway?

Three days before:

There was the usual ripple of chatter at the beginning. It was the moment when a lecture hall is no different than a movie house. But as the man at the front took his place near the podium, the students settled down.

The professor would have provoked interest even if he hadn't been waiting to speak. For one thing, he didn't wear the typical faculty uniform of tweedy blazer with jeans. His suit was a three–thousand-dollar Armani—tailored, of course. And to some, he looked far younger than expected. Many guessed he was about thirty-five years old. He was, in fact, forty-two. The blond hair was beginning to thin, but with the delicacy of his full lips and high cheekbones, he looked boyish. If he had smiled, the effect would have taken yet more years off his face. But he looked at them now with a severe, almost imperious gaze.

This was Professor Timothy Cale, and each semester, his courses on political science were oversubscribed.

"We participate," he started softly, "because we trust."

There was a long pause, and the students didn't look terribly impressed with this opener. A faint cough came from the back of the hall. Then the professor's voice rose, filling the room as if every one of them was insultingly dense not to comprehend what he'd just told them.

"We *participate* because we *trust*," he repeated.

Now they were all focused, each one of them very still in his or her seat, sharply aware they had better keep their attention.

"This room is a new country," the professor went on, now stepping away from the podium. He walked with expansive, long strides, and they imagined he really did intend to claim the room as some obscure sovereign nation. The voice kept hitting them with bullets of staccato emphasis. "I've told you before: every day you walk in here, you will surrender your assumptions to my baggage check of your ignorance, which I assure you is *monumental*."

Then Timothy Cale stepped out of the front area and walked briskly up a couple of steps into the aisle between the seats. He stopped at the second row and yanked a book from the little desk of a student, holding it up for all the others to see.

"Look at this, a biography of Chairman Mao," explained the professor, as he walked down towards the podium. "Good ol' Mao Zedong. 'Power comes from the barrel of a gun.' Oh, really? Bullshit."

He made a point of tossing the book into a trashcan.

"If that was all there was to it, there wouldn't be any literature. Any innovation—hell, there would be no change *at all*. People—we, the governed—may grant or withhold the one thing that cannot be stolen: our trust. We participate because we trust. And we will trust when we can participate. So how do we? How do you define yourself as a citizen? Machiavelli did not just write *The Prince*. In his *Discourses*, he explained that—"

A cell phone erupted in the middle aisles, obnoxiously playing a hip-hop mix. Tim Cale glowered at the twenty-five-year-old football linebacker in the vividly bright polo shirt and track pants.

"Mr. Harding, please bring that down to the front."

The student fumbled with the phone. "I'll turn it off, sorry—"

"No, Mr. Harding. Bring it here."

Shamefaced, the football star came forward like a ten-year-old caught chewing gum. He surrendered the phone to his professor, who efficiently and quickly removed the SIM card and smashed both it and the phone.

"Hey, that's my fucking phone, man! You know how much it cost?"

"Far less than what your father paid for your wasted education, Mr. Harding," the young-looking professor answered. "And this new land that you're in is not a democracy."

But the student didn't know when to quit. "*New country?* So you can do what you like? Fuck that! It's ridiculous!"

Tim shoved his hands into the pockets of his gray trousers and strolled away from the furious linebacker. He was talking to the others now. "Is it so ridiculous? Let me ask—sit down, Mr. Harding. *Sit.* You either comply or face exile from the kingdom. Let me ask all of you: How many people—and at what point when they develop an organization—does it take before you recognize them as a state?"

The students looked to each other, none wanting to debate or challenge him. Barely anyone paid attention to Harding slinking back to his seat. At last, one of their ranks ventured a challenge.

"It's… silly. I mean, it's like, preposterous. With a political state, you know, you got history, you got geography—"

"I have tenure here," Tim cut in, his voice gentle and reasonable. "Same lecture hall I've always taught in. Why can't I be a state?"

With a shrug, the challenger decided to press on. "You already gave us the answer."

"Which is what, Mr. Bell?"

"Maybe we don't trust you."

There was a wave of nervous laughter helping to break the tension and then a sprinkling of appreciative applause.

"I mean, hey, you're an authority," added Bell. "You've demonstrated force, that's all."

"But you *are* participating," Tim pointed out.

"Because we need something from you. We want to learn, so we go along for a while. That doesn't make us citizens—or subjects."

Tim nodded, apparently pleased with the brave reasoning. "Very good. Mr. Bell here has lived in Europe. He knows what it's like to tolerate the rules of others. Oh, don't look embarrassed by it, Mr. Bell. Okay! Okay, here, *right here* is our problem in these United States! And it's in all of you. The assumption that worldly means 'privileged'—that you should actually be *embarrassed* for being smart and having seen other countries."

Tim scanned the rows of faces, seemingly taking them all in and tossing them back, shaking his head as he began to pace again. "Less than twenty-five percent of Americans own a passport, and to me, that is *pathetic*. It means you trust CNN and Fox News more than you want to go see what's out there! Now some in this room want to go save Third World orphans—when you probably couldn't get out of Newark airport if you tried."

He made a point of stopping in front of a lovely young redhead in the first row. Her eyes flicked left and right, and she settled on a patch of the broadloom carpet. Tim mercifully walked on, his stare fixed now on one of the male students in the back row.

"Some of you—God help us—want to run for political office."

Before the others could be sure exactly who he meant, he was already moving on, walking up the aisle and stopping in the middle.

"Some of you are *hiding*. You think education is camouflage, and a degree is a passport. Perhaps. But in this room, you will learn to *think*. And your understanding of what a nation is, what power is, will be broadened as we go along. For instance, how many people here believe in non-violence?"

There was a substantial show of hands from the seats. Tim let out a cruel laugh.

"What a delightful bunch of liberal pussies!"

There was more nervous laughter at this, but above it all was a new whispered chatter over his language.

"Oh, my words are offensive? They're sexist? If you can't handle words, how can you possibly help a man tortured in a cell or who's got a rifle to his head? Every political action in history began as an extreme. Passive resistance is *passive*."

"That's not true!" piped up a girl in the seventh row. "People filled Tiananmen Square and—"

"And what, Ms. Wong? They sat. *Woooowwww!* And when the tanks rolled in a few thousand of your distant relatives got shot. As I recall, you told me your parents immigrated here in 1989. Well, did they leave because they *won*? Do you ever ask them what morally questionable things they had to do so that little Michelle could get her degree in America?"

She glared at him, not bothering to answer.

"Gandhi admitted he could never fight Hitler with his methods," the professor continued. "Why? Because non-violence relies on shame. What if your enemy feels no shame? Non-violence is a political response to a matter of warfare. It means you are not willing to do everything you can for your noble goals, so how important were they? No? Anybody?"

The students traded looks, checking up and down the aisles, and just as it became clear that no one had a response for this, their professor pointed his finger at them like a gun.

"*Bang.*"

As the students filed out of the lecture hall, Timothy Cale packed up his reference texts and files. He was mildly annoyed by the man shifting from foot to foot, hanging back reluctantly like a slow buzzing insect at the edge of his peripheral vision. The man wore a boxy suit with a flat texture, the kind that was a wife's compromise purchased at Sears. He had a weak chin and watery eyes, and his black hair was going silver. He was a man in his late forties who gave the opposite physical impression of Tim—aging faster than he actually was. Everything about him looked like it had been arrived at by compromise.

"Professor, my name's Schlosser. I was sent out by the Justice Department."

If he expected Tim to give him his full attention, he was disappointed. A student with the typical self-absorption of his years pushed forward and asked the professor a question about his thesis. Tim frowned as he flipped through a Steno notebook packed with scribbles, and then he rattled off a time for the afternoon.

"So McInerny must be sending you on this errand," said Tim, already heading for the door.

"No, it goes higher."

"Weatherford then," said Tim, stopping in mild surprise. He made it sound more like an accepted fact than a question.

Schlosser nodded. "Yes, Weatherford. This is right from the top."

Tim arched his eyebrows then started walking again. Schlosser moved fast to grab the door as Tim let go of it, not caring if it slammed in his visitor's face.

"Do you actually believe the ideas you suggested in there?"

Tim allowed himself a tiny smile, perhaps over an inside joke known only to him.

"Mr. Schlosser, don't be obtuse. My job here is to get these cognitive amputees to actually construct a logical thought—perhaps for the first time in their iPad-carrying, game-playing, Netflix-watching lives. Go ask a university student in Vietnam or Zimbabwe what democracy is, and he probably can't give you a textbook definition, but he won't be apathetic in searching for an answer. He'll be invested."

Schlosser shrugged, a way of saying fair enough. "The department has a job for you, but it's not about politics."

"Then don't ask me how I teach political science."

Schlosser bristled. This wasn't the reception he'd expected: curiosity, perhaps even gratitude, maybe a polite rejection with an acknowledgment that it was flattering to be asked. Not this rudeness. Timothy Cale didn't even wait. He was already heading into the hall.

"I asked about your theories because they'll listen—the cabinet secretaries will listen, I mean—in part to what *I* have to say about you," said Schlosser. He tried not to walk so quickly that it was obvious he was struggling to keep up.

Tim was merciless. "No, they won't. The ones making the decisions already know who I am and everything relevant in my career. McInerny does, Briggs does. You showed up on my doorstep because *you* wanted to put your two cents in, and you didn't have anything on paper about me that hadn't made the rounds and could be assessed by others. You need something *new.*"

He suddenly stopped walking and stood in place, waiting for Schlosser to grant his point. Schlosser licked his lips, glanced down the long hallway at the students making their way to classes, and wondered why his impulse was to deny the truth. They had warned him that Timothy Cale had insight. But they had said nothing about him having a laser that bored right into you and got to the heart of your intentions.

"You want to tell me what this job is now so I can say no and stop wasting both our time?"

"No, Professor. Let's talk about India."

"If they had any lingering concerns over India, they wouldn't have sent you. And technically, it was barely in India. It was on the border."

"I have concerns."

"Go to hell."

"You'll want this job, Professor."

"I have a job, thanks," said Tim, on the move again and quickening his step. "And I actually have no ambitions to return to diplomatic service—or to work for government in any other capacity again." He pushed hard on the door leading to the green lawn of the courtyard.

Schlosser followed him out to the sunshine. "You'd be a private contractor on this one."

"Don't care. If they let a paper-pusher like you ask about that incident then that's enough to suggest there would be more interference."

"This is the last time you see me," said Schlosser. "As for how others interact with you... Well, I can't make any guarantees. You'd be well compensated."

Another cocky smile. "I make enough now when I see corporate clients."

Schlosser had disliked the man from his department bio, and he despised him thoroughly now. He felt no one should ever be fully confident in his own security. It allowed him the privilege of indulging his own beliefs instead of following carefully developed policies. When he got back to Washington, he promised himself he would complain about being assigned the task of enabling such a man.

"There are other rewards to consider, Mr. Cale."

"Oh, this is rich! An appeal to my intellectual vanity?"

"Not your vanity, Professor. Curiosity. Now assuming they take you on with my recommendation, you'll do this job not for your own ambition or for any monetary gain, but so you can learn certain things—perhaps some things you've wanted to know for a long time."

Tim didn't break stride, looking straight ahead. "*That's* a hell of a display of logic! Jump to conclusions of motive before you're sure of my course of action! Mr. Schlosser, in less than five minutes, we've learned only two things. One is that you don't know me, and two is that you're a pompous ass."

Schlosser was tired of both the walk and the verbal humiliation. "You're right, I don't know you, but Dr. Weintraub claims he does. He says you'll be interested."

Tim stopped again. "Weintraub could have phoned me himself."

"Departmental formalities."

"Uh-huh. Meaning Weintraub recommended me, but this has to go through the department... whatever it's really about.

Go back to Washington, Schlosser. Tell them I'll speak with the Attorney General myself. *Direct*. I'll send my fee request to his office."

Schlosser pulled out his cell. "Okay, I'll phone and get you the email for his executive assistant."

"Don't need it. I have Weatherford's own email."

"Mr. Cale, I don't know why I ask, since it sounds like I already have the answer," sighed Schlosser, "but they'll want to know: What are your views on capital punishment?"

"I'll make them clear if I ever wind up having to kill somebody," snapped Tim. "It's amazing you can move around at all, Schlosser, dragging all those assumptions around."

"You never answered my question."

"If *they* want to know, they can ask me themselves," replied Tim. "And you wouldn't believe me anyway."

He turned on his heel and left Schlosser standing there.

There were only four witnesses to the Nickelbaum execution that weren't in lab coats. One was the warden. A second was the administrative and theoretical head of the R and D team, Gary Weintraub. The third was a general electrician in overalls, a fellow who had no idea what was going on and was there just in case the power was lost or there was an electrical fire. And like the warden, he had signed a legal statement that prohibited him from telling anyone what he saw. The fourth person was the least known to the scientists, Timothy Christopher Cale.

When the murderer disappeared in the carvings of light and the wretched figure of Mary Ash was led out of the booth like a frightened animal, Tim Cale was as shocked as anyone else—and the most quiet person in the room.

He supposed the researchers had a right to be curious about him because, only two hours before, the head of their team,

Gary Weintraub, had ushered him around without volunteering what he did or why he was there. The researchers all assumed he was a bureaucrat sent to babysit, so they sneered the "Mister" next to his name as if it were an insult. Tim's sense of mischief was tempted to correct them, but he had seen enough class and status nonsense to last him a lifetime back when he was posted in London. And today had given him much to think about, just like the others. He decided to be self-effacing in the circle of experts and lab coats, not gushing over the astonishing thing they had just witnessed and not congratulating them at all.

As doctors accompanying the young girl left for the private hospital in Manhattan, the remaining witnesses filed into a conference room, and Tim joined the slow exodus to a long table. They could barely contain what they felt, and few wanted to sit. This was one of the rare moments when scientists could be children again.

Tim watched them whisper and talk, voices climbing over each other, pairs of hands gesticulating. Others scribbled down estimates and equations. One of them—there would always be one—was the oracle of caution, suggesting the phenomenon might not be easily repeated. Weintraub, now free to talk about certain details more candidly, was busy saying things like "No, no, it will work again."

Tim already knew Weintraub from university symposiums and presidential committees. He was a man in his sixties with a moon face and spectacles who didn't mind at all that his students had nicknamed him "Bunsen Honeydew" after *The Muppets* character. Weintraub had first achieved fame as a documentary host, and since the media liked physicists to be interesting personalities (it was easier than trying to understand what they said), much was made of his distinctive nasal voice, his amateur skill at jazz piano and how as a young man he'd made a pilgrimage to study with one of his scientific heroes, the equally eccentric Leó Szilárd (when Szilárd didn't like someone, he liked to pull out his colostomy bag and show them). Weintraub was arguably the smartest man in the room. Tim Cale was certain he was.

The multiple conversations grew to an insect hum, and at last Weintraub raised his hands.

"Okay, okay, first of all, there is no possible way I can expect this won't leak out, legal documents or not," he said, wearing the same self-congratulatory smile as the staff. "We do have an official announcement drafted and a news conference scheduled—we prepared all this in advance in case things went well."

A new buzz around the table: their director had apparently known what to expect, while the others had been left mostly in the dark. But the lab coats' resentment couldn't last. It was crushed to insignificance by what they had seen.

"The media doesn't always go through proper channels so if you are asked, please, *please*, be careful in your use of language. Don't use any words of religious connotation—I'm sure they'll happily go overboard on those themselves. Make sure they understand we followed a procedure, and it won't be up to us how the transposition booths are assigned. That's a matter for the courts and the legislators."

"We don't even have to go there, do we, Gary?" piped up one of the scientists. "Don't we have years of research ahead of us before we try to repeat what we saw?"

The arguments and counter-arguments all ran for a few seconds with Weintraub unable to restore order.

"Come on, how do you test and research *this*? What we've got to do is ensure the safety of an arrival who—"

17

"People will not want to wait for years of clinical—"

"Look at in vitro fertilization and the stigma that was attached to—"

"You can't compare the social history of decades ago to a completely new radical—"

"*How does it work?*"

The most innocent and direct of questions came from their guest. There was a sudden hush around the conference table, all the scientists now facing Timothy Cale. And he saw a remarkable, almost tangible shame in their expressions. I'll be damned, thought Tim.

Because he realized: *They don't know.*

Weintraub spoke for them all. "We're not completely sure."

"Meaning you don't have a clue, right, Gary?"

He and Weintraub liked each other. Tim knew Weintraub didn't have a molecule of condescension in his body for laymen, nor was his ego so fragile that he couldn't admit to ignorance. They could speak plainly here.

"What you must understand, Tim, is that we had nothing to do with the manufacture of the transposition equipment or its original R and D," replied Weintraub.

"*What?* Are you *kidding?*"

"I assure I'm not. We served as oversight on its health and safety aspects and on the scientific evaluation. Washington gave the green light, and we went ahead and… Well, we needed to figure out protocols, to make sure it does what we were promised it will do…"

Tim was incredulous. His friend hadn't given him a clue what he would see today, and neither, in fact, had Schlosser or those out in Washington. He had expected a bit of a magic act from Gary Weintraub—he always got one. The man's theatrical flair was part of his professional success both on campuses and on television. But nothing like this, nothing with such ramifications!

"Now wait a minute," Tim tried again. "How can you go ahead with something this momentous without knowing how the damn thing fundamentally works?"

"Hey, uh, Mr. Cale," interrupted one of the scientists, an up-and-coming physics star who looked barely old enough to shave. "Before Gary answers that, can you, like, tell us a little bit more about what *you* do and how you came to be here?"

Tim smiled at the naked challenge. "If it helps, I'm here at the request of both the US Attorney General and the Secretary of Health and Human Services. I'm a consultant."

"What kind of consultant, Mr. Cale?"

"The expensive kind."

There was hesitant laughter over the quip, but the faces were so earnest, he knew he should offer a more definitive response. After all, he was asking them plain enough questions.

He made eye contact around the table and explained, "My career is somewhat eclectic, ladies and gentlemen. I used to be with diplomatic services stationed overseas, posted at various legations—mostly in Asia. I conducted investigations that involved any high-profile American national. But over time, I've fallen into what can loosely be called, for lack of a better term, 'risk management.' I don't pretend at all I have your scientific background or anything close it, but because of umm… well, a few personal experiences, which I won't go into today, the White House likes to use me from time to time to write reports and investigate certain phenomena—though up to now nothing on the scale of what we all saw today."

The young expert who had challenged Tim leaned forward. "And where did you have these *experiences*, Mr. Cale?"

Tim looked down the table and met his gaze evenly. "India... South East Asia."

Tim knew the smirks would begin first and then the traded looks. He had seen it all before, and he didn't care. He didn't have to prove his credibility here or with the White House, certainly not at the contract price he was charging, and there were fortunately others in positions of influence who were less dogmatic.

"Dr. Weintraub?" he prompted. "Gary? About my question?"

Weintraub leaned forward to respond, but another of the scientists jumped in.

"Listen, Mr. Cale. Tim, is it? Tim, there have been countless scientific innovations where the discovery and our reaping of benefits preceded our full understanding. Penicillin for one—"

"I am familiar with the history of penicillin, thank you, Mister...?"

"*Doctor* Andrew Miller," answered the scientist. "I'm team leader for Gary's neuroscience division."

His straight brown hair almost reached his shoulders, looking like it could use a wash, and his large hazel eyes were fierce in their direct stare. No doubt, he used all this Byronic intensity with girls. Tim knew his type from his university classes.

"Good for you, but I know about penicillin, *Doctor* Miller," Tim said calmly. "That was a time when—"

Miller wasn't listening. "Fine then, look at the recent tests that demonstrate adrenaline can play a factor in memory. We don't fully understand them, but they began with mice running around a drum full of water. Drug trials went ahead even though researchers didn't know exactly what was going on. Look at atomic energy—"

The Karma Booth

"Maybe that's a bad example," one of the scientists interjected.

"Hippie!" joked Miller, and he got a good laugh.

"We're talking for the moment about applications ahead of full comprehension of potential," said Weintraub, wanting to get them back on track.

"There is only one application," said Miller. He sighed as if satisfied with his judgment and laced his fingers behind his head. "We've seen its potential. We know it! We know the results."

"*Really?*" asked Tim.

Miller leaned back in his chair and pushed a sneaker against the edge of the table, tilting his chair back. "Frankly, even if we did understand the scientific process behind this machinery, it wouldn't be a good idea to tell you. I don't mean *you* personally—I mean any layman."

"Make it personal if you like," answered Tim. "What's your rationale in keeping it secret?"

The rest of those seated around the conference table could hardly believe the naïveté of the question. There were gasps and pens tossed on notepads, more squeaking of pushed chairs and mutters under the breath.

"You've got to be kidding!" sneered Miller. "We're going to catch enough flak from people bitching and whining the old saw that 'just because you *can* do a thing doesn't mean you *should* do it.' Jesus... You want this process out there where it can be abused?"

"That isn't where I'm going," replied Tim. "And your logic is flawed. You assume that by limiting those knowledgeable to a select few, the technology isn't vulnerable to abuse. But here's the thing."

He had their attention.

"By not explaining the science, making it absolutely crystal clear how this thing works, you already begin an abuse of the technology. It makes the whole apparatus into a kind of Ouija board—something occult. It's the natural product of ignorance."

Miller drummed his pen on the table and tipped his chair back another inch.

"Ignorance is something we've always had to tolerate."

He glanced around the table and smiled to the other faces, but they were unconvinced. Tim thought he looked too young to have tolerated much of anything yet.

He rose to leave. He could see he would get nowhere with them for the moment. "I'm sorry, I've worked several years in diplomacy, but I have to say that's one of the most irresponsible, stupid things I've ever heard. You're *scientists*. You're not supposed to tolerate ignorance—you're supposed to cure it. Oh, and trust me, time has a nice way of curing hubris."

2

India. But not India. Not quite. It was what changed every-thing for him, and it was likely why the government needed him now. *Let's talk about India*, that government man had asked him. What was his name? Schlosser. But he didn't talk about India with anybody.

Timothy Cale had been at his mid-level posting in Delhi for a year when the American embassy got a strange request to mediate in a violent ethnic clash. Of course, the details were so few as to be practically useless for any preparation. He was told that a remote village on the border between Nepal and the Indian state of Bihar had been invaded by a group of rebels, their exact affiliation vague and obscure.

It wasn't clear to him even why a US representative should get involved in what seemed like an internal dispute, espe-cially when there were no obvious American interests. It didn't matter. He would go. Sure, the assignment was at his discretion, and as one of the principal secretaries of the embassy, he could have easily turned it down. In looking back on it later, he cursed his own ambition and an almost juvenile urge for thrill-seeking. His Paris and London appointments had been junior postings, but it was the locales that held the glamour, not the office work itself: pushing papers, handling tourist complaints and making sure the colleges for overseas students were behaving themselves. This might be something substantial.

As he boarded an ancient-looking Bombardier turboprop commercial plane, he secretly hoped for adventure, with the equally childish wish that, of course, he'd come out on top and his resolution of the affair would help his career.

All he knew of Bihar he had picked up from the backgrounders written up in neat Times Roman 12 point type from the policy office and from his dog-eared *Lonely Planet India* guide. He stepped off a plane into Patna, gasping over the pollution and the rampant poverty, which was clear from the minute a US Consulate limo picked him up in the Bankipur district. It would take him to where he would rendezvous with an armed Indian escort for the next leg of his journey.

He got a fleeting glimpse of the Ganges, and then the city became another Third World blur with naked, dirty children, a clamor of street noise and sizzling grills for kiosk food, all contrasting sharply with the opulence of the modern glass castles for the city's rich businessmen. There were pungent spices. There was the almost crippling stench of decaying shit in the alleys and backed up sewers, and the coppery smell of stale blood—whether from accident or violent robbery, you could never tell and didn't want to know. Auto-rickshaws buzzed like dragonflies near the Ashok Rajpath, the main market.

Bihar was practically marinated in religion—the Buddha had walked this countryside, and there were lavish Hindu festivals to last you for ages. The last, tenth Guru of Sikhism was born right in Patna. A cynic would have enjoyed pointing out the fact that, amid all this faith, the province had an appalling rate of illiteracy, poverty, inter-caste warfare. The Bihari people faced a revolting degree of bigotry and ridicule in the rest of India.

And here he was, the fair-haired American boy from Illinois, thinking himself sophisticated after his years in Paris and London and a brief stint in Bangkok. *Fool.* He knew nothing. But that didn't stop him. And where he was going was a dot on the map with the name of a Bihari–Nepalese subgroup of a people, a similar but unique culture with a name he couldn't even pronounce, on the knife edge of a border. A no man's land that would make even the Himalayas—so many miles away but still familiar from photos and news reports—a touchstone of reassuring normalcy.

He was briefed in minutes that "the situation hasn't changed," and he didn't even get the chance to ask what the hell the situation was before the Indian soldiers in their neatly pressed khaki uniforms insisted he climb into the SUV. It was monsoon season, but they would have good luck with the roads—little report of flooding. Just potholes.

He couldn't detect the passage of time. Bumped and rocked for hours, with only brief rest stops, he tried unsuccessfully to doze and ignore a pounding headache as the rain hit the vehicle's roof in torrents. There were streaks of glistening drops across the windows, while bullets of moisture dug into the brown soil and made the road into a slippery obstacle course. It was late at night when the engine stopped, and the five Indian soldiers reached for their rifles, the interpreter telling him, "This is it."

"It" was a village of ramshackle houses and a few lights, with a single two-story Victorian building up on a hill and a ring of dark silhouettes, waiting.

His escort had rifles. He could see none carried by the "rebels."

But there were bodies at their feet. Men and women in what looked like traditional clothing, woolen caps and coats associated more with the Nepalese than the northern Bihari. They lay on their backs or with their faces in the mud, and they were all paler than corpses. Tim had seen dead, and this looked worse than dead. Those whose faces weren't obscured by the brown clay of the soil held an expression of demented shock, mouths slack and open. Frozen.

He stopped at one victim then turned to one of the soldiers and asked to borrow his flashlight. If the shadows up ahead had waited this long for their mediator, they could spare a few more seconds. Tim shone the beam of the flashlight on the dead man at his feet. He was clearly Asiatic, yet his eyes, wide in horror, were a vivid Nordic blue.

He swung the beam of light to a woman sprawled a few feet away. Her eyes were open as well. On the blurry halo edge of the light, he could see all of their eyes were open, each and every one of the victims lying dead on their backs or on their sides staring into nothing.

And each one had vividly blue eyes.

He knew next to nothing about genetics, but his instinct told him that was impossible, even as a hereditary trait in a relatively closed community. He read somewhere that doctors believed that light triggered the production of melanin in the irises of newborn babies—it was why baby eyes change color over time. Disease, injury—they could affect eye color, too. But this…

He had no idea what it meant, or if it meant anything at all.

Set after set of bright blue eyes, staring.

It magnified the rictus of horror on each face. The expressions looked almost canine, animalistic in their dread, and their decomposing skin was beginning to look waxy under the constant monsoon shower.

"Mr. Cale," called the interpreter. It was a faintly disguised plea. In other words, let's get the hell away from this place.

Only they couldn't. They were going to meet those who did this.

Their hosts didn't raise any weapons at the soldiers. One of them simply lifted a hand in the universal sign that meant: This is as far as you go. Then the man in the center turned a palm up, closing it with a flip-flip-flip for Tim to step forward. As the interpreter followed half a step behind, a flat baritone voice told the man in fluent English, "Your services won't be needed."

Tim was grateful to at least be out of the downpour. He was led into a sad-looking structure with stained plywood walls but with a tent roof, the light provided by a Coleman camping lamp. He was waved to a rough-hewn table. His chair was the most beautiful thing in the room, elaborately carved, as if by a traditional master craftsman.

Now he at last had a chance to study who was responsible for the crisis, but these people's clothing and manners told him little. Men and women stood in religious robes like those worn by monks—except their color scheme was unusual, not like anything Tim had seen on monks in other countries. They weren't saffron or gold; instead, a mauve and forest green shade that seemed to bleed into the backdrop of the squalid room. And over the robes, they wore traditional woolen vests and jackets and brightly colored scarves of the local people as protection from the weather. Yet somehow they acted as if they barely felt the rain or wind at all.

There were a few young ones, but the older ones stood out to him, their eyes like doll beads and their ruddy golden cheeks lined and cracked with thousands of minute folds and character lines. The man who had beckoned to him took the lead, sitting down in front of Tim, his forehead half in shade, half in light from the lamp. Tim found it difficult to detect an actual personality to the man's face, it was so tortoise-like, ancient and mummified; yet the smile was guardedly polite and the eyes were alert.

Tim was vaguely perplexed over why the man still wore his set of woolen mittens indoors, his sleeves pulled tight to the wrists, as if he felt a chill specifically reserved for him. The gloved hands rested casually on the scratched, worn table.

"Mr. Cale."

Curls of incense smoke floated between them from pink joss sticks planted in a wide pan to catch the ashes. The air was thick with the aroma of sandalwood.

"Listen," Tim started. "I won't pretend to understand the history of your conflict with these people, but if you'll outline your grievances, maybe we can find some common ground. My goal here is to avoid any more bloodshed. Now if you'll tell me who you—"

"That's not important," said a woman near the doorway.

"Especially when you don't know who these people are," said a boy on the other side, close to a corner. He couldn't have been older than thirteen, his golden face round and smooth, almost androgynous.

All three fluent in English. With no accent.

"We will tell you who these people are," said the tortoise-head ancient at the table. "We will tell why they have to die and why some have already died."

"I came all this way to prevent death," explained Tim.

"That is not your function here," said the woman near the door.

Before Tim could ask the obvious follow-up, the man at the table was speaking, his voice vaguely hypnotic with its evenness, and Tim found himself struggling to see him through the veil of incense smoke.

"This village exterminates its girl children. In ages past, it left them to die of exposure in the surrounding hills or took them down to a river to drown them. They spared a few for dowry marriage and breeding and servants. But no love thrived here for daughters, Mr. Cale. When doctors could offer amniocentesis, the villagers used that to prevent girl children. Last year, they sold a group of girls—some as young as four—to a pedophile ring that offers its wares between Sonepur and Kathmandu. Their evils singe and putrefy the air. And there is not one blameless adult, not one that is not stained by this barbarism."

"So your solution to the stain is ethnic cleansing?" demanded Tim quietly. He was incredulous. "Damn it, it's clear you're educated people! And you must *know* these things happen in the rest of India, in other parts of the world. Why are you talking about wiping out an entire village? And who *are* you people?" He calmed down, realizing it must be only a threat. He was here, and if he was here, that meant nothing was decided. "What do you want? What are your terms?"

"There are no terms," said the woman at the door.

"We've explained our reasons," said the boy in the corner.

"At certain times, there can arise a collective evil," said the man at the table. "The rot grows and eats, feeding like mold off the soul of a land. It is not a question, Mr. Cale, of what needs to be done. The course of action will take place."

He didn't understand. They were talking. He could hear them talking, yes, but competing for his attention was the sound of the pattering rain beyond the door of the room, and the incense was making him feel lightheaded. He heard distant screams coming from a street away. The woman didn't turn to look. The boy didn't react at all. One of the soldiers of his army escort stormed into the room, but the people in robes stopped him with a glance. The soldier looked to Tim, making a silent appeal.

"Wait a minute, wait a minute!" Tim pleaded. "This isn't necessary. You can't slaughter a whole village! There must be someone! At least *one* innocent here! And even if they're all complicit, these people must have children who have done nothing—"

He sifted his mind desperately for arguments; tried to summon a bulwark of compassionate rationality to prevent this. Come on, he ordered himself, come *on*. A handful of men with rifles could prevent nothing here if they started their promised massacre—it was up to him. But the situation was unraveling. He couldn't accept that it was deteriorating so quickly, his role reduced to that of an audience member for this grotesque play.

"The children have been removed," said the old man at the table. "They will be cared for at other villages."

"Wait—wait! Why am I here then? Why was there any need for me to come? I don't understand. If you didn't want mediation—"

"You are here because you are still untainted," said the woman.

"We had to go miles to find one who was," said the boy.

"*Untainted?*" snapped Tim. "Do you actually think I could agree with your type of morality? That I'm going to watch you carry out mass murder?"

The eyes of the old man blinked, disappearing briefly into the fleshy pouches of aged skin. The thin mouth pursed its lips, and he said patiently, "That is not what we mean by untainted."

"The word 'receptive,'" said the boy, "might be more applicable. We assumed you would be receptive to us."

Tim knew he wasn't getting anywhere, and it crossed his mind that perhaps he had blundered into a trap. Maybe they always intended to assassinate an American official as their main goal. His panic rose like acid-burning vomit in his throat, and a gloved hand reached across the table and took his wrist. It took his arm gently, with no threat in the motion at all. But it happened so fast.

"You'll leave here safe and sound in a few minutes," said the old man.

"Do you remember your Greek mythology, Mr. Cale?" asked the woman near the doorway. She tugged on the winding folds of her wrap.

"*Argus Panoptes*," said the old man. He let go of Tim's wrist and began pulling off the mitten of his right hand.

"He's a giant," said the boy with a triumphant smile of white teeth, sounding for the first time like a child. He tugged off his knit woolen cap with the strings, and a few strands of his black mop were pulled up for an instant. Just like any boy.

"Servant of the goddess Hera," said the woman. The English and Greek words sounded strange from that wise Asian face. Then her scarf was removed, her neck bare—

"*Panoptes*, meaning in Greek, 'all seeing.'"

The old man's glove was off, and he cast aside his woolen jacket as the classical reference finally clicked in Tim's mind—

He pushed back his chair and jumped up. The wooden legs scraped the floor, and the chair timbered back with a crash.

Yes, Hera's giant, his body covered with eyes.

And in front of him the old man stayed calmly in his seat, the dark forest green and mauve garment folds running like a toga over one shoulder, but the shoulder itself, his chest, his arms covered in *eyes*. There were eyes on the body of the woman. Eyes were blinking from the flat, adolescent chest of the boy. The effect was like seeing skin marked with a pattern of yellowish whiteheads, of boils, but each pupil had a lid and an eyelash, some of them blinking out of sequence with others.

The Indian soldier near the entrance backed away from the woman, one foot out the door.

"What *are* you people?" Tim whispered.

"We told you, it doesn't matter," said the boy. "Not now, in this moment. It's sufficient that you are... receptive."

"There is a cost for the rebalancing," said the old man. "And so we have adopted an eye for each of these villagers who have lived in destructive blindness. Understand: we are not without a comprehension of degrees of guilt. Those who did less are the ones you found as you arrived. For the others..."

His gnarled hand reached into the drapery of his robes and slowly withdrew a dagger.

Oh, God. He grasped immediately what the man was about to do, and because it was impossible, he could not understand how to prevent it.

He was left to watch as the blade dug like a scalpel into the soft white of a blinking egg imbedded in his flesh, and Tim heard himself scream *no no no* as the old man hissed and gritted his teeth in genuine pain. Warm blood poured down the arm, hideously blinding more of the blinking eyes and dripping down to the sawdust floor, and Tim heard the corresponding wails from beyond the shelter.

"*Stop it!* Please stop it! You can't believe this is right!"

"This is for those who did these unspeakable acts," said the old man. "And for those who allowed them to happen, seeing is believing."

The soldier made a guttural sound—not quite a yell but a kind of bark of his revulsion and fear. He ran out, and Tim heard his boots stomp in the moist earth. As the woman and boy brandished their own knives, Timothy Cale rushed past them into the rain. He knew where the soldier was going— the soldier was joining the others who had been guarding the SUV. People ran now into the main thoroughfare of the village as distant screams rose over each other. Shouts grew louder in the native dialect, and there was a string of gurgling cries. The soldiers could do nothing.

Tim couldn't bring himself to step closer to the silhouettes of villagers, some staggering into the road, others falling to their knees.

All of them were clutching their heads, their fingers on their foreheads or at their temples...

Dazed in his shock, he looked back at the rectangle of spilled light from the doorway, and he saw a curving, trickling stream of blood pouring out. It mingled with the puddles of rain.

He couldn't stop the impulse to be sick.

His eyes felt the salt-burn of tears, his forehead still soaked with rivulets of rain, while his throat was scorched with bile. He pulled himself up and forced his senses to register again, but this time the people of the village were missing. No, not all of them, they couldn't be. Could they? The first ones, yes, he could tell that the first ones who had shouted and run into the street were... gone. A mysterious banishment that was the crowning touch of the strangers. But the others? A whole village *gone*. He heard the ugly metal *chunk* as one foolish soldier prepared his rifle to fire, but there was no staccato burst. Something stayed his hand, forcing a reappraisal.

33

You've got to do something, thought Tim. You can't stay just a witness to this.

He started to run through the unpaved narrow streets, his shoes splashing through the puddles of mud and rainwater, looking for... he didn't know what. Survivors, those who hadn't been claimed yet. He had pleaded with them: *There must be someone! At least* one *innocent here!* He couldn't find anyone. Bodies, yes. Bodies and more bodies like those they first spotted on arrival, each one with staring blue eyes, but others were missing. Others were *taken*. He felt a growing hopelessness—then panic, because the soldiers might start up the SUV and leave him behind. Through the *sshhhh* of the relentless rain, he spotted an old woman, curled up, hugging her knees near packed metal chairs behind a market stall table.

Oh, Christ, he didn't speak the language. Maybe... Maybe if he just held out his hand, and if his tone was gentle enough, he could persuade her. "You have to come with me! It's not safe for you here!"

She said something that sounded like a fatalistic complaint. Telling him he was mad, that it was pointless. Her voice was high and sharp and raw, the whine of a gnarled tree branch being snapped off. She was horrified at what was happening around her, but she couldn't see escape.

"*Please,*" he called over the rain, still holding out his hand. "Please!"

After a moment, she picked herself up with an effort, her limbs trembling either from fear or the palsy of her age, stepping out from her hiding place. She could walk surprisingly quickly, but he wished she could run. They had to get away from this place. The strangers in the robes had either over-looked her or were busy reaping other souls. He found himself pulling her along by the arm, cursing himself for his fear.

He heard the small boy from a side alley, calling out for someone. Mother, father, it hardly mattered. Scared brown eyes under a mop of black hair, his tiny limbs at his sides, but his neck turning this way and that, looking, hoping... He was small, and given the diet and environment here, it was difficult to tell the his age. He could have been anywhere between four to seven years old. Tim scooped him up, and the boy cried out, but the old woman said something to shush him and comfort him.

As they approached the SUV, the interpreter looked close to a nervous breakdown. He barely heard Tim calling for them to leave, shouting that there was nothing they could do but go. The man was gibbering and nodding, but he didn't move to call to the soldiers in Hindi. Tim yelled in English to one of the soldiers up ahead in the road, brandishing his rifle but with nothing to fire on, telling him the obvious: *We have to go.*

He heard the soldier call out four names, but only three men returned. They piled into the SUV and drove away, and no one looked back.

There was silence in the vehicle for a long time, and then at last, Tim tapped one of the soldiers on the shoulder. No point asking the interpreter—the man was traumatized to a sobbing wreck.

"Ask her their names." He meant the old lady and the boy.

Most of the soldiers looked haunted by what had happened back there. The soldier he addressed looked vaguely angry, and he took it out on their guests, snapping Tim's question at the old woman. She answered him back in a low but firm voice, and Tim didn't think he needed a translation. She had told him in so many words to go to hell. His kind wasn't trusted in their province, and they would be avoided even more after tonight. The soldier gave her a contemptuous look and shrugged at Tim. The old woman looked out the window, and the little boy moved closer to her, trying to nestle to her bosom. She patted his arm absently.

About twenty miles passed, and then the woman spoke up in rapid staccato bursts of her dialect, pointing out the window. Tim couldn't imagine how she could identify anything through the storm, but she clearly wanted them to stop.

The angry soldier barked back at her, refusing, and Tim leaned forward. "What? What is it?"

"There's another village here," explained the soldier. "She wants to go there, says she and the boy will be safe. I have told her to shut up and do as she's told."

"Let her out," ordered Tim.

"You do not understand these people, sir. They should not be indulged with their—"

"*Let them out.* You're here as my escort, and we have no right to detain this woman. I coaxed her into the car so that she would be safe. She probably knows every village and resident from here to Patna! If anyone can find a relative for this kid to take care of him, it's probably her. I mean, what do you guys want to do? Take the kid back and stick him in an orphanage? Now *stop* the goddamn car!"

The soldier driving pulled up on the side of the muddy road leading to a set of pinprick lights in the distance. Tim opened the car door for the old woman, and she mumbled something to the boy. He slid his small bottom along the upholstery of the seat and jumped out, taking her hand.

"You'll be okay here?" he asked needlessly. He knew she couldn't understand a word, but he asked anyway.

She muttered something back and then made a scattering, waving motion with her hand. *Go away now. Leave.* The soldier reached for the door handle and shut it with a slam. Then the SUV roared away, and Tim could barely see the old woman and boy navigating the muddy path to the new village. There was silence in the vehicle all the way back to Patna.

Coming into the outskirts of the city, Tim pressed the button on his window, listening to the *whrrr* of the electronics for the door and held his palm out to feel the beaded curtain of rain. These drops, he knew, were real. They were the most tangible things in his world now that the old woman and boy were gone, and so he focused on them. Feel the rain, his mind insisted, trying to shut out the memory of the horror they had witnessed. Listen to the rain, feel the drops, feel them...

This much, he knew, was still real.

It wasn't over after he returned to Delhi. The Indian government managed to keep it out of the media, but its leaders, as well as the US ambassador and the State Department, were fiercely interested to know how the entire population of a border village could disappear. After all, the houses, the market stalls and the modest headquarters of the single local official were all intact, which proved no rebel group had gone on a mad spree.

Even the bodies with their blue eyes were now missing.

While pools of blood had been detected from satellite photos near the sad building where Tim met the robed strangers, it wasn't a large enough quantity to suggest this was where systematic butchery was carried out. No, all the people had been taken elsewhere. Everyone wanted to know where.

The soldiers who had been Mr. Cale's escort told a preposterous story, and the interpreter tried to hang himself but botched the job. He was left with the mind of a retarded child after his brain was deprived of oxygen.

What could Timothy Cale tell them? He couldn't say the escort fought back. Their rifles hadn't been fired, and the proof of that was that each gun magazine still had all their rounds. He didn't have a scrap of evidence to back up a plausible lie. For a week, the ambassador let him have compassionate leave, inclined to believe Tim had suffered post-traumatic stress disorder from having seen something terrible. "But when you come back, we need answers," he was told.

Sitting behind his desk again, feeling as if he had been away for years, Tim felt the draft of the rumbling air conditioner and sipped the strong coffee the Indian staff always liked to brew. He looked at his incident reports and knew he had no answers. He didn't know what to tell his boss at his two o'clock appointment.

And then there was "a development," as it was discreetly put.

During his leave, a warrant officer and lance corporal of the Army of Nepal had discovered the old woman and the little boy living not far from where the SUV had left them on the muddy road. They claimed to be from the empty village. The boy turned out to be close to seven years old, and the old woman had been born into a lower caste. She had suffered much from her neighbors. The two were driven to Patna where police and government bureaucrats questioned them. Yes, they had seen the visitors in robes. No, they didn't know who these bizarre strangers were. They had felt searing agony and then nothing.

Obviously, they had been *returned*… Minutes before Tim Cale had discovered them and had them whisked away in the vehicle.

So, thought Tim. Those deadly beings had found two innocents after all.

You thought you rescued them, but maybe you were part of the plan.

The Indians decided the matter was closed. The Americans did not. They sent Tim home under a neat disciplinary rule of the service that involved a gag order, and they kept him on a desk in Washington until it dawned on him that he would never get a foreign posting again.

He had done minor studies in medical ethics, as well as business ethics, and he had a large enough network of Washington and New York contacts that he could launch his own consultancy business. As far as the Beltway was privately concerned (but never to his face), the boy and the old woman who survived the village massacre were a peculiar vindication for Timothy Cale. He began to land assignments that involved the seemingly unexplainable, the fringe science that occasionally spelled disaster when it found gullible congressmen as advocates or when his former colleagues in the diplomatic corps fell prey to "magicians" in Bangkok or Manila.

He racked up a lot of billable hours and air miles casually exposing frauds when he wasn't tapping out reports on stem cell research. He prospered. He didn't think too often about the village near the Indian border. He tried not to think about why the strangers in robes had selected him to be their witness. *Receptive*, they had called him. Whatever that was supposed to mean, it made his flesh crawl.

And now the booths.

The government had brought him into this mess because of what had happened in Bihar. But the border incident years ago fell under the category of the supernatural. These amazing transposition booths were science. "Doesn't matter," he was told on the phone. "You are the only sane American we've got who's had experience with, well, for lack of a better word, *resurrection*."

Word of the booths didn't follow anyone's schedule, least of all the one Weintraub had. Yes, he had an announcement ready in case of a leak, but he argued the biggest issue to resolve before breaking the news was organizing what little concrete data they had.

"Wrong," countered Tim, who argued there was a more urgent priority. "They'll come at you like jackals. But they'll descend even more on the girl."

On Mary Ash. Reporters would expect her to have answers, and Tim guaranteed they would form a mob outside the Ash family residence until they got their clips and their quotes and their background stories on poor Mary's high-school romances, her college ambitions and her day-to-day habits, what music she listened to and who she voted for and any other scrap of useless info to fuel further speculation. Nickelbaum's victim, Tim argued, needed privacy to recover. She was entitled to it.

But the compassionate grace of fate was too much to hope for. By Thursday of the following week, the BBC broke the story first on their investigative show, *Panorama*, admitting they had been tipped off to a possible new execution method that bypassed federal and state requirements. CNN was next, and then Fox News weighed in, suggesting a cover-up. Great, Rupert Murdoch's crew is taking its usual hysterical approach, Tim grumbled to himself.

Matilda, his personal assistant, came into his office without knocking as usual and switched on the news. "You'll want to see this," she told him. More often than not she anticipated Tim's needs correctly, but she had the knack of making it sound like a command, which always amused him.

She was plump and graying, the least likely woman of fifty-eight you would expect to know how to score pot to help her friends handle chemotherapy. Tim hired her on the spot at the end of her job interview—right after she noticed Shelby Foote's three-volume history of the Civil War on his bookshelf and told him how, for a high-school essay, she had tracked down an extremely elderly aunt, blind and half deaf, who recalled Sherman's March to the Sea. Matilda was brusque and opinionated, but she made sure Tim was on time for his appointments. She cleared his desk and kept him organized. She was his secret weapon and professional treasure.

Tim sat back in his leather office chair and deferred to her wisdom in switching the mute button off and changing the channel. Gary Weintraub was on, a weed patch of microphones surrounding him, giving a clue as to how enormous the media scrum was. But Gary was in his element. Tim once teased him about seeking the spotlight, and Gary Weintraub had given him a cockeyed grin and arched his eyebrows.

"Of course, I do, and you should be glad I do," he insisted, jutting his sausage fingers in a tight fist, thumb on top, as if he needed to push an elevator button right away. "You know why the majority of teenagers come out of the secondary education system, and they can't solve a basic algebra equation or know five elements on the periodic table? Because there are so few superstars in science. These children come out with dreams of being in the NBA and the NFL. *Nobody* wants to be in science. It's all government subsidized or academically funded or pharmaceutical-based. Group endeavor. Now I ask you, Tim, who would want to be a part of that?"

But these days, Weintraub could have it both ways. Even those who never watched PBS or read *Scientific American* knew who Gary Weintraub was—their lovably eccentric

41

moon-faced TV "uncle" who hosted shows about space and dolphins. They probably assumed the breaking news was about a discovery of his own. Those who knew better likely felt he was the best of all possible front men.

Tim couldn't help but notice the neurologist, that kid with the cloud of shoulder-length brown hair—what was his name? Miller. He stood behind Weintraub, wearing a lab coat and a self-satisfied grin, enjoying the spectacle. Ambitious enough to learn exactly where the cameras would include him.

"—subject is female, yes," Weintraub was confirming now for the reporters. A question from the scrum was muffled and got lost, but his reply explained what it was. "In her early twenties. No, I don't think it's prudent to specify more than that—"

"Are you denying then that it's—" A reporter threw out the name of another one of Nickelbaum's victims.

For the first time, Tim detected the exasperation in his friend's voice. "I am not confirming it, nor am I denying it," he said with a nervous laugh.

"Come on, Professor Weintraub, there's only one victim he was ever convicted of murdering!" piped up a more aggressive reporter. It didn't take much logic to narrow the possibilities down to Mary Ash.

"All I can tell you at the moment is that the subject is recuperating with the help of doctors and her immediate family."

The reporters weren't ready to let it go. "If it is her, is there a correlation then between the legal system and what the equipment does?"

"Good gracious, no!" said Weintraub, forgetting himself for an instant. "That is to say, we don't know that, and there is nothing so far to even remotely suggest that idea." He began to walk away from the microphones.

"Yes, but—"

"Jesus, people," said Miller with a hand on Gary's shoulder. "He's a physicist, not a metaphysicist!"

There was a ripple of laughter from the scrum. You could tell what would be the top clip used from the news conference on the six o'clock cast, and Tim had to admit it was a good line. Ten points for the smartass.

"Son of a bitch," Matilda muttered under her breath as she stood beside Tim's desk. "This is incredible. And you saw this happen? This is the big thing you couldn't talk about yet?"

"This is it," said Tim, still frowning pensively at the screen. "And so far the wolf pack is keeping to the script."

"What do you mean?"

He waved a lazy hand towards the television set. "They're all asking about the girl. They want to know where she came from, how she came back."

"So do I!" replied Matilda. She sounded mildly affronted that he shouldn't agree with the obvious.

"But no one's asking about *him*."

"Him who?"

"Nickelbaum," answered Tim. "They're not bothering to ask what happened to him."

She stared at him blankly.

"Where did he go?" he prompted, not really expecting an answer.

He waited, knowing it would sink in after a second. He watched her expression and saw exactly what was going through her mind. It would be the same if he asked a dozen of his students or people on the street. Nickelbaum had been dismissed, ignored, forgotten, because he had always been scheduled to die, to be extinguished. Of course, the return of

Mary Ash was more interesting; it was downright fascinating and compelling. And Tim had no more pity for Nickelbaum than others, but—

"He's the other half of the equation," he pointed out, as Matilda looked vaguely embarrassed at forgetting this detail.

"When he went," she started tentatively, "*she* came back. So there must be…" She trailed off with a shrug.

"A connection? Sure, but what kind? People are working on a couple of very tenuous assumptions."

"But he's gone now, and the girl came back from the dead!"

"Which means what exactly?" asked Tim. "Where is 'dead'? How the hell do we even define 'dead' anymore? How did his execution bring her back? There's no logic to it, not at all, because we don't have sufficient information yet. And if Nickelbaum went to the same place his victim was in, then Weintraub's right, and a court decision and our standard morality might play no factor at all in the actual process. Chew on that one for a while! But okay, sure, suppose he went somewhere else. Suppose he went *down there*. That's if you want to get biblical about it. We're still left with a whole mess of problems."

Matilda frowned, trying to think it through, looking at him innocently as she ventured, "I don't see why. Should make the Christians ecstatic."

Tim let the air out of his lungs, lacing his fingers in front of his chin. "Don't bet on it. Again, you're assuming our Miss Ash was busy with the angels. We now have a technology that rudely—perhaps even cruelly—yanked her out of Heaven, presuming that exists, and you're presuming she came from there. That means we're messing around with *the* grand plan. No, Matty, I don't think they're going to be happy about this one at all. This is going to get worse."

After a moment, Matilda crossed her arms and said with a faint note of mischief, knowing her employer's views, "You don't think she came from Heaven."

"No, I don't."

"She was dead," said Matilda gently.

"Yes, she was. And then she wasn't. Which is another thing that troubles me."

Her eyes widened, already guessing his fresh point.

"If she can be dead and then suddenly *not* dead, who says Nickelbaum will stay where he is?"

3

Weintraub sent him an email with an attachment—his preliminary report for the government on how the equipment was thought to work. In the body of the email itself, Gary had informed him in his usual rushed, sloppy typing style: "WE DON'T DARE TAKE THING APART BE A DISASTER."

Okay, thought Tim. They're afraid if they dismantle it, they won't be able to get it to work again. They choose, instead, to learn all they can from experimental use. And they wonder why I'm concerned.

There was a schematic diagram that showed the two chambers, but a picture wasn't worth a thousand words here. Instead, the report had several thousand words, almost all of it conjecture. But there was just enough, Tim realized as he flipped the pages, to suggest Gary Weintraub and his staff had made some brilliant guesses. The white light tinged with blue when Emmett Nickelbaum was executed was perhaps a unique form of Cerenkov radiation—the electromagnetic radiation that's generated when charged particles pass through an insulator at the speed of light. It was why nuclear reactors had their blue glow. This much Tim could follow, and though he had barely passed physics in high school, it intuitively made sense to him. There was, however, no easy explanation for the bizarre light effects and patterns that flashed in the chamber when Nickelbaum was torn apart—nor for the ones preceding Mary Ash's arrival.

But Weintraub and his fellow scientists would have had plenty to talk about even if Nickelbaum had not vanished, screaming, or if Mary Ash had not come back into their plane of existence. As they videotaped and measured the transposition equipment, they discovered it had the equivalent of about seven times the power—all of it contained within the two chambers—that was needed for the Large Hadron Collider near Geneva, the biggest and most powerful particle accelerator in the world.

Within seconds, the booths had proved the Higgs boson was real.

Weintraub and his team had measured other particles that were once only hypothesized in university papers and research: sleptons, photinos, squarks, the so-called "sparticles" that winked quickly out of existence in a ten trillionth of a nanosecond after the Big Bang. The booths proved they could exist. They *did* exist.

The booths proved something else. They proved the existence of a particle that had been the wet dream of physicists for decades, the one first proposed by Gerald Feinberg in 1967, a crutch for science fiction movie plots ever since: tachyons.

These particles had flashed and disappeared in the booths. They were tantalizingly *there* for slices of infinite time, then gone. And the fact that they blinked in and out as part of the riddle of human existence itself made these proofs somehow irrelevant and small and yet desperately essential at the same time.

Jeff Pearce

No, Weintraub and the other lab coats definitely did not want to take the equipment apart.

They don't know, thought Tim.

They don't know how it works. They don't know all that it can do.

They simply don't know.

It was unfathomable to him, too, that the research and development of such a machine could be done and then production carried out with complete secrecy—all benchmarks, findings, assigned personnel, initial test trials hermetically sealed. With not one word of publicity or a single media leak. Tim could hardly believe it. How had they pulled *that* off?

If the machinery had been a government project, leaks were inevitable. Impossible to prevent. If a private corporation had developed the equipment, yes, of course, staff could be required to sign gag orders as part of their contracts. But you would think at each stage of development the company's PR department would want to herald its sensational discoveries from CNN to *Scientific American* to *Nature* magazine. If you didn't want to make a noise for the sheer benefit of branding prestige, fine, then how about the more immediate concern of attracting capital for future development?

But nothing, Tim realized. No story about the booths had appeared until after the Nickelbaum execution.

The booths had seemingly come out of nowhere.

Gary's report indicated that his team couldn't even identify yet what parts were actually included in each of the chambers.

Inside both of them, mounted on the inside roof of the booths, could be seen astonishing equipment that looked "as if someone had miraculously miniaturized a Tevatron." Tim read this line in Gary's report and had to look up what the hell a Tevatron was—turned out it was a huge circular particle accelerator.

Only the guts of the machinery were incredibly more sophisticated. Weintraub's team spotted something akin to a Cockcroft–Walton voltage multiplier—what an accelerator would need first (Tim figured he would have to take that one on faith). But there was no ladder-network of capacitors and diodes. It was more like an insect eye pattern of capacitors, and the whole mechanism had no leads or cords or hook-up to an external power source.

To measure voltage, after all, you need current. But the baffling mechanism suggested the thing didn't run with regular electrical current at all but on *something else*.

Weintraub and his colleagues had to switch on the control panel to start the procedure, and the panel, at least, had to be plugged into an ordinary, humble wall socket.

But they couldn't detect any radio beam or satellite signal linking the panel to the booths.

Yes, there were indicator lights and narrow screens to measure the pulse, blood pressure and EEG of booth occupants, but no one understood either how this data was relayed back.

And that was the sum of their knowledge without disassembling the equipment. They could turn the machinery on and off and start a sequence. That was it.

After turning a switch, they knew nothing about the exchange of a murderer for his or her slain victim.

Not encouraging, thought Tim. Well, he couldn't help his friend Gary Weintraub find technical answers from the booths. But he could speak to the world's first booth arrival.

*

The Ash family home stood in a distinctly rich, white-dominated part of greater Lancaster, southern Pennsylvania. The house at the end of the tree-lined block was distinctive enough that you didn't need to check the rising address numbers. Mary Ash's father was a retired architect, and the long structure with the sloping roof and overhangs resembled one of Frank Lloyd Wright's "Prairie Houses."

The mother came to the door and showed no surprise over finding Timothy Cale on her porch step. Obviously someone in Washington or New York had thought the decent thing to do was to call ahead, whether Tim wanted the Ashes to be warned or not. He could hardly fault the polite gesture.

Mrs. Ash, an older version of Mary in a sleeveless dark sweater and green slacks, seemed to carry a resignation towards the infinite. The resurrection of her daughter was something she would have to cope with long after this stranger imposed on her. Tim took in the dark gray rings under the woman's eyes, her mouth pinched in a line, and he wondered himself how he could have the nerve. He had it, he knew, because he had no choice. He needed answers. They all did.

"Mrs. Ash, I'm not a journal—"

"I know you're not, Mr. Cale," she replied, her words coming out in a tired breath.

"Do you know why I'm here?" he asked, trying to make it sound less of a challenge.

"They gave me some idea," she said. Turning with her shoulders slightly sagged, she walked back into the house before she realized he was still waiting on the porch, needing an invitation. "Come in, Mr. Cale, come *in*."

The décor was what he expected. Tasteful, coordinated, like a layout in a home furnishings magazine, right down to the wooden curios the Ash father and mother probably bought on holiday in Peru. Mrs. Ash waved him to a cream white couch and asked him if he wanted tea or coffee. He didn't want either, thank you. Then Mrs. Ash confirmed that yes, her daughter was home—in fact, she was upstairs in the room she had grown up in, but "you'll want to ask me some questions first."

"I will?"

"They all do," said Mrs. Ash. "Everyone who comes to see her. The doctors, the government men—I think they're afraid of her." Her face looked pinched again for a moment, as if on the verge of either tears or a strained smile that seemed to tell him: *I'm afraid, too.*

She was past the exuberant joy of the miracle, of a reunion with her daughter that involved grateful hugs and tears, of excited confusion over how she could possibly be back. Now there was living with the miracle; with the knowledge that her child was still a victim, even if revived.

"I'm supposed to know her. I'm her mother. Do you have children, Mr. Cale?" But she didn't wait for the answer. "I'm supposed to know her," she said again with more emphasis.

He stopped himself before he offered the clichéd answer, the obvious answer: that even if Nickelbaum hadn't murdered Mary Ash, she had been tortured and repeatedly raped, sometimes with foreign objects. There was no way the girl would have woken up from this horror in a hospital bed without being a different person, forever changed. But he was sure Mrs. Ash already knew this.

She must know it, he thought, because she had made a family impact statement at Nickelbaum's sentencing. She had given a five-minute speech that didn't curse her daughter's murderer or talk about the robbed life of a sweet young girl, only how someone capable of such depraved acts must have so little human empathy that he merited extermination. She had got her wish. And she had got more.

Tim watched her go to the sideboard and pour what looked like a rye for herself. She lifted the bottle to him in afterthought. He shook his head.

"Her fingers are back," said Mrs. Ash, sipping her drink. "The ones that monster cut off. They were just—suddenly— *back*. I noticed them on her fifth day with us. The doctors told us on the second day that all the... damage to her insides was gone, no scar tissue. They chalked it up to some reviving effect of this ... this booth thing. All right, I can accept that. I'm not a religious person, but I can accept that my daughter's privates are healed after the things he did to her and the way he violated her. But people *don't* grow back digits like salamanders."

"No, they don't."

"You think I'm ungrateful." She took another long pull of her drink. Through the French windows to the back yard, Tim saw the shadows growing longer on the grass.

"No, I don't," he said carefully. "It sounds like you were doing your best with your grief, and now a stranger has been foisted on you."

"Please don't patronize me, Mr. Cale."

"I'm not, Mrs. Ash. Quite the contrary. I imagine you have all sorts of people looking to you to help explain what's happened or worse. They pretend they actually know what's going on."

"Yes, they do. But they don't know at all, do they?"

"No, they don't."

She deserved the truth.

Her fingers drummed on her glass tumbler for a moment as she looked out the window to the garden. The shadows were still lengthening, as if darkness could acquire weight. Then she said, "You can go up and see her now if you want to."

He muttered a thanks and went up.

It was quiet in the hall.

He knocked softly on the door to the girl's room, and the light voice that answered adopted a formal tone: "Yes?" No grown-up child that's come home ever answers *Yes* to a knock at the door like that. You call out *Mom* or *Dad* or say *Come in* or say *Hey*. Maybe Mary Ash had heard the doorbell about half an hour ago or was getting used to the parade of visitors.

When he pushed the door open, he found her sitting on her bed with a large charcoal sketchpad. The pad was propped up against the improvised drafting table of her knees. She smiled at him pleasantly but with no effort to rise or to interrupt her drawing. It was the smile of a self-absorbed toddler greeting a polite friend of her daddy's. A pleasant enough smile. The eyes, however, weren't young. They were a wise and vivid green, so striking that he almost took them for another color, one that belonged on a flower from the family garden or on a bright, newly born grasshopper chewing its leaves, knowing what its singular purpose and arrival was for.

"Mary, my name is Tim Cale."

She nodded and smiled again expectantly, reaching out her hand to shake his without a word.

The hand with the re-grown fingers.

Her touch was cool, with a limpness thanks to a tutored grace. And then her eyes were down, back to the drawing.

The room itself told him very little, relentlessly neat and clean like the lounge below. Whatever she was now, Mary Ash had once favored pastel colors, and the acrylic paintings on the wall owed a lot to the European Fauvists. There was a framed computer store ad on the wall—obviously one of her first compositions as a professional graphic artist.

With the high angle she had for the sketchpad on her knees, he couldn't see what her composition was. Not yet.

"Mary," he tried again. "Mary, I know you've had a lot of visitors, and I'll probably have the same questions…"

Her eyes flicked up from the sketchpad and down again as she let out a soft giggle. "I doubt it."

"You do?"

She hadn't invited him to sit, but he sat down anyway in the white wicker chair, making it crunch. *I doubt it.* He could infer a lot from those three little words, and he was instinctively certain he didn't have to explain what his job was or why he was here.

Okay, he thought. If she expects *you* to ask different questions, go ahead and ask them. You planned to anyway.

He wouldn't ask her what she remembered of Nickelbaum's attack. He wouldn't ask if she had any consciousness of the… *transition* to wherever she went. He wouldn't ask where she had been all this time before her return. Others had inquired, and the girl had shaken her head dully or told them she couldn't remember. She was just… *back.*

"Mary, what are you going to do now? I mean, after you've rested. Will you go back to your old job? The design firm will probably be glad to have you."

Her eyes lifted off the paper with new interest.

"What did *you* feel like doing after Paris?" she asked.

After Paris…?

Don't show it, he thought. Don't show surprise. Don't show you've been rattled. It was possible someone had filled in the girl about details of his career.

Her voice remained soft, almost ethereal. The charcoal pencil scratched the page.

"Well, it's not like I was ever murdered and brought back from the dead," he answered reasonably.

"No. But you felt like Europe was ruined for you after she died, and you needed to get away for a while."

Thérèse. The girl was talking about Thérèse. Again, he resisted the urge to ask how she could know anything of his life. Instead he shrugged and replied, "That happened a long time ago."

"*Nooooo*, it didn't," she said, her voice rising in a singsong. "Not really. Eight years ago, August twenty-fifth, you formally requested a transfer to Asia. It was after you knew you couldn't help her. You blamed yourself for the breakup, and maybe if it hadn't happened, she wouldn't have gone out with the man who worked at the consulate in Lyon. He raped her after he lured her up to the embassy's corporate hotel room off Rivoli, and he beat her, detaching her retina. She tested positive for HIV. It's why you delayed visiting me. It's why you feel conflicted about the Booth. You want punishment, but you also know terrible things change people forever. And you felt there was no pattern to life after Thérèse died in a car accident in Hamburg—"

"I think you've made your point," he whispered.

Don't ask how, he ordered himself, his mind racing. *The how doesn't matter right now because she obviously picked up this trick from wherever she went.*

He forced himself to consider the *why* of her spouting the details of his life. She hadn't done it with the others who'd come with their clipboards full of questions.

That meant she had singled him out for this mind game. It also meant he had an advantage, leverage. If only he could figure out what it was and how to use it.

He sat very still, hoping his breathing wasn't fast. He couldn't hear it. He was only conscious of Mary Ash, still drawing but not looking at the paper.

"I suppose you can tell me where I was August twenty-fifth last year," he suggested, playing for time.

"Not an interesting day. You got your teeth cleaned at the dentist's in the morning. You were upset with a foreign exchange student in the afternoon lecture, a Chilean who thought the CIA was right to topple Allende."

"February sixteenth, 1985."

The pale green eyes blinked then held him steady as she recited, "You were twelve and still living in Chicago. It was cold. There was snow on the ground, and you kissed Heather Dershowitz in your family's basement rec-room while working on a history project together about World War One. You were embarrassed because your erection pushed out your jeans. She was eleven and scared she might get pregnant, and you had to show her books that proved it was impossible."

She turned to look out her window briefly and added, "They call it *hyperthymesia*: the ability to recall vivid auto-biographical detail according to dates. I don't think it's very impressive to remember stuff about yourself."

"So you remember it about others."

Her eyes fell gently on him again as she offered another fleeting smile. "Yes. You don't have to worry, Mr. Cale. I'm not reading your mind, and the effect doesn't last. And no, it has nothing to do with the physical contact when we shook hands either."

"You just meet a person and...?"

"You know that quantum physics is responsible for how a television works, but you don't know how. You still go on watching television, don't you? Because you can."

"Do you know about quantum physics?"

"Of course not!" she laughed.

With a flash of insight, he leaned in as he asked in a murmur, "You grew your fingers back, didn't you?"

She lifted the charcoal pencil as she answered pleasantly, "Well, I do need my fingers, Mr. Cale."

He nodded without saying a word, taking it in.

"I need to take a nap now, if you don't mind," she said.

"All right. Thank you for talking to me, Mary."

"Not at all, you're a very intelligent and interesting man," she said as he rose to go. "You've been fortunate to see special things. You'll get to see others."

"What other things?"

She shrugged, just like a young woman trading casual gossip in the street, having run into an acquaintance. "I don't know. I just know you'll be near the center of it. You'll feel better when you remember something."

"What's that?"

"That when you're here, you must be here, Mr. Cale."

"I don't understand."

"I don't know how to explain it better. I volunteered at this daycare once. I went to help blind kids with a sculpture class, and I realized they've never seen red. So how do you explain what red is to them?"

"Have you seen these things you're talking about?"

"No. Sorry. They're for you. You're still untainted."

He stared at her.

Then she broke into a mischievous giggle. "I'm just messing with you, Mr. Cale. *They* didn't send me back. But if I could know about your girlfriend in Paris, I could know about them, couldn't I?"

He was still staring at her.

"You should be happy, Mr. Cale. You learned what you wanted. I had terrible things happen to me, and I'm *not* changed."

He stood in the doorway and saw the mother hovering at the top of the stairs, wearing the same anxious expression as she had in the living room. He had one more question for the girl, but he couldn't bring himself to ask. It was too terrible.

Mary Ash fixed him rigid in her stare, saying, "It's all right, Mr. Cale. I told you I can't read your mind, but you're giving your question away on your face. It's okay. No one else would bother to think of it, not because it's wrong, but because they don't have your way of seeing. And the answer's no."

As he nodded his goodbye, he caught a quick glimpse of Mary Ash lowering the pad of paper.

There was nothing on it. Blank.

But he had heard the scratching of the charcoal. She had drawn, erased, sketched again and shaded with strokes.

There was *nothing* on the paper.

The mother waited until he was at the door before she asked what Mary meant. "She said 'no' to your last question, but you didn't ask it. What did you want to ask her?"

"It's okay, Mrs. Ash," he said. "I'm sorry I imposed on you." He walked back to his car, wanting to get away from the house as quickly as possible.

No, he wouldn't burden the mother with the question that had been on his lips. The poor haunted woman didn't deserve to agonize over that idea, and he barely wanted to consider it himself: whether Mary Ash had somehow actually chosen—from whatever mysterious place she inhabited—to "kill Emmett Nickelbaum back." And if this was what had allowed her to return into their world.

4

The start of the Bolshevik Revolution.

The ends of the First and Second World Wars.

The polio vaccine.

The John F. Kennedy assassination.

The announcement of Mary Ash's return was added to a unique and truly exclusive catalogue, each entry a marker of when people around the world took stock of their era and their place in it. The Apollo Moon landing. The horror of 9/11. Where were you when you heard? What were you doing when this happened? A murderer had been executed, which was nothing new, but for the first time in history, his victim had come back after this was done.

The media dubbed the transposition equipment "The Karma Booth"—ignoring completely that two booths were used in the procedure.

A couple of fundamentalist Muslim clerics in London were asked to comment on the Karma Booth and promised it would be exposed eventually as a fraud. Mullahs in Iran's Assembly of Experts went further, calling it the work of the "Great Satan" and an abomination that could undo the work of countless martyrs. The logic of this official statement was reported without much critical commentary in the West.

The Vatican withheld its judgment for a week and three days. Then at a Mass at St. Peter's, the Pope made a reference to "a supposed scientific development that defies the natural balance of Holy Creation." The condemnation was somewhat veiled, but in a later communiqué, the Vatican openly called for the booths to be dismantled and destroyed as an aberration against God and Nature.

Two simultaneous riots broke out near the Quai D'Orsay in Paris and in one of its more infamous *banlieues*, its lower-income immigrant suburbs, simply because of an Internet rumor. Word had spread that the United States government was willing to export the booth technology to several of its key allies. By the time the French government issued a denial, two policemen were severely injured and five immigrants from Mali and Algeria were dead.

Back in the States, several high-placed Republicans quickly suggested a bill be rushed through Congress that would put Karma Booth executions under federal authority. The rationale was that the Booth would prove too attractive for the state judicial system to resist, and technology of this magnitude should not be needlessly duplicated and therefore left open to potential abuse. The states' rights argument barely rose above a whisper.

A story ran in the *Los Angeles Times* that several Iraq War veterans in Oregon were fleeing across the border to Canada, fearing that the Booth would be used on them if they were ever found guilty of war crimes.

Nothing had changed. And yet everything had changed. Because of fear, because of expectations, because the Karma Booth existed, because a new way of seeing had been created—even if the view was limited and it obscured and raised more questions than it answered. Nothing had changed, except for the possibility that certain people who were murdered could possibly one day be brought back to life.

And none of them would be prophets.

For the sake of security and to cope with the flood tide of media attention, the Karma Booth was carted onto a moving van and relocated to a federal building in White Plains. It was here that Tim, at Gary Weintraub's invitation, saw the second use of the Booth. Weintraub was deliberately evasive over who the selected murderer was or who the scientists expected to emerge as the resurrected victim. "Let's just see what happens."

Tim was late in getting his BMW on the road to Westchester, and only moments after he arrived and showed his ID to the guards outside the test room, he walked in as the process was unfolding. Once again, light carved into the body of a death row inmate, revealing a fissure of amazingly bright pinpoints and whorls inside—and then there was that revolting odor that washed through the room like an abattoir stench. There was enough of the horrified inmate for Tim to identify who was being torn apart. He recognized the young face, the shark-like dark eyes and the peach fuzz stubble on the upper lip and chin.

It was Cody James, eighteen, and for three days of a single week about six months ago, he had been famous—particularly in Texas. In Austin, he had stolen a shotgun and a 9mm Glock pistol from the locked storage case at the home of a friend, whose father was a police officer. He then showed up at his old high school and began shooting. But unlike other school rampages and massacres, Cody James's rage was not that of a nihilistic, disaffected outsider. He was considered a gentle, well-mannered boy. He played guard on the school's championship-winning basketball team and was generally deemed an average if not always motivated student. No, something else had set him off.

At the moment, however, his torment and his grudges didn't seem to matter because his face and body were becoming comet trails and nebulae, changing to tiny stars and dazzling, colored rings. And then a blinding whiteness filled the chamber, gradually fading until all that he was disappeared.

Tim walked briskly over to Gary Weintraub, his friend standing beside the arrogant young neurologist, Miller, watching another couple of scientists work the controls. "Gary, you picked Cody James?"

It was Miller who rose to the defense. "*We* didn't pick Cody James, man," he said testily, running a hand through his halo of unruly brown hair. His worn sneaker tapped the floor tile impatiently as he kept one eye on the Karma Booth chambers. "We picked Geoff Shackleton, the geography teacher he blew away in a cafeteria. His doctor says he was healthy. Forty-two years old, jogged to the park every weekday morning, no psychological or cardiovascular issues we might have to think about. You know...the shock of coming back and everything. And then you got—"

"Not my point," snapped Tim, who went back to addressing Weintraub. "Gary, do you remember the story on the news?"

Weintraub looked like he was going to answer, then made a half-hearted shrug and took out a cloth to polish his spectacles. His round, normally jovial face went blank. He either couldn't recall the details or didn't want to admit he knew them. In the second chamber, bright light was flashing and made its familiar strobe pattern behind the tinted glass. The "secondary effect" had begun.

Tim knew the details of the school rampage well enough. They were sordid tabloid fare, all luridly chronicled before the trial of Cody James. It soon emerged that the young man was friends with one of the school's seniors, Dustin "Dusty" Cavanaugh, who was sleeping with his English teacher—who also happened to be Geoff Shackleton's twenty-seven-year-old wife, Nicole. Dustin Cavanaugh was known around school as "Perv" even without his classmates learning about his affair with a teacher. Young Cavanaugh's sealed juvenile record also somehow made it into the headlines. The most pertinent details involved how at the age of fourteen, he sexually molested both a boy of twelve and a girl who was thirteen years old.

He then played matchmaker between Cody James and Nicole Shackleton, who relieved him of his virginity. But after Cody slept with the teacher, Dustin insisted his friend repay him for the experience by sleeping with *him* in front of Nicole, who allegedly would find it "hot."

Cody, feeling used and humiliated, as well as sexually threatened, went to fetch the guns.

Dustin Cavanaugh stopped laughing when the bullets slammed into his chest, but he lived because Cody hesitated as he pulled the trigger, fouling up his aim. He quickly regained his grim resolve and shot Amber Janssen, who was screaming and pulling out her phone as she rushed to the swinging doors. She survived, but was paralyzed from the waist down.

Geoff Shackleton had no idea what sexual intrigues were going on involving his wife and just happened to be in the cafeteria, talking to a fellow teacher about the latest revised curriculum. He went to tackle Cody, who killed him on the spot with a blast that took off a third of the teacher's skull, leaving a gruesome stain of blood on the floor with tiny bits of bone and brain matter. Cody fired two more shots to keep everyone back and afraid, and then he abandoned the rifle to go hunt for Nicole with the pistol.

The vice-principal of the school had heard the shots, shouted to a student to call 911 on her cell phone, then smashed a trophy case and grabbed a hockey stick from a display. He slashed the stick across Cody James's head as the boy stepped out of the cafeteria, knocking him down and making him drop the gun. Two of Cody's football teammates nearly beat him to death before the vice-principal shouted for them to stop.

Nicole Shackleton was sent to prison for the statutory rape involving Dustin Cavanaugh, who just barely escaped life beyond bars himself over a female student stepping forward with a rape charge that didn't stick for lack of evidence. At her trial, Nicole claimed that her husband had been a closeted homosexual who only needed her for social appearances, and in her sexual frustration, she had turned to a student. It didn't really matter what Geoff Shackleton's proclivities were; he was dead, and she was going to jail.

But now he was alive, naked and disoriented, half-stumbling out of the second chamber as the doctors ran up with a hospital gown and a syringe containing a sedative. Geoff Shackleton was a man entering middle age with a small paunch, a little gray at his temples. His eyes wide, he now asked, "Where...?"

More words formed on his lips, but he lost consciousness. The sedative wasn't really required.

"He's okay," said Miller. Then with less confidence: "He looks okay. He'll be okay..."

He ruffled his hair again and kicked the floor with a sneaker, jubilant that the Karma Booth had demonstrated it would consistently work. Weintraub merely peered through his spectacles, quietly absorbed as if he were watching fruit flies eating a plate of grapes.

They were already wheeling Geoff Shackleton out to the new emergency ward set up for arrivals down the hall.

Tim turned once more to Weintraub and Miller. "You do realize the life you've given back is in complete tatters! From what I've read, the poor bastard had no idea his wife was fucking students. He wasn't gay or cruising bus stations as she claimed, but his rep at his workplace—and oh, keep in mind the guy worked down in Texas as a *teacher*—is ruined!"

Miller was indifferent. "Come on! All that stuff would have come out if he had lived. She would have said the same shit."

"You don't know that!" countered Tim. "And he would have been there to defend himself against her accusations. He tried to stop Cody James at the school, and he probably would have been treated like a hero, which would have mitigated her bullshit. The guy's going to be devastated when he learns his wife is partly responsible for the whole nightmare!"

"And again," said Weintraub patiently, "the man still would have had to face those unpleasant facts had he simply been wounded. What would you have me say, Tim? Do I personally believe Nicole Shackleton and that young man, Cavanaugh, share responsibility? Without question, of course. But the wife and that boy didn't go collect firearms and shoot them in a crowded school—Cody James did."

"Gary, you're missing the point," said Tim. "I don't have sympathy for that boy. The shrinks called him disturbed and unbalanced, and my heart doesn't weep for him at all. The girl he shot in the lunchroom never did a damn thing to him, and the witnesses say the little monster *laughed*. He got a kick out of causing destruction and pain. I don't know what your Karma Booth is but I don't think it's justice! That girl, what's her name, Amber… Amber Janssen. She'll never walk again. What does the Booth do for her?"

Miller stopped tapping his sneaker and folded his arms. In a calm and reasonable voice, he answered, "Nothing—you're right. So you want to ignore what we can do for this guy? Shackleton is alive, and he will think, he'll feel, he'll go on with his existence despite the time gap."

"But we're not talking about minutes, we're talking about months, and *he* could be different," said Tim. Again, he appealed to Weintraub. "I went and saw Mary Ash, Gary. She's not the same person."

"Jesus, you know this after meeting her for the first time?" scoffed Miller.

"Her own mother is afraid of her."

Tim broke off, realizing there was no point. The neurologist wasn't in the mood to listen. Besides, he was learning nothing from this argument and something new had occurred to him—something he had almost forgotten in the light show of the Booth chambers.

"Hold on. Cody James hadn't exhausted all his death row appeals."

Weintraub and Miller exchanged a look, but both were curiously silent.

"How did you speed up the legal process?" asked Tim. He realized as he finished the question, he had his answer already. "You *didn't*, did you? You didn't have to. Did they just give you carte blanche to go ahead and use it for convictions?"

Still, the two scientists said nothing. At last, Weintraub shook his stubby fingers in a gesturing circle, confessing,

"They've sanctioned the Booth for cases where the murders are beyond any factual mitigation or doubt, and yes, I know, Tim, you'll ask who decides that, but we get authorization from the Attorney General. Look, given that you remember so much about the Cody James case, you must know that students at the school caught the shooting on their phone cams. He did it. He was clearly guilty. The appeals were nothing but a formality."

"Oh God, Gary, is *that* why you did it?"

Weintraub sighed. "We needed to know."

Tim understood: to know if the Karma Booth worked on its own laws, not on the laws of Man. And now they had their answer.

The Karma Booth remained a constant source of news, near-news and speculation. You couldn't turn on the TV anymore without hearing discussion about it. It filled blogs and sold magazines. It inspired sick jokes on late night talk show monologues.

Two weeks after the lights flashed and dazzled in the test room in White Plains, Tim walked down Sixth Avenue in New York with Michael Benson, the under-secretary of Homeland Security who had got him involved. Benson was five years older than him, with a tuft of lank black hair at the front of his scalp while the rest had long since retreated. The man's vanity was focused on his body, and he often bragged about four games of racquetball a week and his morning jogs.

"Little shit from the Congressional page staff beat me," laughed Benson, rubbing the hair on the back of his head, still wet from his sports club's shower. "Better play a couple more times a week."

"What's surprising is that you think you can still slaughter seventeen-year-olds on the court," replied Tim.

"*You* go ahead and grow old gracefully, pal. I'm going to fight it every step of the way."

Tim had known the exec as an ambitious player who had moved up through the management ranks of the CIA and then saw the potential in Homeland's growing new department. It didn't surprise him at all that Benson was taking point over something as controversial and explosive as the Karma Booth. The man had always liked keeping a hand in plots to hurt the credibility of the latest Saddam or Osama, and his ego loved a consult from State over how to flatter the newest French prime minister. The Karma Booth offered power over life and death—impossible for a political addict to resist.

"Enough chit-chat about your impending mid-life crisis," said Tim. "Let's talk about this rush you and your pals in the corridors of power have to set off a bomb."

"What can I say, Tim? The Republicans had the Senate seats to pass the bill. It was rushed right through committee."

"Then I'm even happier you couldn't persuade me to move to Washington."

It was a regular friendly and not-so friendly duel between them whenever he was summoned to the Beltway. He had no desire whatsoever to live in the capital. Benson always argued it would make life easier... for him. Tim always reminded him that he charged enough that his clients could, and should, damn well come to New York.

"So they've decided to use it, even though they still don't know how it works."

Benson was philosophical. "Nobody is ever sure how the biggest scientific breakthroughs—"

"Yeah, yeah, I know, I know." Tim sighed wearily, knowing Benson was about to drag out the penicillin defense again. He was getting so tired of that one. "So I take it my services are no longer needed. You certainly don't need an ethics assessment."

Benson pursed his lips, surprised. "On the contrary. We need your assessment more than ever now."

"What on earth for?" Tim asked gently. And Benson's face told him it was just as he feared. The final decider was politics. The technology had to be used because they *did* have it. He struggled for another tack. If they wanted him to do his job, they could at least clear a path for him.

"Look, if you don't know how it works then tell me where you got the technology from. And I'm not going to buy that it's the latest tech toy from the NSA or CIA."

"It's not," said Benson, looking mildly embarrassed. "I suppose the best way to categorize it is... It was a gift."

"A *gift*? A gift from who?"

"Does it matter?"

"You're kidding, right?" replied Tim. "You're telling me an earth-shattering technology is just *given* to American authorities? And no one bothers to do the necessary homework or get briefed on what it—"

"Weintraub was briefed," Benson said tightly.

"He knew?" And as Benson nodded, Tim wondered aloud, "I cannot believe the government gave him carte blanche like this. How could they?"

He ran his hand through the straw-blond comma of hair over his forehead, always a classic sign that he was trying to work something through. It was unbelievable. The technology would be fascinating no matter how the booths had been developed, but to learn of this naïve, irresponsible adoption of them and then blindly putting them to use—

"Weintraub made his case for human trials," Benson was saying.

"*How?* How could he make a case for human trials with absolutely no empirical evidence of his own to demonstrate what they can do?"

"The way I hear it, our good doctor told the cabinet secretaries something like this: 'Put aside all the conspiracy theories, all the bullshit. Just imagine for a moment that there's incontrovertible evidence that Oswald did shoot JFK in Dallas. And that you have the Karma Booth to fix that."

Tim sighed in disbelief. "Aw, come on, that doesn't fly. That whole hypothetical shows you exactly what problems we're going to get with this thing. There are *still* doubts to this very day over Oswald's involvement. Great! What happens when you *do* have a case that sparks public outrage but the evidence isn't clear-cut?"

Benson offered a lopsided smirk. "Come on, Tim, that's why they invented appeals. Yes, I know they fast-tracked the Cody James case, but they'll come up with a new process. What? You think if they fried Oswald, and he didn't do it—"

"Go ahead, tell me what happens."

"Nothing happens!"

"Nothing happens? You're sure? How do you know? How can you possibly know, Benson, until it happens?"

And as he saw Benson grapple with that one, he nudged the man's elbow, urging them to keep walking. The walking always helped him to think. He just wished it worked for others. He didn't want to be distracted into the tired arguments for or against capital punishment. Those in the pro-Booth camp had the ultimate trump card, and yet no one was pausing over the enormity of a far more humbling truth of the machines.

"Benson, listen to me," Tim tried again. "I'm not a physicist or a medical doctor, but it baffles me that I should be the only person waving the red flag here. Let's say these things work properly—they bring back a victim while they execute the murderer. Then we have *physical laws of Nature* that may actually follow a *moral principle*. Can you wrap your head around that one? Because I can't!"

Benson licked his lips, eyes downcast, clearly wanting to speak some truth to the issue. "Tim, listen, the Booth can still be used," he said slowly. "If it does follow a moral principle then we have scientific means to guide us in—"

Tim cut through him brutally. "Project past your wishful thinking. The Booth has this enormous power. It was built—by a man or a team—somewhere. That means somebody already has insight into how these mind-boggling principles work. They may even be able to manipulate these principles, whatever they are. You comfortable with that one, too?"

Benson allowed himself another long pause to consider. "Maybe that's why the tech is a gift. The responsibility is so huge."

"So I'll ask again: Who gave it to you?"

"Orlando Braithewaite." Benson waited for the surprise then nodded as he saw something else on Tim's face. "That's right, they say you met him once. Had some kind of enlightening special meeting with him and your dad."

"I wouldn't go so far as to call it that."

Benson shrugged. "Call it whatever you want. Find him, and you'll get your answers."

"It's not like I have Braithewaite on speed dial and can get an appointment."

"That just makes you the same as everyone else who's tried," replied Benson. "He gave us the goods, briefed Weintraub about it and then nicely buggered off on his Gulfstream. Anybody else, yeah, of course you ask about a gift horse in the mouth, but…"

"Yeah, I get it," said Tim. "Bill Gates, Warren Buffett, Michael Bloomberg, Orlando Braithewaite."

Yes, he knew about Braithewaite. He had known about him for decades.

"Look, if you can find him, more power to you," said Benson. "The cabinet secretaries are expanding the parameters of their—*your* investigation. We need more than just your input as an ethicist. We need you to figure out how this damn thing works, Tim. What the long-term effects are, what kind of trouble we could get into, what our billionaire's real agenda may be—everything, everything—"

"You need a scientist to make those kind of evaluations," argued Tim. "And you've already got one with Weintraub. I'm not an investigator for State anymore, pal—I'm not even a diplomat. I'm busy raising the next crop of Oxfam workers and correspondents for *The Economist*."

Benson stopped at a corner and dropped his voice to a whisper, pointing a finger into Tim's lapel. "You are exactly the guy we need. You think for one second we're going to get an objective view from Gary Weintraub? Are you shitting me? Get real! Yeah, sure, he'll tell us what he knows for equations and physical effects, that's it. I mean… Jesus, they go on and on about Oppenheimer and those other guys and their conscience over the bomb. Well, they still built the fucking thing, didn't they?"

Benson stepped back and looked around them nervously, as if he had just confided a dirty little secret. "You get your retainer plus twenty-five percent above that. We're giving you unlimited travel—first-class commercial when it's regular business, private Hawker Horizon when it's a priority, on loan from Justice."

"What do I need a jet for when the Karma Booth's right in New York?"

And as soon as he started the question, he heard his own words trail off, as if someone else had spoken them in a distant room. He had his answer. "Jesus Christ…"

"You got it," said Benson.

"There's more than one out there."

"There's *several* of them," said Benson. "We should have known Mr. Braithewaite wouldn't play Santa Claus only with the United States. The Japanese came to us on their own about *their* Booth after Weintraub's news conference. The Israelis won't admit they have one, and we're not holding our breath over Saudi Arabia either. I've got a list of the others. Intelligence ops confirmed pretty early that Moscow has one. The liberals at State are bitching how Russia signed the European Convention on Human Rights, so capital punishment ought to be outlawed there already."

Tim rolled his eyes dismissively. "It's not like we can claim the moral high ground when *we* execute people. And these same geniuses should remember that Russia never ratified the protocols. Anyway, there hasn't been an execution there in years—the last one was in Chechnya."

Benson shrugged. "Hardly makes a difference, does it? I'm sure everybody's rulebook is getting thrown out the window. By the way, we've discovered the regime in Iran is a complete bunch of hypocrites—their mullahs denounced it, but Iran's got one." He crouched down and snapped open his briefcase, fetching a file and passing Tim a large photo blow-up. "Do you know what this is?"

Tim pulled out his reading glasses and looked. The color photo took in a large swath of a city skyline, and it took him only an instant to recognize the Montparnasse district of Paris. After all, he used to keep an apartment there. But then he saw in the foreground what the picture was really about.

"La Santé Prison," offered Tim. He tapped the grim, brown blockhouses stretching out like spokes on a wheel. "The French have a Booth? It's one thing for the Russians to have one, but capital punishment is definitely against the French Constitution."

"They do," said Benson. "They're taking the view that they'll use it for terrorists—same rationale as the British, who, incidentally, are keeping their Booth in Wapping or some godforsaken place, can't remember. But we have a new headache in Paris."

He handed Tim another couple of photos. They were surveillance shots from CCTV cameras, ones looking down on a young woman who couldn't be more than thirty years old. She had an ethereal beauty, with long black hair and pale skin, her lips full and her blue eyes inquisitive. And there was something else about her.

"How did she come back?" he asked. But he sensed he already knew the answer. It was about to be confirmed.

Her clothes. That was the first tip-off. The woman was wearing a green cotton dress and a broad-brimmed straw hat with a bow, almost as if the legendary Madeleine had grown up and left the old house in Paris covered with vines...

"The French claim there's only been limited use of the Booth, and no executions of prisoners are held at night," said Benson. "We have to take that on faith, but they seem genuinely stunned. After seven o'clock, there are no researchers in the facility wing containing the machine, so there's no need for any guards to be in the actual room. But closed circuit cameras stay on in there just like everywhere else—"

New photos. Tim flipped through them and stared at the flare of white light in the grainy shot, the Karma Booth impossibly turned on, functioning with no scientists in attendance—and no condemned inmate to be executed. In the next shot, the woman appeared. She was nude, stunningly beautiful, but clearly disoriented as she staggered out of the second chamber. More photo stills of the surveillance. *Snap...snap... snap*, and she walked out of camera view. Tim looked up at Benson, who saw his new question forming.

"They haven't determined how she got out."

"It's a *prison*," said Tim. "She shouldn't be able to get out at all."

"We know. So do they. There's no footage of her in the entire complex beyond that room. Then the street cameras pick her up from the Rue de Sèvres—how and where she got the clothes is also a mystery. She went into a Métro station and disappeared—no footage of her inside. *Anywhere*. But the Police Nationale had the presence of mind to lift fingerprints from where she touched that bench."

"She doesn't have a criminal record," said Tim flatly. "She was a victim."

"Okay, you're so clever," replied Benson. "If you've guessed that then maybe you've guessed the rest."

Tim skipped back to the first shots of the woman walking along the street. Wearing the green cotton dress that was simple, stylish. No, this woman wouldn't be in the regular database of unsolved murders. He could see it now, a subtle difference in the line of her jaw and in the oval of her face. People really did once look different thanks to diet and environment. Benson handed him a photocopy of a newspaper clipping, and he looked at the same beautiful woman in a posed photo and saw that the story had been printed in 1928.

The dress wasn't signature flapper apparel, but similar enough to be from that era.

"Her name was—is—Emily Derosier," explained Benson. "The last name is French, but she had a British father. She was a socialite and painter—or so the article says. I've never heard of her. She hung out with the celebs. Got stabbed to death in her Paris apartment, and the killer was never found."

Tim scanned through the article. It was mostly a bio that recapped the highlights of the victim's life. He would have to read it more thoroughly later.

"Great. So I've got to find Orlando Braithewaite, and it looks like I got to locate her as well. And I better find her fast."

"Maybe 'fast' is overstating it," said Benson. "Hell, she may rattle off the same gibberish as Mary Ash."

Tim shook his head. "I don't think so. Weintraub's crew pulled Mary Ash from the other side. This woman is different. She walked back into our world of her own accord, after more than eighty years. She must have come back for a reason."

5

Tim had Matilda book a transatlantic flight for him in three days. Before that, he wanted to go and visit Geoff Shackleton, curious to see if the schoolteacher was "different," as he had warned Weintraub and Miller.

It was raining as he drove back out to the White Plains facility, the sky a strange twilight blue behind the dark charcoal clouds. On his car stereo, he played *Kind of Blue*, the signature Miles Davis album. Tim's father had heavily influenced his jazz tastes. Piano, bass, drums—that's all you need, Dad said. Tim had found him to be right, and small 1960s combos were always the best musical sedative for him. Lee Morgan, Davis, Bird—yes, he had been right about music even though his father had never learned to play a note. But he had been wrong about so many other things.

His father was an electronics engineer, a man who believed in the firmly tangible and who spent the decades of his life at a workbench in front of an oscilloscope and a spot welder over circuit boards. His work was unfathomable to his son. It wasn't until his twenties that Tim realized his father's world view was almost entirely shaped by the evening news. Maybe that was what drove Tim to learn

French and to grapple with Hindi, to pursue a career in exotic locales.

His father had died of pancreatic cancer last year, refusing to see his son in his final emaciated stages, and Tim had never told him about India. It was not something they could talk about: intrusive concepts of otherworldly realities or of life after death. His father was an intelligent man, but not an intellectual. He had been one of that last generation of superman dads; the kind who kept three saws in the basement and who could fix his own car, a man who could easily sail Lake Michigan when they took the family's tiny boat out. Tim wouldn't be able to find the carburetor in his BMW if he tried.

Tim's mother had died ten years before from multiple sclerosis. Frightened and confused near the end, she had asked for a minister. Dad refused to get her one. Tim wasn't religious and didn't even consider himself spiritual—he was no seeker. But he had hated the old man for a long time over that denial of comfort for his mom. More than that, he hated how his father had easily accepted the doctors' diagnosis of his own fate—that cruel sentence of three months left—and just obediently, quietly, died by their schedule.

He didn't think about his father much afterwards. Theirs had been a distant relationship once Tim had grown up. The Karma Booth stirred up all this old business.

On the stereo, the Davis album ended and he heard Dexter Gordon play "Cry Me a River." Serves you right, thought Tim, smiling at the irony. It was fitting on this drive for another reason. The music had come from Gary Weintraub; his friend had found a rare live performance by Gordon in a Berlin jazz club and had the old vinyl converted to digital for Tim. A wonderful Christmas present three years ago.

Tim parked across the street from the federal building and held his valise over his head, trying not to get soaked as the security man in the navy blazer held the door open for him. After his postings in Asia, rain was always a time-travel mechanism for him, making him recall the monsoon seasons in Delhi and Mumbai and the way drops hit the tin roofs of squalid huts and formed instant lakes out of the cracked alleys.

He thought fleetingly of the night in the remote village, pushed it from his mind.

"It's really coming down," said the security guard.

"Yeah."

"Everything quiet here?"

The security guard nodded, knowing what he meant. He had been staffed to the project even before the Booth had been shipped out for its first use at the prison, and he had watched the mushrooming of publicity, protests and curiosity seekers since Mary Ash's resurrection. He had also become Tim's first antenna for when Weintraub and his scientists were excited over a development. Today he gave Tim another stoical nod. All was quiet.

Tim went up to the seventh floor and discovered the guard was right. He walked into the test center's infirmary room, and an ordinary middle-aged man looked up from his hospital bed at him with the curiosity you give any visitor. Geoff Shackleton had been prescribed mild anti-depressants—that was after Gary Weintraub felt he ought to explain the background of the shooting and what had happened to Shackleton's wife.

Tim wondered if he had "guilted" Gary into breaking the news personally. It didn't matter. Shackleton deserved to know the truth, and he would have learned in time. At least the guy was in a controlled environment where he could get counseling and any medical follow-up. He was affable towards Tim, though he looked a bit subdued, even drained, by the mood drugs he was on. That was probably to be expected. Tim began to relax, figuring the teacher's responses must be very much those of a coma patient on waking up.

"They'll probably keep you in this facility for a couple more weeks," Tim informed him.

Shackleton pulled the food tray on its swing arm and brought a bottle of water within reach. "That's okay," he answered with his mild Texan drawl. "I mean, it's not like I have anywhere really to go. They let me call my insurance company, and that's... What a mess! They said technically I'm not injured even though I was pronounced dead, and since I'm back alive, they invalidated my life insurance policy. Thieves. Goddamn thieves. Just as well—my wife was the beneficiary."

"I'm sorry."

"No, no, I'm... Hey, I shouldn't bitch like this, should I? I ought to stay grateful. I'm *alive*. What they did, it's amazing. And I'm only the second person to go through this? They told me there's a girl from Manhattan who got killed by some psycho, and she was the first, right?"

"That's right."

"My God. Incredible. How's she doing?"

Tim decided to be neutral. "She's fine. Have you spoken with your wife at all?"

"Not much point in that, is there?" Shackleton stared at the beads of water pattering on the room's windowpane, withdrawing into himself for a brief second. Tim waited patiently.

"My bank accounts have been closed," the teacher said slowly. "They tell me my house was foreclosed on when

Nicole went to jail. I can't afford a lawyer—not yet. The only word I want her to get from me is in divorce papers."

"I can make a couple of phone calls," Tim offered. "Your situation is unique, but there are already victim services in place, and I imagine if they keep using the Karma Booth, they'll have to set up a whole new extension of those programs for people who come back. Help them make a transition back into their old life."

"Or a brand new one," said Shackleton.

"If that's what you want. I'm sure it'll take time, but you'll find your way."

Tim rose to go, muttering about how he wanted to beat the traffic into the city. As much as he felt sorry for the teacher, he felt oddly reassured by this meeting. This man seemed fine. Then what had happened with Mary Ash?

Shackleton was talking to him.

"Mr. Cale?"

"I'm sorry, my mind was elsewhere."

"That's okay. Umm... You said you were hired to assess the impact of this thing, didn't you? What do you plan to recommend?"

"I don't know," said Tim honestly. "I've barely begun to examine all the issues involved and learn about the Booth. It's early days. How do you feel about it?"

Shackleton made a small, self-deprecating chuckle. "I don't know. I'm kind of the lab rat in the maze, aren't I? But it's bigger than me. You know I actually used to be against capital punishment."

"You still can be, Mr. Shackleton. Your beliefs haven't been compromised—you were never given a choice about being brought back."

"Yes, but who would say no?" asked the teacher.

"There are bound to be those who will," replied Tim. "Maybe we'll all have to carry around little cards like they do for organ donation, ticking off whether we want the procedure. Maybe we'll see 'wrongful life' suits in the courts. Are you upset by the fact that they executed Cody James?"

Shackleton sat in silence for a moment, mulling over the issue. Tim could hear a distant thunder roll through the window.

"Are you a God-fearing man, Mr. Cale?"

"No, I'm an agnostic."

Shackleton nodded. "Yeah. New Yorker, a professor, a diplomat—didn't peg you as a church-going fellah. Honest truth is I don't know how I feel about Cody. Or God anymore."

"Oh?"

"Men resurrected me, Mr. Cale. Not God. That's clear."

As Tim left, he marveled at how it was the last thing he expected a Christian schoolteacher from Texas to say. Well, he had warned Matilda the Booth was guaranteed to upset the whole range of belief systems. He punched the button for the elevator, and still distracted by the conversation, breezed through the sliding doors—

He felt the rain first, drops pelting the shoulders of his coat and wetting his forehead, jolting him back to attention to his surroundings.

He had been in the elevator.

Now he was on the street.

No, he couldn't have just sleepwalked his way out of the building. There were security checks and sign-out sheets before he was ever allowed to hit the pavement. But when he whirled around, he was facing the eastern wall of the block, the front entrance around the corner. There was a *kra-koom* of loud thunder, and a fork of lightning hit the ground behind the skyline of shiny boxes of office buildings.

Blink, and you're standing outside.

You've been moved. Plucked out of a point in space and a linear direction in time. Shifted elsewhere. What the hell...?

As he walked briskly back in, the security guard matched his confusion over how he could have got past him. Tim flashed his ID and snapped, "Forget it, it doesn't matter."

"But you were *inside*. How did—"

"Look, I'm here now, just let me through." Then he was back on the elevator, heading for the infirmary.

"Forget something?" asked Shackleton, looking genuinely surprised to see him.

"We're seven flights up," said Tim. "I stepped out of the elevator onto *the street*. You did it."

Shackleton's features went blank, as if he were a foreign tourist trying to decipher the words of a hotel desk clerk. "You said your mind was elsewhere."

Tim stared at the schoolteacher, hearing the words but no sense in them. Shackleton repeated it as if now it might sink in. "You *said* your mind was elsewhere."

"So you helped me? To get there...? Into that moment when I wanted to be outside...?"

Shackleton's expression was still innocent. "It's so simple, if only people would pay attention."

Tim nodded a silent goodbye and walked out again.

Benson's words came back to him in the car on the way back into the city. *We need you to figure out how this damn thing works, Tim. What the long-term effects are, what kind of trouble we could get into, what our billionaire's real agenda may be.*

Oh, is that all? Surely they had to know themselves that to understand the Karma Booth meant finally learning the nature of existence itself. Maybe they did.

83

We need you to figure it out, Tim. Everything, everything.

He felt he was back on familiar ground, conducting an investigation that was international in scope yet had clear "suspects" to find and interrogate. This specter of a woman who had slipped from the 1920s into their own century—she must know things. Mary Ash did but either couldn't or didn't want to communicate them with him and the rest of the world, at least not yet. Without a doubt Orlando Braithewaite knew things, if only Tim could find him to ask his questions.

That's right, they say you met him once.

Braithewaite.

Had some kind of enlightening special meeting with him and your dad.

He had lied to Benson. A small lie, but a lie nonetheless. It had indeed been a special meeting, back when he was a boy. But his father hadn't been present at the time.

Tim had been nine years old. Old enough to know who the Great Man was, and the touchstone of that experience prompted him to follow the billionaire's career in the news ever since. It was almost as if he felt a vague curiosity or obligation to keep track of a notable relative. The software developments of Braithewaite's computer corporation. The acquisition of rare works of Leonardo da Vinci by one of his foundations, to be donated to a modest school for girls in Pakistan. The astounding development of yet another Braithewaite foundation, setting up a research facility in Norfolk, England, where a lichen-like biomaterial organism would grow into a livable structure decades and decades into the future.

And now here Braithewaite was again, back on the world's radar. Tim couldn't help but feel that Braithewaite had unleashed on the world an alchemist's trick, what looked like blindingly bright gold but was, in fact, a lead anvil of new responsibilities and new horrors.

He got into town, checked his messages and emails with Matilda, and it didn't surprise him at all when the office receptionist for Orlando Braithewaite told him she would pass on his message, but that he shouldn't expect to get an appointment. Mr. Braithewaite wouldn't care that Timothy Cale was calling on behalf of the White House. Mr. Braithewaite didn't have to care because he was in Africa. It afforded him the luxury of keeping the arrogant, developed world at a distance, the same way the developed West had ignored the continent for decades.

Tim decided the only thing he could do was besiege the man's personal assistant in New York with messages and more and more requests. But of course, eventually, he would have to go to Africa. A trip there would be such a small thing. Especially to find out what waited beyond the whole world.

He had been nine. Though his father didn't like to travel and he absolutely *hated* flying, one of Braithewaite's companies had thrown enough money at his dad to lure him out to Thailand, of all places. Tim had begged to go with him, his imagination so easily fired by exotic locales, and since it was summer and the boy was already fairly independent, Henry Cale had caved in, while Tim's mom had stayed at home. Thailand was lush and green and humid, and there was plenty to dazzle an impressionable nine-year-old boy.

The project his father was working on had to do with robotics—mimicry of animal movement to get machines to be more graceful. Most people would have accepted that purpose, but even then, Tim was suspicious. "But Dad, what's it all for?"

"What do you mean, kiddo?"

"Well, does this Braithewaite guy want 'em for weapons to sell to the Pentagon or give everybody a robo-butler or what?"

His father had laughed. "I actually don't know, son. If you got enough money, you can pay guys like me to tinker around and figure out what you want to do after."

Fair enough. A long flight to London then their connecting flight to Bangkok and then a trip by car to a remote spot in the vast green expanse of jungle and rainforest. There was the lab complex, a neat row of bungalows for senior staff like his dad, and a village about a mile up the dusty road. It wasn't long before his father had to leave him to amuse himself. It was fun for a couple of days to watch the *whrrring* and screeching steel beetles and animatronic dogs scuttle around a gravel and sand courtyard for a while. But the novelty soon wore off, and Tim turned to his packed books and to exploring the village. When he had got his fill of the strange looks of the local people, he trudged and crunched his way through the magnificent vegetation.

After a while, he learned to pick his way quietly and more carefully because he realized if he did, he would take more in; fabulous insects and animals that wouldn't start at his approach. On the fourteenth day of his trip, he gasped in surprise as he spotted a great hornbill on a low tree branch. *Wow.* The most stunningly vivid yellow, white and black bill, reminding him a lot of a toucan, and according to his travel guide, the bird not only ate figs and insects, but it would even hunt small squirrels and birds. It looked to be hunting a gecko right at that moment.

Then Tim heard a buzzing drone. It would have been comical if it weren't so inconvenient and irritating. One of the robotics models from the R and D team back at the facility had somehow strayed into this jungle. This kind of thing happened when a command pathway got stuck in its programming, and the engineers and assistants had to go forage for their escapees. Now Tim was sure this fluttering metal *thing*, designed to look like a bird, but flying more like a drunken bumblebee, would spook both the hornbill and its prey.

"Not to worry," whispered a voice behind him. "It sees it, but it's not scared."

Tim looked over his shoulder. Just behind him stood Orlando Braithewaite. Tim would remember that even then the billionaire seemed ancient, though he could only have been about fifty that year. A man in an open-necked white dress shirt and tan khaki pants, his doughy face topped with a frosting of white hair, he smiled at Tim as if they were both partners in this casual expedition, and Tim felt himself smiling back, grateful for the company.

Every so often, Tim had spotted the CEO strolling the compound and knew he was supposed to be polite to this important man. Now Braithewaite gave him the impression that he was fleeing the tedium of the engineers and scientists just as much as he was.

"You're Henry Cale's son, aren't you?" The tone of his voice suggested he already knew.

"Yes, sir." Distracted by the bird, Tim burst into a happy laugh. The hornbill seemed to be studying the lazy, droning model. Tim thought perhaps he should go back to whispering, but the hornbill didn't seem to care anymore that he and Braithewaite were here. "Huh! Look at that! It doesn't know *what* that thing is!"

"Oh, I don't know," said the CEO gently. "Maybe it's getting inspired."

That was when things turned strange. The gecko padded nimbly away up the branch, along the thick, knotted trunk and to a neighboring limb of another tree. The hornbill lighted to another branch, stalking it. Tim and Braithewaite stepped cautiously, slowly, forward to watch, and then the impossible happened. Another hornbill was suddenly *there* on the branch, close to the gecko, only it couldn't be real. It "ghosted" in its movements, and if laptops and computers had been as advanced back then as they were today, Tim would have compared it to a screen icon shaded by the arrow. And stranger still, the "ghost hornbill" made the same buzzing drone as the robot model.

The robot model. No, he wasn't confusing the two. The drone was on the jungle floor, seeming to have run out of juice.

The hornbill—the real hornbill—fluttered its wings slightly and hopped a little further on the branch. Tim grasped what was going on—the impossible copy was *herding* the tiny lizard toward the genuine bird.

"How... how can it do that?" whispered Tim. "No bird can do that!"

Braithewaite said nothing.

They watched as the hornbill caught the gecko, tossed it in the air and caught it, gobbling it down. The ghost version of it was suddenly gone, abruptly vanished, dispensed with.

Tim turned away and began trudging back to the lab compound and the bungalows, Braithewaite walking along beside him. "You knew," he said with a faint note of accusation.

"No, I didn't," answered the CEO.

"But you said it—you said the bird got *inspired*."

"I was making a joke, young man, that's all. I'm sure we both must have been seeing things. The light can play tricks on you in the rainforest. We saw *two* birds, not one. No big mystery about that."

Tim was irritable all of a sudden. "I *know* what I saw. It watched the robot thing and then it came up with an idea—it *made* that other bird somehow! You say it's a trick of the light or whatever, but it made the same sound, too. It—it imitated it."

Braithewaite smiled. "You ever hear of the lyrebird of Australia? It can actually mimic all kinds of machine sounds. A car alarm, a chain saw—it's amazing."

"I know what I saw," Tim insisted.

The businessman stopped, putting a hand on Tim's shoulder. "I saw it, too."

Braithewaite seemed to read what was in his face, as if Tim waited to be told it had all been an elaborate joke, or that the billionaire's other engineers had improbably perfected a more convincing animatronic creature. He looked down at Tim as if the two shared a unique new perspective on reality.

"No, I'm not humoring you. And yes, I saw it. I threw out other ideas just now because I was curious to see how strong you are in accepting the evidence in front of your eyes. Not what other people will tell you. You know that we can fool ourselves, can't we?"

"Well... sure."

"But not this time," said Braithewaite, again flashing a smile that assured Tim they were in it together. "Are you any good at math and science, Tim?"

"No, sir," answered Tim, slightly embarrassed. He knew his dad was brilliant, and there were times when he genuinely did wish he was better at these subjects. But he just didn't seem to have the knack for them.

"It's okay," said Braithewaite, putting an arm around the boy's shoulder and leading him back to the compound. "Neither am I really. But you can take a scientific approach to things even if you never pick up a test-tube. They give you some poetry in school, don't they?"

"Some," said Tim, and they were close enough to the settlement now to hear the scientists and engineers talking, some sharing a smoke with the Thai staff.

"Look up a fellow called Blake," urged Braithewaite. "*To see a world in a grain of sand...*"

Tim went off to get a snack from his bungalow's Thai housekeeper, and for the rest of the day, he sifted over in his mind the bizarre thing he had seen in the jungle with the eccentric businessman. He hadn't learned the word *sentience* yet. He couldn't even articulate for himself how the bird, a simple bird, could possibly have the higher intelligence to do what it did, let alone the physical impossibility of what it had accomplished. He only knew that Orlando Braithewaite must have had something to do with it.

He did not speak to Braithewaite again during the rest of his stay in Thailand. There were occasional nods and polite smiles as the important man went to this building or that, always in the company of assistants or his management team, but Tim Cale would never share another one-on-one moment with one of the richest men on the planet.

So he was quite surprised when, four months after Tim and his father got back to the States, he learned that Orlando Braithewaite had arranged for him to get a full college scholarship. That was how Tim could afford to go to Yale. Word leaked out from the registrar's office about who was paying the bill, and so a minor legend evolved that the CEO had been so charmed by young Timothy Cale that he wanted to fund the boy's education. No one ever heard about weird animal behavior in the tropics or cryptic conversations walking back to a remote lab facility. It was enough that a billionaire had briefly been impressed with him.

Driven by conscience and good manners, Tim's father had tried through company channels, and then through his own personal efforts, to reach the CEO so he could thank him. But it was around this time that Orlando Braithewaite moved out of the public eye, staying more and more outside the United States.

Tim spent the next three days poring over court documents and forensic case files, looking for commonalities between Mary Ash and Geoff Shackleton, between their murders, between their lives… He hoped to find some clue, some distinguishing factor, to explain why the Karma Booth did what it did to Mary Ash and then what it did to Shackleton. He discovered nothing. Three days of fruitless research, but then something occurred to him. Maybe there was a common element. Maybe—

His musings were interrupted by a phone call from Gary Weintraub.

"I think we need to talk."

"We certainly do. Why don't we talk about Orlando Braithewaite?"

"Tim, I—"

"Then I need to know what you're doing about Geoff Shackleton, if there's any new phenomena shown by Mary Ash—"

"*Tim.*" He heard Weintraub made a sharp intake of breath, and then his old friend said tightly, "Look, I have some idea of the things you're going to say about Braithewaite. I imagine some shouting will be in order. But you need to get back here ASAP."

"Why?"

"To meet the newest returned victim—if it *is* a returned victim."

Tim didn't understand, and he didn't expect an explanation over the phone. He hung up, and as he reached for his black valise, Matilda put through another call, this time from Benson. He was trying to warn Tim about what was already breaking on CNN, Fox and NBC. The US Attorney General was "stepping down" to be with his family; the truth, according to Benson, was that the President had pushed him out for not being hawkish enough over the Karma Booth.

The new man stepping in—not yet grilled by the Senate but his confirmation all but a rubber stamp—had made it clear the Karma Booth executions should go ahead as planned. He was a former Kentucky prosecutor and one of the most conservative law professors to ever teach at Harvard. But in a careful maneuver of "cover your ass," the President was willing to keep the more cautious Health Secretary in the cabinet, which meant that Tim's contract and his investigation would still go forward.

As Tim turned his car onto the highway, he knew that Gary Weintraub would probably push hard to stay in his place, researching the Karma Booth. If executions were to go ahead using it, someone had to be the gatekeeper of Pandora's Box. *Damn it*, thought Tim. The Karma Booth's potential could be felt by the whole world, and it was forcing the politicians' hands.

When he got to White Plains, Weintraub insisted on giving him a short briefing first on the latest reports of Booth usage in other countries. "You need to see what's happened in context," he pleaded gently.

"What context?" asked Tim. He didn't know what his old friend was building up to.

According to the papers in Weintraub's hand—which detailed both US intelligence efforts and direct reports from other countries—the Karma Booth had presented a unique problem no matter where it was used. One of the first natural motivations with the Booth was to execute child murderers and bring back their small victims. Those whose lives had ended alone—tortured, pitifully crying, with no one responding and coming in time to save them.

In France, three years ago, a mother in Avignon had gained international sympathy by pleading on television for the safe return of her twin girls—it was later proved she had drowned them both in the Rhône. They sent her through the Booth, and her girls didn't return.

Nor did the seven toddler victims of pedophile murderer Avi Schacter in Jaffa.

In Tokyo, a *nisei* girl pushed onto subway tracks by a nineteen-year-old member of a *bosozoku* biker gang also failed to come back through the Booth.

A scientific consensus was slowly emerging. The Karma Booth couldn't (or wouldn't) resurrect any murder victim younger than twelve years old. The age appeared to be fixed, yet like so many other things, could not be explained.

Thirteen-year-old Sunil Ghosh, molested and strangled by his uncle in Mumbai, had stumbled out of the Karma Booth in New Delhi, more coherent than the usual arrivals and asking for his parents.

Fourteen-year-old Ali Khal, killed on the spot with a dagger when he burst unsuspectingly on his family's store being burglarized in Riyadh, had emerged from the Booth, his eyes haunted and wide. He was able to whisper after two days, "Are we poor now?" He had assumed the burglar had got away with it.

The Booth would not bring back eleven-year-old Bobby Tyler, beaten to death in Little Rock.

It would not bring back Maria Cobos in São Paulo, who had just turned nine before she died in a fire started by arson.

"Twelve," said Weintraub. "The arbitrary age of resurrection seems to be twelve. Any victim younger than this doesn't come back."

"Okay, understood," said Tim.

Then Weintraub moved on to a lengthy explanation about the latest execution using the Booth. He rattled off the background details, his voice betraying the strain of nerves and a new emotion: genuine regret.

"Armed robbery five years ago in, uh... in San Francisco." Like Nickelbaum, the latest death row inmate had been especially sadistic, which fueled the justice system's drive to put a lethal injection in his arm.

Tim nodded, impatient to see the new arrival and get the rest of the facts later. Wasn't it enough that the victim had returned? No, insisted Weintraub. "Just listen to me, please, Tim. You must realize—you have to *know*—we never expected anything like this."

And on he went with his background description. The story went that in a wild machine-gun rampage with accomplices, the convicted bank robber had taken a thirty-five-year-old Asian police officer captive, shooting off Constable Daniel Chen's right kneecap and beating him half-senseless with the butt of his rifle. Then the man shoved the barrel into his victim's mouth in front of witnesses.

Daniel Chen had been on the force ten years. No commendations, just a responsible, regular cop. His young wife, May, had come over from Hong Kong through the arrangement of Daniel's parents and in-laws, and his two daughters were aged three and five.

The inmate was torn apart by the white light of the Karma Booth, his body ripped into the blue and violet whorls of the mysterious equipment.

Gary Weintraub showed him the videotaped execution, but only the footage of the first booth. "Now let me show you 'Daniel Chen.' We have him waiting in the prison infirmary."

When the professor drew back a curtain on an observation window, Tim saw a boy of about three years old with sunshine-blond hair and bright blue eyes.

6

The boy stared curiously around the room, dressed in a hospital gown, his small feet dangling over the side of the examination table. Weintraub's team had electrodes on the boy's head hooked up to an EEG monitor. They were watching for any unusual activity, something like what Tim had seen from Mary Ash and Geoff Shackleton. The boy's eyes were certainly haunted, like those of Mary Ash, and like the first returned victim on her emergence, there were moments when the face went blank with disorientation, the lips trying to summon speech.

Tim stared at Gary. "Oh, my God…"

Weintraub ran a hand over his perspiring bald dome and clicked a button pen nervously. He swallowed hard and grunted, yanking back the curtain to obscure the observation window. He was partly responsible for bringing this child here, and he clearly didn't want to look at the boy anymore.

"I am imagining right now how some public relations flak in DC will panic over the 'message' from this."

"What the hell has the machine *done*? Did it yank Chen out of the middle of…of… what?"

There had had to be a reason for this, thought Tim. There *had* to be. "Mary Ash was dead less than a year, wasn't she? But Chen's killer…"

Gary Weintraub nodded. "The time elapsed, yes, I see your point. The Booth must have pulled Daniel Chen out of his next… incarnation, I guess, for lack of a more precise term. Or maybe it is the right word. We're standing here, accepting the actual assumption on a scientific basis that reincarnation is *real*. I feel a fool just for saying it."

"Your evidence is sitting in there," Tim reminded him, suppressing a shudder.

"But it's not instantaneous," said Weintraub. "Something else happens before… I mean, the process has an interval. And the equipment pulled him from wherever he was supposed to be. The ramifications of this thing! It's got to stop."

"It won't stop," said Tim. "Benson called me so your higher-ups must have called you, didn't they? We've got a new Attorney General, and he wants this thing to be used. There's an election year coming up."

"I know, I know," answered Weintraub, still staring at the curtain as if he could see through it to the child. "But surely the man has to face the truth. If we showed him that little boy…"

Tim let the air out of his lungs in a long sigh. "He'll make the same conclusion. That we've stumbled onto our 'first rule,' and the Booth should be used only on murderers whose victims are deceased less than a year. As if that'll save us from more chaos. Gary, listen. Please tell me you haven't notified Daniel Chen's family."

Weintraub looked mortified. "Are you *joking*? The idea alone is grotesque! And from what I understand, Daniel Chen and his wife have children of their own."

"It's going to leak out," said Tim. "It's inevitable."

"I'm making arrangements to have the boy placed with special needs personnel in a different city," offered Weintraub. "For now."

"For now?" prompted Tim. "What, so we'll have a whole generation of foster children brought into our existence by that thing?" Something occurred to him, prompting a fresh chill down his back. "Gary. Suppose the Booth didn't pluck him out of the 'other side,' the hereafter, wherever—suppose it scooped him up from *here*? *This* plane of existence. Suppose this kid is destined to be on a milk carton in New Jersey if we don't find out who he belongs to?"

"He's not talking yet," Weintraub protested.

"What's he said so far?"

"Nothing. We tried speaking to him in English, French, German, Spanish, Italian, Mandarin, Cantonese, you name it we've tried it just on the off chance that some piece of Daniel Chen is still in there, will react - and yes before you say it, I know Chen grew up in San Francisco, and that's all counter-intuitive, but we didn't know what else to try... But the boy doesn't engage with anyone who walks into the room, doesn't make eye contact. We're not sure if there's a mild form of autism at work here, but it's still too early to be making assumptions. If the boy did disappear from Norway or whatever, well, for all we know, it could take months to discover his parents—if he ever did have parents. Good gracious, listen to what we're saying."

"Terrific, you've invented a whole new category of orphan."

"Come on, Tim, what else would you have us do?" demanded Weintraub. "Every new technology causes upheaval in the world, and in ways mankind can't begin to predict."

Tim waved away the rationalizing. Outrage would get him nowhere.

"Okay, let's try something else for the moment. What did Orlando Braithewaite tell you when he showed you the Booth? I mean, didn't he give any kind of understanding of its limits, what it could do?"

Weintraub collapsed into a metal chair in the hallway. "It wasn't that straightforward."

He rubbed his eyes, and Tim could see his friend's exasperation growing again. "Braithewaite flew me out at his own expense to Sierra Leone. I had no idea why he chose that particular country—last I heard, he was living on the other side of the continent in Ethiopia. He had the transposition booths set up, and he never introduced me to his technicians. He just went ahead with his... demonstration."

"Demonstration?"

Weintraub's round face lost its color, his eyes glaring at the floor tile. For a moment, he was back in Africa, reliving the experience of the first time the Booth was used.

"Braithewaite claimed the Booth had undergone trials with animals: wild pigs in Kenya slaughtered by lions on the wildlife preserve and brought back to life. I never saw them. I did hear things from an animal pen nearby that squealed and snorted—it was a peculiar, warped sound, as if it had gone through some kind of electronic mixing equipment. Looking back on it now, the poor things sounded terrified. But I merely assumed they were bleating away because one of them was being taken away for dissection or something else. Animals *know*. They always know somehow. Then they hauled in this wreck of an African convict in rags... They dragged him in cuffs right to the first booth. Braithewaite said the man had been a henchman of one of the warlords years ago, during the blood diamond era. He shot an army soldier in his last escape attempt.

"And I watched Braithewaite manipulate the controls himself. The soldier had only been one month dead, and I examined photos of the crime scene, Tim. They even showed me where the man was buried. They had a Portuguese doctor who had worked as a medical examiner in Lisbon—he checked the DNA from bone marrow to confirm it was the right person. And then I watched the lights in that second chamber, and this pitiful, mumbling victim shuffle naked as an infant back into our world! I swear I don't remember what questions I asked Braithewaite. I certainly can't recall his answers, but I do know this soldier after sixteen hours was lucid. He was absolutely awake and coherent—he was *alive*. He asked for a friend in his unit, and he wanted to know about his family."

Tim didn't say anything. He simply stood and listened, knowing Weintraub wasn't finished.

"Before you ask, the poor man couldn't tell us anything about where he had gone. He might as well have just woken up from an anesthetic after surgery. No white light beckoning him forward, no coma dreams, nothing. He was just... *back*. If you had seen the evidence of his death, pictures of his actual corpse, and then to look into the eyes of this fellow! Not like Mary Ash, Tim. I didn't conceive of a Mary Ash, coming back so strange, so affected..."

"You wanted this."

"Yes, it's true, I wanted it! I thought the whole world wanted this—that we *needed* this technology! Every day the network news is an unspeakable recital of carnage."

"Gary, it's always been that," replied Tim. "History is a steady roll call of plague, butchery, intolerance, war, and yeah, mass murder. So we live in a bloody age—what else is new? Except for *this*. Can you reach Braithewaite? Can you ask him how we control this goddamn thing?"

"Don't you think I've tried? It's impossible. He has a whole corporate army of receptionists to keep you at bay. They take messages, but he never responds."

"Okay, but do you think he foresaw this? That he knew the Karma Booth would have these effects with the way it's being used?"

Weintraub looked up. His helpless expression told Tim he couldn't be sure of what Braithewaite had thought.

"Damn it," muttered Tim. "Okay, I need to talk to that boy."

"He's not talking to anyone."

"I've had some luck so far with Mary Ash and Geoff Shackleton."

Weintraub nodded. "Fair point. But if I were you, I'd be worried about why *you're* the one who connects with these people."

"For now, let's just use it to our advantage."

"Very well. But he's still a child, whether he was reincarnated in Germany or born into some other realm of existence. Assuming he'll talk to you at all, what do you expect to learn? He'll probably tell you even less than Mary Ash."

"If he really is a child, he won't lie well," replied Tim. "Maybe I'll get something."

Tim walked in, offering a friendly smile to the boy, who snapped to attention as the adult closed the door. He looked as anxious as any three-year-old in a strange place without parents or a trusted guardian. His tiny mouth opened in surprise and expectation, and his little feet still dangled over the side of the examination table as if he was sitting on a fishing dock on a summer holiday. He fidgeted and shoved a couple of fingers in his mouth. Whatever else the new arrival was, Tim thought, he was a small child.

"Hi, buddy," Tim started, sliding over a chair. "We want to get you home. I know you haven't talked to anyone here, but maybe your mom and dad told you not to talk to strangers. So okay, we'll do this properly. My name's Tim. And you are?"

He held out his hand to shake. The blond boy smiled shyly and looked away.

"You know," Tim tried again, "I've lived in all kinds of places all over the world. Maybe you want to start differently. We can bow like they do in Japan—" He bowed. "Or maybe you come from another place where they don't shake hands. Hey, maybe they start with hand puppets. You come from the land of hand puppets?" He started to pantomime a horse galloping and a goofy bird. "Is that it, you come from the country of Gooney Bird?"

The little boy began to giggle at his antics. *Contact*, thought Tim.

"Come on, buddy, I'm acting my heart out here! If we can't use gestures, do I have to sing my name and you sing yours? *Tiiimmmmmm...*" He imitated a long humming chime.

The boy laughed harder, and then his small hand reached out and touched the side of Tim's head. Tiny fingers lifted in a fluttery brush of movement, carried out with a three-year-old's coordination, but there was an intent, a purpose.

Contact.

It was not telepathy, not quite.

"Whoa, wait a minute," muttered Tim. "I can't... I don't know how to... How are you doing this?"

Music. He *tasted* music. He wouldn't have thought such a thing possible. The notes and sounds seemed to have a weight in his mouth and throat, as if the emotions of melody can have a taste. The music itself was disturbing, barely anything familiar to him. He tasted Arabic melodies, Armenian and Turkish woodwinds, but only later, much later, would he be able to identify the cultures behind what was being passed to him. Or pin down what he guessed were the instruments. As if they mattered at all. Arabic *duduks*, Indian *tablas*, arghul drones, finger cymbals, Persian *kamanches*. But he suspected the Middle East flavor of the melody in his throat wasn't important. It was the feeling, the feeling rushing from the boy. Anxiety, little lost animal fear.

The music sounded at first like a cacophonous wail to Tim's ears, so used to his diet of jazz, classical and pop. But these melodies would have sense and precision to those who grew up in Cairo and Tehran. He wants to go home. *I know you want to go home*, thought Tim, swallowing, trying to say the words. *We want to help, we need to know your name, who you belong to*, and then the music changed. The taste in his mouth became bitter, with a garlic tang. The notes grew dissonant, harsh. A child's frustrated banging on a piano keyboard—

Weintraub and Miller were rushing into the room, their faces showing concern. "Tim, step back," said Weintraub, an arm already up to gently urge him aside.

"What? What is it?"

"Look at the monitor," said Miller, his hand in a surgical glove lifting a tiny flashlight to check the boy's pupils.

Tim looked. There was an earthquake on the small screen, the lines for brain function jumping and stuttering. And he knew what this was. He had actually seen it before—at fourteen years old he had watched, helpless and panicking, as a cousin experienced what doctors called an absence seizure. They used to call it *petit mal*. A thunderstorm in the brain even as the person's eyes stare vacantly ahead for seconds, occasionally a limb twitching or the sufferer moving on his own to a different spot for no reason. It was chalked up to a form of epilepsy.

But this boy was not disconnected as his cousin had been. He was *in there*, a piece of him communicating with him on a subliminal level.

"He's alert," said Tim.

"No," mumbled Weintraub, his reaction automatic.

"No, he's right!" piped up Miller. "Look at him, Gary!"

The boy was moving his head, studying the room, not engaging with any of his visitors. For Tim, the music was gone. He tried to make eye contact once more with the boy, but there was no sign of interest. By the time Miller told a nurse to fetch a sedative for the child, the seizure was over, and the lines on the monitor showed normal brain activity.

Outside the room, Tim tried to explain what he had just experienced.

"Sounds like *synesthesia*," reasoned Miller.

"What?" asked Tim.

"Neurological anomaly," explained Miller. "It's really kind of cool. It's like, two body senses coupled together. Some people with one kind of synesthesia have talked about, like, *seeing* music on a kind of screen in front of them, in wavy lines. I mean oscillations. People with another kind can associate colors with certain numbers or letters. It's not like it's a consistent thing, but many of them, you know, think of 'A' as red. So imagine if every time you see nine, you associate nine with blue."

"But I don't have this synesth... this neurological thing," complained Tim. "The boy made me *taste* music! He caused it." He turned to Weintraub. "I think you can forget about the milk cartons, Gary. I can't believe he's from this plane of existence. He communicated that way because he expected it would make sense to me."

"Well, that's a huge assumption," snapped Miller. "You don't know that for sure, man."

"You think a three-year-old boy could do that, and this would be the first we learn of it?" Tim shot back. "Every child *wants* to communicate. He just did. He didn't use language—he used what was available to him. And I felt him telling me he wants to go home."

"But he couldn't tell you where."

"He's a child," said Tim. "Imagine you're a tourist lost in Athens, and you can't read or speak Greek. Now imagine you're a little kid who's separated from his tourist parents. I couldn't speak his language."

"But he chose to speak with you," Weintraub pointed out.

"I know, and I don't quite understand that either. I don't know how to read or play music. You do, Gary—you play jazz piano. You're a more fitting choice. You'd know the underlying mathematics to possibly communicate with him. I don't know why he singled me out—maybe because I hummed my name as a joke for him. There is a pattern emerging, though, from the three we've seen come back."

Weintraub shoved his hands into the pockets of his lab coat. "I don't detect one."

"I can't pretend I have it completely figured out," admitted Tim, and with a sideways glance at Miller, he added, "and I'm willing to admit this is purely subjective. But Mary Ash could tell me what I was doing on any given day of my life. Geoff Shackleton was able to detect my impatience to get on with things, and he transported me out of a building with a single thought. That boy made me taste an instrumental piece of music in order to understand what he felt. Each of the Booth victims has come back with extraordinary skills informed by heightened empathy."

Miller folded his arms and tapped out a nervous, distracted rhythm with his sneaker. "Hey, that's great, but I don't see what that observation gets us. I mean so what? So like, they understand *us* better because they've been to the Great Beyond? We got to understand *them*. I'm happy for you that you're making connections, man, but I'll feel so much more satisfied when I got raw data in my hands."

As he walked away, Tim turned to Weintraub. "What was that supposed to mean? What's he talking about?"

Weintraub watched Miller go and said, "Oh, since we can't figure out yet how Mary Ash and Shackleton can do what they do—and now we have to include the boy as well—Miller wants to do full workups on every returned victim from the Booth, as well as their murderers. Perhaps when a victim returns, he'll find something in their brain scans, something that can give us insight into these extra... functions."

"That's actually very clever," said Tim, impressed.

"Only if it gets results," Weintraub reminded him. "If our young genius wants to insist on miracle productivity for everybody else, we should hold him to the same standard."

"Damn straight."

"I have to say, Tim, your pattern theory puts a nice, positive spin on what they do. But these people are returning with enormous power. I can't say I'm comfortable with anyone being able to rattle off my daily biography or move me across distances, especially if they turn out to be a child who wants to move me around like a Tonka Truck."

"They don't belong here," said Tim, staring at the little boy through the window. "Even if they are benign, they're not supposed to be back with us."

"Will you tell that to Mary Ash?" asked Weintraub.

"I think she's suspected it herself for a while now."

"Then what are our conclusions? You're making it sound like there's a plan behind it all, and I'm telling you there isn't one. There never is. It's the kind of chaotic fallout you always see with a new technology."

Tim moved to go. "I happen to think someone planned for chaos."

7

Tim checked his BlackBerry, which assured him there were no more sightings of Emily Derosier, the murder victim of 1928 who had stepped out of a Karma Booth and onto the streets of modern-day Paris. He didn't give a damn. He was still convinced, as he had told Benson, that there was *purpose* behind her return without any execution. The investigation had to move there. He rang Benson's cell to explain it to him, and to his surprise, the White House official agreed. Best to pile on the favors while the man was in an accommodating mood, thought Tim. He needed something else.

There was a pause on the line, and then Benson asked: "Seriously?"

Yes, seriously. Tim wanted him to ask the authorities in India to find the boy and the old woman—the ones who had been "returned" after the mysterious robed strangers had massacred the village residents. The boy wouldn't be a boy any longer; he would be a young man. The old woman, he expected, would probably not even be around anymore, given her hard living conditions and the life expectancy of her caste. Still, it wouldn't hurt to look. There was always a chance.

"Oh, for fuck's sake, Tim," said Benson, "do you have any logical reason to think these two people on the other side of the world are connected to this shit?"

"None at all—except for the fact that this is all about those who come back, the 'arrivals,' the returned, whatever the hell we're calling them. And these two were returned years before the Booth was ever used. I don't have logic, I just want to play a hunch."

"Sounds like a grasp for vindication."

Ugh, thought Tim. He should have expected that one. "It's *a lead*. It's one lead. I'm having you chase that lead so I can do my job for you."

Christ. A grasp for vindication. Hardly. If he hadn't been trapped in the firefights over his career after the episode, doing his best to salvage his credibility, he would have gone back to the border region himself to interview the two survivors. In the years since that rainy night, he had castigated himself plenty of times for not returning. Over time, he recognized that a part of him was on the side of the strange monks. Part of him appreciated their swift if brutal justice.

Because they had returned the boy and the woman.

On the line, Benson clucked his tongue but at last relented. "Aw, what the hell. I'll have the embassy in New Delhi make inquiries."

"Good. I'll call you from Paris. And I think it's time to put that Hawker jet to some use."

"Our arrangement was for business class if it's lower priority of—"

"Get real. If I fly out somewhere on commercial, and then the shit hits the fan, not much good having the jet back in Washington and not with *me*, is it?"

109

Benson groaned and said, "Fine, I'll fix it. But you should stop over in London first."

"Why?"

"I promised I'd get you some help. Your help is in London, and you'll have to pick her up."

At the Borg El Arab airport in Egypt, the guards who handled the night shift belonged to the Special Forces Regiment attached to the army's field headquarters in Alexandria. And they were bored. They were doomed to another stretch of hours guarding the peculiar equipment in the aircraft hangar at the newly expanded runway. Being soldiers, of course, they would do as they were ordered. They were well trained to anticipate and deal with almost any attack from terrorists in the region or a civilian uprising. But discipline relaxed a little during a lull.

In the cafeteria and social area, a couple of men played backgammon, while in the corner an earnest young corporal argued with a sergeant over which channel to keep on the portable television. The debate was over Al Jazeera versus *Eal Beit Beitak*, the popular game show with a title that translated as "Feel at home." The game show won.

When the Russian-made Mi-17 helicopter thundered in on its unscheduled approach, the two curious soldiers who stepped out to greet it recognized their own air force's markings and colors. It wasn't a case of the bird not being allowed here, but *why* was it here in the middle of the night? The soldiers assumed there must be a malfunction. That would be enough to prompt an emergency landing, and one of them jogged inside the hangar to fetch a technician on call.

The soldier who walked under the blades towards the cab of the aircraft didn't suspect anything wrong until the door opened. The occupants of the copter were next to invisible behind the tinted glass, but now a white man of about fifty with curly brown hair and weathered features smiled at him affably and jumped out. The man kept right on smiling until his commando knife sliced across the soldier's brachial plexus and then across his throat. The soldier died within seconds, and the man eased his body gently down in the shadow of the copter's landing struts.

"Typical," sneered the man in his Ulster accent.

Having read about Israel's pre-emptive strike that devastated the Egyptian Air Force in the Six-Day War, he felt completely justified in his contempt towards any Arab soldier.

"Right then, let's *move!*"

His handpicked team jumped out of the copter, machine guns ready, and raced towards the hangar. Desmond Leary stayed by the aircraft because he wasn't bloody stupid, thank you very much (first perk of management: less risk). Plus, he fancied having a smoke. The boys would do fine and could handle a minimal guard detail, and while he'd prefer to have no casualties, his men would open fire if one of the bastards felt like he needed his seventy-two virgins early.

Unbelievable, letting *this* country have one of these things. Christ in His Heaven, he'd be tempted to take the fucking thing away from them even if there wasn't a higher purpose in mind for it. His client was plugged in enough to have politicians, intelligence officials, diplomats, all feeding information to him, and the intel—which he promptly passed on to Leary—had been bang on. These buggers had a Booth. Well, they wouldn't have it for long.

He checked his watch. Five minutes. Mere seconds to cut the phone lines and cables for Internet, ninety more seconds to scout the location while the Egyptians were herded into their barrack rooms and locked in, with their cell phones and sat phones confiscated and dumped in a bag. Leary had actually padded his estimates when planning the operation, expecting trouble of some sort, and he heard distant shouts of anger and shock from the Egyptians. But his team leader sent him a brief text for the first check in, and it looked like there were no heroes today. Good.

The men he had hired were experienced; some had stayed with the IRA as it shifted from holy cause to holy shit, let's get rich off of organized crime. Others were veteran contractors from the conflict in Somalia, the Fiji uprising, Libya's upheaval and, naturally, Iraq. They wouldn't hesitate to fire.

Neither would he if he were in there.

Leary couldn't suppress a tingle of nervousness, checking his watch again. He dropped his cigarette and stubbed it out, grateful for the chime of a second text. It meant the boys were on their way out, their target acquired. Wonderful. Now all they had to do was escape an entire bloody air force screaming for blood and on their arses probably ten minutes after they were airborne.

He turned his head and spat, thinking: We'll make it. Made it out of all the other shit-holes, and at least life would come out of this, not just death. Remember that. They would be well paid for the job, too. It was safe now to check out his men's progress, and he strolled into the hangar.

He smiled as his men pushed—as rapidly as they could—an electric skid lifter with a maximum weight capacity of two thousand pounds over to the west corner of the vast room. This was where the first chamber of Egypt's Karma Booth rested, and Leary felt a swell of pride at having guessed right about its size and probable weight. His men got to work, and the second chamber was loaded on another skid, close behind. The remainder of the team jogged backwards with their guns ready for any last-minute nonsense.

"About fucking time," said Leary, grinning.

His mate, Colin, rolled his eyes and bared his teeth, a friendly fuck-you expression on his face for his long-time commander. They had killed together and drank together, and it had taken Desmond Leary weeks to talk his old friend into this job, but now he was proving he was worth all that endless nagging and plying with pints. It was Colin who had done enough ops in the Middle East to know Egypt was the most vulnerable place, and he had declared, "No worries, mate" when Leary suggested flying the Booth chambers away on the Mi-17. "It'll be fucking elegant."

So far, it was. They got the chambers onboard the copter, but as those bringing up the rear piled in, some damn fool of an officer decided the prestige of the Egyptian armed forces was more important than a long life. *Stupid bastard.* Leary yanked his legs up from the ground as bullets strafed the cab's open door, and he barked at the pilot to open fire with the Mi-17's guns. The roar was like a dragon's bellow, the rounds cutting in half the fearless men trying to keep the copter on the ground.

"Idiots!" yelled Leary over the engine.

This is not what he wanted. He didn't respect the uniformed men lying in their blood on the tarmac, but he wasn't one of those sadistic cretins who relished casual slaughter. It was always intended to be an op with minimal casualties, and now it was tainted. The blood he had wanted to spill was that of the butchers, the guilty ones.

"It's a war, Des," said Colin at his side, sensing his regret. "You talked me into this, and I knew there would have to be sacrifices."

"Christ, I know," sighed Leary. He clapped his friend on the shoulder and said, "Let's go sacrifice the right people, yeah?"

He put the dead Egyptian soldiers out of his mind. It was that simple, and it had to be, especially for what they were doing and what they had planned. He took comfort from the fact that the merchant marine ship should be reaching the designated rendezvous coordinates right about now. They would be home free soon, and then they would *really* change the world.

Waiting for takeoff of the private jet, Timothy Cale flipped open his notebook computer and checked the news websites. BBC, CNBC, Al Jazeera, HuffPo, ABC... The story links were demoralizing. In Nebraska, a ranch hand and part-time mechanic who beat a homosexual to death in a bar had been convicted of manslaughter—manslaughter, not murder. Despite the fact that no premeditation was found for the crime, there was an outcry to use the Booth to bring back the victim. It had turned out during the trial that the killer had been a closet case, taking psychiatric drugs over his suicidal thoughts, but abusing the pills with alcohol. He allegedly demonstrated genuine remorse. No one knew what to do.

In Naples, Italy, where assisted suicide was still illegal, a fifty-nine-year-old woman took a kitchen knife and stabbed her husband to death—he had been slowly dying from multiple conditions, including kidney disease and Parkinson's. No matter what the authorities told her, the woman firmly believed there had to be a secret Karma Booth kept by Italian officials, and they could use it to trade her life for her husband's. Tim clicked away from the link with a grunt. This, too, he thought, had been inevitable—the progress of the world's anger. First, people resented the assumption that the United States held the technology alone, and now they suspected other Booths were out there. And they were right.

His flight was uneventful. He dozed, read the newest pop history book by Giles Milton, and wondered about his tax dollars at work when the third flight attendant brought him a lavish breakfast meal, one normally reserved for a cabinet secretary.

Still, he didn't regret bullying Benson into letting him use the Hawker.

A car was waiting for him at Heathrow, and he noticed the drive into central London had grown even more excruciating. At last the car pulled up in front of 10 Broadway near St. James's Park Underground station. The world knew this address as Scotland Yard, the headquarters of the London Metropolitan Police Service.

The trouble was that Benson's "help" wasn't there to greet him. A staff sergeant came out to speak to him, and from his years in London, Timothy recognized the man's Yorkshire accent. "Oh, yeah, on her downtime she likes to hop on the Tube and run over to Embankment. She hangs out in a café in Villiers Street called 'Good Timing.' When you exit the station, just stay—"

"I know it, thanks," said Tim, waving as he left. He had the hired driver run his bags over to his hotel near Russell Square.

It was easy to pick out his contact from the daypack-toting tourists and the shop girls on break at the little café. She was a black woman, no older than thirty-two, her hair cut stylishly short and straightened. Her complexion was a light brown, her nose angular, and her brown eyes were wide and challenging with their intelligence. This, Tim guessed, had to be Detective Inspector Crystal Anyanike. As he opened the door, she was absorbed in a book, sipping tea, but now her eyes caught his approach. He doubted much ever got past her.

"You would be Tim Cale," she said, her voice a pleasant mezzo-soprano.

Tim smiled, another American who was a sucker for the educated accent.

"I would be Tim Cale," he answered, shaking her hand and sitting down.

"Well, I hope you didn't expect me to sit around on my arse waiting for you to show up!" she laughed.

"Not at all. I'm actually surprised to find you sitting still. You have quite the reputation."

Benson had emailed a file. Crystal Anyanike's career had been unusual to say the least. By fifteen, she was enrolled for her undergraduate studies at the University of London and then went to Cambridge, where she got what they call a "starred first"—first-class honors with distinction on her exams. Her thesis—that early African civilization was much more advanced than previously thought—started a small bidding war among publishers.

She could have become a pop historian or academic superstar, but instead she got an unusual call from what used to be the London police's Special Branch. They liked her mind. They also liked the fact that she was fluent in Arabic and could get inside the heads of extremists (a second book, aimed exclusively at academics, looked at terrorism in Africa). And they liked very much the fact that she was already a *nidan*, a second-degree black belt, in Yoshinkan aikido.

So they sent her to the police training center north of Colindale in London and then put her in the black cap and uniform in Lambeth, where she handled everything from domestic disputes to hauling off the yobs that broke windows after last call at the pub. But she was on a secret fast-track program, with just a brief stint in the trenches, so that there would no question that she had the basic skills to join the new Counter Terrorism Command.

No one doubted her abilities after she was on the job for a month. She broke a case involving a small cell of Algerian terrorists planning another airport fire like the one in Glasgow in 2007—this time it was meant to be at Gatwick, with the intention to kill as many people as possible. When officers raided a house in Ealing, one of the suspects took them by surprise and shot a member of the team point blank. He was about to strafe the others with an M4 assault rifle when Crystal Anyanike grabbed his arm, spun him around and sent him flying through a second-floor window. The suspect suffered a broken leg and a cracked pelvis, but he was alive and could be interrogated.

The story, according to Benson's email, had become something of a legend within the ranks of the police forces across the UK.

From all that he had read, Crystal Anyanike was smart, insightful and tough. He only had a couple of doubts, and as he sat across from her at the café table, her large brown eyes held him steady. He had a feeling she was well aware of the question marks he had saved up on his flight.

"Tell me what you're reading."

She passed him the book. It had leather binding, with uneven cloth pages that had yellowed with age. The copyright for it was 1897, and a stamp inside told him it belonged to the University of London's School of Oriental and African Studies. A heavy tome on various African mythologies. Crystal's bookmark was in a section dealing with life after death in various cultures.

"You think there might be answers in there?" he asked politely.

"I don't know, but I thought you would approve, given what I hear of your own experiences. India and such."

"I do," said Tim. "I must say you're not what I anticipated." He gestured to the gold necklace dangling a crucifix.

She stiffened a little, her full lips parting to reveal a generous smile. "Is my faith a problem for you?"

"No, but if we're going to work together, I think I'm entitled to ask if it will be a problem for *you*. The Karma Booth is upsetting the principles of every major religion I can think of."

She nodded, offering him a sunny smile. "All I can do, Mr. Cale, is quote Saint David of Bowie here: 'Just because I believe don't mean I don't think as well.'"

Tim smiled back. "'Word on a Wing' from the *Station to Station* album. Yeah, I have it. We're in England, so... Were you raised Anglican?"

"I was," she answered, her eyes darting to a corner, searching memory. "But I had a lot of problems with the long-haired white dude they gave us in plate portraits. When I was a teenager, I started to question religion—as you do. And I discovered the stories of Makeda."

"Queen of Sheba."

"Ah! You are good. Anyway, I went and found all the other biblical instances that took place in Africa. You know, the ones that somehow never top the list in the King James Bible."

"So for you, Jesus is real but was black. And Heaven is really up there."

"You have a problem with Jesus being black?"

"On the contrary, if he existed at all, I'm sure he wasn't white, but he's not the issue we're confronting with the Booth."

"Heaven is somewhere, Mr. Cale. I don't give a toss really how the road signs point to it. But if you're asking if I need that comfort of a supreme being, an overall plan, then yes, I do. Interesting... They warned me you're an atheist."

"They told you wrong," replied Tim. "You would probably classify me as an agnostic. I don't believe in any human-manufactured God, if you want to pin me down, but of course, I can't prove it, and frankly, I'm not even interested in the subject."

"But what you claimed you saw in India...?"

Tim let out a soft groan. It was always hard to explain to others his thinking on the episode. People wanted to bring in God, like a stubborn gatecrasher at the party.

"DI Anyanike—Crystal? Crystal. The two subjects don't suggest a link to each other in my mind. What I saw suggests to me there are other realms of existence, that there may be laws of the universe we haven't learned yet. For now, they simply defy our current scientific thinking. Don't get me wrong, I'm not a materialist. But you're looking for a Divine Plan, and I don't see one, any more than I see a single intelligence responsible for a whole human city when you compare it to a troop of gorillas out in the jungle. It's just a different community beyond us. Nicer furniture, better satellite TV."

"Yet here you are. Looking into the Karma Booth."

"Yes, I am," he answered. Maybe this woman would understand. Maybe she would get it.

"Here's the thing. What I saw in India was wondrous. And horrifying. And a mystery. I don't need the answers to fit my way of thinking. I *would* like explanations for the phenomena, sure, but I don't need the ego boost of some big confirmation of my world view."

"Then why...?"

He finished the question for her. "Then why take this job?" He laughed. He was surprised to hear himself give her a truthful answer, one he hadn't even shared with Matilda back in New York. "I took this contract because they handed me a compass nobody knows how to use—this Booth thing—and essentially told me to go explore. I just want to know what's there."

"I see."

"So now that we're getting down to it, why did *you* take this job?"

She sat back and folded her arms, sincerely considering the question. "I can't pretend I'm not curious on a religious level..." Slowly, she leaned forward again, lacing her fingers on the table. "The rumor is you actually do care about the Third World. We have plenty of nice white men who affect concern, but I checked on you, Mister Cale. You tried to stop a slave ring smuggling in Africans for prostitution when you were stationed in Paris. Back in the Nineties, you tried to force certain oil companies to stop doing business and hiring militias in Sudan."

"Then you know I wasn't very successful. And the Republicans were running the show back then. What's your point?"

"My point is you might understand *my* point." She offered another brilliant smile to let him know she wasn't being irritable. "Six months ago, I had to go down to Africa for Counter Terrorism Command—make contacts, swap intel. I can't tell you what specific countries I went to but... Let's just say it was depressing enough for me to almost quit. The big corporations are still in there, right up to the elbows getting dirty. And people still get slaughtered.

"Now along comes the Karma Booth. And everyone thinks in terms of a single maniac who strangles a girl or the nutter who shoots down a police officer. But this Karma Booth may actually balance the scales with the *real* mass murderers. You know—the corporate execs who hire mercenaries to wipe out whole villages so they can mine the countryside. The ethnic cleansing bastards. These fellows who run around without fear of the UN. And now you're telling me *other* countries have this technology…"

Tim nodded, comprehending where she was going with her story. Justice. Strip away all the discussion about potential, the Karma Booth still had to be about justice if it was used at all. And she had put her finger on perhaps the most deserving of functions, that those who committed the most unspeakable acts be traded for the populations they eradicated.

"If we can get those answers you want," said Crystal, "maybe the dead don't have to simply rest anymore. Everyone sees Africa die on the news. Imagine if it could live?"

"I think we're going to get along just fine," said Tim, offering his hand for her to shake.

She took it. "Charmed, I'm sure, Mr. Cale."

"Tim."

Crystal slid her antique volume into a cloth bag and said, "They briefed me that you want to concentrate on finding this woman in Paris—the one who stepped out of the Booth and disappeared. How do you want to proceed?"

Her question threw him for a moment. He realized that he hadn't actually developed a plan of attack, knowing his old notebook full of contacts with Interpol and European police forces had been gathering dust. On his flight over, he had spent some time sifting over his encounters with Mary Ash, Geoff Shackleton and "Daniel Chen," trying to formulate better questions to ask Emily Derosier when they tracked her down. Now Crystal had the good sense to ask: Shall we find the lady first?

"I, uh, was assuming you'd liaise in Paris with the French authorities—you must know people there. And we could ask to review their own CCTV footage from the Montparnasse cameras, perhaps we—"

"How much do you know about her actual murder?" Crystal broke in.

Tim shrugged. "Not a lot. They showed me photocopies of old newspaper stories. Her murder and a brief bio."

"Technically, it's still an open homicide," explained Crystal. "It's the coldest of cases, but maybe there's an actual file and an evidence box lying around somewhere. I saw the same camera footage you did. That woman didn't wander out in a daze. She was going somewhere."

8

They took the jet early the next day, and by noon, Tim and Crystal were sitting having lunch at La Tour d'Argent in the Latin Quarter of Paris. Their table faced the window with its breathtaking view of the Seine and the Notre-Dame cathedral, and Tim didn't give a damn what the Michelin Guide had to say these days, he always enjoyed the duck here.

Crystal looked bemused by the rich surroundings, her eyes darting here and there but the corners of her mouth carefully flat and neutral. Tim recognized the expression; he had worn it himself years ago. It was secret delight that you can barely contain, but you still did your best to play it cool. The young detective inspector sitting across him no doubt lived on a budget in London, and she didn't often get to see such places unless she was taken on a date or for a special night out.

Then she surprised him with her own insight. "Your family wasn't rich, was it?"

"No," he answered. "What makes you ask?"

"You ordered our meals like you were taking revenge. Shall I assume you're charging this to the American government?"

"You assume correctly."

"I take it we're here mostly because Emily Derosier kept an apartment in the Latin Quarter. I understand that, but I hope you're not expecting her to just pass us by on the street."

He shook his head, slightly embarrassed, then offered, "I wanted to get a feel for where she lived and spent a lot of her time. I know it doesn't make a lot of sense. The shops are different, the streets are different—it was almost a century ago. But you can still get the flavor sometimes, the essence of a place and its history and roots, by standing on the actual ground. I'm not a cop like you, but I always hear that people go back to what's familiar. They can't help themselves. We have no other place to start except with the idea that maybe she still is who she *was*."

Crystal nodded in sympathy. "That's true. It's also true that sometimes intuition is all we have to go on. Fortunately, who she is—and was—still leaves fingerprints and can be caught on CCTV. The Paris police are cooperating. I had my department send them a special algorithm for facial recognition software—we usually reserve it for terrorism suspects. If she's still here, we'll likely get some hits after a few days. We'll still be picking up breadcrumbs from where she was, but we may get lucky with a sighting in real time. This is what else we know…"

She handed him the case file and a couple of newspaper feature bios as the waiter asked if they wanted coffee. Tim asked for the dessert menu and invited her to "go crazy" as he perused the faded, typed pages from almost a century ago.

In the final year of her life, Emily Derosier was twenty-nine years old and at the height of her fame. Like certain celebrities today, she had become known more for simply "being" rather than for her accomplishments. Unlike today's star crop, however, she could boast genuine talent (her paintings, with dream-like images, were reminiscent of Miro, only the iconography held Asian religious themes instead of Jewish). She was also known for a sometimes mischievous wit. When a notorious male prude complained about young women flashing their legs with the rising hemlines, she replied, "Keep complaining, and we'll never flash you anything else."

She also had an impetuous, bold attitude over social wrongs. In 1926, a couple of tourists from the American South complained in a restaurant because famed black singer Josephine Baker sat at a nearby table. Emily got up and poured a silver bowl of Béarnaise sauce over the man's head.

As Tim read out this anecdote, Crystal declared, "Yeah, saw that. I like her already."

So did Tim. Even from the clippings and book photos, you could understand the woman's allure. There was a luminescent quality to her oval face, framed by the flapper's blunt cut. Only a couple of years later, she set a new fashion trend by getting her brown hair cut short. But Emily Derosier had staggered out of the Karma Booth nude, with tresses at shoulder length. Wherever she had been, time definitely passed in measurable increments there.

In 1927, she had returned to Paris after a half-year trip to Sri Lanka, known back then as Ceylon. She had gushed in interviews that she felt "changed by the place" and that it had heavily influenced her work. A couple of her paintings were displayed ahead of a planned show at a gallery not far from the Jeu de Paume, but one week before the premiere she was murdered in her apartment in the 6th arrondissement. The newspapers made much of the fact that she was discovered in the nude, with multiple stab wounds to her chest and neck.

The case file suggested she must have been sleeping, and as the door was forced open, she hadn't bothered to reach for a robe but had stepped in surprise into her own sitting room—as if modesty wasn't required. Or she simply didn't care. Maybe there was a touch of fatalism in how she confronted her attacker, brazenly parading herself before the inevitable happened.

The police took photos of her body, but neglected to take shots of the door, and the file included the pencil notation: "Front entrance smashed in; looks strongly like blood was up." (Crystal rolled her eyes. "Forensics," she muttered. "The early, *early* years.") There had been a struggle. Emily Derosier's fingers and palms showed several defensive wounds, and a wide puddle of blood had indicated exsanguination.

Tim looked up from the file. "Well, you're the detective. What do you think we should do?"

"I need to check where her paintings are still being shown," said Crystal. "Somebody must have done a coffee table book on her or something—maybe that will do."

"Why?"

"Right," said Crystal, tapping the file. "It says here that on the night of her murder, the canvases in her apartment were slashed and vandalized, and the gallery where her show was supposed to be held had a break-in. Her paintings were found in a pile and burned."

Tim nodded. "Okay. Which means what?"

"It means they got it wrong ages ago, this wasn't a crime of passion," said Crystal. "An ex-lover destroying her work as an act of spite? Not buying it. The murderer—it couldn't have been anyone else—didn't want the world to see the new inspired visions of Emily Derosier. Her killer was afraid of something back then. What was it? What was she hoping to show the world? Maybe we can get a hint of it. The other question is what is Emily Derosier afraid of today? Why hide?"

"You're convinced she's hiding."

Crystal leaned back and took a sip of her coffee. "Try this. Say you walk along an iced-over lake. It cracks, and you fall through a hole. You nearly drown, but the doctors get to you in time before you die of hypothermia. You lose time. You wake up, and any normal person would thank his rescuers and say, 'Oh, my God, I nearly died, I have a new appreciation for life' or some other rubbish. You would, wouldn't you? But our lady of the lake doesn't speak to a single soul in this new world and simply *leaves*. There are only two reasons you flee after you come back from the dead. One: you have something to hide, and two—"

"Whoever tossed you in the water might still be around," said Tim.

"Exactly."

Tim folded his arms, impressed. For all the compliments he got from people over his alleged great insight, he always wished he had a more logical mind. He could see how Crystal Anyanike would complement his skill set. Still, he felt a peculiar urge to tease her, always a sign that he liked a person.

"You're not suggesting the killer is still a threat when he must be over a hundred years old?"

"Very funny," replied Crystal. "I'm pointing out this woman walked out of the Karma Booth the age she was murdered. Not older, not younger—as if her death fixed her in time. You can fear many things but high in the top ten is death or injury. Well, she's defied both, hasn't she? If she can walk back into our era, you'd think she has nothing to worry about from any human being here. Unless there's someone else who doesn't have to follow the rules…"

"I'd like to know why she's still Emily Derosier," said Tim.

"I don't follow."

Tim explained to her about the three-year-old blond boy who was supposed to have returned as Daniel Chen. Crystal listened without interrupting, her mouth opening in wonder. He knew what he was telling her ran contrary to all her Christian beliefs, but she had dared to take on the assignment. Well, she was the one who claimed she could handle it.

"This woman has been gone for close to a *century*," explained Tim. "So why hasn't she stepped through the Booth as someone else? Why not someone we know nothing about or have never heard of? Why not someone completely new?"

Crystal reached for the folder with the breakdown of CCTV cameras in Paris. Answers would only come when they found the woman.

The waiter stepped up with the exquisite piece of cheesecake she ordered. Crystal clapped her hands like a little girl. "*This* is Heaven. Chocolate..."

Tim sat back and laughed. For a moment, the weight of Karma was briefly lifted.

Dieter Wildman stepped out of his men's health club onto Rue Saint-Denis in Montreal, mildly cursing the rain. He hadn't brought an umbrella, and his hair was still wet from the pool. Well, he should be happy, he supposed, that he still did have hair at his age. Well into his eighties, he swam several laps at the club three days a week, and his doctor declared that he had the heart of a fifty-year-old. Not bad. Now, if he could only escape this demanding lecture circuit that was less work than his clinic but more of a pain in the ass. He scratched his salt and pepper beard and decided to walk.

He never knew why he bothered to weigh his options. He always walked. Now and then, faces turned—brows crinkling, mouths open in recognition—but the curious on

The Karma Booth

the street didn't bother him most of the time and let him
go on his way. He had made his home in Montreal partly
because the attitudes here were more progressive and people
supported his work. And there was the fact that the beautiful
architecture here, the circular da Vinci staircases and the old
buildings, made him sometimes feel he was in a tiny corner
of Europe preserved in Canada. It kept the ghosts nearby,
all the haunting reminders in little, innocuous things—gray
slabs of stone, the way the rain washed a pair of men's boots,
a menorah in a shop window. Keep the little things close,
where they become familiar and mundane, and the ghosts
lose their power.

Tonight, in fact, he was not only giving a speech but
dedicating a new exhibit for non-Jewish Holocaust victims:
gypsies, Communists, homosexuals—all the forgotten ones.
Wildman himself was Jewish, but his father was arrested
and put in a camp primarily for his labor union activities.
That was in 1937. Staring at barbed wire had bred in him
the habit, the joy, of going for a stroll whenever he liked.
But he didn't buy into the myth of the "superior nobility of
the oppressed." He annoyed the B'nai B'rith when he spoke
out about Israeli bombings in Gaza, and he had picketed
the US consulate in the 1960s over the Vietnam War. Of
course, neither of those activities were why he was famous
in this country.

He stopped into a drugstore to buy some mints and a
newspaper, and when he jogged in a slow, easy gait across
Saint-Denis, they were waiting for him.

A man walking in front of him slowed down, his back to
Wildman, and too late, he realized this stranger was nothing
more than a distraction. He was there to block any curious
eyes up the street. Behind him, an arm yanked him hard off

129

the curb and a fist clubbed him on the nape of the neck. He staggered with the blow, and like any mugging target, he stammered surprise and went into denial. This can't be happening. There was no reason for it.

"Uhh! What...? What is this? What are you doing?"

"What does it look like?" barked the voice of the man pushing him to an open car. He had an accent, but as Wildman struggled for his life, he didn't recognize it. "We're dragging your arse off the street."

"What—what do you want?"

"What do we *want*? Me personally, I'd like ten minutes alone with you in a room to beat the shit out of you, you genocidal son of a bitch! But we need you alive!"

They punched him in the nose and again in the temple, and as he lost consciousness, Dieter Wildman felt the fresh spit on his face and heard the words that explained the attack. Desmond Leary was still yelling at him, *You fucking baby killer!*

Tim's computer woke him up. He had dozed off with a book folded open on his chest and the lamp on the night table still on. In times of stress, he liked to go back to the rationalists: the writers and thinkers whose prose was acerbic but logical, reasonable. He found them to be a comfort in an age when people's ultimate defense was "I *feel* it's true" rather than a thought-out argument. If a student in his lecture hall talked like that, Tim couldn't help but pounce.

When his notebook computer pinged, he lifted his head, and an old paperback copy of Gore Vidal's *Julian* slid off his chest onto the floor with a pulpy thud. He had read it before, but had bought it out of a sentimental whim while on a date, strolling with a prospective girlfriend through

New York's cavernous Strand bookstore. He and the woman didn't click. But he kept the book.

He'd received another security-encoded email from Gary Weintraub, this one with an attached video file. The professor's message started: "We're told this was smuggled out of Tehran by a member of the *Majlis*."

Impressive, thought Tim. And dangerous. But if anyone could get valuable information out of Iran, it would be a member of the *Majlis*, which Tim remembered was the Islamic nation's legislature.

Iran's Karma Booth, still a carefully guarded secret kept from the country's population, was only to be activated by the will of the Special Clerical Court. The court had unique powers. It normally handled alleged crimes by clerics but could also hear cases involving ordinary Iranians. It couldn't be overturned by any appeal and answered only to the *Rahbar-e Enqelab*, Iran's Supreme Leader. The MPEG allegedly showed a use of the Booth last week.

Tim detested the fanatical regime in Iran. It wasn't because of the continued saber-rattling against the US. It was because he had several friends who were Persian expats, and they had told him horror stories of their lives back there. Tim scrolled down, preparing himself to be disgusted over the details of the background behind the execution. Iran's warped version of justice was regularly featured on the websites of groups like Amnesty International and Human Rights Watch. This isn't going to be pretty, he thought.

The man sentenced to step into the Karma Booth was a father pushed past his breaking point. His eleven-year-old daughter had been raped and choked, leaving her severely brain damaged. Her assailant was a sadistic university dropout who turned out to be the son of a powerful mullah.

Jeff Pearce

And the girl's father had beaten him to death in a storm of rage and grief.

Tim, disgusted, hissed aloud over the decision of the court. In their infinite wisdom, the clerics had decided—despite physical evidence gathered by police, as well as forensics that were on par with the standard in most countries in Europe— that the young man couldn't have dragged the girl into the Tehran cul-de-sac where she was found later, glassy-eyed and barely breathing with her clothes torn. Two chums of the young man claimed he was with them. It didn't matter that they had clearly lied and that both had been spotted in their classes. The mullah's son was deemed innocent.

So the girl's father took his revenge. And now he had to be executed. Not by the usual method of the gallows at Tehran's Evin Prison—no, the Karma Booth would be used. Intelligence operatives had learned the clerics preferred to call it "*Divan-e Ahlee Keshvar.*" The Chamber of Justice.

Gary Weintraub ended the summary there. He made no comment on what was in the video footage except for the cryptic line: "This may give us another fixed rule for the Booth." Then came his signoff. There was a quick post-script, informing Tim that the National Security Agency had provided translations of the voices on the footage. They ran at the bottom as subtitles, like in a foreign movie.

"So let's go to the video replay," Tim whispered to himself, rubbing his eyes as he launched the clip.

Orlando Braithewaite must have given every country the same "model" of Karma Booth. Tim recognized the twin chambers, and the angle of the camera on the tripod took in the hands of a technician running the control board. Tim ignored the backdrop—he suspected it was part of an infirmary wing just as American officials used a hospital ward for

132

their Booth at Sullivan. It was quiet until a loud disturbance could be heard off camera, and then a portly man in a gray inmate uniform was dragged into frame by two guards. They must have informed him he was about to die.

He kept shouting and fighting with every step. "No, tell me, just tell me! What would you do? If it was your child defiled like that? Your child, your blood!"

The guard was telling him: "I don't give a damn. And we don't have time for this—"

With all his dignity now stripped away, the man was still hoping to break through the guard's indifference. "This is not justice! God will punish you for this! Don't! Don't—"

"Are you a woman?" Barked the guard, telling him to shut up.

He smashed the man across the cheek and jaw, his blow angry and wild. He used the back of his fist, and the condemned, middle-aged father staggered. It gave the guards the moment they needed to shove him into the chamber and lock the door. As the man recovered, he reached instinctively for a knob or a grip to slide a panel. There was none. Now he hammered on the tinted glass. Tim knew what would come next.

But this was not why Gary Weintraub had sent him the footage. There were a couple of inaudible comments from the guards as the father disintegrated in the blazing white and swirling colors, and no translated subtitles were offered or needed. Then came the familiar secondary effect: more bright light and dazzling swirls. Someone unseen, perhaps another technician who had stood behind the camera all this time, picked the camera up off the tripod and held it, walking forward.

Tim waited.

There was a slight jerkiness to the hand-held shot of the camera as it approached the second chamber, and the belligerent guard who had struck the father looked into the lens, his lip curled in an expression of prison staff stoicism. It was clear they had expected their new arrival to be conscious, perhaps even alert.

"Mahmoud Bahonar?" called the guard.

Tim recalled that this was the name of the girl's attacker, the mullah's son who was traded back into existence for the life of the father. The guard opened the door to the chamber.

"Mahmoud—"

The camera angle jerked again, and then the technician found the zoom and moved in. But there was nobody in the Booth. Then the second guard let out a sharp cry and said, "Look, look!"

He swore and gasped, stepping away. Tim could hear the voice of the camera operator demanding to know what he should be looking at. *What is it? What?*

The first guard's face was ashen. It sounded like the second guard was vomiting in a corner off camera. The lens finally tilted down as the technician understood. The focus blurred, and then the zoom—

"*White worm,*" whispered the technician. For an instant, Tim was confused. Then the image sharpened, and he understood.

It was a maggot. Crawling on the floor of the chamber.

Emily Derosier spoke to Tim and Crystal the next day—through oils on canvas.

At university, Tim had taken art appreciation courses, thinking they would be easy undergraduate electives, and for the most part they were—but he'd also been surprised to find he genuinely enjoyed them. The lectures on art had pushed him to mull over the canvases at the New York Met and not merely take them in like a fast-food consumer on a package tour.

For so long, he'd had a chip on his shoulder at college, thinking that as a lower-middle-class boy, he could only *pose* as someone with cultural knowledge. His scholarship only went so far, and each night after studies, he'd had to rush off to wait tables. But instead of adding another social skill to further his diplomatic career, he had fallen in love with art. He learned a humbling appreciation for a heritage of brushstrokes and verses and classical music (though he'd always prefer jazz).

While living in Paris, the perks of working at the American embassy got him countless comps to all kinds of gallery shows, and he'd built up a nice, informal network of curators as friends. Crystal had told him how she wanted to check out Emily Derosier's paintings, so he used his network now to track down the modest gallery on the Left Bank, one that amazingly still kept a tiny collection of Derosier originals. But "collection" was probably overstating it.

When Tim and Crystal showed up, they were greeted warmly by the frumpy but pleasant, sixty-two-year-old manageress of the gallery, who had a distracting, almost de-Gaulle-like beak nose. Grateful for any visitors, she led them to seven paintings waiting on individual easels, and with a flourish, pulled the dusty sheets off each of them, one by one. Few ever came to see the work of Emily Derosier anymore except for an occasional student working on an obscure, unreadable master's thesis. She muttered a self-satisfied "*Bon*" with her hands clasped, then primly walked away to leave Crystal and Tim to examine the pictures.

The ones placed on the front easels had clearly been deemed to be the best of the artist's work, almost as if the gallery matron had wanted to hide the others in case they drove any visitor to leave. There were scenes of a Paris market, with lonely figures, their faces obscured as they shopped. One sentimental composition depicted a lonely girl wandering a bridge while lovers nuzzled in the background under an umbrella.

"They remind me of that fellow who did a picture of this couple dancing while some servant holds an umbrella over them," remarked Crystal. "You see it in postcards and calendars all the time, but I don't know who the artist is."

"Jack Vettriano," replied Tim. "Yeah, I can see what you mean."

"They're not brilliant, are they?" she asked, and when he looked mildly surprised over deferring to his opinion, she added, "You know what to order in a posh restaurant. I reckon you know about art, too."

"A little," he answered modestly. "No, they're not brilliant."

He stopped in front of one composition that showed French locals having a smoke in a lobby, just beyond where a movie theater showed a black and white film. Emily Derosier had painted on the screen her friend, Josephine Baker.

"I always liked the Twenties," said Tim, unable to hold back a smile of appreciation. "They make a lot out of the Depression, but it didn't last as long as people think, especially here. Good music, more flexible morals than people are told, passionate politics… It would have been an interesting period to live in."

"Yeah, I suppose it would be great," mused Crystal. "If you were white."

"Point taken."

"You Americans are so funny about history. I never think about what it would be like to live in Elizabethan England or like, Victorian times. You can't trip over something in London without it being historical. We're knee deep in it."

136

"And for you, it's something to escape?" he asked.

She stood next to him in front of the painting. "The Karma Booth would have us believe we never do, wouldn't it?"

He didn't know how to respond to that. He carefully moved the easels with the city scenes out of the way and considered the pictures behind them. He and Crystal both took a step back, surprised by these new compositions. Well, these made their trip to the gallery worthwhile.

"Different," whispered Crystal.

"Very."

There were a couple of watercolors of Buddhist temples against countryside backdrops, but what made Tim and Crystal gasp were the oil paintings next to them. Expressionist, Futurist visions of...*what*? It wasn't clear. In one painting, a woman in a flowing diaphanous robe, which Derosier had clearly modeled after herself, crouched to step through a window, which in turn was a mouth of a fantastical being, its eyes and nose Cubist shards of blazing white and glacier blue. In another composition, the angle of the viewer was from below, looking up, as if submerged in water and seeing a bather paddle above. But the gorgeous nude's body was half cut away, as if part of the painting was to be used as a *Gray's Anatomy* anatomical study. The water was a storm of violent, vivid blues, greens, violets... swirling nebulae.

They were eerie. Compelling yet disturbing. They didn't testify to the inner peace and spiritual transformation Emily Derosier boasted about to reporters after coming back from Sri Lanka. Tim could imagine why these surviving canvases had been locked away for so long. With her scandalous and brutal murder, and the discovery of her nude stabbed corpse, the great socialite's friends must have thought these paintings would ruin her reputation further, hinting at mental illness.

"These were painted before she was murdered," said Tim, "and almost a full century before there was any Karma Booth."

"But that means there's no context."

"What are you getting at?"

"Let's presume for the moment her killer knows something about the afterlife," reasoned Crystal. "Why bother to murder her at all and destroy her paintings? You can't tell a thing from these about the Karma Booth. It hadn't even been invented yet. These pictures wouldn't have made sense to anyone."

"Not on a rational level, no," agreed Tim. "But when it comes to imagination... There's a book by a guy named Leonard Shlain—it's called *Art and Physics*. Shlain makes a compelling case that various artists anticipated certain breakthroughs in science and how we see the physical world. Da Vinci's drawings of flight are hundreds of years ahead of time-lapse photography. Surrealism foreshadows Einstein's theories of relativity and space-time. Abstract art anticipates the concepts of black holes. You get the idea. Ever read George Orwell? Take away the words to express freedom or independence, and the mind will have trouble even articulating the idea. You see Picasso or Seurat, you think differently. I think what her murderer really wanted to do was to kill the inspiration for a new way to conceive reality."

Crystal was pensive for a moment. "Right. Well, that presumes the Karma Booth—or whatever's beyond it—is a good thing for human evolution. I thought you were against it."

"I like Fourth of July fireworks as much as the next guy," replied Tim. "That doesn't mean I let little kids play with blasting caps. We're children with this technology. We don't know what the hell we have. Emily Derosier, when she was on this side of mortality, must have got an inkling."

"And maybe somebody else knew more. Or *knows* more."

Tim heard a musical ring tone, and Crystal reached for her cell. She looked up from scanning a text message on her screen, her large and lovely brown eyes widening.

"They've spotted her. She's in the Beaubourg."

9

The Beaubourg was what local Parisians called the Centre Pompidou, the museum and library complex near Les Halles and the Marais. The building looked like someone had torn the skin off a metal beast, leaving all its piping, plumbing and ductwork on display in different colors. It was a high-tech abstract colossus opened in the late Seventies, one that became a landmark in spite of its critics, and almost every day jugglers and buskers entertained small crowds in the gently dipping courtyard in front of its façade.

As the rented car zipped them over to the square in the 4th arrondissement, Crystal saw the looming structure of the Beaubourg and remarked, "Didn't someone once call this thing a sewer on stilts?"

Tim chuckled, grateful for a comment that broke the tension. Crystal had asked the police to hold off, to simply watch the Derosier woman and contain her. If the officers moved in, nobody had any idea what she would do. And in point of fact, she had actually done nothing wrong, let alone criminal, in coming back from the dead. They simply needed to talk to her.

Crystal's cell rang again, and Tim heard her say, "*D'accord*" and quickly push the button to end the call.

Their subject, explained Crystal, was up on the third floor in the Bibliothèque publique d'information, the vast public library in the center. And she appeared to be no threat at all, sitting quietly using a computer. Emily Derosier may have stepped into a new century but it seemed she was quite capable of navigating the Internet. Crystal steered the car for the quicker entrance to the library from the Rue du Renard.

A uniformed officer was there to meet them at the door and escorted them as they hurried up the escalators. The library was massive, and the study tables with their picture-window views of the surrounding neighborhood were so inviting. Too bad they were here for another purpose. They passed high shelves of books, yet more shelves, and then they came to an open space for computer terminals and saw her.

And Emily Derosier looked up and saw them.

Tim shivered with a jolt of electricity down his spine, a sensation of uncanny knowledge that struck him right between the eyes. He had met celebrities and political figures before. He had felt the strange jarring that comes from a famous person resembling their photos but they always looked a little different in the flesh. Shorter, more lines in the face, reduced to the smallness of reality—plus some little difference, some tiny factor. The woman yards ahead of him was unique.

He had watched the video of her stepping out of the Booth and had seen only a beautiful nude woman. But after days of looking at her in black and white photos from a bygone age, she had taken on a mythic physicality for him. It would be as if Ingrid Bergman had suddenly stepped off a screen showing *Casablanca* and sat there at the computer terminal. No, it was even beyond that. Someone more impossibly distant: Florence Nightingale or Arthur Conan Doyle, an anachronism suddenly introduced to you.

And now here she was, monochrome flesh made living flesh: pink and young and healthy. Slender arms, the unmistakable oval face, full lips, green intelligent eyes. She wore a modern, beige halter top with a brown peasant skirt, the long hem on the skirt a vague reminder of her place out of time. As they walked up, he noticed her posture was unusually straight, her fingers poised over the computer keyboard *downward* instead of flat. It was the way he typed, too, because he had learned on an old Underwood typewriter in high school, not an ergonomic, plastic keyboard. They hadn't been invented yet. The woman had kept a few habits of her past.

Looking right at them. And she smiled at them.

No, not at them. At *him*. Crystal caught it, too, whispering, "How does she know...?"

And then Emily Derosier stood up and moved to go. But she wasn't fleeing them. Her eyes were elsewhere, and now Tim and Crystal saw who was making her bolt, and the uniformed cop was shouting *Stop* but it wasn't clear who the order was for. Crystal yelled to the intruders in French, "Who are you?" Her small hand touched Tim's shoulder, giving him the briefest of pushes to go after Emily Derosier. She and the officer would take care of—

A man and a woman were running down the open room after their mystery woman, but they suddenly faced Crystal and the policeman in their way. Their clothing was nondescript, semi-formal. They might have been plain-clothes detectives for all Tim and Crystal knew, but there was clear aggression in their manner. It was the man who stood out, with his long lantern-jawed face and broken nose, his eyes canine and seething. He didn't seem to care at all that a cop was *right there* with his hands raised, asking him where he was going. The woman was a redhead with a washed-out, sallow complexion, her tangled red curls wild and bouncing with her long jogging stride. What the hell did they want? As Tim looked over his shoulder, Crystal reached inside her jacket for her service weapon.

Emily Derosier had also paused, looking beyond Tim to the confrontation about to explode. Then as she turned on her heel, she vanished.

Incredible. Her body seemed to pass through a funhouse mirror, frames taken out of the strip of film. *Gone.*

He was on the same spot in seconds, right where she had stood. Nothing there. If he had taken his eyes off her, he could understand it, but she had started to run, and then *nothing.* Damn it.

He was frozen for an instant, not knowing what to do, but the strange couple was still there, at least, and he had to help Crystal and the cop.

Crystal couldn't pull out her gun fast enough because the lantern-jawed man closed the distance and knocked it out of her hand with a grunt. Tim watched, amazed, as the petite detective didn't betray any shock, any outrage, but smoothly grabbed the man's wrist and spun in place in a tight circle. Then he was flying in an undignified tumble against a wall. Aikido.

The uniformed officer was left with the redheaded woman. It happened so fast, so fast—her right hand came up in a mauling action, and the policeman staggered as his face was raked with vivid, bloody lines across his cheek. The woman screamed something guttural, no words in it, and then she was sprinting away. Tim rushed over to the strange man as he picked himself up from the floor. Crystal was now yards away, her eyes on the cop. Tim knew nothing about fighting—hell, he hadn't been in a fight since he was a kid. The blow that walloped into his temple was an explosion, and the carpet rose up and slapped him in the face.

Distantly, he heard Crystal crouched down by the policeman, grabbing his shoulder radio, calling for the two suspects and the Derosier woman to be intercepted at the exits. Then she retrieved her gun as Tim recovered.

"Well, that was bloody stupid," she said matter-of-factly. "You're not a cop—you're not anything here. When there's a perceived threat, leave it to law enforcement professionals."

"Can we save the lecture for after we stop them?"

"Let's go!"

A library security guard was already hurrying over to help the wounded policeman. Tim ran as fast as he could. He jogged four times a week, but he was still fifteen feet behind Crystal. She didn't slow down until they were in one of the glass walkway tubes of the Pompidou Center, and the gunshot made a terrifying *crack* in his ears. He heard her shout something like "Down!"

Then he felt her body tackle him and push him for the best cover they could find in this naked, open space. Glass shattered, and suddenly there were large holes in the transparent curves above their heads. Tim heard rapid footsteps again, and Crystal took off once more after Lantern Jaw.

They were in the signature piping that winds its way along the façade, running against the stream of the escalator when Crystal shouted, "I see our girl! She's in the courtyard!"

Emily Derosier. But the redheaded woman had managed to escape to the street as well. Lantern Jaw was at the bottom of the escalator, shoving a tourist out of the way, and there were screams as he fired his gun point blank at a policeman calling for him to halt. He aimed the gun again, trying to shoot Emily Derosier. But in the courtyard the crowd was soon busy shouting over something different.

The redheaded woman had caught up to her target, her hand clawing and raking at her. Emily Derosier cried out and fled towards a set of book and magazine kiosks. A handful of tourists were frozen in shock, most of them frightened by the gunfire, while others stampeded in every direction along the courtyard. Then the man and the woman tried again to corner Emily Derosier—

And it happened once more. Frames cut out of context from the running loop of film—she was gone, then back again.

Whatever magic trick she pulled, it was as if the redhead could see through it, past it. The woman pulled a knife out, a stiletto, and people stopped and stared in bewilderment as the lantern-jawed man raised his gun arm. Time crawled. The gun arm raised...

But as Tim and Crystal hit the street, Emily Derosier gave him another look, this time a bizarre expression of grief, as if she were asking him silently for an apology. When she looked back at her attackers, Tim suddenly understood why.

Because it hit them all.

Whatever she did, it was like a blast hit Lantern Jaw, the redhead, Crystal, himself and a few of the confused, frightened pedestrians and tourists in the courtyard. It staggered them, making Crystal fall to her knees, bending over as if about to be sick, and causing Tim to crumple onto his side, his brain on fire, worse than any pain he'd ever felt before. He couldn't see past his own agony to what was happening with Lantern Jaw and the redhead—

Emily Derosier. She invaded him. She invaded them all. Filling them up until there was nothing left of them.

He felt it. He felt it as the *he* of his being became a communal *you*. And then something came into him as it must have come into the others like a searing metal bolt of psychic force, it burned and scalded, scraping the core of him. His mind flared with images but not only his own. A confused jumble that must have come from the minds of the crippled, sobbing and screaming others. His fingers touched the cobblestone dust, his mind trying to focus, trying to repeat that they were real, not the images, the cobbles. But still the onslaught persisted.

Blinded by the intimacies of others and feeling his own pour out of him into this pool of collective consciousness, he tried to force out words for what felt like hours until he finally found the strength to yell, "Enough!"

Emily Derosier turned, and he saw her face go blank, shocked back to the immediacy of the moment. Her lips parted in a small *o* as if she'd only slapped him out of a flash of temper. It obviously took her a second to realize how vast the impact had been.

He looked into Crystal's eyes and saw a mirror reflection of haunted self-loathing. Let it pass. Jesus, let it pass like a bad aftertaste. Where was she? Where was—

Gone. When he looked over at the murderous couple, they, too, were recovering, and a police car came to a screeching halt in the middle of the square.

Lantern Jaw still had his gun and fired wildly, running for his life now. The redhead looked around her, and she didn't have enough time to escape the newly arrived cops getting out of their car. Panicking, she completely ignored their orders and moved to grab a hostage, one of the bystander women who still trembled and shrieked over the psychic devastation.

There was another loud *crack*, and the redhead dropped to the pavement.

Tim and Crystal ran over, Crystal waving her credentials and trying to explain in breathless French, but it was too late. The redheaded woman was dead. Tim heard the radio chatter of the cops trying to box their other suspect in, but the man had already run right past Les Halles.

"Damn it!"

"Who the hell were they?" asked Crystal.

"And how the hell did they even know Emily Derosier was back?"

They didn't talk about what Emily Derosier had just done to them.

It took forty minutes for the police to take down their statements and ask all their questions. Precious time was lost, but then did it really matter? They had no idea anyway where their mystery woman had escaped to. Tim paced a furious circle in the square as the sun fell behind the shopping centers of the 4th arrondissement, while Crystal tried to reassure him.

"Patience," she told him.

"I've never had much."

She gave him a mildly scolding look. "Well, this is law enforcement. Tracking people—even if they're people who aren't... normal. You're either patient or you go mad. And hey, we might get another sighting off CCTV footage."

"I suppose."

She drove her knuckles gently into his shoulder. "Don't sulk, Mr. Cale. I was just starting to like you."

When the cops were done with them, they walked back to the floor of the library where the first confrontation had happened.

They *didn't* talk about what Emily Derosier had done to them. Neither of them wanted to.

But both knew if they found the woman again, she could unleash that same kind of mental fury.

What Tim found interesting as he tried to get past his own revulsion over how he was violated was that it didn't seem to be a decisive blow against her attackers. The psychic blast had been scattershot, and when she had stopped it, Lantern Jaw and the redhead still recovered just as he and Crystal did.

Or maybe because they were surrounded by innocents, she hadn't given them full force. Or she couldn't focus it to a lethal degree.

"What was she checking on the Internet anyway?" asked Tim.

Crystal swiveled the computer monitor so that he could see for himself. "You."

On the screen, several windows were open with old news links on his diplomatic and his university career.

Crystal got the police to show them the CCTV footage of the courtyard in front of the Beaubourg, and when it cued up to Emily Derosier fleeing the center, Tim spotted the mysterious couple emerging seconds later. Then came Crystal and himself. Emily Derosier ran—but that wasn't what was interesting in the video. As he watched himself and Crystal suddenly freeze in place, he recognized these were the moments when their Booth victim seemed to disappear before their eyes.

But on the footage, she just ran quickly to a different spot. Other pedestrians were reacting as well. They were all shocked, startled by her disappearance and wondering how she seemed to phase out of one spot and reappear in another. But the man and the woman who were chasing her looked more frustrated than surprised—

As if they knew to expect this, but didn't have a way of combating it, thought Tim.

The same thought occurred to Crystal, plus something more. "They don't know how to deal with her."

"No," whispered Tim.

Then on the footage, Emily Derosier walked faster. And *faster*. Until she was a blur to the police surveillance cameras as well.

"Whatever she did to get away, she did this to *us* first," Crystal pointed out. "Some sort of illusion. She screwed with everyone's head before she actually had to move faster than the cameras' motion detection."

It was still afternoon back in New York, and Tim emailed the footage to Gary Weintraub with a note about what they saw. An hour and a half later, it was Andrew Miller who responded, suggesting he talk to Tim and Crystal live through Skype so he could offer his feedback more quickly.

Crystal immediately picked up on Tim's lack of warmth for the young neurologist. Tim told her they'd be lucky if Miller didn't have his ratty sneakers propped up on the desk in front of the webcam, and as the link came up, the scientist didn't disappoint. He was leaned back in a chair, burrowing through a bag of Lay's potato chips, and his eyes widened over Crystal seated next to Tim. Miller tossed his bag quickly aside.

"Hiya, I'm Andrew," he said nervously, dusting his hands of crumbs and doing his best to offer a winning smile.

"Yes, how are you?" said Crystal, ignoring his attempt at charm. "DI Anyanike."

Tim allowed himself the faintest smirk, unable to resist. "What do you have for us? *Andrew*."

"Uh, yeah," said Miller. "Inspector Anyanike is right. You could call it an illusion, I guess. What you guys experienced is known as *akinetopsia*. The inability to perceive motion.

You said you saw comet trails, right? Fuzzy sort of waves from that chick's limbs? That's what people with *akinetopsia* see. You normally get it from a lesion in a spot of the extrastriate cortex or if you're popping certain antidepressants. But nobody's ever heard of *mass akinetopsia*—let alone somebody 'strobing' a crowd like that. Jesus."

"She did something else, too," said Tim. "Can Gary give us a clue as to how she just blipped out faster than the cameras?"

Miller shrugged. "It's guess work. Gary says the blur looks faintly—and he said to emphasize this, *faintly*—like part of the light show of the Booth."

Tim and Crystal traded a look.

Crystal leaned forward. "Are you saying this woman has the power of transporting herself the same way people were brought back from the dead?"

Miller's face broke into a happy grin. Tim winced, expecting him to make a foolish comment about loving her accent. Fortunately, their science geek restrained himself.

"Look, it's purely speculative. We don't know, and cut us some slack here—we're working off a digital transfer of a street camera! We're already using advanced video equipment here in New York to try to catch stills and progression of the light spectra for the next Booth transpositions."

"There shouldn't *be* any more Booth transpositions!" snapped Tim. "Not until we figure this out."

"Not up to us, dude," replied Miller, bouncing in his chair. "Can't believe you're still pushing that, Tim. Look at what you've seen so far! You got people coming back with incredible abilities. Mary Ash, Geoff Shackleton, this chick! We're not just bringing people back—we're bringing 'em back *better*."

Tired, Tim ran fingers through his comma of blond hair and asked simply, "There's nothing more you guys can give us to help track her down?"

"Sorry, man."

Miller didn't look very sorry at all. But then Emily Derosier wasn't his problem.

Tim thanked him and clicked off the Skype program.

"She was looking into your background," said Crystal. "Maybe it's a matter of waiting until she comes out and makes an approach."

"Assuming she gets to us before that weird guy finds her."

"Yes, well, *he* doesn't give people *akinetopsia*," said Crystal. "He struck me as quite mortal. So I say we add him to our list of people to find. And I say he might prove easier than the others."

10

Two days later, to their surprise, Miller was getting back to them in the flesh, fidgeting nervously at the front desk of Tim's hotel. The concierge had phoned up, and Tim came down from his room and naturally asked what the scientist was doing here.

Miller groaned. "Weintraub sent me over. He thought we ought to check to see if that redhead the police shot in the street was anything special. You know... If the Derosier woman came out of nowhere, maybe this one's an arrival we just didn't know about? Man, I knew you'd be in decent digs, but you get to stay *here*? Shit, I'm at a two-star dump in this Pigalle district! Over by the Rue de... de..."

He couldn't remember the name and dug into his pocket for the hotel's business card. Tim wasn't interested. "Andrew, I'll talk to Gary about getting you better digs. Listen, there's nothing about this woman to suggest she came out of a Karma Booth, if that's what you two are thinking. It was Emily Derosier who flitted away and dazzled all of us. Her attacker bled and died like a regular person. And her boyfriend was ordinary enough to use a right-cross. Take my word for it on that one."

Miller was still gaping up at the chandeliers and the gilt-framed paintings as he chomped away on his gum. "Hey, I don't have a friggin' clue if she's special, but Gary called over to the Pasteur Institute and got me a place I can work in. This Center National de la Re-church—"

"Centre National de la Recherche Scientifique."

"You know it?"

"It's the largest government research organization in France," replied Tim. "It's also one of the biggest science agencies in all of Europe. You don't have to be a doctor to know it. They should be able to provide you with anything you need."

"I need the dead chick's brain."

Tim nodded. "So that's why you're here. You want to peek inside her cranium."

Miller's face lit up in a happy grin. "Hey, what if she *is* unusual? What could her brain tell us? This could be an amazing opportunity! Man, if the scientific community knew, they'd be clamoring for papers!" Catching Tim's look of disapproval, he added, "But that can wait. Anyway, Gary spoke to Benson, Benson spoke to the Health Secretary, who got on the horn to Paris. I don't know what the French word is for 'Sorry, we are going to drag our asses like zo,' but the consensus is that your babe of a London bobby knows how to sweet-talk the frogs. And I would be hugely indebted to you, Mister Big-shot Freelance Consultant, if you'd let *me* ask her to ask them."

"Be my guest," said Tim. "But if you'll take some friendly advice for your approach, a London police officer hasn't been called a 'bobby' in maybe a hundred years, and you guys might save yourselves a lot of diplomatic aggravation if you stop calling French people *frogs*."

"That's right, you were this big diplomat."

"Yeah, call me crazy—I try to be polite to other cultures and meet them on their own terms."

Miller was only half paying attention. "Finally!" he cried out, looking over Tim's shoulder.

Tim turned. One of the hotel bellhops was pushing a dolly that carried a *very* large box. He watched as Miller rushed over, telling the bellhop, "Thanks, thanks a lot." He signed a form in a frantic scribble and rushed to tear the sealing tape off the box and open it up. Tim didn't understand.

"You had equipment brought here?" he asked. "Your hotel's that bad?"

"Real shit-hole," muttered the neurologist, dumping some bubble wrap on the foyer rug. "They lure the tourists in on their website, claiming Toulouse Lautrec or somebody once lived there, and then you show up, and it's communal bathrooms and a fucking tiny sink in your room. I think that mattress has bugs, too. *No way* I want to keep anything valuable there! So I had them ship this to your spot. Jesus, I hoped it survived—"

Out of instinctive manners, Tim took a step forward to help him lift whatever it was out of the box, sheathed in another layer of protective wrapping. He couldn't imagine what it contained, Miller chanting all the while by his side, "Careful, careful, careful." He half-expected a portable 3-D printer, but it was the wrong size and shape for that. Then the neurologist triumphantly peeled away some of the clear plastic and gasped in delight.

"Yes! It's okay."

Tim could hardly believe it.

Miller needed two arms and one of Tim's hands to hold up his treasure. It was about five feet long and heavy, and he talked about it as if he were boasting about a favorite son's Little League championship.

"You had *this* shipped over?"

Miller beamed with pride. "USS *Missouri*. Laid down in the Brooklyn Navy Yard in 1941, launched in 1944. Nine sixteen-inch Mark 7 guns firing armor-piercing shells. This baby saw Iwo Jima, a *kamikaze* attack, the Japanese surrender…"

"Well, not this particular baby," drawled Tim.

Miller tilted his head and smirked. "Cute. My granddad served on the *Missouri*, and my dad used to work with me on models—not as big as this. Plastic, rickety shit. This one's got over seven hundred individual wooden pieces, been working on it every day for months, not about to break my streak now."

"And you bring something like this over every time you get on a plane overseas?" Tim asked in disbelief.

"Oh, no," chirped Miller. "I've never been out of the States before. Getting a passport was a real pain in the ass, but Gary helped. Hey, everybody's got to have a hobby, right? Helps me think."

"But you might only be here a few days. Pretty expensive to ship it over."

"Government picked up the tab. They'll pay for it, too, when I go home."

"You're *expensing* this?"

Then Miller squared off in front of Tim and adjusted his glasses. "Hey, from what I hear, you like to go for long lunches at pretty chic places and have Uncle Sam pick up the tab. How is this different?"

*

Tim, feeling a bit more respect for the young neurologist, let him tag along to his dinner with Crystal Anyanike that evening at one of his old haunts on the Île de la Cité. Miller wore an ear-to-ear grin through the wine serving and was still singing Tim's praises for including him after dessert. Two hours later when Tim had returned to his hotel, Benson called him on his cell.

"Our embassy in Delhi found out what happened to the boy—well, the young guy—and the old woman from that village."

The ones returned by the robed strangers.

"You're not going to like it," Benson went on. "There's no chance of follow-up."

"Why not?" asked Tim. "Don't tell me the Indians have them in protective custody to keep the lid on—"

"They're both dead."

Tim shut up, mildly stunned. The return of the boy and the woman had been a constant for him, as if their lives must be strangely blessed and would vaguely go on. They were two innocents to whom nothing else bad could happen.

Wrong.

"Animal attack," explained Benson.

"*Both?*"

"Given the weird shit you've been telling us about them, this is in the ballpark. And it's been confirmed. Just a second—"

Tim heard the blip of a text file sent along. Benson had just given him a translation of a local police report. According to the Indian authorities, two snow leopards had come down from their habitat above the tree line of a nearby mountainous meadow on the Nepal side. The new settlers—the ones that moved into the shacks of the village since that nightmare with the robed strangers—insisted the beasts had *deliberately* gone after the woman and the young man.

They came down in great loping strides, and then the big speckled cats singled them out, ignoring completely the easy prey of a toddler child and of a goat in their paths.

My God, thought Tim. They targeted them.

The woman was the first to die, her throat torn out by one of the animals. But the cat didn't stay to feed. It caught up to its companion as the other animal ran down the young man. People screamed and sobbed as the two cats mauled him to shreds, and they later reported the pair was strangely oblivious as a farmer raced out with a rifle. The cats didn't even stir from their feast as he let out his first shot. He killed both of the animals quickly.

The attacks didn't make sense, thought Tim. The Indians were equally baffled. Snow leopards don't hunt in pairs or packs, and while they can take down animals three times their size, it was out of character for a pair of them—let alone one—to approach a busy human settlement. More often, they hunted domestic livestock when humans encroached on their domains.

It couldn't be coincidence that the old woman and young man were chosen.

Tim felt frustrated for much of the next day. The others had their own set tasks, leaving him to think he was stuck with unnecessary downtime. Crystal was busy with the police, sifting through CCTV footage to look for Emily Derosier and "Lantern Jaw" as they now called the surviving assassin. Meanwhile, Andrew Miller had finally managed to navigate the French bureaucracy to do tests on the dead redheaded woman.

There was one bright spot for Tim. Before Miller left to fiddle in a borrowed lab in the 16th arrondissement, he mentioned how the French police had managed to identify the redhead.

"Her name was Ana Tvardovsky. Whoever the hell she was. Don't know if that gives you anything."

"It gives me enough, thanks."

The name wasn't familiar at all, but the fact that the woman had been Russian stirred a distant memory.

Thanks to his consultant status and his old diplomacy contacts, he had access to the right databases. Nothing... nothing... nothing. And then he got a hit. Punching in the name 'Tvardovsky' prompted a nice page of links to research papers and analysis files, a spot where academia met espionage and tweedy professors did the grunt work for MI6 and Europol. Tim clicked on one, and up came a photo of the dead woman with her washed-out, sallow complexion and tangled curls. In the photo, she was a brunette; the red hair had been a dye job.

Once upon a time, Ana Tvardovsky had been that rare creature, a female enforcer for the Russian mob. She had started out on her back as a high-price call girl. Then she showed talent for putting others face down dead in the Volga. It figured, thought Tim. He recalled how the woman had turned vicious, raking her nails across the face of the cop back in the Beaubourg.

What had Emily Derosier been to her? Tim didn't know yet. But a clue was perhaps in how Ana Tvardovsky had made a career change five years ago.

"Viktor Limonov," he said aloud, staring at his computer screen.

Ana Tvardovsky had left the Russia mafia to go work for Viktor Limonov, one of the most notorious arms merchants to come out of the broken rubble of the Soviet Union. She had served as first contact for his new clients, had set up his meetings and made sure his money got into offshore accounts. But when Limonov was finally captured in Thailand so that he could be dragged before an international court, she had quietly slipped away and boarded an overnight flight for Phnom Penh. And then her blinking light on the detection screens of law enforcement faded out. Gone. Inactive. Out of sight.

None of what she'd done for Limonov would have made her any more special, except for Tim's inside knowledge that Viktor Limonov was supposed to be executed by the Karma Booth later in the month. Just like the snow leopards, this couldn't be coincidence either.

He sent Crystal the links and files and got a smiley face back in response. Huh. He had expected a *THX* or a one-line text, not such an upbeat playful reply. Maybe he was acting a little too stuffy around her. You don't have to be the serious prof *all* the time, he chided himself.

Even their third wheel, Miller, was better at breaking the tension. The neurologist could go from revelling in the wonders of the Karma Booth to a throaty, less-than-worshipful remark about Crystal being a "goddess." Tim and Crystal had both watched in fascination as Miller giggled with delight over a familiar *Big Bang Theory* episode playing on a bar's TV set.

"This one's a classic!" he told them, and then recited the dialogue of the Sheldon character in English over the French dubbing.

Crystal had the information now on Ana Tvardovsky so if there were any leads to Lantern Jaw, she could find them. He re-read his notes from his talks with Mary Ash and Geoff Shackleton, and then he found himself wandering back to the small art gallery to study the paintings of Emily Derosier.

He was willing to bet her murderer had never known of the existence of these pictures. The killer had slashed and vandalized others. *Why?*

He stepped up to the canvases, close enough to inspect the texture of the thick strokes of paint. What had Emily Derosier been trying to say?

The paintings: a woman in a diaphanous robe moved through a window, which was actually the mouth of an impossible creature of light. A view offered through a tempest of water of a hauntingly beautiful dissected nude. *And now you've come back.* You checked up on my background, thought Tim, but you ran when I found you.

Perhaps because you knew I wasn't able to protect you in that moment. And yet you seemed to protect yourself well enough, he thought.

Was it possible...? That she had run because she had wanted to protect Crystal and him? There was no way to know until he could ask her in person.

He stood staring at the pictures for a long time, as if he could divine answers from them with just this mental guard duty, and then he felt he wasn't alone anymore. He turned, expecting the manageress, but instead saw Crystal at his shoulder, smiling at his faint surprise.

"Sorry, I didn't mean to sneak up on you," she told him. "But you were concentrating so hard."

"Nothing to show for it, though."

"If it makes you feel better, we have no more hits off the CCTV footage. Wherever she disappeared to, she's lying low."

Tim nodded. "Dinner?"

"Somewhere cheap and cheerful this time," suggested Crystal. "All those wine sauces and rich desserts are too tempting. And when I go back to my real job, I better fit through the doors if I have to go out on a raid."

She and Tim walked to the door of the gallery. "Somehow I doubt you'll ever have that problem," he answered.

"I hope you have better lines than that, Mr. Cale."

"It's not a line at all, I'm serious. The way you took after those creeps! I was breathing your dust. By the way, I called Matilda and had her FedEx me your two books. I like how you've extended Cheikh Anta Diop's ideas on African civilization in your first one. I also like the way you think. It's… three- dimensional. You'd make a great sub-contractor for my business if you ever get tired of police raids."

"Is this what passes for flirting in the consultancy world?" she asked him. "Casual job offers?"

"It's a serious job offer," he replied. "And certainly not a casual come-on."

"Glad to hear it. I'd expect only a serious come-on from a man of your stature, Mr. Cale."

As they hit the street, she took a couple of quick steps ahead to hail them a taxi. As it pulled to a stop in front of them, she had a glint of mocking in her eyes. "As for the job offer, it's appreciated. But we should wait until this is over to decide how well we work together."

"Understood," he said. "Then dinner's on you tonight!"

She stayed on the curb, blinking at him in surprise.

He opened the door for her. "Coming? Cheap and cheerful, you said. I'm sure a detective inspector can afford cheap and cheerful."

She swatted him with a hand as she got in.

*

When Tim and Crystal came out of the Metro on their way back to the hotel, there were ten urgent text messages from Benson, all of them insisting that Tim call right away. He and Crystal sat down in the lobby café and ordered coffee, and Crystal booted up her laptop.

A minute later, Benson's voice over Beltway traffic was urging Tim, "Drop whatever you're doing and get back here."

"What now?" asked Tim. He hit the speakerphone function on his cell so Crystal could listen in. They heard Benson honking at an intersection five thousand miles away.

"A Christian radical group has kidnapped this high, muckety-muck doctor in Montreal. You ever hear of Dieter Wildman? He's a German immigrant and Holocaust survivor who opened several abortion clinics. Very big in the pro-choice movement. They even awarded him the Order of Canada, which didn't go down well with the far right fringe."

"Well, Canada's right wing is usually still left of anything south of the border," Tim put in.

"Doesn't matter anyway, I guess—this group isn't Canadian. It's an *international* coalition of whack jobs. They took Wildman because he's one of the few pro-choice advocates who won't go into hiding. You remember how some doctors were assassinated? I suppose the lax security helped when they grabbed the guy."

"On *your* side of the border," Crystal pointed out. She swiveled the computer screen around so that Tim could see. Her London superiors had already sent her a briefing note on the Wildman kidnapping.

"The word is the Canadian border guards *did* put them through their paces as they drove into New York

State—something off about the vehicle. The Americans didn't even stop them, just waved them on through. They smuggled Wildman onto a Cessna owned—get this—by one of the big televangelists. Phony flight plan and manifest, of course."

"Excuse me, Detective, but where the hell are you getting your information?" demanded Benson. "How did you get these facts?"

"It's *Detective Inspector*," she corrected him. "And you might want to remember the kidnapping occurred in *Canada*. Sovereign nation? Still part of the British Commonwealth, remember? Ottawa was good enough to send us a briefing memo—*they* don't mind cooperating in matters of international law enforcement. Just because you asked for me doesn't mean I work for you. *Mate!*"

Tim picked up his spoon and banged it against his coffee cup. Benson barked a curse and said, "I can hear that, you know!"

"Good. Can you forget the territorial pissing match? We've got bigger issues here. They flew Wildman out. Can we all agree Wildman is no longer anywhere near the United States or Canada?"

"Makes sense," said Crystal. "They must have thought it was easier to bring Wildman to the Booth than bring their stolen Booth to America."

Tim nodded. "Right. They could move it, but to bring it to the States would mean dismantling it to avoid suspicion. No one fully understands how the Booth works, so they have no idea if they could put it back together again and make it function." He groaned in disgust. "Benson, you there?"

"I'm here, Cale."

"You know he's dead, don't you?"

"That's not Ottawa's official position," replied Benson. "And it's not ours either."

"But it's probably the reality," said Crystal softly, more for Tim's benefit than for the official on the speakerphone. "They're going to keep on using this thing like a weapon. It has to be taken back. We'd be better off staying here in Europe."

"Well, the President wants you to get your ass back here for a briefing," said Benson. "Meaning you, Tim. The *Detective Inspector*—as she just reminded me—doesn't work for us so her invitation is optional. I should add our Commander-in-Chief did *ask*. You know the President is very big on manners—and on international cooperation."

They would both be going to Washington.

They made good time on the jet. Their two-hour reprieve to freshen up was less a granted mercy from Benson than a sudden scheduling delay from Pennsylvania Avenue. Crystal confided to Tim that she had never seen Washington before, and as much as she tried to hide it, there was still a bit of the wide-eyed tourist in her as the limo whisked them around Dupont Circle.

He was amused to see her lose interest as they were ushered through the security checks. As a British citizen, she had no idea that she was getting special treatment. They were definitely off the standard tour. Tim had come here as a visitor himself several times, but that was years ago when he was still with the State Department.

Then they were led into the Oval Office, and Tim noticed the President working at the famous Resolute Desk. You usually saw a President posed in front of it, speaking behind it, consulting with a staff member near it, or leaning over it in near-silhouette the way Kennedy had done in the iconic photo. But the current holder of the office now sat at the desk, and maybe "working" wasn't the right word. The President tapped keys to make farm animal noises on the latest model of iPad, while her "assistant"—five years old with golden curls and wearing pink overalls—shrieked happily, perched on the edge of the green blotter. Miranda Grant was many things besides the highest elected official in the land, including, at fifty-three, a grandmother. She glanced up at Tim, Crystal and Benson and waved them on in.

Tim knew her from years ago, a time when he could still call her "Miranda." She was once one of the high flyers on Wall Street, working in risk analysis for a major insurance company. Her career in the US Senate was launched when she correctly diagnosed what it would take to lift Detroit out of its horrible economic depression. She was sharp, kept a steely focus on her election agenda of banking reform and infrastructure renewal, and she didn't think twice about firing cabinet secretaries if they stepped out of line or became a liability on the six o'clock news. And she always encouraged insiders to speak their minds—up to a point.

All these qualities brought the inevitable snide whispers from the opposition about her being "hard" or "pushy"—or worse labels. She could suffer them all, except being compared to Margaret Thatcher. She *hated* that. Damn stupid cliché, she complained, every female leader being compared to Thatcher. So even though she genuinely loved her grandchildren, she wasn't above using them as props for photo shoots at the White House to soften her image—it was one of the reasons why she made a point of having the kids visit her in the Oval Office. Now she looked up from the tablet and the toddler on the desk, handing the little girl off to an aide.

"Timothy Cale! Haven't seen you since the Foreign Affairs Committee days." As they shook hands, she stood on her toes to give him a polite kiss, barely brushing his cheek.

"Well, it was a struggle uphill I've tried to forget, Mrs. Grant," chuckled Tim.

The President made small talk with Crystal, who made a point of complimenting a hand-carved wooden sculpture from Nigeria on display—a gift from the new ambassador. Then she and Tim were waved to the cream couch near the presidential seal, and it was time to get down to business. The Health and Justice secretaries briskly walked in to join the meeting.

"I would be grateful, gentlemen—and lady," started the President, the flint in her voice clear and sharp, "if anyone here could offer a solution for how to shut this fiasco down. Are we talking another huge manhunt around the globe for nutcases? Dr. Weintraub and his team *still* don't have a clue what the actual power source is for these Booths, so we can't come at the problem that way. The Egyptians are hanging their heads in embarrassment and covering this up from their own people…Tim, I thought you were brought in to deliver some answers when the first signs of trouble happened. Do you have any answers *at all?*"

Tim did his best to hide his surprise. He hadn't anticipated he might end up the fall guy for this cock-up. What the hell was going on? Was it Benson who set him up? But he realized in that split second, it hardly mattered. The President was waiting to be enlightened, and Tim could appreciate how she deserved a response.

"Answers, no, Ma'am," Tim replied calmly. "Inspector Anyanike and I have turned up a few leads. We were running them down when we were called back here."

"You're saying I interrupted you doing your job?" asked the President, a faint smile of challenge on her lips.

"I'm saying the job isn't done, Ma'am, and we're eager to get on with it."

166

He'd be damned if he'd back-pedal here. Even if he was called in to answer to the President of the United States, the woman was still his *client*, not his boss. If they thought he wasn't doing a good enough job, they could always find someone else.

Oh, Christ, he told himself. Who are you kidding? You want the answers, too.

"Tim, just tell me if you're getting anywhere," said the President, who seemed to pick up his meaning. "Tell me you need more resources, I'll get them for you. You need an army, fine—we got an army. What I can't give you is much time. This is going to leak out. You might say it's unfair that you have to figure this out. Too damn bad, I've seen your fees."

That prompted a mild ripple of laughter around the room.

"I'm asking you, please," said the President, the slight chill in her tone now returned, "if you have anything so far to make sense of this disaster. This could start a panic."

"I do," said Tim, and he looked briefly to Crystal, whose face for an instant betrayed just as much anticipation as the others.

Perhaps because she mistook his expression for an appeal, Crystal leaned forward and perfectly matched his bluff.

"We've found a possible ally," she started gently, "of sorts. A returning victim. She's the one who stepped out of the Booth in Paris without an execution, and she's shown an interest in Ti—Mr. Cale. That suggests—at least to me—that there is sentient knowledge on the other side, wherever that is, *whatever* it is, that must know what is going on here. On our plane of existence."

The President looked to her cabinet secretaries. "What are you saying, Miss Anyanike? That you two have made contact with this person?"

"No," Tim offered quickly, and Crystal gave an emphatic echo: "No, no." They briefed everyone quickly on what had transpired in Paris, and Tim threw in the details about the two survivors in India hunted by the snow leopards. As the others in the room demanded impatiently to know the connection, the President, to her credit, held up a hand for calm and quiet.

"That disappearing village in India is why we knocked on Tim's door in the first place. Because he's the only who's ever had confirmed dealings with this kind of phenomena. And you're right—I don't buy that it's a coincidence they get viciously attacked while all the rest of this is happening. Not at all. There's a connection. Maybe you're right, Miss Anyanike, maybe we… Well, humanity has an ally. So now I understand your testiness with your Commander-in-Chief, Tim."

Tim nodded, understanding the code: You get one break, old friend—you won't get another one like it again.

The Health Secretary, perhaps feeling too much like a spectator and needing to make a show of contributing, piped up for all to hear. "We've got to get a moratorium on this thing. Something like a non-proliferation treaty with other countries for safety and prevention purposes—"

"That's fine for the long term," said the President a little impatiently. "We're still left with the urgent problem of these fanatics in possession of a Booth. Tim, Miss Anyanike, what do you think? We need you both available for when these jokers turn up. And they're bound to turn up with threats and demands."

"No doubt," said Crystal. "But we'll be of the best use to you in Europe."

"I agree," said Tim. "Once we're back there, hopefully Emily Derosier will find a safe window of opportunity to contact me. I can't see why else she would dig into my background. Plus I suspect the terrorists who captured Wildman are nowhere near North American soil anymore. You offered an army, Ma'am—I think we need one. For the obvious: a strike force to take the Booth back. I assume the guys in Langley are using satellite surveillance to look for them."

The Director of the CIA offered a curt nod.

"Has anyone got a lead on Orlando Braithewaite?" asked Tim. "He's the one who's been handing out all these Pandora's Boxes."

"In the wind," said the CIA Director. "We still think he's somewhere in East Africa. No confirmation yet."

Tim sighed. "I have a few volumes of questions I'd like to ask our friendly billionaire."

"We pin him down, you'll get your chance," said the Director. He shook with a rumbling wet cough, making a little hammer gesture with his fist against his sternum. He was the kind of dedicated, old-school spy who drowned all his moral questions in double-Scotches and plenty of steaks cooked medium rare. "We can have a crack team ready for rendition as soon as the boys give us a bead on Braithewaite."

"You can't do that."

The Director knew about Tim's less than heroic departure from the State Department, and his hackles rose over a liberal in his midst.

"*Can't?* You just asked for a strike force, Cale. But you don't want to throw a net over the guy who started this mess? Why? Because 'he's an American citizen with rights?' Gimme a break! Word is that Braithewaite plans to rescind his US citizenship and throw in with one of the African regimes!"

"Interesting distinction you're drawing there," replied Tim, tilting his head slightly toward Crystal, "especially when we have an international guest in the room. So according to you, the only people we can go ahead and kidnap are those who *don't* have an American passport. Nice!"

"Let's just cool the tempers," put in the President, raising a hand again.

"My objection was a practical one, not moral," added Tim. "You're talking about a covert operation on foreign soil to extract the man who developed this thing. A man who may have access to other technology *that can tamper with what we understand about reality.* I want to go ask him questions. You want to go fuck with him. Sure, let's try that and see what happens!"

"What *does* happen when someone goes through a Booth without a formal execution order?" asked the President.

Everyone was suddenly stone quiet.

The President of the United States looked from face to face, her voice still reasonable. "Does anyone know? What happens if someone goes through the Booth who hasn't murdered anyone?"

The Health Secretary spoke up. "No country's reported ever having tried it. I mean... Why take the risk? What would be the rationale?"

"But we know someone can travel *back* through a Booth," said Crystal. "Emily Derosier. She's used it as a means of transport. That suggests we could be right: Braithewaite may have the means to use a Booth for escape."

All eyes were back on Miranda Grant. She seemed to be staring at a patch of carpet, but Tim suspected her eyes were on a detail of the presidential seal. *This is yours*, it must have reminded her, *it's all up to you.* As much as Tim chased the effects of the Karma Booth, her decisions over it would be written up in history books.

At last, she looked up, coming to a decision. "Storming in to capture Braithewaite could be disastrous. We need him to tell us what he knows willingly... As for Dr. Wildman and the stolen equipment, you'll get your strike force, Tim. It's officially a rescue mission. Wildman could end up being the first non-murderer to go through a Karma Booth."

"Well, not convicted," muttered the CIA Director.

The President shot him a look. "We're *not* having that discussion, thank you! However you personally stand on the abortion debate, Mr. Capanelli, you'll pardon me, but I am not interested. It doesn't matter what any of us think, *Roe* v. *Wade* is still the law of this land, and if I remember correctly, what you're talking about isn't against the law in Wildman's adopted country either. This administration categorically does *not* condone tactics of intimidation like bombing of health clinics, assassination of doctors or kidnappings! We'll keep on labeling this a terrorist attack in all communications to the media."

She stood up, a signal that the briefing was over. As the other officials filed out, the President gestured to Tim and Crystal to hang back.

"Tim, I have no idea what kind of dangers all of this presents to you and Miss Anyanike. If you want, I can order a Secret Service detail to accompany you."

Tim turned to Crystal. Was it bravado if he turned it down? The strange couple hunting Emily Derosier made him think he ought to consider accepting the help.

On the other hand, no one could have anticipated what he and Crystal faced outside the Beaubourg. And Crystal, standing just out of the President's line of sight, was giving him the slightest shake of the head: *no*.

She had developed a working relationship with him one-on-one. The last thing she would want, he recognized, would be to have to negotiate with more Americans over this crisis.

"We'll be all right, thank you, Ma'am. But I do think we should keep Weintraub's fellow, Miller, on in Europe with us. He's head of the neuroscience group and has been involved with several of the resurrections. We'll need him."

The President nodded. "I'll get Weintraub to understand."

Benson started to usher Crystal out of the Oval Office, but Tim hung back, lowering his voice. "If I may..."

"What's on your mind, Tim?" asked the President.

"If the teams do get lucky and track this group down—say they confiscate the stolen Booth, what then?"

"What do you mean?"

Tim frowned. He wasn't comfortable with his own position on this, but it had to be said. "Is it wise to let the Egyptians have the Booth back? Nothing against the Egyptians per se— maybe it's an opportunity to rid the world of one less device."

The President smiled. Tim had once played poker with her years ago after a UN conference, and she'd gone home with more in her wallet than he had.

She paused and said carefully, "We'll cross that bridge when, God willing, we get our hands on the thing."

11

The briefing with the President of the United States was sobering enough that Tim and Crystal hardly spoke as the limo whisked them to a hotel. Then Tim remembered his manners. "Thanks for your help in there. I didn't realize I'd been set up for a call on the carpet."

She smiled faintly and muttered, "No worries."

It was understood that they could have two days' rest, enough time that hopefully fresh intel could be gained on the terrorists, and then the jet would return them to Paris. As their new hotel's façade loomed in the tinted window, they said nothing more to each other, both seemingly drained. Then Crystal leaned on her armrest and finally sounded him out.

"I got the impression you weren't too keen on our young Dr. Miller."

"I'm not," replied Tim. "In terms of social skills, he's an ass. In terms of his field, he's allegedly brilliant. I want to learn what Emily Derosier is once we catch up with her."

"You don't think she's human?"

"Well... 'human plus' maybe."

Crystal didn't say anything for a moment, and there was the steady, lulling noise of the limo engine, the sunlight crisscrossing over the car's sunroof. She pulled out her laptop, switched it on and showed him a downloaded file she said had just come in while they were busy in the Oval Office.

"Nine weeks ago, Somali pirates captured a merchant marine vessel in the Gulf of Aden, but they didn't demand any ransom, not right away. That's unusual—obviously. Her Majesty's Government, like everyone else, has had it up to here with these thugs, and though the ship doesn't belong to a British concern, it's been put under our surveillance. And it rendezvoused, interestingly enough, with a Greek yacht."

"They used it to transfer the Booth. Clever."

Crystal nodded. "MI6 is now sure the terrorists have the Booth on the yacht here." She pointed to a spot in the middle of the Mediterranean. "They're headed in this direction."

Tim clucked his tongue. Son of a bitch. Right through the Strait of Gibraltar.

"Okay. But they're not stupid enough to bring a Karma Booth all the way across the Atlantic where they could be nabbed. Why not bring Wildman to Egypt and throw him into the Booth *there* to make their point?"

Crystal was silent, wondering this as well.

"In fact, why not just video his execution and escape?" Tim went on. "Why risk moving the Booth? And where would they—"

"Northern Ireland."

"What?"

"Northern Ireland," she repeated. "Look at the route— through the Strait of Gibraltar. Exactly the way they'd have to go to reach there. It's one of the staunchest anti-abortion spots in Europe. Unionist and nationalist groups both oppose it, and Sinn Féin only wants a limited relaxing of the laws. They'll have allies there who can look the other way at customs, and when they execute Wildman they'll be in the thick of supporters who will believe the ends justify the means. A terrorist attack is always meant to be theater. They'll want an applauding audience."

"That's why you didn't want the Secret Service guys to tag along," mused Tim. "You suspected this is where they'd take the Booth."

Crystal looked at the laptop screen. "Did I?"

"So this is a show for the SAS."

"They're the best in the world, Tim—no matter what Navy SEALs claim. If they're making for Northern Ireland, you can bet my people will insist they handle the op."

"Fair enough," said Tim. "So at what point do we keep up the pretense, and I let Washington know we're on our way to Ulster?"

"Let's wait until we're halfway across the ocean."

"Before we go, I think there's one other place we should visit tomorrow so that you fully understand what's going on here."

"Right, then," she said. "Where?"

"Pennsylvania. I want to introduce you to someone."

When Mrs. Ash came to the door this time, she didn't bother with a greeting and showed no interest that Timothy Cale had brought along a stranger. She merely gestured for them to walk through the house and out the French windows to the expansive back garden.

Mary Ash knelt barefoot on the grass in a flower print dress, her palms cupped protectively as if cradling a baby bird. Certainly, they could hear a high-pitched mewling and feverish shrieking, but the girl didn't let whatever it was go. Her expression was blank, almost like that of a lab technician's clinical detachment. She only looked up and smiled when Tim and Crystal drew near.

"Hello, Inspector Anyanike."

"Hello, Mary," Crystal answered politely, showing no surprise at being recognized.

Tim had warned her about the girl's jarring habit of knowing intimate things; about the *hyperthymesia*, what Mary Ash herself had defined as "the ability to recall vivid autobiographical detail according to dates"—only she'd rather do this with others.

"I'm not sure I have anything new that can help you, Mr. Cale," said Mary, her eyes still on what was in her cupped palms.

"It's all right," he answered. "What are you doing?"

"Oh… Looking for perspective."

"On what?"

"On me."

She took her left hand away, and now they saw there was no baby bird or tiny creature in her grasp. *Mary Ash* was contained within the flat island of her own hand, growing out of the palm heel, close to the wrist. It was a miniature version of herself from little more than a year ago: naked with her filthy, lank hair hanging down over her eyes as she screamed in agony, her forearm and belly splattered with the blood of her amputated fingers. There was no version of Emmett Nickelbaum in this hideous portrait, just the tortured girl and her agonies, self-contained as if in some demented invisible snow-globe.

Crystal screamed and staggered back.

Tim jumped back as well, muttering, "Jesus Christ…!"

"He kept making me ask him," said Mary Ash. "He wanted me to ask him, 'Are you hard?' I had to ask over and over. After a few hours I just said it anyway. He didn't even have to prompt me."

176

"Mary," said Tim, trying to reach her.

"He made me small," said Mary Ash softly. "So I thought this scale fit better. I could make it larger, but that would be disturbing."

"*Why* would you want to see this?" Tim demanded. He was shaking. He looked to Crystal, and saw that they were both shaking, mirrors to each other's shock.

"I'm sorry," said Mary Ash. "I kept it small."

Crystal swallowed hard. "Please... Please put it away." She shut her eyes and looked down at the grass—doing all she could to avoid the image in front of her and expunge it from memory.

"Mary, we came to talk," Tim started again. "And see how you're doing..."

For which they now had their answer.

Mary Ash brought her left hand back and pushed against the tiny version of herself, but it didn't dissolve or shimmer in the mode of a cruel hologram joke. The mouth and clawing arms squashed and rolled into a grotesque ball of bizarre human Plasticine. The young woman was literally rubbing and smoothing the tortured version of herself back into her hand.

"When he returns, he'll look for me," she explained. "I have to carry him around in my head anyway. So I thought, you know, if I can understand the appeal for him of what he did, maybe I'll have a weapon. For what's coming."

"Mary, Emmett Nickelbaum is *gone*," Tim put in quickly. "We can protect you. I can call now and get a police detail to watch your house and your family, but if you know things—"

Mary Ash looked up at him. "I can't see the future, Mr. Cale. You know what I can do. May twenty-third, he eats fish. May twenty-fourth, berries of some kind, I don't know what they are. May twenty-fifth, fish again, but you'd expect that. Crystal Anyanike's father is knocked down and bruises his hip against the curb of Whitechapel High Street after the police constable uses the N-word. It was so... nasty. Coarse. He won't tell her mother because he's had two other episodes like this already, and she can't understand why he's angry all the time. She thinks he must bring the trouble on himself. They never speak of it to their daughter."

"My father's dead," said Crystal.

"Your mother isn't," replied Mary Ash. Her voice was sonorous; it could have recited a death toll. "I'm sorry. I can't tell how the pieces get preserved but the memory is there. They're all there. I wish I could describe it, but I do art. I mean I *did* art. I think in pictures. I don't want to die again in an ugly way."

"You won't," said Tim. "We'll protect you. But Mary, how can you know he's coming back?"

Mary Ash sighed. She seemed to be making a great effort to stay patient with them, as if she had to simplify the blue of the atmosphere and the ripples in a lake for a child. "I have to carry him around in my head, Mr. Cale. People say, 'We're all connected,' and people always say that as if it's a good thing."

Crystal shot Tim a look. She knelt down and sat across from the girl with a slow wariness, as if fearing their Booth victim might decide to shift the ground beneath their feet. And Tim couldn't say she was wrong to be cautious, not when Geoff Shackleton had moved him outside the White Plains building weeks ago.

"I miss drawing," the girl said sadly. "But there's not much point anymore."

"Why?" asked Crystal.

Mary Ash let out an amused theatrical groan. "*Ohhhhh*, too many steps. He'll be coming back, Mr. Cale, because he's not part of the cycle. Same as me. I didn't tell you before because I didn't want to think about it too much. It still hurt but it doesn't anymore. I want to fight back this time, if I can figure out the best way how. Others can go like spilled milk, but you know, I've always wanted to matter while I'm here, and maybe I can in a little way." She offered another sad little smile. "My mom would probably like it if I matter."

"You're talking like you're going to die again," said Crystal.

"I told you," Mary Ash reminded her. "I can't see the future."

"But you're still being cryptic," said Tim.

"I don't mean to be," replied the girl. "You've tried to talk to the boy but you can't."

Tim marked this. So she could see into the head of the blond boy, too; the one who was once an Asian police officer. Constable Daniel Chen.

"It's not so magical, is it?" she went on. "You've tasted his music, but that doesn't mean you can cook a symphony." She suddenly laughed, but the tinkling notes from her throat were dissonant, a sudden pounding on piano keys. "You know he's miserable, right? He's miserable because, yeah, he knows he's visiting, and you have no way of getting him home where he's supposed to be. And before you ask, Mr. Cale, there's nothing I can tell him on your behalf or translate for you." She sighed and added, "I told you before. Sometimes you wear your questions on your face."

Tim didn't know what to say. It was clear neither did Crystal.

"I don't want to be this way to you." Her fresh laughter sputtered and collapsed into something like a sob, more human and reminiscent of what cried out minutes ago in her palms. "I want to help, but it takes every ounce not to *float*. You can see that, can't you?" She looked at Tim with moist eyes and added, "I mean, you tell your students that old line. You read it at thirteen years old. It was a day in March, with the gray snow still on the ledges of the brick buildings, and your boots made a crunch—just like when you feel the old plastic sleeve on a library book. That crunchy sound. '*The past is a foreign country.*' It is, Mr. Cale."

He knew better than to respond; he and Crystal knew nothing of how she lived these days.

"But I want to live," she said after a pause. "I just have to think of a way to fight back this time."

"I told you, Mary. I'll get a police detail arranged as quickly as possible."

The girl nodded. "Thank you. I told you last time, didn't I? I've never seen Paris."

Tim looked back towards the house, where Mary Ash's mother hovered with a fresh highball, too scared again to go near her daughter. He should have had answers for this woman by now. Damn it, there was still no comfort he could offer her in terms of information. Then he was distracted as his eyes wandered to the ground, and alarmed, Tim tugged on Crystal's arm, urging her to rise.

"Hey!"

The grass was red underneath her legs, yet it didn't stain her skirt or limbs. Crystal got to her feet and quickly inspected herself but assured him, "It's not mine."

Now they could see the pattern. The blood in the grass formed a vivid new composition. The soaked red blades stood in for the wire-mesh stubble, and the eyes soon coalesced into their sadistic familiarity in clotted pools. But the expression in them was very much like the last one Emmett Nickelbaum had in life as the Karma Booth tore him to atoms.

Mary Ash didn't bother to shift from her tranquil spot on the grass. She looked up at Tim and Crystal and said with the faintest note of self-conscious humility, "It's a work in progress. I'm using what I can remember."

A video was placed on YouTube claiming responsibility for Dieter Wildman's kidnapping. Wildman, roped to a chair, looked very frail but defiant. His left eye was swollen and livid with a yellowish red bruise, but apart from the doctor's slightly elevated breathing, the consensus was that the victim was all right, all things considered. Now if they could just reach him in time...

Unlike other terrorist groups, the ones who had taken Wildman didn't force him to read out their demands, and they didn't even bother to wear ski masks or scarves. One of them with curly brown hair that badly needed cutting and a craggy weathered face—a man who looked like he'd spent his life planning in basements—addressed the camera.

"Last year, there were more than a hundred and fifty thousand abortions across the United Kingdom," insisted the man on the screen, his seething outrage carrying a discernible Northern Irish lilt. "Abortions performed by Nazis like this old bastard here."

"I'm the Nazi?" asked Wildman, his voice weak.

"*Shut the fuck up!*" roared the man.

But still Wildman softly demanded, "I'm the Nazi?" And his exhaling breath held a croaking laugh, bitter and pitying for the unrecognized, forlorn irony.

Tim remembered reading in a background note how Wildman had survived Auschwitz. Christ, imagine coming through that horror only to endure the ignorant screaming and barbarities of these troglodytes.

"Um, not that it matters," said Crystal, "but the figure he cited is wrong. And ridiculous. The group he claims to be speaking for here is notorious for inventing their figures. They also like to pad them with 'suspected abortions.' They throw in estimates based on pharmaceutical sales of the morning after pill."

"Terrific."

Crystal tapped the screen. "This is Desmond Leary, former IRA. terrorist turned bank robber—then mercenary after peace finally broke out. Sudan, Democratic Republic of Congo, Kosovo, Pakistan… Mr. Big Conscience for Babies doesn't mind if the ones already born in Africa wind up child soldiers. He's muscle, not brains."

"How do you know?" asked Tim. He clicked the little slash mark across the icon for the video's sound. Leary's rant was irritating noise, not providing them with anything useful.

"You have a reputation for insight," said Crystal. "You tell me."

Tim paused to consider. Then: "He's showing his face. This is a guy who rationalized for years that he was slaughtering and bombing for a cause, and he didn't want to be a spokesman in all that time. He'd have the strategic and tactical common sense to hide his identity. But I doubt even mercenaries like him earn enough to pay off Somali pirates. Someone knew exactly which of his buttons to push—the whole angle that unborn children are the perfect innocents. No gray lines, no compromises… He's been primed for a long time to work for a cause that's personal to him, and someone took advantage of that."

"You'd make a fair counter terrorism analyst."

"Only fair? I did work in the American foreign service."

Crystal smiled fleetingly at his witticism then reached for a file. "The cash behind Leary comes from this American televangelist, Parker Scott Thompson."

She held up a publicity still of Thompson looking towards Heaven with a smug grin of personal knowledge, then a surveillance photo of the forty-eight-year-old preacher in a polo shirt and beach shorts.

"Mr. Thompson is a cliché," she went on. "Argentine authorities have known for a while he's had an affair with one of their top actresses in Buenos Aires. We're guessing he forgot to mention to Leary that he arranged an abortion for her at a clinic in Holland. Whether he's funding this out of demented guilt or he likes having the power, we don't care. He was stupid enough to fly back to Argentina as Wildman was kidnapped, and the Argentines don't mind at all having him extradited to us."

"And your people don't mind him becoming your problem?" asked Tim.

Crystal laughed. "He's small beer as far we're concerned. He has no ministries in the UK. His show isn't carried on any of our networks. The second he screams 'atheist persecution,' we'll leak the story about the actress—photos and all. Leary's the bigger threat. He'll have whole Facebook pages of supporters in Northern Ireland, and for years, he's had a network of safe houses he can rely on."

"But something tells me you have an idea where he is."

"There's that famous insight." Crystal shut off her laptop. "You think Miller has ever been to Derry?"

Derry. The Troubles had once been bad here. According to the files, Desmond Leary learned to hate the British and became radicalized as a thirteen-year-old boy. That was after he got caught in the shooting gallery of the Bogside Massacre known as Bloody Sunday. But as the Nineties started, the violence died down, and by then Leary had long moved on to plant bombs in London. Derry survived the Troubles and him.

There were—and it seemed there would always be—shoppers at the world's oldest department store of Austins, and there were even more tourists these days coming to see the old walls on the river's west bank and St Columb's Cathedral. In Maydown, far from the city's landmarks, there was an empty factory warehouse a couple of miles up from the old DuPont manufacturing plant. No one had paid much attention to it since it was quietly bought up two years ago.

The British were sure the merchant marine ship was sneaking into the estuary leading into the River Foyle and ultimately into the port of Lisahally, where the Karma Booth would have to be moved by truck. Eighteen counter terrorism officers back in London had pored over the prison and arrest records of Leary's associates, along with their financials. And they had turned up the warehouse in Maydown bought by one of them. It was a warehouse that, according to satellite images, had a couple of security cameras for its perimeter and yet absolutely no business at all going in and out of it during the day.

The SAS team drove only so far up to the building, and then their vehicles stopped. Tim, Crystal and Miller were to wait, and it was made clear that God bloody help them if they didn't. "You don't contradict these guys," Crystal warned. "They go in like Batman, and you never see them coming."

Still, mostly thanks to Crystal's position and influence, they were allowed to follow a hundred yards behind with an escort once the SAS team had disposed of Leary's point guards with sharpshooters. Miller, deciding discretion was the better part of valor, followed two hundred yards behind.

Tim hadn't worn a Kevlar vest since one of his assignments in Asia. It was heavy and hot around his torso, and when he tapped it with his knuckles, it felt like he wore a hockey pad. Crystal handled hers more gracefully, but still she looked half-swallowed by the gray vest.

Her hand urged him to stay back. They shouldn't follow too close behind the team. So they watched the SAS squad burst into the warehouse with their rifles raised and their flashlights sweeping the green walls, and then they heard shouts and a thunderclap of staccato gunfire, loud and long and ugly.

"*Hands on your head, down on the floor! Down on the floor right—*"

More gunfire, and now between the eruptions, Tim and Crystal heard another sound. A metallic ringing and a hum, getting louder.

"What is that?" she asked.

Tim knew. He tugged on her arm, and when she resisted, he sprinted ahead. "Shit! That's the Booth! *They're using it now!*"

"Tim, wait!" she yelled. "They haven't cleared—Tim!"

But he kept running. She was still calling his name, warning him, and then she was at his side, and her eyes widened with shock as she came face to face with the Karma Booth for the first time. Tim was already familiar with what would happen next. There was nothing he could do. Dieter Wildman was in the first chamber as it filled with dazzling flares of color and light, but his expression remained inexplicably calm. Tim understood. The doctor's face was set in a firm resolve to preserve his dignity.

"Oh, God," whispered Tim.

Decades ago, Dieter Wildman might have been forced into a claustrophobic space like this one to be exterminated, and so now he had decided on his posture of farewell. He had lived with a rehearsed knowledge of his potential end for decades. Now that death was coming, he knew how to act. There would be no screams. There would be no yells or even an outraged final look. He would simply be going...

Tim waited for the inevitable.

The officers in helmets and protective gear had two surviving terrorists on the floor, one wounded and being handcuffed, while the other was still fighting with his nose in the dirt of the cement floor. Tim recognized Leary from the video sent out on the Internet.

"You'll see in a minute we did the right thing!" Leary was shouting. "We're bloody heroes, and you should—"

"Shut up!" barked the officer with his knee in Leary's back, light flickering and bouncing off his helmet.

Miller stood timidly outside the doorway, the only civilian to heed Crystal's warning to hang back and let the assault team do their work. Now she hurried over to him, desperate and close to panic, grabbing his lapel.

"Can you shut it down? Can you do something?"

"No, no, it's hopeless—"

"*Miller!*"

"It's too late, Crystal! They started the process, Weintraub and I have no idea how to reverse it!"

They were helpless, impotent in the blinding spray of colored molecules from the first chamber. Tim felt more than saw Crystal stepping over to him, looking to him for answers, for a solution. But he had none. Leary, still struggling on the dusty floor, was able to crane his neck to see the fruits of his labor. His face broke into a delighted grin, sure that he was about to be vindicated. Then his expression went blank as did everyone else's.

Because the process wasn't going as planned.

Dieter Wildman was still whole. The light of the Karma Booth refused to carve into his body and transform him. The doctor, resigned a moment ago to his fate, now betrayed a look of confused bewilderment. He knew instinctively that whatever was supposed to be happening *hadn't*.

And Desmond Leary, still fighting the knee wedged in his back and resisting the handcuffs about to be slapped on, bellowed with rage over being cheated. "Fuck! Fuck, fuck, *FUCK*!"

He rolled and wrestled out of the officer's grasp, kicking a heel into the man's head and scrambling to his feet, breaking into a sprint. It was blind, mad dog insanity—running up to the first chamber of the Booth and yanking the door open. Leary was actually *getting inside* to choke Dieter Wildman as if this would prompt the kaleidoscopic, dazzling bursts to do his will and execute his hostage. Crystal ran forward. One of the SAS men ran forward.

Then Leary screamed. The doctor's eyes were wide with horror. He was less than an inch away, his wrinkled, liver-spotted hands trembling in a panicked gesture to comfort, to help the man, no longer his tormentor but a human being now attacked by the light. Light reflected and bounced around the chamber, taking Desmond Leary but not Dieter Wildman. The door still open, Crystal and the SAS man shouted for the doctor to come out, get out of there, and they were pulling the doctor to safety—

Leary was gone.

The second chamber began to hum. And now light—flashing, pulsing, signaling an arrival. Everyone waited.

12

Crystal gasped as the necrotic, sickening odor from Leary's execution assaulted her nostrils and provoked a reflexive gagging. Tim had to cover his own nose and mouth at the smell. The team officers, fiercely disciplined, stifled their reactions, but he caught their sharp intakes of breath as they stood in awe of the flashing chamber.

Tim noticed another smell, one that was different from what he remembered of Mary Ash's resurrection.

Wildman, still very much alive, stood next to them, and Crystal panted for breath and asked, "Are you all right, sir?"

"Yes. Yes, I think so... What happened to him?"

She couldn't answer, looking again to Tim, but he didn't know. She nodded to the SAS man, who merely hustled the doctor away, following procedure. It didn't matter if Wildman said he was all right. He needed to be rushed to their medic and checked out. Tim and Crystal barely noticed them leaving, their eyes still fixed on the second chamber, waiting for the motes and whorls to coalesce.

The Booth had taken Leary, but if it took Leary, then who was coming...?

The odor. It was faintly reminiscent of childbirth. Tim had witnessed deliveries in Third World villages. He could instantly recall that smell, even though he had never had any children of his own. Then it took on a sickening sweetness, like the flesh of burn victims. The shadow emerging now behind the tinted glass of the second chamber was adult in height...

No one stepped forward to open the door panel of the second Booth. The arrival itself pushed the door, banging it open with the limp claw twitches of dinosaur limbs, of a visceral fetal anger.

Then it shuffled wetly out of the chamber, and there was a *pat, pat, pat...* It left a *puddle* of fluid, a disgusting brown pool, as if meconium flowed in a river from a pediatrics ward. One of the officers let go of his rifle and vomited. Crystal, next to Tim, let out a short, sharp cry of horror at the thing that now walked into their world.

Tim stared, and a distant part of him recognized he was numb, stupidly staring, but he could do nothing else. *Oh, my God* was the thought that kept playing over and over in his mind.

It was Leary. Desmond Leary reborn in the second chamber as a grotesque parody of a resurrected victim. But no, it was more horrible than that. In his fanatical career, Leary must have passed around his share of inflammatory pamphlets, with the kind of disgusting propaganda images that could be seen on placards protesting outside abortion clinics. And the Booth had reshaped him in the image of his hate.

He was still Leary, but now he was more *it* than man. And several *its* at once.

Here was Leary, with more than one pair of eyes, but so many pairs that were clouded with milky white cataracts, and what wheezed and drooled very much like a mouth on the misshapen head sucked in the air and made an angry hiss. There were atrophied limbs. There were curves and rounded growths of elephantiasis and greenish, scaly flesh of leprosy. There were twisted parodies of bone that were beyond spina bifida. And inside an orifice was what appeared to be a second, more regular face, revolting because it could still *be recognized as Desmond Leary's face.*

Its beaded eyes and thin lips were twisted in an expression of pure malevolence. Eyes like abandoned shining pearls on a hellish landscape, with multiple mouths that belonged more on insects or reptiles. It was not a single creature; more of a community that was never intended to grow, forced together and now feeling the rage of a mob, a mob of things that weren't supposed to be here, in existence. Desmond Leary had hated so much and for so long, even while he screamed high and shrill over "life."

So the Booth gave him life. All his twisted, warped conceptions of it.

Tim staggered, his head suddenly on fire. It was a rush of migraine-like agony that stripped him of his rational senses, and he looked towards Crystal with a primitive need for her to help. But she was already holding her head in equal pain. They all were. Miller dropped to the floor on his hands and knees, yelling out.

It was not the same as what Emily Derosier had done to them in Paris. This was not a probing but a silent *scream* inside their skulls. The Leary creature was demanding, pleading to die.

One of the officers found the strength to save them, firing his rifle. There was a jackhammer roar as bullets sank into the soft, bloated pink mass with its leering mouths and limping gait. The Leary-thing squealed and whimpered as it died, and worst of all, it laughed. The deformed thing actually *laughed*. As if its existence were a great joke, and it was happy that it won a reprieve.

Crystal burst into tears and cried out, "I've got to get out of here! Get me out of here!"

"Okay, okay," said Tim, shaken as well. "We'll get out of here—"

"I need to get out of here now! Right now! *Jesus, please!*"

They ran back to the car, Crystal wracked with sobs in the passenger seat. Tim didn't say a thing. He left her alone, deciding it was best to give her a few minutes. His own hands were shaking, and he had to stand a moment in the quiet Irish countryside in the crisp night air to center himself. Then he went to find the SAS team's vehicle, where its medical officer was peeling the Velcro of a blood pressure cuff off Dieter Wildman's right arm.

"How are you?" he asked.

"I'm fine," answered Wildman, looking tired. And haunted. "I'm fine, really."

"They'll get you home," said Tim. "I'm very sorry this happened to you. Your government will likely suggest you don't talk about this, in case it gives other psychopaths any ideas."

"I would expect them to say that, yes. But... Mr. Cale, is it? I'm sure you know that madness never lacks for creativity."

"True. But I prefer we don't give madness any more inspiration."

He nodded a goodbye, and it occurred to him he should check on Miller. The young scientist was perched on the hood of one of the army vehicles, his laptop open, but he wasn't typing. His hands were steepled over his mouth, his eyes blinking, struggling to focus, blinking again.

"Hey," called Tim. "You all right?"

"Um, sure, yeah—of course." His body shuddered with a nervous release of energy. "No. No, I'm not. Are you?"

"No."

"That was… It was… I've got to write Weintraub. I've got to report what happened."

"Yeah."

"I don't know how to do that."

Tim couldn't think of what to say.

"I'm going to go with the doctor. Hitch a ride back in the medical truck. I'll see you guys in the morning, okay?"

"Okay, Miller."

Tim walked back to the car and didn't say a thing as he slipped inside and buckled his seatbelt.

"If people knew what the Booth did to Leary…" She paused, seeming to gather her thoughts. "God damn that bastard for making me pity him."

"Yes," muttered Tim quietly.

"Even Wildman pitied him."

"Yes. Yes, he did."

"These machines," she said. "These bloody machines can't be good for humanity."

Tim nodded, and he let his voice drop like a hammer. "Then *destroy* the one we found. The SAS have it. It's in your jurisdiction—let's walk back there now, and you tell them to smash the thing, bust it up so that it will never work again. There's one in London, sure, but there can be one less of those things in the world."

"I… I don't know, Tim. I don't think I have the authority."

"Crystal, the only authority needed to stop a bomb from going off is a human being with a sense of decency. Tell them Leary planted a hidden explosive, and we just learned of it now. Make something up. Any excuse. I'll back your play."

He waited. She stared straight ahead, and then she clapped a hand on the steering wheel decisively and opened her door. They trudged back together towards the warehouse, their steps slowing as they got closer. Neither of them wanted to go back in there, but it was necessary. They would need to see this task done, witness it being obeyed. Crystal flagged down the team leader of the strike force, holding her phone out as if she'd just got a call. Tim wandered a few feet away, only half paying attention to their conversation. She was reminding the SAS man that, according to Whitehall, she was still in charge.

"Listen to me, Captain," she was saying. "I need you to put a flamethrower to that device. A controlled demolition, however you want to do it, but do it fast."

Cold out here, thought Tim. The wind slashed at his cheeks.

"We have new intel, that's why…"

The captain finally accepted the order, and they all went into the warehouse.

The unworldly stench was still there, still in this lonely place.

The corpse of the *thing* that used to be Leary was still there, still lying on the floor.

Tim noticed Crystal hovering close to him, but it wasn't for protection or comfort. Her eyes were dry, and she was once more calm, contained, a professional. She stayed close, but it was almost as if she stood ready to protect *him* in case some new danger—a missed member of the terrorist cell, something else horrible from the equipment—leapt out to confront them. She's so strong, he thought. This is a strong woman. She's seen astonishing, terrible things even before tonight's nightmare, and here she is, not bolting, not shirking—staying on the job. It had taken him years to get past what he saw in India, and she had seen more in the space of days, and she was planting her feet by his side. Amazing.

The soldiers prepared to destroy the booths.

As they got on with the job, everyone was on edge again. No one touched the control panel, and yet everyone half-expected that the booths might glow and pulsate...

They didn't. Dark, lifeless metal and glass.

The SAS men took their time setting up, moving about and measuring at an excruciatingly slow pace, carrying out chores beyond Tim's understanding, and then one of them loaded base charges around the chambers. Suddenly, the captain was shouting for them all to clear out, get some distance. Tim and Crystal were rudely shoved towards the door, told to run down the hill, and by the time one of the soldiers informed them that was far enough, they turned, and there was an orange-red blast, a roar that must have woken up farms miles away.

Smoke cleared, and they went in to inspect the rubble. The metal panels of the booths were blackened and twisted, looking a lot like plane wreckage, but there was a surprising lack of electronic debris.

"I thought there'd be more," said Crystal.

Tim had thought so as well. The lack of pieces, of parts, bothered him.

They drove back to Belfast, and when she pulled up in front of their hotel, he asked her if she felt uncomfortable with her decision. She asked him back if he felt guilty for pushing her into it. Not at all.

"Me neither," she replied.

*

A day later, they learned that the SAS men had taken away the misshapen, cackling Leary-thing that shambled out of the Booth, now mercifully dead, in a large biohazard bag intended for agricultural disposal. Crystal said it was horrible to think it would be preserved somewhere. Like a deformed pig in a jar of formaldehyde. Tim told her it could never be anyone's idea of an exhibit. It would be, even in death, a grotesque warning. Only they didn't know yet of what.

They went back to Paris, the three of them. Tim, Crystal and Miller. Miller's way of coping was to announce loudly that he was going to work his way through the minibar in his new suite, two floors down from the ones for Timothy Cale and DI Anyanike. When Tim went to check on him, he found the neurologist was in his room, but he wasn't drinking. Miller sat on the edge of a chair, deeply focused on the wooden pieces for his model of the battleship, *Missouri*, resting on a glass coffee table. Tim watched him for a long moment.

"Must have been great," Miller told the glue stick in his hand.

"What? Being in the navy back then?"

"No…"

Tim waited for more. Miller applied a wooden panel to a tiny gun on the stern.

"Knowing so little, having everything to look forward to," said Miller, studying his battleship. "Better microscopes, the invention of lasers, polio vaccines… Did you know they didn't even discover Pluto until 1930? Gary told me. There was still bad shit, like famines and racism, sure, but this is as bad as it could get. Planes and ships. You could destroy a country, but you couldn't break the world."

"No. Not yet."

"You—you just *couldn't.* It means in theory, you could run away, you could find some place to hole up, change your name if you like, start over. Wait for the world to get its shit together."

"You find the right place, and yeah, you'd be okay," said Tim, playing along. "Switzerland, Portugal if you kept your head down. You could, sure."

"And now you can't."

"No." Tim didn't take him for being nostalgic.

Miller's hand brushed along the selection of wooden struts. His chest lifted, and he let out a long sigh. "And now you get to put me in my place. The biggest 'I told you so' ever. Because there's nowhere to run, and it's our fault, right? Science. We never learn our lesson. Dynamite, atom bombs— we keep taking it to the brink."

"Andrew, that's not what I've—"

"Only you're wrong," said Miller, his voice calm, almost dead of feeling. "That psycho didn't know science, he didn't know physics or engineering, he didn't know *anything.* He was just a nutcase who found a big gun and blew himself in the head. And him running off with a Booth doesn't make you right."

He was gripping another wooden panel so tightly, his forearm shook.

Tim was getting concerned. Miller, finally conscious of what he was doing, put the tiny piece down on the table. He flexed his hand, checked it with an index finger to make sure he hadn't cut into his own palm.

"Sorry," said Miller.

Tim waved that away. Nothing to be sorry for at all. They were all trying to cope. He said goodnight and left the young doctor to his model.

Back in his own room, he must have stood a full forty-five minutes under his shower, good and hot, as if the pelting beads of water could wash away the images from that warehouse. He had just slipped into one of the hotel's plush cotton robes and had switched on the large flat television screen when there was a knock at the door. It was Crystal. Her hair was up, and she wore a London Met sweatshirt and black leggings, padding around the hallway barefoot. Well, they did keep the carpets scrupulously clean here.

"Oh, I thought you'd still be up," she said apologetically.

"I am. It's okay."

"I—I didn't mean to disturb—"

"No, it's fine," he said, motioning her in. "I was only going to switch on a movie. You can get a few English channels on their satellite package here."

"Oh, wish I'd known that," she chuckled. "I can barely figure out the remote."

"I can show you how to work it," he said, scooping it up from the coffee table. "Sorry, what's up?"

"Nothing," she said with a shrug. "I... I just didn't feel like being alone. What were you going to watch?"

He was suddenly conscious that he was in a bathrobe. He ran his fingers through his still-wet hair, switched the TV to a movie channel and said quickly, "You choose, I'll be right back."

Then he ducked into the bedroom and flipped through his bag. He kept a couple of T-shirts and a pair of sweatpants for just being comfortable if he wanted to read or work at his laptop, but now he realized the state they were in. He didn't want to wear these ratty clothes in front of her. So he put on a dress shirt with rolled-up French cuffs and a set of Armani trousers without a belt. As he walked back in to join her, her face broke into a wide grin of happy bewilderment.

"You're joking," she said.

"What?"

"You can't possibly wear that for when you want to relax."

Busted, he thought. Now he was actually embarrassed. "I don't... But my usual dress-down clothes are kind of sad and torn and..."

"Go change," she ordered.

"Yes, Ma'am!"

He went and put on the sweats, and when he returned, she nodded her head and snapped, "Better." And so they sat watching a six-month-old Hollywood thriller. They didn't talk, not even to comment on the film. It was comfortable enough—no awkward tension, both of them needing each other's presence but still feeling subdued after Derry.

He was half-asleep on the couch when he felt more than saw her leaning over him, squeezing his shoulder in an improvised goodnight. Then there was the click of the door as she left.

He looked for her at breakfast down in the hotel's restaurant, but she wasn't there as usual. He eventually found her in a patisserie around the corner from the hotel. They exchanged good mornings, and he watched Crystal thank the lady behind the counter, pocketing her change and offering him a newly bought croissant. They stepped out of the shop and by silent agreement began to stroll the boulevard.

He saw her expression darken and ventured a guess. "Please tell me you're not still thinking about Northern Ireland."

"No," she said. "I don't want to think about what happened in Derry."

"Then what's on your mind?"

"Mary Ash."

Tim nodded, waiting.

"I have a theory. I don't know which is more terrible: if I'm right or if I'm wrong."

"And?"

"And I've been racking my brains on how to test it."

"Tell me, and then we can come up with something together. Or I can get Weintraub to look into it."

"You remember your basic physics?" she asked. "Yes, I know, it seems as if it's all gone pear-shaped, but what if they *still apply*? The rules, I mean. What if we're afraid to look at how they're actually working here? The law of conservation of matter says it can't be created or destroyed, only rearranged."

"Okay, but I don't know where you're leading me."

Crystal bit her bottom lip, furrowing her brows as she started again. "Don't you see? Forget for a moment whether there's an actual *soul* for each individual, where did the *mass* come from for a physical body? I read the reports. That police officer, Daniel Chen, was *cremated*. Mary Ash was in a funeral plot and must have decomposed down to bits of flesh on bone by the time they fried Nickelbaum. I can't pretend I know exactly what's going on, but the Booth works because a murderer goes through, yes? We can't just summon a victim out of thin air by putting his killer in proximity to the device!"

"No. We can't."

"What if... what if something from the murderer comes back as part of the resurrected victim?"

At first, Tim took the chill down the back of his neck as a signal there could be truth in Crystal's notion. And she was right; it was horrible to contemplate. There was something disturbing, he'd always thought, in the enigmatic behavior of

Mary Ash, of the boy that was once supposed to be Daniel Chen, the others, and the things they could do now. God, how revolting it would be if Mary Ash carried a piece of Emmett Nickelbaum's charred soul in her.

Except it could not be true.

"Why not?"

"Our flapper wandering the City of Light," Tim reminded her. "Emily Derosier. There was no execution in the Paris Karma Booth before she walked back into our world."

Crystal countered that if the rules of physics had to be thrown out, they could hardly maintain firm belief in DNA. Maybe she wasn't the Derosier woman. Maybe there was another factor that resulted in a delayed resurrection. Maybe the reason had to do with a million other speculative things; but her pained expression suggested that she knew it was a weak argument.

No, thought Tim, it *was* Emily Derosier who had staggered out of the prison in Montparnasse. It had to be. And whoever had killed her must have died almost a century ago.

Crystal's "murderer ingredient" theory, he suspected, was his new partner's way of preserving her Christian faith. After all, if it were the Booth's fault—bringing back human beings but getting them wrong from borrowed pieces of killers—then the alternative would have to be rejected. The shattering idea that there are other levels of existence, and that we're possibly recycled back into this plane. He had his own problems with accepting that.

But it was one thing to intellectually entertain the concept, quite another to have a scrap of possible proof. Life after life... You assume there would be rules, conventions. And so far, they could find none of any comforting certainty. Damn it, he thought, what if the other worlds were just as defiant of explanation, wonderful and tantalizing yet with new inexplicable horrors and pains and beauties and pleasures all their own? But no simpler, no clearer. Because who the hell could promise that the next world equaled the truth?

And if the Booth was tearing down the Gates of Saint Peter then who could keep their head in the clouds?

If it were true.

They went on with their separate chores of research during the day, but that evening, Tim left a note for her with the hotel concierge. Crystal was to step into a booked shuttle sedan that would take her to a spot near Jussieu Métro station in the 5th arrondissement, where he stood waiting for her, umbrella in one hand, a gym bag in the other. She looked at him completely puzzled, which was what he wanted, and he smiled and handed her the bag.

"Here you go, evening clothes," he said.

"What, for dinner?"

"Uh, no, not dinner."

She unzipped it and checked inside. Now she was really confused. "This is my *gi*."

"Yes, it is."

He had made arrangements to have her white practice *gi* top and trousers and the black *hakama* she wore as a senior black belt in aikido flown by courier over from London.

Now he casually turned and led her up a flight of stairs to a surprisingly airy studio. By day, the beautiful, polished hardwood floors and the mirrors on the wall were for dancing, but at night, mats were laid down, and the place became a dojo. He watched as she peered inside and saw about twenty students in the white *gis* of juniors, some in *hakamas*, already warming up and practicing. There was a short, spry, barrel-chested Japanese man in his seventies with silver hair, wearing a *hakama*, watching them all with his arms folded. He could have been a general surveying an army, but when he noticed Tim and Crystal at the door, his face became cheerful, almost elfin in its delight at finding them here.

"Oh, my God, that's Gozo Tanaka!" said Crystal. "That's *Gozo Tanaka*."

"Uh, yes, I believe it is."

"He's, like, a legend in aikido!" Crystal babbled on excitedly. "He's tenth dan, studied with Shioda, opened the first Yoshinkan aikido school in Europe. He was *there* when the founder Morihei Ueshiba visited Hawaii, and—oh, my God, how did you manage this? Oh, no, he's coming over here."

"A friend in the Quai d'Orsay owes me a favor, so I set this up," explained Tim.

Tanaka stood in front of them now, and Crystal bowed low, Japanese-style, saying, "*Osu!* Sensei Tanaka, it's an honor to meet you."

"The honor is mine, Miss Anyanike." Despite the years, Tanaka's English had kept a heavy accent. "Your students are waiting."

"*My* students?" echoed Crystal. "I thought…"

Tim smiled. "You're going to teach them. You're a fourth dan, right? Sensei Tanaka would like you to lead the class, and then he'll give you an hour of private instruction." He added mischievously, "I mean, if you have the time."

"Good!" boomed Tanaka, smiling brightly, and he began to walk back to the edge of the mats.

Crystal was over the moon. "Yes! Yes, I have the time." She turned to Tim. "This is amazing. This is one of the best gifts I ever… Why?"

Tim shrugged, feeling suddenly self-conscious. "We've both been through a horrible ordeal, and... I thought of finding a special church for you, but that seemed too presumptuous. Have you seen Miller's crazy ship model that he brought over? It gave me ideas. We all need a distraction. If you painted, I would have got you the best paints. If you played guitar, I would have found you a hot rock band to jam with. You do this, so... I made a couple of calls."

She beamed at him, took a step forward to reach out, then thought better of it. There was a pause of a second, and then she turned back to Tanaka across the dojo and called, "Sensei, do you have a spare training *gi* for our *kohai* here?"

"Me? Whoa, wait! I don't know this stuff, Crystal, this is your thing—"

"You're here. My class, my rules. C'mon, we'll go get changed. Ten bets to one, you've never put on a *keikogi* before."

And then she was tugging him by the sleeve as someone handed him a folded set of top and trousers, plus a white belt. Tim remembered a pal from the State Department once dragged him to a karate dojo fifteen years ago, and he'd been kind of interested but never got beyond two, three lessons because of the demands of his job. He had long since forgotten how to put on the outfit. But no sooner than they were in the locker room than Crystal was stripping off her shirt and unbuttoning her trousers, completely comfortable with the quick change in front of him. All at once, she was in a purple bra and matching panties, and he could take in every flowing, gorgeous curve of her body, her full breasts almost spilling out of the bra cups, the shape of her strong legs...

"Hurry up, they're waiting for us!" she said, fixing up her hair.

He swiftly unbuttoned his shirt and slipped off his pants, and she said behind his back, "The trousers have a drawstring.

Those are simple enough. It's the jacket and belt that give novices trouble."

When he turned around, naked to the waist, she was already dressed, looking incredibly elegant, even regal in her *gi* top, trousers and *hakama*. He put on the jacket, and she moved in close, tying the strings, then wrapping and knotting the white belt around his waist.

"There," she said softly, smiling up at him. "Done. Let's go see how you do."

He laughed, because she had deflected all of her nervousness over being here. He would have been content to sit on a bench as a mere spectator, but she was letting him into her world.

For the next hour, she was in her element, guiding the class in fluent French, showing them moves and throws with technical precision completely beyond his understanding. Every so often, Tanaka would interject with a point of his own, but more often than not, the teacher nodded approvingly. Tim was dazzled by her ability. It was one thing to catch a glimpse of it back at the Centre Pompidou, quite another to see the range and breadth of her skill. She would spin in a graceful arc, her subtle hand movements too fast for Tim to follow, and an opponent would go flying through the air, thumping to the mat and rolling away. She was incredible to him.

Rolling was something he wouldn't master in this one hour, landing in a heap—dizzy, sweating, bewildered. Every so often, however, his eyes would catch hers, and she flashed him a bright smile of gratitude and pure joy.

They said that Viktor Limonov liked Shakespeare. Though born Russian, he was fluent in English, French, Arabic and could boast a working knowledge of some African dialects. He appreciated literature and didn't just pose as an intellectual. His circle of associates claimed he could rattle off the entire scene from *Henry V* when the king demands a governor open a town's gates, promising lurid horrors if the soldiers are forced to sack it.

"The blind and bloody soldier with foul hand, desire the locks of your shrill-shrieking daughters," Limonov recited, giggling. His accent elongated the *o* vowel into *lawks*. "Your naked infants spitted upon pikes, whiles the mad mothers with their howls confused do break the clouds..."

For most, these were lines from a play. But Limonov's employees had actually witnessed him take a baby three months old in Chechnya away from its sobbing, hysterical mother. They had seen him jam the baby's pink, soft body onto the sharpened point of a five-foot high wooden spike. And leave it there.

Viktor Limonov didn't simply trade in weapons. He also enjoyed using them in civil wars, coups and rebellions from Eastern Europe to Africa to Asia. It was Limonov's weapons that had armed the Janjaweed militias that had made Darfur a hell on earth, and it was his rifles that had slaughtered entire villages in the Congo region so that companies could retrieve minerals for computer microchips. The military regime in Burma once paid him two million dollars in opium to help teach a lesson to the ethnic Shan people, who infuriatingly insisted on staying alive.

Limonov, according to Human Rights Watch investigators, had ordered refugee girls to form a line in front of his tent. Some of the girls were as young as twelve. "Tell each mother," he instructed his interpreter, "her daughter can lose her cherry or lose an arm."

When a woman ran forward, sobbing pitifully and throwing herself at his feet, Limonov's long face cracked into an amused grin, and he said through the interpreter: "I thought all you people were supposed to be Buddhist! Don't you know the Buddha says life is suffering?"

The rapes by Limonov's men and the Burmese military units had gone on into the morning.

He stood six feet, three inches tall, and had the carved, muscular physique of an Olympic athlete. There was a tautness to him as well that suggested he trained for survival, not for the sake of any masculine vanity. The face was long, with cruelty in the thin mouth. He had the nervous habit of scratching his chin with the backs of his knuckles, as if testing to see if his razor had done a good enough job in the morning.

For close to two decades, he was practically untouchable as the UN failed to disentangle its red tape. It didn't help that during the first Gulf War, Limonov was considered a valuable "asset" by the US military. But he didn't play favorites, and Washington decided he had to be stopped when he counted among his customers the Taliban and Al Qaeda. They lured him to an arms contract negotiation in Bangkok, and he was escorted in leg-irons and cuffs and whisked off to an international criminal court in The Hague.

Jetting around the globe to sell weapons, he had worn a series of racquetball polo shirts, faded jeans and high-top desert boots. Reduced to a gray prison jumpsuit, Limonov had served three years of a sentence at a maximum security prison wing on a military base outside Amsterdam. That was until it was decided by the powers that be that he should be sent through the Karma Booth.

Before the procedure, he was kept in isolation from other prisoners but was allowed the privilege of books and newspapers. A guard asked him smugly if he knew what the Karma Booth was and what it was for.

Limonov grinned to show he could take a joke. "As I understand it, you want to open a toilet that washes down to Hell and flush me."

The four guards escorting him burst out laughing. That's right, they agreed, that's *right*.

"A man should know what he really is before he meets his end," laughed a guard, trying to be profound.

Limonov grinned at that remark, too.

As the guards led him to the first booth, he looked past them to the technicians minding the controls. A woman at one panel averted her eyes. The man next to her kept his face poker-calm. He considered his work a distasteful but necessary duty.

"Do you actually think," Limonov said to him, since he seemed to be the only one paying any attention, "that all those people I supposedly killed will just dance naked in a... a what? A conga line out of that tube over there?"

"If one innocent person steps out, it's worth you going in!" answered the technician.

The argument ended because the first chamber's door was sealed with Limonov inside. He was manacled now to the metal rail. Lights and color danced behind the glass, and then the most infamous modern arms dealer and mercenary of recent times was gone. The guards and technicians waited. But it seemed Viktor Limonov had been right about one thing. None of his victims stepped out of the second chamber.

Limonov's execution had been anti-climactic, and everyone present wrote it off to another puzzling case where the scientists were left with more data, even if it was data about something that didn't happen...

*

In Paris, Tim's cell phone went off at five thirty in the morning. The display told him it was Weintraub.

"Viktor Limonov is still alive."

Tim rubbed his eyes. The words Gary was saying didn't make sense to him, not yet. Limonov...?

"Alive. Wow. After they sent him through the Booth? Did they give him a medical exam afterwards?"

"They couldn't," answered Weintraub, "because Viktor Limonov stepped out of the second chamber of a Karma Booth in New Delhi."

13

The authorities in India had followed closely how the news of the Karma Booth had evolved in other countries, and they didn't want the headache of riots and controversial demonstrations. It was decided that instead of a prison facility or a military base, India's Booth would be housed in a restricted wing of a hospital on the outskirts of the capital. This was why, officials explained later to their American and the British counterparts, that Viktor Limonov was able to escape as easily as he did.

He emerged from the second chamber of India's Karma Booth still in his prison jumpsuit, not naked like other arrivals. The single guard in khaki uniform turned on his heel as the light flashed in the chamber, his eyes popping and his lips swearing an epithet in Hindi. Limonov rushed out, swinging his elbow into the man's jaw. As the guard dropped to the tiled floor, Limonov's running shoe stamped into his throat, and there was a sickening crack of bone and crushed larynx. Then he snatched up the guard's automatic rifle and fired two quick bursts at a pair of hospital staff rushing in from the monitoring room...

As he pushed the doors of a fire exit, starting an alarm, he walked—purposefully, calmly, not in a rush at all—out to the parking lot with the rifle looped over his shoulder. By the time the gun registered with the young couple dropping off the man's mother for gall bladder surgery, Limonov had shot the husband point blank in the head.

The wife ran screaming as Limonov muttered to the corpse at his feet, "You nearly bled all over my new shirt..."

He quickly yanked off the man's trousers and shirt. Then he left his latest murder victim in his jockey briefs on the cement, driving away in the man's Tata car. Police found the vehicle abandoned on the shoulder of the main highway to Mumbai.

"You can't blame the Indians, really," said Weintraub as he briefed Tim over Limonov's return. "After we let other countries know about Emily Derosier, attention has been focused on having medical standby. There's round-the-clock surveillance, and guards are put *outside* the test room. It's because we presume victims will show up, not..." He didn't have to finish his sentence.

"You're right, it's not their fault," said Tim. "No murderer has ever stepped back out of the Booth."

"Until this one," said Weintraub.

Tim asked his friend to keep him posted and hung up. He thought of calling Crystal's room, but the news could wait—no point in ruining her sleep, too.

Ugh. Of all the psychopaths and murderers who could conceivably have knowledge of the machine's secrets, it had to be one of the world's worst genocidal maniacs. If the Karma Booth couldn't exterminate Viktor Limonov, Tim had to wonder if anything on earth could.

He knew he shouldn't get ahead of himself. They still had to find the bastard. Others could solve the problem of how to contain or execute Limonov (again) after they had tracked him down. But now there was Limonov to find—plus they had to find Emily Derosier *and* Orlando Braithewaite.

He stayed up for an hour, but with no epiphanies, he crawled back to his bed. He was woken again at eight by a call from the front desk. The hotel's concierge asked, "Monsieur Cale, we need to know if you wish the package to be kept in the hotel safe or if you want it brought up? If you prefer, we can arrange shipment back to New York City for you. You have trusted us in the past."

"Yes, I have," mumbled Tim, still half-asleep. Package? He wasn't expecting a package. On other visits to Paris, he had taken advantage of the chance to shop for antiques, a few first editions and the occasional line drawing by one of the second-string Impressionists. As much as he was told art should be treated like an investment, Tim preferred to buy what he liked. If his personal finds ever depreciated monetarily, well, at least he had the comfort of enjoying what he hung on his walls.

But he hadn't made any shopping trips this time.

"If you can give me half an hour, I'll come down to take a look and decide," he told the concierge.

"Very good, Monsieur."

He took his usual breakfast in his room, glad that his European assignments had "civilized" him to appreciate things like a good meal. He munched on a croissant and ate his eggs, perfectly fluffy the way he liked them, while flipping through a set of the morning papers. He was unashamedly old school. To him, hard copies were easier than checking the online news links.

The *International Herald Tribune* was leading with a story about corruption in the World Bank, plus the death

211

of an influential French director who hadn't made movies in twenty years but who still attended festival galas. Its third major item on the front page, matched by *Le Figaro* and the *Telegraph* from the UK, was a peculiar story about the murder of fourteen-year-old boy in Rhodes City, Greece—a Karma Booth resurrected victim. It immediately got Tim's attention.

The teenager had died the first time when an older boy stabbed him to death, all, predictably, because of an argument over a girl they both liked. There had been protests in Athens over the use of the Booth, not because of the technology, but because of an execution of one so young. But the Greek government, which had swung to the right in the past couple of years, wanted to remind its citizens of the deterrent effect of capital punishment. And so their fourteen-year-old victim came back. He didn't, incidentally, get the girl who inspired the whole ordeal—she apparently found him "disturbing" after his return.

She claimed that he frightened her now. That when they walked along down by the harbor, she would talk of her mother or a mutual friend or a teacher at school, and he would... change. His features would blur and suddenly *be* that of the friend or teacher, except that she was the only one who could see it. She thought for a while she was going mad.

The boy didn't seem to be doing it on a conscious level. Instead, it was some kind of sympathetic impulse of temporary transformation.

The boy was later found beaten to death and sodomized in a dark, cobbled cul-de-sac of the Old Town. The police had a theory that friends of the executed teenager had exacted revenge, thinking they'd never be caught or that the Booth couldn't be used to bring him back a second time.

"So they're not immortal," Tim muttered to himself.

The articles said nothing about whether the boy had been jumped from behind or not, but even if he was, he might have still used that frightening face-changing ability on his attackers. Who wouldn't back away from that? Run away from this bizarre being?

And yet if he had used it, it didn't seem to buy him any time or allow him to escape. Maybe the boy had expressed that peculiar detachment Time had noticed in Mary Ash.

He tore a couple of the articles out of the newspapers and looked up a website for the Hellenic Police, the *Elliniki Astynomia*, to make life easier for Crystal. She was the one who should liaise with them to find out forensic details. By now he could anticipate what she would say: That if you took out the boy's resurrection, the case wasn't exceptional and didn't merit their interest. He could only counter that the Booth's role in another anonymous life made all the difference in the world.

The *Guardian* newspaper had learned about the suicide of Desmond Leary and was demanding to know in an editorial what had happened to the Booth stolen from Egypt—and the fate of poor Dieter Wildman. *Shit*, thought Tim. Well, he'd know there'd be heat when he'd pushed Crystal to have the damn thing destroyed. The President and a couple of cabinet secretaries would pretend to be pissed off over him causing friction with London, but in the end they would be privately glad there was one less of those things in the world beyond the reach of the United States.

In the background, the news of Limonov's startling escape was being played for all its worth on CNN, where the head-line at the bottom read: "MALFUNCTION OR MESS-UP?" Fortunately, it looked like the news services had only half the story and were running on the assumption that Viktor

Limonov had—for reasons nobody could quite pin down—been transferred from Amsterdam to Mumbai.

Tim reached across his plate and tapped quickly on his tablet. Fox News was suggesting Holland had deliberately let Limonov out of its jurisdiction—part of a sinister agenda to undermine US foreign policy. After all, weren't these Dutch all pot-smoking, prostitute-frequenting leftists who believed in assisted suicide and abortion?

Maybe, thought Tim, this is better than people knowing the truth, though it was only a matter of time before Limonov's... what? Teleportation? Leaked to the world.

He dressed and went downstairs. The concierge greeted him like a long-lost brother. Of course, at four-star hotels in Paris, AmEx Black Card holders are always long-lost brothers.

"Ah, Monsieur Cale! Did you sleep well?"

"I always sleep well here, Marcel," he lied.

"Right this way, Monsieur."

He led Tim into a convenient back storage room, where one of the desk clerks pried open the five-foot-high crate, then clipped the twine and ripped away the brown foolscap wrapping.

It was a painting; a stunningly beautiful painting of a blonde, nude woman, her breasts and legs blurring into the tableau of a café scene with street musicians. The light in the composition was an afternoon ocher, a four-in-the-afternoon time when the evening promises infinite diversions, a time Tim loved. The picture was Miro-esque and Picasso-like, but at the same time it wasn't, because he recognized the style in the shimmering colors.

Emily Derosier.

"There's a card, Monsieur," said the concierge, plucking it from the wire on the back of the frame. He handed it to Tim, who tore open the small envelope.

Both the paper and the envelope were special stationery, quality stock, like the kind once used by people who had the money to impress. In a tidy, swirling handwriting, the note urged: *Thursday, Au Dauphin, 1 pm please.*

Au Dauphin. He knew the place.

Tim shoved the note in his pocket and turned to the concierge. "Can you please have it brought up to my room for now?"

"That's not a problem at all, Monsieur. It's an exquisite piece you will enjoy very much, and if you ever decide to part with it, I think the manager would be most interested in making you a handsome offer."

"You flatter my taste, Marcel." He clapped the man on the arm and headed towards the foyer. He wanted to take a walk and think.

Crystal could talk to the French police about the painting. He wanted somebody—somebody good at forensics—to examine it carefully. Whoever had sent that thuggish couple to hunt Emily Derosier at the Beaubourg might know by now that Tim and Crystal were also searching for her. They might also feel like playing games. So he wanted to know all about that painting before Thursday. If Emily Derosier had painted it, he wanted to know if it was one of her compositions from almost a century ago or if she had painted it last week.

He wanted to know *everything* before he dared to sit down at a table in Au Dauphin.

On an impulse, he turned and walked briskly back to the hotel, impatiently closing the doors to his elevator before the newest Hollywood ingénue and her Pomeranian could glide in. When he used his pass card to enter his room, he saw that the hotel staff had thoughtfully brought up an easel to display the painting. It was still an astonishingly beautiful piece of work. But it was different.

He stepped closer to it. The colors still appeared to shimmer, the texture lifelike. But the actual composition was *different*. The nude woman's expression was now a little sad. A face had also changed on the Cubist-block of a street musician. The hour of the day in the painting looked closer to noon. Was he kidding himself? He hadn't looked at it that carefully down in the storage room. Maybe he was reacting unconsciously to a *pentimento*, traces of a previous painting or drawing under the finished work. Frankly, he didn't delude himself that he had that good an eye.

He carefully picked up the painting and brought it closer to the window. The painting switched again, and this time he was sure of it. There were subtle changes in the hues of light and the expressions of the Futurist figures.

Damn right he would have a forensic expert examine this.

Twenty-five-year-old Gudrun Merkel laughed at the two young men clumsily dueling in chain mail. This was great fun, she thought as she stood in the Royal Library courtyard. They were all students at Humboldt University in Berlin.

The duel was supposed to be for an experiment for one guy's thesis. He didn't even go to Humboldt, but everyone thought the courtyard was a perfect site for it, and, of course, the fooling around with mock swords made for great horse-play. The library was used for Humboldt's Faculty of Law, and Gudrun took studies here, so she was happy to take in the show early before morning classes and to casually accept the joint passed along by one of her friends. The pot would take the edge off.

She and the others made *Monty Python and the Holy Grail* references, jokes about *Highlander* and of course, *Lord of the Rings*. All of them were getting nicely toasted and barely taking any notes for even the appearance of doing homework. Gudrun laughed and told the friend next to her that the clanging of undergraduates worked better with the retro-ska music on her iPod. It would be hard for anyone to believe that the brunette girl in a heavy woolen sweater and jeans, who didn't take life seriously but expected she'd drift into academia or museum work, had emerged from a Karma Booth six weeks ago.

No one treated her any differently in this moment because no one with her now actually knew.

In fact, Gudrun Merkel's parents and doctors had taken elaborate steps to make sure Gudrun herself didn't know. She had been beaten to death by an abusive boyfriend, and in the moment she returned to existence in the second chamber, the doctors had fired a tranquilizer dart into her bare midriff. The poor naked girl had collapsed to the floor before she could feel the shock of resurrection—the doctors *hoped*. When Gudrun Merkel woke up in a hospital bed, she was informed she had been in a coma for four months.

She asked for water. She complained of a slight headache and dryness of mouth. After ten minutes, because everyone kept assuring her that she was physically okay, and that her muscles hadn't atrophied significantly from her "coma" and that the swelling from her head injuries had been successfully treated, she asked about Rudy, her boyfriend.

Rudy committed suicide, they told her. It had been decided this was the most plausible scenario yet one that would allow therapists to help Gudrun Merkel move on and hopefully break the cycle of involvement with abusive partners.

They certainly couldn't tell her they had traded his young life for hers. Or that Rudy, whom she swore she loved so much, had insisted before his execution that he hadn't done anything wrong, and that "if she just did what I told her to do I wouldn't have to hit the bitch at all!" He had escaped going to prison for assaulting another girlfriend two years ago because his father was a member of the European Parliament and had called in a few favors. But there was no way his father could clean up the fallout over what was done to Gudrun Merkel.

"Poor Rudy," she had whispered in her hospital bed. With a wet sniff, she had rubbed her moist eyes.

The truth was that the German government had been waiting for a case like the murder of Gudrun Merkel. Her boyfriend's fate was sealed as soon as her time of death was declared. Declared, but never announced—not to anyone beyond her parents, who had to sign official documents ensuring their silence. The Merkels were happy to do so, given the lurid stories about Karma Booth victims in America and other parts of the world. So all those involved in the ruse— the physicians, the authorities, her parents—felt Germany was taking a mature, enlightened step that other nations with this technology should have tried before: minimize the trauma and sensationalism.

They would try bringing a victim back but simply not tell the individual. They would see if the intelligence from the Americans and British was true about Booth victims returning with unusual heightened perception. The Germans were skeptical. Somebody in Washington or London had wanted to start an urban myth, that's what all the nonsense was about. Take away the astonishing flashes of light in the procedure, the noise and drama, and we'll see if these victims are still special when they wake up in a gown in an ICU bed, won't we?

But Gudrun Merkel wasn't a foolish girl, despite how her boyfriend had gradually whittled away and eroded her self-esteem, isolating her from her friends and family before he stole her life. She paid attention. She saw things. Her last few nervous months in her previous life had developed her radar for the nuances of evasive rationales and secretive behavior, even if it couldn't save her from her boyfriend's lethal blows.

At the hospital, her parents and the doctors and everyone else seemed to treat her coming out of the coma as if such a thing were banal. Their responses were muted, guarded, which she thought was extremely strange. There was a man with a briefcase who often came around, and in the patients' recreation room, she asked a young woman on chemotherapy if she knew who this man was.

"Oh, the nurses say he's from the Chancellor's office," her new friend explained.

Was there a political celebrity in their wing? Why else would someone that high up come to visit?

But no one knew at all why the man came around two or three times, always intently listening as he was briefed by doctors—Gudrun's same doctors. No one knew why the man often drifted past the doorway of her room, doing his best not to stare—at her.

She could read the papers. She watched the television news. They thought she couldn't make the connection, that by simply having her admitted and placed in this bed and not mentioning the details, she wouldn't put it together. She wasn't a complete idiot.

She realized she was one of them.

And there was something else, too.

Because of her ordeal with domestic violence, Gudrun Merkel knew not to talk to people about subjects they didn't raise in conversation. She was nothing, nobody. Whatever this was about, there was a purpose that was more important than her, and she should keep her mouth shut for them. It was like her law studies. Her father had told her since her mid-teens she must be in a profession that was *secure*, and though she found the law crushingly dull, she knew Daddy was right. Her father had always been right.

So now in the courtyard of Humboldt's Royal Library, Gudrun Merkel didn't pay much attention as the tall man walked up to her, fishing a badge out of his inside pocket. Viktor Limonov was shaved, his hair trimmed, and instead of his signature polo shirt and jeans he had opted for a dark navy blue suit and tie.

He held up the badge, saying briskly in fluent German, "*Polizei*. Gudrun Merkel?"

She stared into space for a moment, barely looking at him before she responded. "You're not police."

"True. But you're not running away."

"It wouldn't do me much good, would it?"

Limonov's blue eyes closed to slits, his mouth opening a little in a canine impression of a smile. "Not much. Where were you just now? Meditating?"

"There are people dreaming," answered Gudrun. "In Mexico City, a girl lies sleeping in the back of a pickup truck under a blanket. She's four. In her mind, she's thinking of fluffy rice while a puppet character comes to the dinner table and sings for her—he's one of those famous felt puppets from American TV, I can't remember the name. In Munich, there is a twenty-four-year-old systems analyst having a nocturnal emission, only he's confused because he became aroused over the idea of his coworker friend, Ludger, naked. In Australia, an aboriginal woman cleaning houses is dreaming she's on holiday in Sydney. There are no strangers' toilets to clean, no disappointment in her son's eyes, and her sister has married far better than she expected. She'll wake up in a few minutes but feel rested."

"How nice," said Limonov. "I suppose if I drifted off right here, you could tell me what's in my head."

Gudrun swallowed hard, really seeing him for the first time. "There's no need. You're very proud that you make nightmares real. You've said it—you've said you make nightmares real, but people think you are self-aggrandizing. They don't know that you have lucid dreaming, or that you can exercise conscious control over your REM atonia. For most people, release of specific neurotransmitters is shut down, so that the body's muscles don't move while they dream, and they don't hurt themselves or others." She paused a moment, swallowed hard again and added, "I don't know how I know that. The point is: you're already asleep."

"What a clever girl. And you know this because I'm dreaming now, aren't I?"

"Yes. You're about to come out of it. It's because you're summoning the images of raping me and stabbing me to provoke a reaction, and it's getting you excited, making you lose some of your control."

Limonov chuckled, and then he heard his laughter and blinked once, twice, truly awake now as the girl predicted. She looked at him with eyes of dread, suppressing a shiver. It was nice that they could feel fear, he thought, even if her type had come back with special advantages.

He had expected this conversational intimacy, both of them knowing oh-so-much more than the *true* sleepwalkers walking around them, going about their mundane lives. But the girl's rising terror was a bonus. Sweet.

"It won't be like your dreams," she warned him flatly. "The rape. The blood. I don't sound like that when I scream."

221

"That's very good. I wonder if you were this assertive and confident before your lover killed you."

"No."

"If you know all these things, you should know why I'm really here."

"You think murdering me will help you get what you want. But it won't. You'll find out you can't see the way I do. You have a... You're blocked."

Limonov studied Gudrun Merkel carefully, noticing her eyes were moist with grief for herself but still she showed no impulse to flee.

"It's not a gift for you, this extra life, is it?" he asked. He meant no cruelty in his question and was genuinely interested in the answer. "You didn't think it was a gift at all, being brought back. You don't have to fake gratitude and joy over your second chance—not with me. We can be honest with each other."

"Yes."

"I suppose this is why you do not run. Because no matter what I do to you, in the end, when your heart stops, you will be rewarded with what you didn't get last time. Peace. Final peace... You assume I will fail, and I won't change things."

"Yes."

"And I suppose if I tear off your clothes, push up your legs and defile you, if I slash at your breasts with my blade and cut your face, you will simply float away in the heads of someone in Peru or Albania, won't you? You will disconnect and defy me with a stupor."

"Yes," she mumbled.

There was a boy of thirteen in Norway, his mind replaying a hiking trip through lovely woods. It was very green and bright there. It would be enough for the duration of what he would do to her. She would focus hard. Woods. Sunshine. Crunching leaves under boots and the birds twittering, calling to each other across the gorgeous trees...

Limonov sent his knife in a vicious arc across her throat. He felt cheated out of pleasure, cheated out of what he had come for, but... Like he always said, spare the blade, spoil the victim.

14

"It's not paint," said Miller flatly, studying the picture.

"It's a painting," laughed Tim. "It's got brushstrokes, it's on canvas, it's got a nude for Christ's sakes."

"I don't care if it looks like a painting," said Miller. "That's *not* paint. The forensics guys over at the French police looked at it, and then they gave it to a couple of biochemists at the Pasteur Institute, and I've confirmed their findings with my own tests. It's not paint, but it *is* organic. It's fucking freaky is what it is."

"Well, then it's a nice conversation piece," replied Tim, shrugging. "I guess everybody picked up on that weird 3-D effect or holographic…"

"Tim, there's no hologram in there," insisted Miller. "For 3-D, you need three different compositions going on to create the illusion, and for a hologram, you need lasers and shit and—look, I'm sure Weintraub can explain it. There are *no* other images in this picture except the one you see—at the moment. And then the next moment. I told you, it's organic."

"Right, okay, you're doing that thing again," piped up Crystal.

"What thing?" asked Miller.

"The thing where you confuse the bloody hell out of us."

Miller clicked on YouTube on his computer. "Check this out. It'll make things easier to understand."

Tim waited as the scientist brought up links to a couple of videos pirated from BBC Nature documentaries. Soon they were watching footage of a floating octopus. The creature drifted along the bottom of the ocean, past spiky plants and alien-looking fish. Then it suddenly shifted and transformed color with all the whimsical choice of a disco ball, switching patterns to blend in with a patch of algae.

"Whoa!" said Crystal. "*That* is freaky!"

"An octopus uses chromatophores," explained Miller. "They're cells with pigments that reflect light. Cephalopods like the octopus have complex chromatophoric organs controlled by muscles and their nervous systems. An octopus can also change the texture of its skin, by the way, which makes for even better camouflage."

"So what are you saying?" asked Tim, still mystified.

"The picture has *this* stuff?" asked Crystal.

"Or something like it," said Miller, "but yeah, essentially, it's a painting of chromatophores. When you brought it near the window, it adapted to its surroundings and in reaction to the changing light source. I'm saying this whole painting is a living organism."

Tim looked again, as did Crystal. The colors stayed brilliant, the nude locked in place, wandering in her frozen graceful stance amid the street musicians of this Futurist café scene. They looked at the picture, waiting unconsciously for its colors and composition to change. They couldn't help but wait, now that they knew.

*

The next day they were on the move. While Tim, Crystal and Miller had dealt with Leary and the stolen Booth in Northern Ireland, the French police had been quietly, patiently circulating the photo of Ana Tvardovsky to one- and two-star hotels and short-term rental apartments in Paris and its suburbs.

It turned out that despite her grim mission to track down Emily Derosier, their redheaded assassin preferred to stay in relative comfort. She had booked a room at a beautiful wine warehouse from the 1800s converted to timeshare suites, one located out in Bercy in the 12th arrondissement in the west. They were in luck. A caretaker for the property recognized Tvardovsky as "Ana Cara," a woman who supposedly held a Romanian passport.

It was clear from the moment they let themselves in that Ana Tvardovsky had done little in these rooms except eat and sleep. Her overnight bag was unzipped and still open on a chair, and the remains of a Thai takeout meal were still in a recyclable plastic container in the fridge. One jacket and skirt set was hung up in drycleaner's plastic in a closet.

"Nothing much here," said Crystal flatly, surveying the rooms. They had been told by the French police not to expect much, but she had insisted on being thorough.

"She was a genuine mob hitman—I mean hit*woman*," remarked Tim. "She'd know enough to cover her tracks in case she had to bolt, wouldn't she?"

Crystal began to sift belongings out of the brown leather suitcase on the chair. The Paris cops had tagged it as evidence but hadn't taken it away because they knew she would want to inspect it. "There's always something. People can't help being who they are, and they show themselves in tiny ways. Had an old criminology professor hammer that into my brain. Knickers, pantyhose, skirts, blouses, trousers, and in the pockets—"

She yanked out a packet of tissues still in their plastic wrap, a pen, a jingling collection of coins and a few bank notes. "Nothing."

"Maybe not," said Tim. He scooped up the money to take a look. One of them didn't look right, and when he fanned the packet, there was more than one of them. "These aren't euro notes."

Sri Lankan rupees. Crystal plucked a couple out of his hand and shrugged. "Pretty money. Emily Derosier had her big transcendental change while traveling in Sri Lanka. Maybe Lantern Jaw and Tvardovsky thought they could find her there."

"Maybe," said Tim. "But these notes look fresh. They feel like ones you'd get at the foreign exchange booth. I don't think she came from there, I think she expected to fly there soon."

Crystal nodded. "You're right. Good catch. I'll ask the Paris cops to check if her alias had any booked tickets to Colombo or—hang on. Why go to the trouble of changing your money if you think you're going to catch up to Derosier in Paris? That's pretty negative thinking."

"It's a good question," said Tim.

The answer waited at the abandoned hiding spot of Lantern Jaw. It had taken the authorities longer to piece together his identity, and they had only got so far. The redhead's partner had rented a squalid one-bedroom flat in the *banlieue*, or suburb, of Clichy-sous-Bois. Obviously, they hadn't traveled together as a couple. In this neighborhood of mostly Algerians, Tunisians and Moroccans, Lantern Jaw had tried to hide in plain sight as one of the poor whites, calling himself "Gogol." Because of the 2005 riots, the building's super had installed a hidden security camera in the parking lot, and the police had a clear shot of his face.

227

"Gogol" was the name on his phony passport, but Crystal suggested they cross-match the man's photo against known associates of Viktor Limonov. After two days, it worked. Lantern Jaw had been born in Minsk as Dmitry Zorich, one of Limonov's merry band of psychopathic mercenaries working in Syria, Congo, Afghanistan and other war zones.

"Polar opposites," said Tim as he and Crystal rummaged through Zorich's belongings. "She was practically a ghost at that timeshare. Few clothes, no keepsakes. If she hadn't been killed, she would have left nothing behind for us. And this guy is—"

"A slob," Crystal put in.

"Right."

Clothes were strewn over chairs, on the floor, in piles in the bedroom. While Ana Tvardovsky had settled for takeout, Dmitry Zorich liked to cook, and there were a couple of French cookbooks on his counter and elaborate spices bought in the neighborhood as well. Judging from the lingering odors, Tim suspected he wasn't a half bad amateur chef. But Zorich didn't like to clean up, and dishes encrusted with curry sauces and old food bits were stacked in the sink.

When the French police had driven up to the *banlieue* block with sirens in full wail, Zorich had been forced to leave everything behind. The old luggage strip was still taped around the handle of his bag, which gave them the details of when he arrived and from where—a morning flight from Croatia three weeks before the showdown at the Beaubourg. As he and Crystal explored, Tim collected the moldy paperbacks that Zorich had been thumbing and marking with a yellow highlighter in virtually every corner of the apartment, all of them in either French or German translations.

"According to MI6, this Zorich is what you Americans call a real piece of work," said Crystal, nudging a stained sweater on the carpet with her shoe. "He would have been kicked out of the Russian army if the Cold War had lasted. Fits of manic paranoia and one diagnosis of bipolar disorder. Likes junk science, even flirted with joining a New Age cult. Then Limonov found him, and the briefing notes say Zorich became an almost fanatical devotee of his, always by his side. He would have been arrested in the same raid in Bangkok, but it looks like Tvardovsky warned him in time."

"He doesn't fit any kind of profile I've heard about for these mercenary Blackwater types," answered Tim, still checking the paperbacks. "These guys come out of war zones, and they know what they know. They're practical types—adrenaline junkies. They like the concrete, the tangible. Look at this—"

He held up the only book in English, Arthur Koestler's *The Roots of Coincidence*. Tossing it aside, he recognized a French translation of *The Book of Lies* by Aleister Crowley and allowed himself a sardonic smile. His late ex-girlfriend, Thérèse, had briefly been infatuated with Crowley's mysticism through his books until Tim found her some other volumes—biographies that showed her how the author was a vicious racial bigot and misogynist. She didn't speak to Tim for a week but eventually came around.

"We've got a couple of books in French about parapsychology, a biography in German of Carl Jung, a French translation of *The Holographic Universe*... Something in German about dreams. And this one."

He showed her a French book on Wilhelm Reich. "You ever heard of this guy? Psychoanalyst who hung out with Freud. Believed there was a cosmic energy called 'orgone.' I had to learn about him for my psych minor in university."

"Oh, yeah," said Crystal. "He built these mad machines, didn't he? He thought he could fiddle with his orgone particles to make it rain."

"Uh-huh. So I guess somebody else took psychology as a minor."

Crystal smiled. "Nope. Had a mate in uni who was really into Eighties retro and Kate Bush. She used to play 'Cloudbusting' practically every weekend. I thought she was pulling my leg until I checked it out—the song really *is* about the cloud machine."

Tim rolled his eyes and sifted the books.

"What?" prompted Crystal. "You had the album on vinyl, did you?"

"I'm not *that* much older than you, Inspector."

"Well, you have always seemed fairly spry to me," she said, laughing mischievously.

He smiled back, allowing her to score the point. They looked at each other a moment, Crystal still eyeing him warmly, and then she turned her interest back to the book in her hand.

Tim decided he would take the paperbacks back to his hotel and go over the highlighted sections. Maybe they would give him a clue to what Dmitry Zorich was after.

"Our Russian slob comes to Paris to kill," he muttered, half to himself, "but he uses his spare time to soak up all this 'beyond reality' stuff. You'd think if he was trying to kill Emily Derosier, he'd already have his answers."

"The guy follows Limonov," said Crystal, approaching the dirty kitchen and then thinking better of it. "And our war criminal is a master manipulator. It's possible Limonov tapped into whatever insanity this fellow has and is using it. For Tvardovsky, he could have used something else, like plain greed."

"You and I both know what we saw that day," Tim reminded her. "Emily Derosier got into everyone's head, and I mean *everyone's* head. I can believe Zorich is bonkers, sure, but Limonov must have fed him and the woman *some* answers to motivate them."

"You're preaching to the choir," she answered gently. "We'd be hell bent to get them off the streets even if we didn't have this madness going on. Gives me the creeps that Limonov stepped out of a Booth!" She flipped open a fresh paperback. "Tim, look at this. Check this out."

He thought she had found a passage in the text, but no, what had captured her attention were notes scrawled in Russian on the inside title page of the book. Zorich had doodled tiny quick reference maps next to a paragraph of scrawl.

"I can't read Russian," said Tim.

"Neither can I, but look—this is our intersection here. And this is a sketch of where the Beaubourg is. He's even put an 'M' for Rambuteau Métro station. Zorich's a mercenary. He thinks in terms of figuring out terrain and geography. Force of habit."

"Is that so surprising when he comes to Paris to kill somebody?"

"No, but look at this separate little map here," answered Crystal, taking a pen out of her pocket and using it as a pointer. "This is odd. Whatever this place is, Zorich must not be familiar with it, so he's copied a map out of a book for a visual aid—he's even labeled a couple of streets in English because he can't think of a phonetic version in Russian. But this… this can't be Paris."

"You're right, it isn't," said Tim.

She looked at him, curious.

Tim tapped the page. "He's written 'Chandni Chowk.' That's a big market in the old part of Delhi. I used to shop there for gifts for friends when I was stationed there. Wait a minute…"

He began to search the other books. Crystal understood. Zorich might have drawn himself a map in the other titles. "Here, he's done it again. The thing I don't get is why doesn't he simply buy the damn maps? They can't be that expensive."

"But he needs to learn these places," explained Crystal. "Terrorists rehearse their routes, Tim. They do recon on areas. Maybe he doesn't have the luxury of time. You *invest* in a map when you need to stay a while. But it looks like Zorich and Tvardovsky have been globetrotting all over the place, stopping at a bunch of specific spots in a rush. He drew himself the map of the Beaubourg just so that he and Tvardovsky could hunt Derosier down. They were tracking her—and trying to box her in."

Tim nodded, impressed. "Well done, DI Anyanike."

"Thank you, sir. Now it's your turn to be clever. If that was part of Delhi, what's *this* a map of then?"

Tim studied Zorich's sketch. "If I'm right… Colombo in Sri Lanka."

"You've been there, too."

Tim shook his head. "Nope, wanted to—never got there. But I have read the list he's scribbled next to his map. I've seen it before. These are all luxury property areas in and around the capital. Crystal, I don't think our creepy couple was headed there for anything to do with Emily Derosier. This property list… Benson told me that CIA operatives and the NSA were checking these places to find out if Orlando Braithewaite lives in one of them. I think they're trying to find Braithewaite for Viktor Limonov!"

"What could Limonov possibly want with him?" asked Crystal. "He's gone through the Karma Booth unharmed. He's laughing at the world. The most he could want with our billionaire is to thank him."

Another good question, thought Tim.

If Washington wanted to keep on pressuring him for answers then Tim was determined to push back over his multiple objectives. What progress had the NSA and CIA made, he demanded in a text back to Benson, on pinning down the whereabouts of Orlando Braithewaite? Any? Not so far, he was told.

That evening, Tim strolled around Paris because it always helped him to think when he walked, but he found himself dwelling on the old personal ghosts that still lurked here. He must have come back to Paris more than a dozen times since his posting here early in his career, and while, of course, he had thought of Thérèse once or twice on those trips, the echoes of his cynical youth had collected to hiss and snarl at his conscience more than usual this time. He wanted to damn the Karma Booth for that, too.

He had told himself later that he was intoxicated on the city more than he ever was on her. Thérèse had been fun but flighty, the girl who knew the best ancient elevators without security cams for risky sex, but who got herself into trouble with credit card debt, with the wrong friends holding drugs in a Belleville apartment, with being pegged as an accomplice to her shoplifting model friend.

Tim broke it off after seven months. There was no way his rationalizing explanation sounded like anything else but betrayal. She was brilliant, he told her. She had so much potential. But he couldn't afford to stick around and wait for her to get her act together. Didn't he have a *career*? Didn't he have a position that couldn't afford any public embarrassment? Six months after he let her go, she went out on the date that had ended in her brutal attack.

And wasn't what had happened to her so similar to how Mary Ash had been savaged? He hadn't wanted to think about it before. The Ash girl had not come back the same. Never mind what she could *do*; she was a haunted shell. And Thérèse, so doomed with her grandiose ambitions and erratic behavior—long before she was raped and beaten and infected—could never be called a survivor. The label implied ultimate triumph and acceptance over the worst, but the spiral for her had merely intensified.

The Karma Booth wouldn't have saved her because it insisted on death before it settled accounts. How could the Booth restore the wounded and broken like Thérèse? He recalled Mary Ash's clinical recital of his opinions the first time he had stepped into her room: "*You want punishment, but you also know terrible things change people forever. And you felt there was no pattern to life after Thérèse died in a car accident in Hamburg...*"

Life after life. This is the pattern the Karma Booth exposed and disrupted.

So where did you go, babe? What life do you lead now, and are you even aware of what happened before? Are you here, he wondered, or are you somewhere in that strange place where Daniel Chen graduated to flavors of music in his throat?

He strayed into the Latin Quarter, and as he made his way along Saint-Jacques, he found himself drifting by force of old habit into Rue de la Parcheminerie. He liked to go into the Abbey Bookshop, stuffed with more than 35,000 titles and where Leonard Cohen was usually groaning on the stereo, or he would take a few steps further to Exiles Bound, where he was on a first-name basis with the owner, Ron. Ron was a Brit and a retired Foreign Office secretary who treated his bookshop like a salon, happy to argue conspiracy theories, the virtues of socialism or the joys of Sufi poetry with any student from the nearby Sorbonne.

But the lights were off as he approached the shop. Ron often kept the place open until one in the morning, but he was certainly entitled to a night off. Tim turned on his heel and swung back for an hour of browsing in Abbey Books, and he wouldn't have thought twice about the gray sedan parked down the street except that he heard its engine starting up.

There had been a gray sedan, too, on Rue Saint-Jacques.

He didn't like this. He didn't think of himself as a paranoid, and it was entirely possible that the President had had a change of mind and sent along a couple of suits to keep a discreet eye on him. But unlike in the movies, they would have had to liaise with French authorities, and he couldn't believe Benson or someone else wouldn't drop him a line.

Screw you, whoever you are, he thought. You want to follow me, let's see you keep up.

He still knew these streets pretty well. The obvious Métro station to hit was Cluny–La Sorbonne, but he doubled-back and walked briskly over to Rue Dante then onto Rue Domat. Any car tailing him had to circle around and would give the game away in the narrower avenues. Or they would have to guess where he was going and head east on Boulevard Saint-Germain. But he was already fishing out his *Carte orange* pass and heading down the steps of the Maubert–Mutualité station.

He debated whether he should tell Crystal. But he wasn't sure about the car; he had merely felt the déjà vu of its presence.

If he was being followed, he knew he must make one hell of a disappointing surveillance target, that's for sure. All he'd done tonight was eat out and wander around bookshops.

What would Thérèse make of his quiet life these days as a consultant and professor? After all that she'd been through, she would have probably deemed it splendid. Good things had always been deemed "splendid" to her. Tim preferred to think of the pre-attack Thérèse, the young woman who would have turned up her nose at his drift towards middle age. Oh, yeah, how she would have chided him for that! He would give a lot right now to hear her teasing laughter.

It occurred to him that the Karma Booth might soon invent a new kind of grief. Death was supposed to be irrevocable, but now there would be that peculiar ache of loss with the still living, always so tinged with its irrational resentment and contradictory bitterness. *Right now he is getting on with a new form*, you might be told by counsellors. *She is growing up somewhere else with a different name.* All the things unsaid, unresolved, undone. Tim stepped out of the Métro and his head was swimming with all the personalities of his life gone and perhaps renewed—parents, aunts and uncles, casual colleagues and beloved friends.

If we leave this life, he thought, then what, if anything, do we keep? He didn't know whether to mourn or celebrate. Because a door beyond the dazzling whorls and nebulae of the glass chamber had stayed stubbornly, frustratingly closed.

Edward Brewah had a favorite spot in his home city, one that bordered the less affluent section of the West End but overlooked Freetown's spectacular natural harbor. The harbor was one of the jewels of Sierra Leone. Here, watching the endless blue that stretched beyond Queen Elizabeth II Quay, the forty-seven-year-old former soldier could be by himself. He preferred to be alone more often these days, ever since his wife had left him two months ago, taking their small child with her.

He shifted his weight as he sat on the artificial mountain of dirt left by the construction machines. Someone wanted to build something here, but there must have been bureaucratic delays or bribes not duly paid, because he had made his pilgrimage for weeks now and had never been disturbed. That was good.

He could sit in peace and watch the ocean, and *it* could feed. Its belly was never full.

His wife didn't need to explain her decision when she left. Edward Brewah could see the dread in her eyes. It was always there, and one morning when he returned from the night shift, she had announced in nervous breaths, "I'm leaving... Edward."

She added his name with a peculiar note of formality, but then she had never truly believed this was her husband. He didn't stop her from going. Somehow the impulse simply didn't come; not when she picked up their little boy, and not when the gypsy taxi whisked mother and child in the direction of Lungi airport, where they would board a plane and go stay with his wife's sister in a squalid town in Liberia.

The *gnawing*. He never got used to the jaws and didn't want to; the discomfort was just right and the pain had a twisted comfort of *penance* in the action. It would never get its fill. The back of his head felt wet. Of course.

He had tried to adjust to life back home; he had, really. Ever since the shock and the nausea and looking up into the startled eyes of the white man with the spectacles and the melon-shaped head, the one they told him later was quite famous in America. He had never asked Edward his name, only questions and more questions about *Where have you been? How do you feel? Where did you go? But you must remember something.*

Yes, he remembered things, but they were all moments from his old life. The voices of Krio in the market; the smell of diesel oil at the garage and stale takeout food on the mechanic's bench before he and a friend drove over to their commander's office at the Murray Town barracks. The war. Of course, he remembered the war.

Wet, squishing sounds now. He didn't look. There would be *regurgitation*. And there was a mild pounding in his head.

The end had come with the stink of male sweat and the concussive wave of bullets, like a weight slammed into his chest. The last sounds in Edward Brewah's ears had been cries of alarm over his injury and more shouts to go after the escaping criminal. The thug was one of the last of "Mosquito" Bockarie's RUF butchers who amputated limbs and slaughtered children. *Get him. Get him now.*

Then there was whiteness that blanked out everything, and the squeak of limbs falling and sliding against thick glass. His arms. His legs. Whole. He recalled the sudden shame over losing control of his bladder and the feel of his warm urine down his leg. He was crawling on a dirty, cold floor for a few seconds before men in lab coats rushed to lift him onto a gurney.

Before that day, Edward Brewah had believed in the Lord and in his only son, Jesus Christ, and so he could not hate his wife for recoiling from him when he came through their door. He had not asked for this great sin to be done. The army would let her keep his death benefits, and the kindly old white foreigner—who had so much better manners than the American scientist—had spoken to the army.

Orlando Braithewaite, he discovered, was a billionaire and a man of great influence. He arranged for Edward Brewah to get an honorable discharge from the army with a modest pension and a new job as a security guard at Connaught Hospital downtown.

Then Orlando Braithewaite was gone and so was the American scientist. Edward Brewah was left with the baggage of his questions, such as *Will this feeling stay?* The detachment. The lack of joy or even casual pleasure that he somehow knew intuitively belonged to anyone coming back. It was wrong to return this way. But it hadn't been his decision.

He could make a new decision. But suicide was a mortal sin.

Teeth again. And the pain in his head that told him something would never reach its climax.

When the civil war was over in Sierra Leone, there were thousands dead and two million displaced, and Edward Brewah in his *first* life realized he had spent half of it with a rifle in his hand, trying to put an end to evil things. He had woken up many nights screaming over the severed limbs he'd seen left in a ditch, and the rapes he'd interrupted with the butt of his rifle slamming into a villain's head. Rapes plural. Boys without souls, stoned on drugs beyond all instinct of self-preservation, running in a legion-of-scarecrows charge that insisted you fire. His wife had helped him banish these nightmares. He had thought their child was an unspoken declaration of new hope.

His son was entitled to a happy life.

He watched the eternal blue beyond the port. The sucking changed to clamping and more gnawing. The migraine reasserted itself, but he sighed and focused on the blue.

"Survivor's guilt," said a voice in English, except it had a peculiar accent to it; not like a British person's English or the kind spoken by the occasional American mining executive who flew in.

Brewah looked up. He didn't recognize Viktor Limonov but somehow he knew him. The tall Russian was back in a signature polo shirt and jeans, favoring high-top desert boots, because he could dress as he liked in this small corner of Africa where no one cared about the UN and war crimes. The thin mouth grinned pleasantly, and the husky dog blue eyes inspected Edward Brewah and betrayed no shock or revulsion at what was happening.

"You feel guilty because you live," observed Limonov. "I'm sure you had the same guilt after the massacres and after the war ended, but you didn't have a way of expressing it."

"True," said Edward Brewah warily.

Gnawing again. He had no name for the thing but *it*, and *it* was forever hungry. With its scrotal sac of a head and its disgusting beak-like maw, its many beads of eyes stared up at him as it fed on the stump of his arm. It slurped and gnawed until it regurgitated a mess of half-digested tendons and flesh back into his lap, as if it needed to feed invisible young. These bits *oozed* and coalesced back into the formation of his new hand and forearm. He wasn't disgusted the first time this had happened because even then he knew he was creating it, even while he was responsible, too, for creating the slug *thing* that crawled and slimed and pushed its way into a freshly ruptured gash in the back of his head... never fully entering.

These things repeated themselves like a manic-depressive's endless monologue. Feeding with vulture tenacity, violating without climax.

"It's rather disgusting what you do," commented Limonov, and Edward Brewah was annoyed at the arrogant way the man scratched his chin with the backs of his knuckles. "But then I suppose you want it to be wet and mixed up with biological fluids and meals for carrion. Guilt is a gorging, isn't it? But it's also a stain. And the way you violate your-self! The Americans talk about a—what do they call it? A… a skull-fuck! But you really do it!"

Brewah put *it* away. And he stopped the headache. "What do you want?"

"It's what you want," said the Russian. "I can help you."

Edward Brewah sat still. He hadn't felt fear or appre-hension when he died the first time, but now he began to tremble. "There was a girl in Germany who understood this loneliness. You murdered her—that one I felt. And there is a man in Texas who does not carry the sense of drifting like some others…and me. He is perhaps living fully awake for the first time, but you want to kill him, too."

"No one here on this plane of existence is fully awake, I promise you," sneered Limonov. "Not them, not you. Not even me, as that girl in Germany pointed out. And *you*…! You who wasted your second life with your self-indulgent masochism!"

"Squandered…"

Limonov shrugged. "Yes. Others squander it, too, but you make me sick more than the others. They're merely *bored*, and I can appreciate that. Now you… Ugh."

"There is a Heaven and a Christ!" said Brewah, getting to his feet, knowing he would have to fight in a moment.

"I might have met him," answered Limonov, stepping closer. "If I did, you can trust me, he bleeds like the rest. Of course, he would say, 'That's the point.' Your kind is always so clever before you go. Do you have a witticism for me?"

"They'll know," insisted Brewah in a shaky voice, backing away. "The teacher is strong. So is the artist in Pennsylvania. If I know of them—"

"They can know you, yes," said Limonov impatiently. He took out his knife and swung it into a wide vicious arc.

"People say, 'We're all connected,' and people always say that as if it's a good thing."

Brewah jumped back, escaping the blade, but he stumbled and fell against a tower of piled cinderblocks. He took a deep breath and concentrated. He had never focused this hard before, but it seemed to work. The flesh of emotion and tissues of sympathetic outrage grew and presented themselves on Limonov's skin like reddened hives and malignant growths.

And then the Russian was fine. Grinning at him as if his effort had been a practical joke. Viktor Limonov stood unchanged, this monster who had sold weapons to Foday Sankoh, Bockarie, Augustine Gbao and others in his country during the war. And yet he was clearly not of this earth.

"That's a very good tactic," chuckled Limonov. "The boils, the growths. Maybe I'll use it on the next one. My turn. Let's see now! I think you go too easy on yourself with your migraine…"

Edward Brewah concentrated, and his skin was smooth and without blemish as he anticipated what the Russian would try to do. Nothing grew, and nothing attacked, not *it* and not the slug from his own torment. But he had guessed wrong about Limonov's intentions.

He *tasted music*. He stared in horror at Limonov as the cyanide octaves and melodic botulism seared his throat and lungs, making him sputter and choke and fall to the ground, helpless. He should have realized it before because he hadn't felt the strange boy like the others, not the Texan or Mary Ash or, the most mysterious of all, the beautiful Englishwoman. The boy was dead, and Limonov had got what he needed as toxic chords choked off his breath. Edward Brewah wept. It was over. He'd *failed*. And now this enemy was stronger.

Edward Brewah died weeping. He knew the guilt would stay hungry forever.

15

In Tim's hotel room in Paris—which had become their base of operations—he and Crystal sifted their email reports. They offered a grim breakdown of the Karma Booth victims being murdered by Limonov. Benson sent along CCTV footage of Gudrun Merkel in Berlin, and it was clear she had done nothing to defend herself. And Crystal's network of sources in Africa reported that Limonov had bribed his way through customs into Freetown to reach Edward Brewah.

"He's hunting them," said Tim.

Crystal frowned at her laptop. "It doesn't make sense! Viktor Limonov is the king of the mercenaries. He brokers weapons. He goes out and wages wars as a soldier of fortune. If anything, he should be accessing Swiss bank accounts and laughing his ass off in a country with no extradition treaty."

"Jesus fucking Christ!" muttered Miller, sitting on a couch in a corner in front of the TV. When the two glanced over at him in surprise, he looked up sheepishly. "Sorry! It's just... Think about it. Psycho mercenary guy's gone through the Booth. I mean if Mary Ash and Geoff Shackleton come back with abilities...! That must be how he's tracking 'em—"

"Let's not jump to conclusions," warned Tim. "Limonov wasn't a victim resurrected. Yes, he beat the Booth when they tried to execute him, but he didn't walk out as some kind of god. Everything we've learned so far suggests he's still a *human being*. Thanks to his shady connections and his arms sales, he's got contacts all over the world, including India. We know he boarded a private Cessna jet to get back into Europe. He's human, Andrew. He's got to be."

"You've got nothing to base that on!" complained Miller. "You just want it to be true."

"Yes, I do," Tim conceded. "You're the science guy. Isn't it better to reserve judgment until we have more information? I do think you're right about one thing. He shouldn't be able to even *know* the Booth victims, let alone be able to track them down all over the world."

"Especially Gudrun Merkel," added Crystal.

"*We* didn't even know about her," said Miller.

Tim sighed. They were right. How could Limonov know about a young woman who was a resurrected victim when she might not have even known herself? Though given that certain authorities in Germany had known, it was possible that word had leaked out.

"He was an arms dealer," said Crystal. "You said yourself he has shady connections."

"What are you thinking?" asked Tim.

"A hunch. I don't want to say any more until I speak to a few friends in London. But trust me, Tim, if I'm right, his 'how' is a very mundane, familiar how. I'd like to know more why he's going after them."

It got worse. It wasn't only Limonov going after them. A day later, Weintraub sent text messages to let them know the resurrected victims weren't safe in the United States either.

The three-year-old blond boy who was once Daniel Chen had been sitting in a local playground three blocks from the home of his new foster family in Myrtle Beach, South Carolina. Gary Weintraub had chosen the family himself because he was a friend of the oceanographer father and the mother who was a software firm accountant. The couple had a seventeen-year-old daughter who was in her first year of university in Charlotte and had taken care of an autistic nephew for a couple of years (so they had experience with special needs children), plus they were affluent enough for a full-time nanny who could take the boy on outings like the one to the playground.

No one could have prepared these surrogate parents for what happened.

The little boy usually sat on the lowest rail of the jungle gym and never actually climbed it. The other children left him to himself most of the time, though one afternoon a two-year-old girl giggled and ran to her mother, chanting, "Bells, bells!" And if Gary Weintraub and Timothy Cale had been there, they could have explained to the little girl's mother what the boy had done.

Children tasted the music and somehow *knew*, but their parents simply dismissed what they were told with the knowledge that their sons and daughters were being precious.

No one could agree on a physical description of the suspect, except that he was a big man, unshaven with greasy, lank hair. But all the witness accounts said that he had pulled up in his Honda car, not even bothering to park properly, and had got out with two large Dobermans on leashes. He stopped and quickly, efficiently, unhooked the leashes from the animals, and to the stunned horror of parents there, the dogs ran in greyhound gallops into the playground. The dogs had *deliberately zeroed in* on the toddler.

A woman screamed. A father rushed over in a selfless effort to save the boy, and one of the dogs sank its jaws into his arm. He yelled in pain and staggered back.

What was stranger still was how the little boy turned to face the dogs, and as one savaged the heroic father, the other actually retreated for all of a moment. The animal vomited onto the grass. Then it was snarling and slobbering as if it had got its hideous second wind, having purged itself of whatever sudden poison had overwhelmed it, and by now the other dog had joined in. It was no longer interested in the father cradling his bloody chewed arm. The two of them set on the little boy the way they would tear open a rabbit—

All the while, the screaming, hysterical nanny, a woman of thirty-five from El Salvador, was held back by the man who had driven up in the car. She had the strength of the traumatized and desperate, but the man… He was like a brick wall, preventing her from risking her own life for the child. Hair. Blood. Torn flesh and tiny limbs. It was too awful, and she was on her knees, sobbing when his thick, callused hand slapped her, knocking her unconscious. The man went back to his car in long, easy strides and he actually *whistled* for the dogs to get in.

As Tim and Crystal left their latest briefing with the French police, he reminded her about the snow leopards hunting down the two survivors of the village on the Nepal border. She nodded slowly, gathering his meaning.

"From what we understand," Weintraub's new text read in the scientist's typical rushed style, "the boy was attacked two days before Edward Brewah. So impossible for Limonov involvement."

Not quite true, thought Tim. There was the terrifying possibility that Limonov had allies for whatever sick game he was playing.

"I think it's time you let me in on your hunch," he said to Crystal.

"I've spoken to my mates back in London," she answered. "They reminded me of something that happened at the Pentagon a while back, sometime in—"

But before she could finish, her cell rang. It was Miller, telling her that he needed to see them both down at the lab facilities borrowed from the French.

"Can it wait until tomorrow?" asked Crystal. "It's going to be a nightmare to get over there at this time of day." She covered her phone with a palm and whispered to Tim, "His lab's near the Parc des Princes, and there's a football match on tonight. Did you know they dumped him over there?"

Tim shrugged. "I was told it was the best facility they could offer."

Tim could hear Miller through her cell, sounding increasingly desperate for them to come.

"Andrew, hold on," Crystal told him. "Andrew... Andrew... All right, all right, we'll be there as soon as we can!"

As expected, it took them a good forty-five minutes to beat the rush hour traffic and the soccer fans driving in to see the Saint-Germain football club. At the lab facility, an irritable security guard led them in, and they were taken to where Miller waited, sneakers pushing against the edge of a worktable as usual. His face was ashen. Their American genius sat with his hands laced close to his mouth, trying to solve a new puzzle that he alone understood.

"Well, what is it?" asked Tim. "You sounded like you were having a nervous breakdown or something."

"Maybe I am," replied Miller. "It's not possible. I'm sorry I dragged you both down here—someone must have fucked up. I'll get Sims to review everything back in White Plains. It's impossible, it's completely—I must have misunderstood something or—I can barely think anymore!"

Tim didn't know him well, but he did know the young scientist didn't admit easily to making mistakes. "What did you find?"

"It's wrong. Doesn't matter, it's wrong—I'll have someone else review everything."

"What's wrong?"

"Okay. Look. Back in White Plains, they did *full* DNA profiles of victims and executed criminals. Complete physical work-ups, CTs and MRIs. *Every one.* Weintraub insisted we do full brain scans before Emmett Nickelbaum ever got pushed through. Jesus, we had Mary Ash's profile even before she came back. And I finally had a chance to go over the results on different subjects and... Well, to do some comparisons."

"Okay then, what did you find?" Tim demanded.

Miller didn't answer. With no response forthcoming, Tim reached across the worktable and scattered the pages in front of him.

"Come on, what? Is this it? What did you find?"

Miller looked more and more agitated. He pulled out a tattered Kleenex to polish his spectacles while he rocked in his chair. "We must have screwed up..."

"Come on, Andrew," sighed Crystal. "What are you getting at?"

"Hey, I know how to read a fucking axial MRI. I went to Johns Hopkins, and I got the student loan payments to prove it! I'm on half a dozen peer review groups for—"

"Andrew," prompted Tim, losing his patience.

"Okay, okay. Listen... Thirty-nine years ago, a wild grizzly bear in Montana mauled a tourist on a camping trip and was put down. It was one of those freak animal attacks—the bear just came out of nowhere and slaughtered the guy. No reason for it. I mean, the tourist wasn't being an asshole or doing anything wrong like taunting the thing. You with me? So around that time a database got started for protected wildlife species, and the bear got all kinds of tests done on it, and then it got carved up, and tissue samples were sent to the Howard Hughes Medical Institute in Maryland. Some records are with the Center for Disease Control, other places..."

"That's very interesting, but why do we care about a bear attack in America decades ago?" asked Crystal.

"Because I got to thinking about the snow leopard attacks on that guy and the old lady," explained Miller, standing up and gathering his notes. "You asked for samples from the victims, Tim, but you neglected to ask for samples or tests done on the animals."

Tim and Crystal traded a look.

"The animals?" asked Tim. "Why would you want tests on the animals?"

"Jesus, you guys don't see it. It's right there in the report from Delhi. Those snow leopards went after the old woman and the guy. The folks in that village said those cats went after them *specifically*."

Tim shrugged. "I know. It's creepy, and we've talked about it ourselves, but we still don't understand where *you're* going with this."

Miller tugged on a shock of brown hair near the base of his scalp, a brief gesture of nervous self-destruction. He was still frustrated, still unable to say what was wrong. He hammered his fist on the table. Then he snatched up two sets of stapled pages and placed them side-by-side.

"They look pretty much the same to me," said Tim. "Are they from the same patient or something?"

"No..." Miller flipped each stack of papers back to the cover page. "These are both scans of human brains, okay? Only the one on the left is the scan for that damn grizzly bear in Montana!"

Crystal was shaking her head. "That... can't be possible."

"Welcome to where I've been for the past three hours!" snapped Miller. "Hey, we share hormones with mice, pigs, all kinds of other critters. And scientists have been fooling around with hybrids—chimeras—for years now. The guys at Stanford grafted human glial cells into newborn mice, but this...*This!* We are talking human brain structure in another species! The *shape* of the entire brain is wrong for Smokey out in the woods! It's insane! And it gets worse..." He trailed off, turning his back to them, giggling as if to cover embarrassment. "I'm a fool. I've done something wrong, or they've done something wrong, but it's all *there*."

They stared at him, waiting.

"You haven't guessed yet?" asked Miller. "Two scans, remember? They're both for Emmett Nickelbaum."

"What are you saying?" Tim asked, utterly bewildered.

"I'm saying—and I can't believe I'm saying it—that Emmett Nickelbaum used to be that grizzly bear."

16

Crystal fell into a chair. "No. No, no—this can't be right. If you could tell me a person was once a fish or a bird or vice versa, there would be more. Just the human brain scan thing alone—"

"You tell me!" barked Miller. "This breaks every scientific rule I know about biology, genetics... I mean, shit, what about the sheer common sense of *scale*? Brain capacity plays a role in allowing higher functioning, so how the fuck would this even work if someone comes back as a bird or a fish or whatever? The structure could be the same in theory, but cognitive abilities would be extremely reduced, and... I mean, shit, do we run CTs on every damn wolverine or camel or bear or gorilla from now on to look for your Uncle Charlie? Why would you before? However this happened, there must have been a glitch in the system, the grand scheme, and maybe that's how we stumbled over it. We wouldn't know of this until..."

Until the Karma Booth.

"Oh, God," said Tim.

"What?" asked Crystal.

"Mary Ash," he explained. "She *knows*. Somehow she knows this! She told us when we visited."

Crystal was still confused. "How? She was so cryptic. I mean, she did say she carried Nickelbaum in her head."

"Yes, she did, but remember what else she said? *May twenty-third, he eats fish. May twenty-fourth, berries of some kind, I don't know what they are. May twenty-fifth, fish again, but you'd expect that.*"

"The diet for a grizzly bear," Miller put in.

Crystal shuddered. "Oh, my God…"

It was a macabre joke, thought Tim, except that Mary Ash had been deadly serious in her casual recital. She had rattled off from her impossible otherworldly memory the mundane facts of Emmett Nickelbaum's life in his previous incarnation. She had all the events linked to individual dates because, as she had plainly informed them, she carried him in her head. She carried *all* of them, every single soul. And damn it, she'd *told* them, but they just hadn't put it together.

"*Fish again, but you'd expect that.*" And then she had moved on to an incident in the life of Crystal's father.

"I don't understand," said Crystal, her voice cracking with feeling. "She talked about Nickelbaum, and she sounded mad—like a schizophrenic. But then she started talking about my father. My dad!"

"Contemporaries," said Tim with a flash of insight.

"What?" she demanded. "Tim, what are you…?"

"Thirty-nine, forty years ago," he explained. "Mary Ash has the ability to rattle off your bio for any day, for any minute. She jumped from talking about Nickelbaum in his previous incarnation to where your father was *at the same time*. She picked a fixed point and told us what was happening with each soul."

"She's making sense," said Crystal softly, understanding. "Sense from her weird perspective, because she sees it all."

"Yeah."

Mary Ash, their haunted lens on the past. Offering the dark day of racism against Crystal's father while miles and miles away, simultaneously, Nickelbaum had foraged and hunted and lumbered his way back to the soundless screams of his true nature.

Tim looked to Miller. "You mentioned the snow leopards in Nepal."

Miller shrugged. "The cats were put down, destroyed. That's what the Indian authorities say. We've got nothing to test. But I think…"

"They used to be human, too," Tim finished for him.

"Yeah. The way they went after their targets. And they were targets, not just prey."

"What do we do with this information?" asked Crystal. "I mean, how do you tell the world? *Do* you tell the world?"

She instinctively turned to Miller, who went back to clasping his hands in front of his face, still overwhelmed.

"I don't know," he mumbled.

Then she stood, seeming to gather her strength. "Maybe that can wait. Here's a better question: How do *we* use it? It tells us more about them all, but I'm not sure what it says."

Now she was looking to Tim for the answers. He didn't have any. It was almost too much to comprehend. Life after life after life.

He thought of Daniel Chen, returning as that little blond boy who did not seem to belong in this world, unable to communicate except through the excruciating beauty of mixed senses. *How many lives do we get? How does that even get determined?*

And if it were true that Emmett Nickelbaum had gone from animal to human form, he had still remained a beast.

So what were they to make of those religious doctrines of the East that claimed you *earned* your way up from the dung beetle and the goat?

The Booth. The Booth broke more rules than they could have imagined.

"I don't know what Andrew's findings will mean for all of us," said Tim. "Who can dare to even guess? Maybe the public got the name right. It is a Karma Booth in a way, screwing up the natural karma of human beings."

They all fell silent a moment.

"Wait a minute, wait a minute," said Crystal. "Mary Ash is afraid of Nickelbaum coming back. But the Karma Booth exchanged him for her—it ripped her back from wherever she went after she died. Either he went *there*, or wouldn't he bounce back to a lower incarnation?"

"She said it herself to us," Tim reminded her. "He's not part of the cycle—same as her."

"But guys, none of the other killers are who were sent through a Booth!" argued Miller. "Why he's so special? Geoff Shackleton's murderer, Cody James, all the others... We haven't, like, seen them or heard about them returning. I mean, have you?"

"No, that's true," admitted Tim. "But I got a terrible feeling about this. Maybe, just maybe, Nickelbaum had help coming back. He was a genuine psychopath, and who do we know who recruits psychopaths?"

She caught his meaning and shivered. "Limonov."

"Viktor Limonov is the only person we know to ever go through a Karma Booth and pop right out, with nothing happening to him," said Tim. Then he added quickly, "That we *know* of. Okay, suppose there's an in-between stage, a waiting room, a place that's... I don't know. If you like Dante, a Purgatory of sorts. Zorich and Tvardovsky were human believers—Limonov woke them up to their true nature. But when Limonov stepped through the Karma Booth, he went in and showed Nickelbaum how to come back."

"That's a lot of conjecture," said Miller.

"After the bomb *you* dropped on us today?" asked Crystal, holding up his findings. "I could almost believe anything now!"

"Nickelbaum matches the description of the man who put the dogs on the boy," Tim pointed out. "I know it's thin, but *he* fits. And if it is Nickelbaum, he has no motive to go after that boy except as a task for Limonov. Mary Ash is convinced he's back in this world. But Nickelbaum was an auto-mechanic, not very bright, just pure sadistic appetites and cruelty. I'm convinced Limonov is using him as a pawn."

Miller sat up, clapping his thighs, his voice bitter. "This is great. This is just fucking great! Psychos come back and can't die, people walking around with weird shit happening... Terrific! I helped set off a worse disaster than global warming and nuclear holocaust. The whole fucking universe gets screwed! How do we fix *that*?"

"We've still got an ally," Tim reminded him. "We got interrupted with Leary and his demented crusade, and so we've got unfinished business."

Crystal read his mind. "Emily Derosier."

"We find her," said Tim, "before Limonov and his cronies murder her like the others. I, for one, never like to keep a lady waiting."

That night, Tim trudged wearily back to Exiles Bound, hoping to chat with his old friend, Ron, for a bit of conversational comfort food. But when he reached Rue de la Parcheminerie and Saint-Jacques again, he grew annoyed. Not a gray sedan this time—a different car, but it was parked with its engine running, and he knew, he just *knew*, it was idling across the street for him.

"Hey!" he shouted. "Hey, what do you want? You want to talk or play games?"

He jaywalked in a self-righteous march across the street, but before he could bang on the windshield, the driver got out and raised a hand for him to calm down.

"*Crystal?* Jesus! What the hell's going on?"

"Tim, please get in the car before you make a complete scene."

He slipped into the front passenger seat, and she turned the engine off. "Right, listen to me. I'm not here over you, I'm here for Emily Derosier."

"I thought we'd built up some trust," he said tartly. "Especially after what happened in Northern Ireland. Crystal, we're supposed to be finding her together."

"Listen to me, Tim. You are very good at what you do, the whole analysis thing, but you nearly got your ass blown off outside the Beaubourg. I told you before: when there's any kind of danger, leave it to law enforcement professionals. This is what *I* do. Watch the bad guys, go after the bad guys—"

"We don't even know if she is a bad guy," he broke in.

"No, we don't. Fair point. But I've seen this before, yeah? I've seen plenty of times how a witness or suspect can have a go at messing with someone. And I think your judgment is impaired over this woman."

"You don't find it interesting that she comes from almost a hundred years ago and walks back into our time?"

"She's playing you!" said Crystal. "She researches *you* at the library. She leaves that weird octopus-skin or whatever painting for *you* at the hotel. The appointment on Thursday is with *you*. I happen to think we should find her and talk to her on our terms, not hers. She'll *know* the police will show up at the restaurant—she can anticipate that. Easily. So I reckon she might pop up when you're unguarded, maybe at one of your old haunts. Here…"

She passed him a printout of a web page. "Do you remember this? The article's about your mate, the bookshop owner, but *you're* mentioned in it, and there's you in the photo with the others. 'The unique bookstore was saved from bankruptcy when a group of friends stepped in to offer Ron James a much-needed infusion of capital.' Well, nobody does that unless they shop at the place. It doesn't take much to figure out you visit here, and I bet she might come around to check."

Tim stared out the windshield. "Well, then we have a problem because you're not the only one who got this idea."

He pointed across the street.

"Oh, no."

Lantern Jaw. Same broken nose, same constant menacing threat in the eyes. Dmitry Zorich. He was no longer in a suit but a plain brown windbreaker, T-shirt and jeans. He was headed for the bookshop, his hands stuffed in his pockets.

Crystal got out of the car. "Stay put," she ordered. "Call the police."

He yanked out his cell, but he'd be damned if he let her go all by herself against a demented Russian mercenary. Call it macho bravado or chivalry, but either way he couldn't just sit there. Plus his friend Ron was in the bookshop, a retired antiquarian who wanted nothing but to sip his Scotch while enjoying a quiet life and tending his books. Christ, he thought, if his friend got hurt, it would be his fault—

He ran up just as Crystal informed Ron to leave as quickly as he could. The silver-haired bookseller was in the street now, looking confused and in mild shock. He was even more surprised to see Tim sprinting across the street to him.

"Ron! You okay? You need to get out of here!"

"Tim, what the hell's going on? She says she's a DI with the Met—we're in bloody France! She pulls out a gun and—"

"Ron, there's *no time*. Get up the street and try to flag down a cop car. She really is with the London police. Go now. *Go!*"

And as his friend mumbled a defensive "All right, all right," Tim opened the door to the bookshop.

The glass pane above his head exploded—gunshot. He dove for the floor.

Beyond the overstuffed shelves and messy piles, he couldn't see Crystal or Zorich, but there was another loud crack, and this time wood splintered and sheared away from a display cabinet. Where was Crystal? He still couldn't see her.

There was a back fire exit, but either Zorich didn't know this or he had to shoot his way to get to it.

Footsteps. Running, tripping over something... And another shot.

Then he heard a high-pitched grunt and fumbling, and there was a metallic clatter. Bodies collided against the back wall and framed photos were bounced off their nails, shattering on the floor. Tim rushed in, having to turn sideways to get past the wooden ladder, and he spun around the corner to see Dmitry Zorich. The Russian yanked a vicious little blade out of a hidden sheath under his sleeve and slashed out at Crystal. Both their guns had been lost, knocked to the floor in the struggle.

The blade sliced across her belly, and she yelled and jumped back. But there was little room to maneuver in here, and as she slipped to the floor, Zorich crouched and slashed again,

258

slicing her right arm. Now he stabbed out to finish her off, and Tim kicked a thick English dictionary soccer-style into Zorich's head, which bought Crystal two seconds of distraction to scramble out of the way.

As the Russian went from surprise to full-blown hatred at his intrusion, Tim realized he had no other trick or weapon to save himself. Zorich sprinted towards him, and Tim spun around behind the shelf and pressed his weight as hard as he could—

There was a thudding cacophony of books raining down, and the Russian growled and slipped out from underneath the fallen slab of wood. Then Tim heard his quick footfalls along the creaking floorboards. Zorich was trying to find his way through the rabbit's warren of other shelves to escape.

"Cops are coming, Zorich!" he shouted. "You don't have a lot of luck in places like this, do you? Bookshops, libraries— *she's* not here, and we know who you are now!"

He dropped to his knees, looking for Crystal, and after a second, he found her already tying a makeshift tourniquet around her arm with a handkerchief. She was breathing hard, gritting her teeth against the pain of her slashed stomach. The wounds Zorich had inflicted were superficial, but they were enough to take her out as a threat to him.

"Are you all right?" he whispered.

"What did I say?"

"Let the nice psychopath carve his initials in your arm?"

"You're not my bloody backup!" she snapped, but he sensed she was more embarrassed over getting hurt than truly angry with him. "If there's a way out the rear, *take it*. Even if he gets out of the shop, we'll have him this time."

"Yeah, like last time. He got away from a full contingent of cops in a public square!"

"*Tim.*" His name as both warning and plea. "That's bloody commando knife fighting he used on me. Don't you dare take him on!"

"I'll just delay, I won't fight," he promised.

"Tim!"

You've got to do something, he told himself. Doesn't have to be goddamn heroic or even brilliant, but the bastard was dangerous, and that outweighed his fear. As he stood up, he spotted Crystal's fallen Glock 9mm that had slid under a cabinet of first editions. She was hurt. He wasn't fooling himself; it really was up to him. But he would use the gun only if he had to.

"Zorich!" he called.

He didn't bother to wait for an answer. The surge of adrenaline was making him sweat though he had done little so far, and he tried not to think of the Russian's blade sinking into him if he failed to pay attention. Stupid to die like that, he told himself. It'll only happen if you don't watch out, and she's hurt back there, and this psycho mercenary should have some answers so don't fuck this up. Don't let him get out.

"Zorich?"

One second, two.

"What do you want, Cale?"

So. I know him, and he does know me.

Zorich's English was reasonably fluent, but with the vowels stretched. He asked again, "What do you want, Cale?"

"What do you want with the artist?"

"Go fuck yourself, American! You think I explain myself to you?"

"You want to kill her for yourself or for Limonov?" asked Tim. He followed the Russian's voice back towards Political Science and History. "Which is it, Zorich? I'm guessing you're on a chore for Limonov. I mean, you followed him to every crater of hell around the world, so why not do one more errand for him, right?"

"*He* will *free* us!"

"Free you?" asked Tim, genuinely mystified. "What the hell is Viktor Limonov going to free you from, Zorich? He's on the run! What, you think he's indestructible or something after the Booth? They'll just shoot him or gas him or—"

The knife flew and sunk into a book past his left ear. *Son of a bitch.*

"You talk too much, Cale."

Tim rounded a corner, raising the Glock. Zorich had made the mistake of going down an aisle with no way out.

"He didn't free Ana Tvardovsky, did he?" asked Tim, holding the gun level at the Russian.

Zorich was backed against a bookshelf but looked coiled, ready to spring.

All you have to do is hold him here, thought Tim. You told Crystal you'll just delay, you won't fight.

There were sirens in the distance. Sirens were good. He took a deep breath and tried to hold the gun steady, but the Glock shook in his hand with the tension of the moment, and Zorich smiled.

"Whatever Ana Tvardovsky was or could be is gone because she went on that fool's errand with you," said Tim. "And that was for Limonov, too, wasn't it? That was all in the name of whatever bullshit he sold you."

"You never fire gun in your life, have you, Cale?" chuckled Zorich.

"It's simple, I press the trigger," bluffed Tim. "Like you change the channel on your remote."

"And you think that will finish me, yes?" asked Zorich.

"You were an animal before, right? Like Nickelbaum. So you'll be an animal again. Or my guess—something lower."

Zorich took a step, still looking as if his whole body was loaded for a desperate tackle. "Clever, clever! You learn a couple of things."

"Just stay right there," warned Tim.

"Do you have any idea of how ignorant you really are about existence?" demanded Zorich. "Most everybody—they forget. They do not know. You do not know what *you* were before—or what you were before that and before that and so on and so forth! Now imagine you remember."

He took another bold step.

"Be smart," said Tim. "Care about *this* life you have in *this* second. Because I *will* shoot you, asshole!"

"You see on television, Cale? When animals go insane and attack human being for no reason? Out of blue, they kill and need to be put down. You never wonder why that is? Think of waking up in lower consciousness, knowing where you are…"

And Tim tried to keep his hand steady, but still he took a step back to keep the distance. Yes, he could imagine it. He knew what the Russian was driving at. Maybe it was true. Maybe most people didn't remember, they couldn't *know*. And if there was an order to things, it stood to reason that the slate was wiped clean, memory gone. But suppose there were ones who *did* remember? Imagine your soul, your sentience still with you as you were startled awake in a lower incarnation.

"Trapped in body of what you call it? Snail. Or ape. Or leopard. Whatever. You know that you were once human and are now in this form."

He took another step forward.

Trapped, thought Tim. A human mind suddenly aware of where it was while surrounded by creatures that communicated and filled their needs on regular animal terms. Surrounded by beasts, living their beast lives, and you are trapped. With *them*. A mind trapped with a soul that self-aware would go mad. He thought of the Montana grizzly making its rogue attack…

Yes—yes, the news had reports almost every week these days of such senseless, unpredictable rampages. A gentle elephant at a zoo in California tramples the handler who cared for it for years. A killer whale swims into shallow waters to turn on a vacationing bather for no apparent reason.

"Don't you wonder, Cale?" taunted Zorich. "They kill because they need to *die*. We become desperate, mad—locked in lower forms of incarnation. Murder is the door out."

"Maybe that's how *you* climbed up to the next rung," answered Tim, and he willed his arm to stop shaking, to hold the gun level. "But hey, you're also insane. Now step back, damn it!"

"You know these things, these incredible things," said Zorich, shaking his head at him as if Tim were the fool. "*I remember! I know!* And you *dare* ask me why I follow that man?"

"Last warning, maniac."

"I don't fear death anymore, Cale. I fear the cycle. But *he* is not part of it, and so he can free us. Shoot me, and it doesn't end. It delays. Why don't I prove it to you?"

"Great, you mean I have to wait around while you grow up in your next form? *Step back!*"

"No, I think you will tell me from *your* next incarnation!"

The Russian let out a cruel laugh as the cloth of the windbreaker's pocket bulged out, and Tim suddenly understood he'd been played all along. Zorich was only waiting for his moment. Tim had been spellbound by his relentless steps, when all Zorich wanted to do was to slip his hand into his jacket—

The shot was impossibly loud, bursting through the cotton and polyblend of the jacket, but Tim ducked out of the room at the last second, cursing himself for a fool. *Idiot.* Sucked you in. But what he said... The madness of a trapped soul in lower forms.

He needed to duck back to find Zorich again and aim, but as he made his quick shuffle, an impossibly strong hand gripped his wrist and pushed up, and his shot went wild. Zorich was bellowing, using his body weight to ram Tim into a set of shelves, and he was too strong, far too strong, and the gun was twisted out of Tim's grip, skidding under a book trolley. Zorich was a mercenary, a trained assassin and soldier for hire, and there was no contest. Tim felt a blow in his stomach, and he doubled-over, suddenly desperate for air, and then the Russian was hurling him across the room. Tim fell in a heap, with books in a landslide striking him in the head and on the arms. And then Zorich was on top of him, his big hands around his throat, his teeth bared as he strangled him...

The blade of Crystal's hand swung like a cleaver into the side of Zorich's neck, and anybody else would have fallen in a heap. Zorich staggered, but he didn't collapse. Crystal whipped her leg in a blur, and her boot nailed the Russian in the ribs, and that was what finally got him off Tim. He roared in pain and fresh rage, standing up, ready to fight the detective. Tim was in a daze, coughing, gulping air and rolling on his side. He watched as Crystal leaned against a bookshelf, her service Glock now in one hand, the other cradling her slashed belly.

"Don't be stupid," she told the Russian. Her voice was flat, matter-of-fact. She was making it clear. She wasn't Tim; she wouldn't hesitate.

Zorich gambled. The Glock roared, and then he was staring up at nothing as his jacket bloomed with the wet, crimson petals of flowing blood.

Tim tried to get to his feet. Crystal hissed through her teeth, feeling the pain of the knife slash.

"If you want to borrow my things, make sure you hang onto them," she told him, breathing hard. "I had to crawl on the floor to get this back. Your friend should dust his place more."

"I'll be sure to tell him," promised Tim.

Zorich lay gurgling in pain, and he didn't have long—Tim didn't need to be a doctor to see that. Jesus, how awful to die like this, bleeding life away, thanks to a gunshot.

"This wasn't necessary," mumbled Tim. It sounded insipid in his own ears, but he didn't know what else to say. The Russian was dying in front of them.

Zorich struggled to speak. "I won't fall far. You think... I will? I have strength now... Grow old, Cale... Twenty... Twenty-five years..."

Tim grabbed a dusty cloth off a shelf, needing something to put pressure on the wound, staunch the blood. Hopeless. He felt a hypocritical fool for even trying. But he had to try. If only for the sake of the information the thug might give them.

"Grow old, Cale," Zorich softly implored him again. "I'll be somewhere... doesn't... Doesn't matter. I'll wake up to the truth... again. And I'll find you as an old... man, and slit your throat."

"Or maybe I'll teach him how to shoot properly," snapped Crystal.

"Or maybe we get an ambulance, and you'll rot in a cell," said Tim.

"No… No, we will win… He'll find her, Cale… before…" Then Zorich was gone.

17

All at once, it was pandemonium with the new shouting voices and the blue of the cruiser lights flashing along the walls and book spines. Crystal put up a fuss, but she finally lay down on an ambulance gurney, and then there were too many questions from policemen, Ron, paramedics...

Tim's mind was still busy with a pair of snow leopards in India from years ago, coming down from the mountains to tear open the throat of an old woman and a young man. An attack that was all too deliberate and coincidental.

It was a two-hour wait at the hospital while Crystal was patched up in the emergency ward. He sat in one of those ugly molded plastic chairs, listening to a six-month-old baby cry, stuck with his own inner debate on Zorich's revelation. Contemplating, brooding over those "locked in lower forms of incarnation"—and those who woke up and realized where they were and what had happened to them.

What, he wondered, is truly behind a cat's eyes? Cat brain, cat consciousness or something more? Were Hindus right that we commit genocide with every oblivious wave of the fly swatter? Too simple, and yet part of it was true according to Miller's latest findings.

He thought of the Russian's final taunts. So Viktor Limonov was, indeed, keenly interested in finding Emily Derosier. Zorich and Tvardovsky had been his catspaws. So what did the war criminal need her for? Or was it that she was an enemy who could defeat him?

The baby kept on crying. *Who were you before you were this infant?* Then there was Zorich's pitiful threat, like a mafia don, to come back and avenge on Tim himself in twenty, twenty-five years. Zorich "feared the cycle," yet he sounded sure he would be human in his next incarnation.

A baby crying. An older couple bickering. In a distant corner, a ragged, filthy man held his gashed arm swathed in toilet paper and rocked back and forth, humming. His years in Europe had made Tim sympathetic to a national health care system, but he could have done without the interminable Soviet-era waiting periods you seemed to get with one. His cell phone rang.

Tired, he was surprised to see it was Benson on the call-display, and then he reminded himself of the obvious: the man was six hours behind Paris. Not that Benson ever remembered that.

"You know, I might have been sleeping." He didn't care if he sounded cranky. Crystal had saved his life yet again, now getting stitched back together, and he hadn't even saved the situation by keeping Zorich until the cops swooped in.

"Tim, what are you doing, going after Limonov? You asked to rush back to Paris so you could chase your socialite ghost! And track down those thugs at the Pompidou Center."

Tim groaned. He could tell Benson now or save it for a report. He didn't feel like a late night debriefing. "We can multi-task, Benson. Why are you suddenly micro-managing your contractor?"

Over the line, Benson let out a calculated weary sigh. Its effect was useless in swaying Tim's confidence. "There are countless Interpol agents, not to mention assigned special agents of the FBI, staff for the International Courts of Justice, plus Christ knows how many other alphabet soup law enforcement types who can chase down Viktor Limonov. He's not your assignment."

"He is my assignment," said Tim patiently. "He's killed at least two people resurrected from the Booth. He's the only convicted murderer to be executed and not die. That dumps him squarely on my plate. I'd think you'd want me to track down this nutcase with the same zeal we had for Desmond Leary."

There was a pause on the line and then Benson's voice came back, now more reasonable. "You're right. I guess that wasn't fair of me. Thought you might be stretching yourself too thin. Oh, and I've been trying to allocate you some additional resources."

I'll bet, thought Tim. Into the phone, he said, "Thanks. But I still get to decide where and how I deploy those extra resources you send me. There's a damn good reason I make my contracts airtight so that I'm calling the shots."

"Hey, Tim, come on! No one would ever to try to tell you how to do your job—"

"Glad to hear it."

"But come on, these are unusual circumstances. So whatever your contract said, buddy boy, the lawyers can sort that out when the smoke clears. Jesus, Tim, you sat in the Oval Office with the President basically telling you, 'Don't fuck it up.' You think she didn't tell us right after you left, 'Don't *let* him fuck it up?' I'm sure the lady will want to know if you've made any headway in reaching Braithewaite."

Terrific. The one task he could definitely report no progress being made.

"Not yet... It's late here, Benson."

"Yeah, sure. Look, Tim, I'm on the five o'clock Saturday into de Gaulle airport. I need you to bring me up to speed by ten thirty that morning, and please don't give me your regular shit that you're busy. Try to be a team player for once in your fucking life, will you, man? Honestly, I've got your back, but I also got a job to do."

He made a quick goodnight and hung up.

Tim shoved his cell back into his pocket. In retrospect, he should have expected this. The intrusion was probably overdue, even with the dubious "success" of taking one of the Karma Booths out of terrorist hands. Of course, Benson could have stuck his nose in far earlier. Was he rushing over now because of pressure from the White House? Tim doubted it. Melinda Grant was the kind of commander-in-chief who would have dialed Tim's cell if she were unhappy with how the job was getting done.

Saturday morning. Just as well. Benson would be coming *after* he was due to meet Emily Derosier at Au Dauphin on Thursday, assuming their artist showed up for her appointment. Maybe by then they'd have more information to placate their Washington handler.

Benson's timing still struck him as odd. And why shouldn't they go after Limonov?

Tim scribbled the 10:30 morning appointment into his day-planner and wondered if he shouldn't place a couple of calls to trusted allies in DC to find out what might be going on.

It was time to panic, as far as FBI Agent Gordon Fraser was concerned.

They had warned him about Mary Ash, how creepy she could get and the disturbing things she could say, but no one had suggested she would become difficult regarding Protective Detail. From what Fraser had been told, the girl wanted protection, ostensibly from a man who no longer existed.

Gordon Fraser had ten years invested with the Bureau. A black man who stood six foot two with a rugged frame, he had once had a shot at a professional basketball career until a minor tendon injury. He liked Protective Detail because it was not routine, though lately he'd been taking courses so that he could move on to the white collar fraud unit (friends assured him it was a good career move). Fraser was known to be patient. He had a mortgage, a sixteen-year-old daughter who struggled with dyslexia, and he wasn't at home as often as he liked, but in every personal activity or professional job, he prided himself on being committed to the moment.

They had "given" him Mary Ash to look after thanks to his reputation for not being easily rattled or baited. Gordon Fraser was steady. He listened to traumatized witnesses without giving away too much of his personal life or letting himself get sucked into the vortex of their grief. He ignored the taunts and manipulative comments of the Klansmen, fanatical terrorists and prime time psychos he occasionally had to escort to facilities. He knew better. *You take down what they say discreetly, but don't engage. You do your job.*

Mary Ash, however, could grow things out of her hands. Horrific, bleating, misshapen things. And she had talked—incessantly—when Fraser walked by her side along New York's Sixth Avenue.

"Not India," she'd muttered. "They'll think it's India because of *him*. Or somewhere closer in Europe, like her. Doesn't have to be—doesn't have to be at all. He's still

271

limited, but he's got enough strength. September fifteenth. Olives are off the trees. The fridge is cold."

"Take it easy, Mary," Fraser had said, with a calming hand on the girl's shoulder.

Stupid thing to do: agreeing to day trips out in the open, where any fool reporter could stroll up and complicate things or a whack job could appear with a gun. Word was that the parents couldn't take it anymore—they had "thought it best" that Mary graduate to the next step in her recovery. And that meant the girl should move back to New York and try to find a new job as a graphic designer.

In the time it had taken with continuances and motions for Mary Ash's killer to be brought to trial, then convicted and to lose his only appeal, the girl's old roommate had naturally found someone else to share their old apartment. But Sita had generously agreed to help locate a new one for Mary in Brooklyn and help her get back on her feet.

"The fridge is cold," Mary had announced once more in her sleepwalker's drone.

And Gordon Fraser had thought: Who are they *kidding*? Girl's a train wreck. One second lucid, wanting to hit an art store for pastels or some shit, and the next rambling on about—

"Mary, you want we should get some coffee or something?" he asked with genuine compassion. "I don't know anything about India, sweetheart. I don't know anything about Europe or elsewhere or olives, okay? And most fridges are supposed to be cold. I thought you wanted to get your art supplies? Look, why don't we take a break and—"

"September sixteenth, he doesn't know, he doesn't *understand*," said Mary, suddenly more agitated.

She pulled away from him, and for a moment, Fraser thought she might cause a scene. Fraser hated scenes. But the currents and eddies of unflappable New Yorkers swirled around them and then past, and there was not a single, second glance of regretful interest from the human pilot fish on the move.

"Okay, there's the store, let's do it."

"September nineteenth, contact made," said Mary, her eyes scanning the shelves full of black leather portfolios and taking none of it in. "He gets a print-out article by Vikram Raj Singh Chauhan, a copy of Gerald Kersh short stories. The book has been left in a puddle, and blackish-green mold grows and festers on pages eighty-six through hundred and twenty-five. The fridge can't hold it safe. There is no caring because he's not a reader, the other one's the reader, and he wants to *do*, wants to act—"

"Mary, we came here for your supplies."

"You don't see, you can't see," said Mary Ash, her head shaking nervously with a Tourette shudder. Her fingers fidgeted with a button on her coat. "You want photographic precision, edges that are clear and defined. You do not know what *you* were—or what you were before that and before that and so on and so forth. Now imagine you remember."

"What *I* was?" demanded Fraser, and then thinking better of it, he asked, "Mary, who are you talking about?"

"They kill because they need to *die*. They become desperate, mad—locked in lower forms of incarnation. Murder is the door out. I'm not strong enough yet, but I have to try."

"Okay, that's it, I'm taking you home."

"Look there," said Mary Ash quietly.

Fraser couldn't help but look.

Slumped on the floor was a brunette girl of about twenty-five with high cheekbones, dressed in a heavy woolen sweater and jeans, looking past them. A fountain of arterial spray shot from her throat. Blood, so much blood, but what rocked

273

Gordon Fraser even more was how the girl gazed at him with the expression of the nodding addict, with a faint smile of the anesthetized patient counting down from ten, as she said, "*It won't be like your dreams...*"

"Oh, sweet Jesus!" yelled Fraser, dropping to his knees, and then he shouted for the store clerk to call 911. He vaguely heard Mary Ash behind him announce quietly that the victim with her throat slashed was called Gudrun.

"I should have been there to help her," he heard Mary Ash say behind him as vivid liquid red poured through his fingers and down his wrist, over the sleeve of his jacket. "I could see it. In my head, I mean. Before I could... just make things that happened to me. But I'm getting stronger. That's why I can make you see stuff now that happened to other people. This one was bad."

"*Mary, help me!*"

"I can't... Not for her. It's already over, you see. I just wanted you to understand."

The guy behind the counter saw what he saw, and what was Mary babbling about? The store clerk recoiled two, three steps, and rushed back to the front counter in his scuffed Doc Martens to grab the phone and call for an ambulance.

"There are others," said Mary Ash. "I'm not really strong enough yet, but I have to try."

Gordon Fraser pleaded for the hemorrhaging victim to *hold on, hold on*, but the girl in his arms literally bled away. Fraser didn't understand how and why her flesh became a pulpy, spongy and bloody mass in his trembling fingers like so many rotting peaches. He didn't know anything about how this girl had once *focused*, willing herself to stand in clean woods and sunshine. Crunching leaves under boots and birds twittering.

Then she was gone completely.

And of course, Mary Ash was gone.

Fraser groaned as his colleague in the New York office, Dorfman, came on the line of his cell phone. He knew he had to be honest. "She's in the wind."

"For fuck's sake!" barked Dorfman. "How the hell did that happen?"

"I don't know! One minute she's looking at charcoal pencils, and the next I'm on my knees, trying to help this chick with her throat slashed, only she wasn't…"

"Wasn't real?" ventured the condescending voice on his cell. "Damn it, Gordon, you read the brief."

Yes, he had read the brief, damn it, and he knew his practically spotless record couldn't insulate him from the recriminations over this fuck-up. But it was one thing to read what the Ash girl could do, quite another to be mesmerized by the result.

"Look, will you get Zabalotny and Ingram to swing by the parents' place? Tell 'em—"

"Fuck, Gordon! We're not going to tell them *anything*. We'll say we're doing a follow-up on her mental state."

"Oh, God, oh, God," muttered Fraser. He'd thought… He thought he could handle it. Handle her.

"Get it together, man."

"The shit she comes out with. All she needs is a shopping cart and a filthy blanket. And what she can do…"

He heard Dorfman sigh on the line. "Well, is there anything in what we said we can *use*? You know that Cale guy they hired is going to have both our asses. What did she say, Fraser? Come on!"

"I don't know!" answered Fraser, wanting to do anything but relive his failure. "Shit about India and Europe—no. She said 'Not India' and—"

"What's not India?"

"She didn't say, man. She said, 'They'll think it's India because of *him*.' Uhhhh, 'somewhere closer in Europe, like her.' Whatever that means. Started talking about olives off the trees. She kept saying the fridge is cold. What's her deal with fridges?"

"Fuck… Oh, Christ."

"What? What is it?"

"She didn't mean a fridge. She meant 'The Fridge'— as in a nickname. The guys at the garage where Emmett Nickelbaum worked called him '*The Fridge*.' She's told people that Nickelbaum isn't dead—he'll be coming back for her."

Yes, it was definitely time to panic.

Then something occurred to Gordon Fraser. Mary Ash had known this, but she had chosen to slip away from him anyway.

"She doesn't want to hide anymore," Fraser said into his cell phone.

Dorfman was skeptical. "How do you know that?"

"I feel it's true," Fraser replied, knowing it was an anemic answer, that he had nothing to base that on. "She said there are others, and that she had to try. Dorfman."

"Yeah?"

"Something terrible is going to happen."

Sarcasm coming down the line: "You feel that, too?"

"Yeah. Dorfman, when we find her—*if* we find her—I need to go on sick leave. You know something? Tell 'em I got to go on sick leave *now*. I'm coming in."

"Gord, there's nothing wrong with you. You lost the girl, and the assignment went to shit, that's all. You'll be okay!"

"No, I'm not, Dorfman. I'm really not."

Because he couldn't stop thinking about what the girl had said. He didn't fully understand how he was aware of what

Mary Ash was about to do, but she had cursed him with the gift of being able to put it together in this moment.

There was no way to follow the girl to prevent what was going to happen, and worse, far worse, was his growing conviction that it should happen, and that he had no right to even dare to interfere.

The Italian girl, Maria Gigliotti, had spent four hours in excruciating terror in a closet, stripped nude and with her wrists and ankles bound with electrical tape. In the moments between the crushing tedium of the darkness alternating with blind fear over what would happen to her, she still couldn't piece together what was her mistake. The great wall of an American with his veil of wiry chin stubble and his stolid dome with the bad comb-over had approached her with an open guidebook.

She should have known better, because his nails were dirty and his clothes didn't look very clean, but it had been eleven o'clock in the morning, and they got so many tourists in Brindisi. He had picked her up like used furniture, his huge mitt of a hand covering her mouth even before they got to the shadows in the narrow alley.

She had cried so hard and for so long in the closet that her reddened eyes ached. The big man had gone away, and hours had passed. She had tried to hold out from natural instinct, making noise through the coarse rag stuffed in her mouth, but in the end she had been forced to urinate in the tiny, black space. It stank in here. It reeked of piss and sweat and fear.

And then she was suddenly elsewhere. Still nude and bound, but it was as if a great hand had scooped her up in the night of the dank closet and opened its palm to reveal

277

her new place. She was somewhere else… She didn't know where, and at the moment it hardly mattered.

But there was a girl here who sat on the gray broadloom carpet across from her and against a wall. She looked about her own age but made no effort to crawl over and *help*. To tear away the sticky electrician's tape and free her or declare she would go and fetch the police. No, she just sat there with her elbows on her knees, two idle fingers playing with a split end of her brunette hair.

Maria Gigliotti noticed there were two bloody stumps where the fingers should have been on her other hand.

"I've been where you are," said Mary Ash in her thin, ethereal voice. "You're right, it's about to get worse. I've been thinking lately… about evil. You know they say soldiers guard us while we sleep, and they have to kill indiscriminately to preserve democracy, liberty, whatever. Whole shebang, right?"

Maria Gigliotti, eyes wide and struggling in her bonds on the carpet, could only *Mmmmmm-mmmmmrrrhhhmmm* as she tried to wrench herself up to a sitting position. She couldn't sit up and fell with a painful thump onto the ragged carpet.

"I've been thinking a lot about that," said Mary Ash. "I used to watch the news, but…" The corners of her mouth turned up in a shy smile. "But I don't really need to watch the news anymore," she added lightly. And she rocked with a singsong laugh at her own joke.

Maria Gigliotti pleaded with her eyes. *Please. Please, help me.*

"I think about little kids in war zones," said Mary Ash in her dreamy, distracted way. "They get hurt or killed, and people just accept it. That's war. Collateral damage. But I'm thinking, no, that's wrong."

"*Mmmm-mmrrrhhhmm.*"

278

"Why do collateral strangers have to die in a war but not when you fight, you know, something else? A single evil? You get what I mean, right? War's a collective evil, but you can fight evil one on one." In a whisper, she added, "We both know about the singular kind..."

Maria Gigliotti watched as the stumps, the two bloody stumps, lifted and brushed through a strand of hair.

"Oh, these. I know. I don't draw anymore so I thought I'd go back to what he left me. What was I saying? Oh, yes... Little kids. Innocents. Evil. Like, nobody thinks about the scale. They'll say it's different, but it isn't. I mean, it's just the scale that's different. It's a scale of one."

Maria Gigliotti sobbed quietly, lying on her side.

"My mom says they found splinters in me," said Mary Ash.

Maria Gigliotti kept begging with her eyes.

"I have to send you back now," the strange girl told her with what sounded like genuine regret. "I don't want that for you, but this is a war. And you're going to be my *bomb*."

The crying, terrified nude victim on the floor strained harder at her bonds, screaming now through the muffling rag that *No, she couldn't go back, please, please, please don't send her back, don't send her—*

But then it was done.

18

Crystal stayed one more night in the hospital and then was discharged. She put on a brave face over how close she had come to death, telling Miller and Tim back at the hotel, "I'm glad that bloody Russian's dead! Doctors tell me I'm going to have a scar."

"I'm sure it'll fade," offered Miller, hovering like an anxious puppy.

She stepped on her toes and gave him a peck on the forehead. "You're a sweet little geek, Andrew. You really are."

Then she casually announced that she had to get some air and strolled out of the hotel lobby.

Miller went upstairs, back to the decks of the *Missouri*. Tim retreated to his own room, checking emails and returning a couple of phone calls from the university back home. An hour passed. Then it was two hours. Then three…

The three of them hardly ever passed much time without checking in with each other, and Miller called Tim to ask if he knew if Crystal was all right. Tim thought he should find out for himself. He had his own concerns. Their detective inspector was tough as nails, sure, but she could have been murdered by Zorich. True, the same could be said for him, but Zorich's blade hadn't sliced into his stomach.

Paris in the late afternoon. Each cobblestone of the tourist areas was glazed with the ocher light of restaurants and shops. The traffic was picking up, and there was a cacophony of voices and marching feet outside the Métro stations. Tim sent a text message to Crystal, wondering where she was, and within minutes, she replied with a one-word text that surprised him: *Beaubourg*. She hadn't written anything else. That could mean *I'm fine, leave me alone*, or it could mean she expected him to come around.

When he arrived, he found her hanging out in the gently dipping courtyard in front of the Centre Pompidou, listening as a young black busker with dreadlocks played acoustic guitar, singing Bob Marley's "Redemption Song." The busker's voice was gentle and clear, and Tim watched for a little while as Crystal smiled and sang along under her breath.

"Hey."

"Hey," she echoed.

"Something we missed here?"

"No, no." She sounded surprised by his question. "I came here for me. This place always felt special for me. I mean, before we ran into Zorich and Tvardovsky…You could see jugglers and musicians and street performers. It used to be magic here. I wanted to find that again."

He sat down beside her on the gently rising slope of the cobbles. The reggae ballad mixed with a bell from a passing cyclist, and a young girl ten feet away laughed as her boyfriend lifted her in a hug and swung her around. And it was all fine. It was special, just as Crystal wanted.

Her fingers played with the gold crucifix dangling from her necklace. "You used to work in London, didn't you?

Do you know the Notre Dame de France church right off Leicester Square? I used to love popping in there. I mean, you know I'm not Catholic, but there are certain beautiful places... Doesn't matter what you are."

He did know it. It was an unassuming little treasure of a church in a narrow street off the movie theaters, the Häagen-Dazs outlet and the rowdiness of the square. In one of its chapels were simple but stunningly beautiful modern murals by the French writer and poet Jean Cocteau. Those who didn't know his work probably mistook them for Picassos, but they probably enjoyed them just the same. Tim had often felt the impulse to stroll in and refresh himself by gazing at those murals. They were so simple—like a child's foolscap drawing—yet lovingly rendered and spiritually inspiring. It was nice to know that he and Crystal, unknown to each other back then, had shared a similar taste in one of London's overlooked gems.

They sat there for a long moment, and then she turned to him and asked, "What did you want to be when you grew up? When you were very little—you know what I mean."

Tim laughed. "Got to think about that one. Huh, let's see... An astronaut."

"Really?"

"Yeah, why not? My dad was an engineer, and I suppose that influenced me. I liked space stuff, read books on Mars. But by junior high school, it was clear I was terrible at math and sciences."

"And a diplomat was born."

"I couldn't get away from physics quick enough. What about you? Little Crystal with her hair in braids."

She smiled and watched the crowd in the square. "I wanted to be a teacher. My dreams seem so modest now, but that's the way it was for us. My mum had a good job as a nurse, and that was all you could hope for sometimes where I came from—a good job. And when I got older, I thought it would be amazing to be a uni professor. Respect, tenure, working on *ideas*... Never even imagined being a copper."

"You can still be a professor, if you want to leave the force."

"Yeah."

The busker played on, and he noticed in the dim light that her eyes were wet.

"Crystal..."

"I'm fine," she said. "It's stupid, really. I've had close shaves before—well, you know some of it. They fast-tracked me for a unit that faces some scary, dangerous people—terrorists, gangsters—and you don't fight them alone, you have a team, you have resources, and... I don't even know why it's bugging me. Yes, I do. *I do*. It was just us, you and me, and Zorich wasn't some stupid thug, he's evil, he's part of real evil. And he cut me..."

"And you put him down."

"Barely," she said, and her body suddenly shuddered. "Christ, Tim, why don't you have someone better? Why don't they have the good sense to throw someone *bloody better* at this?"

"I don't think there is anyone better."

"That's sweet, and no offense, yeah? But you're not qualified to know."

"I know a little something about evil, because I met it before," he answered. "I know that I was a clumsy, terrified idiot that night, and you saved my ass. I know that I don't *want* anyone better."

She leaned in and kissed him.

Her mouth was soft, her tongue exploring his with an eager grace, and he felt her fingertips on the back of his neck. As she broke from him, he felt suspended in a powerful moment of intimacy playing over and over, the busker music now somehow faraway, and yet he was still in the present, watching her lean away and smile.

It was a brief smile, one to cover her nervousness as she asked, "I bet you were a shit boyfriend when you were younger, weren't you?"

"I was," he laughed. "Ambitious workaholic. I took her for granted. Her—them, all of my lovers."

"I was rubbish at relationships, too," she said, and he felt her warm, soft hand still on his neck. He loved the touch of her fingertips on his skin. "And now?"

"Now I like to think I've found a balance. At least I hope so."

"So do I," said Crystal.

Without a word, they rose, both knowing they were headed back to their hotel.

They went to his room, and before he could say anything as they stepped inside, she was in his arms, kissing him passionately and coaxing him towards the bedroom. Their mouths hardly parted as he wrestled free of his jacket, and she kicked off her shoes. She tugged and worked his buttons, opening his shirt and then taking his hands to put them on her breasts. He felt his legs collapse under him as she sat down on the edge of his mattress, and on his knees in an almost worshipping posture, he sucked a nipple into his mouth.

Her breasts were exquisite, and her waist was a perfect hourglass beneath her clothes, her brown tummy flat and perfect. Tim's index finger idly traced a line along the black stitches. *You won't scar*, he assured her. *You'll heal.* She smiled at him but said nothing. From her face, he could tell she wasn't really that vain, worrying about a seam of old injury along her belly. Hungrily, he tugged on her unzipped skirt, taking her panties with it. She was wet to the touch, shuddering with the pleasure of his fingers exploring her core. Then he climbed on top of her, already hard.

"Wait a minute," he said huskily, knowing any self-control was fading away.

"Oh, no, please," she said, not wanting the moment to break. "Tim..."

"But I don't understand."

"The world is going to hell," she answered, her soft hands slipping up the small of his back to feel his shoulder blades. "And I want... comfort. Tenderness. Warmth. I know you're a good man. And I like you. What more do you need?"

She kissed him again, their mouths opening for each other with a more languid energy. When her head fell back against the pillow again, she said, "I haven't seen good in a long time, Tim, and you've been acting decent and keeping your head while all this chaos is going on around us. I don't know what to believe anymore, so I want a break. I want time to stop for a little bit."

"Okay."

Au Dauphin often got the word "unassuming" attached to it in reviews, but it was a likeable bistro in Paris facing the Place André Malraux and the Palais Royal. The chefs were from Biarritz, and the dishes were French and Basque. Enough tourists came in that Tim and Emily Derosier could talk and be ignored—that is, if she showed up.

He had learned enough about her by now to order a Cabernet, what he suspected was her favorite sort of wine. This is beyond surreal, he thought. You're about to meet a woman from the flapper era in twenty-first-century Paris. Surreal, but not impossible, because he had stood facing Emily Derosier once before as she sifted through research online at the Centre Pompidou. He half expected her to plunk down in the seat across from him wearing a large sunhat and a movie-star smile, as if her cryptic gift of the painting had been an overture to a romantic chase, and he had now somehow proven himself.

Thanks to the ever-cooperative MI6, Crystal had set him up with spy gear in the form of a pinhole camera in his lapel pin and a carefully hidden mike in his tie. Since Derosier had seen her before, she would monitor the conversation from a surveillance van a block up from the restaurant. As well, a couple of French plain-clothes detectives fluent in English sat at a table only four feet away.

He should have watched for his approaching guest or anything out of the ordinary, but he found his concentration wandering. From his research, he had discovered that Emily Derosier had frequented an Italian bar around here, now long since gone. The story went that she "shared" a handsome young pâtissier with Cole Porter in a rear booth. Another story went that the American writer and arts patron Max Eastman, while on a visit over to Paris, had talked the innocent young socialite out of wasting her time with a Communist organization by telling her horror stories about Stalinist Russia. Then there was the time she was supposed to act in a silent movie written by Jean Cocteau, one promising a more frank and provocative depiction of sexuality than Hedy Lamarr in *Ecstasy*. But two weeks before shooting was to commence, she had been murdered.

She intrigued him, this flapper whose story was cut short before it became legend. While stationed in Paris, Tim hadn't given in to the romanticism that was a packaged product for tourists here, but he was still amused by the idea that, once upon a time, you could rub shoulders with so many future bohemian giants, seeing them as ordinary human beings before they were trapped in sepia photographs like moths in amber.

"Ditzy," said a voice in front of him.

He snapped to attention.

Emily Derosier. Seated. Relaxed. Here, without him seeing her walk up.

Wearing a simple cream blouse and beige skirt as if she had come in for lunch from an insurance office up the street. The French detectives seemed to take no notice of her, and Tim realized they had been foolishly naïve in planning surveillance. What she had done back in the courtyard in front of the Centre Pompidou…

"Ditzy?" he echoed.

"You were curious what my friend Josephine Baker was like," she answered coolly. "She was feather-brained, but she had a sweet soul. She enjoyed life—food, sex, animals, travel, men. And women. When you grow up as poor as she did, wearing the same dress and going barefoot every day, I suppose it gives you appetites for more than just luxury. She was the most vivacious woman I ever knew."

Tim paused, thinking he had to tread carefully. "You miss her."

"That's not nearly as subtle as I expected, Mr. Cale. You were doing so well. You have genuine interest in what my life was like, my *time*, and that made you so much more interesting than others. I would expect them to pester me with the usual."

"Where you went and what happened to you after you died," said Tim, nodding. "But those are reasonable questions."

"But not *your* first questions, which is why I wasn't expecting you to be a bore."

She flashed a winning smile at a waiter and picked up the wine menu. "The Cabernet was a good choice, it was very thoughtful of you," she said to Tim. "Let me return the compliment by getting us a Merlot I think you'll like."

The waiter nodded and went away.

"I think you would have liked the age I lived in very much," she said, resting her chin on her laced fingers. "You're right—there *was* far more sex going on than historians believe. Far more open-mindedness and of course, far more silliness when it came to politics. More literacy and more wit, but I'm trying to be fair. I can't say I like all the people running around now with their tiny earplugs, recreating privacy and sense stimulation because they lack the time and the room for recreational pursuits. Josephine, Cole, Max—we lived in the moment. We never had to learn about Zen for that."

Tim watched the waiter fetch a new bottle from the wine rack and said, "They don't see you. I mean those I came with. The same tricks you pulled outside the Beaubourg you're using to disguise your presence here now, aren't you? The *akinetopsia*, the mind reading—"

"You over-estimate what the resurrected victims can do."

"You're not a resurrected victim."

She looked at him sternly. "I am, Mr. Cale, in my own way. I'm merely one who's come back after a significant delay. As for 'tricks': what's being done is the planting of a suggestion. The detectives, the others—they're under the impression that Miss Anyanike has stepped in to talk to you. Even she thinks she's making casual chit-chat with you at this table right now and will go back soon to her seat in that vehicle. It's not that they can't or don't see me, it's that this temporary idea is overriding their senses."

Tim studied the plain-clothes detectives for a moment. Amazing. They remained perfectly oblivious. He wanted to call out to them, but her eyes asked him silently to give up on the idea. He could tell that she would interpret this as some sort of mild betrayal.

"It's not such a clever trick. Did you know that two percent of the population has what's called *prosopagnosia*?"

"I have no idea what that is, but you're starting to sound like Miller."

"Face blindness. These poor people... They literally can't recognize others."

"But that's not what you're doing here," said Tim. "You've substituted Crystal for you in their minds."

"Yes. I just find the other condition interesting as a point of trivia. It's interesting how we see people. Your friend, Dr. Miller, will tell you that when you first spot a friend in the crowd on the street, you may not really *see* him either. Your mind has to play catch-up and match the physical description in front of you with your image of the person from memory. I suppose it gets more technical than that, but you get the gist. I can't maintain it for long."

"Good to know."

"It's not a slip of the tongue in admitting weakness, Mr. Cale. I'm not your enemy."

She reached across to rest her hand on his. Tim felt the softness, the quiet charge of sensual electricity as he'd feel with any attractive woman, and though he didn't move his hand, he knew he showed surprise.

"Yes, Tim. I'm real."

The waiter brought back the new bottle, placing it next

to the Cabernet. Out of pure habit, Tim waited for the man to go, though he wondered if the waiter saw Emily Derosier or the illusion of Crystal Anyanike. He poured glasses of Merlot for both of them. She was right. It was a nice wine, and seeing his reaction, she crinkled her nose at him, biting her bottom lip. This was the mischievous British expat that had once weaved her spell only a couple of streets away.

Don't get seduced, he told himself.

"What do you want?"

"Ah. Not 'Why are you here?' You'd rather be impertinent."

"Fine," he shot back. "If you like, we can start with 'Why me?' The only reason for you to make contact is because you must have information related to the Karma Booth. That's an assumption, but I think it's a reasonable one. The resurrected victims—sorry, *other* resurrected victims—have no memories of what happened to them between their deaths and their returns. You didn't come out of that Booth scared and confused by the future. You *hid*, and then you sought me out. Maybe you are Emily Derosier, but you're also something more, and you have an agenda. So why not seek out Weintraub? He's the physics genius who understands the Booth. For that matter, why not go to Orlando Braithewaite? He gave us these damn things, from what I understand."

She paused, seeming to choose her words carefully. "Orlando Braithewaite is not your immediate problem."

"And you're here to help."

"Yes," she said.

"So I ask again: Why come to me?"

"Do you know why you were given this job?" she asked back. "You think it's because you're one of the few they could trust who has seen the impossible. But what the officials trusted—what is serving you best now—is that more elusive quality of insight you're famous for."

He didn't want to be distracted by flattery and pressed again: "You said there was an immediate problem. What is it?"

"You were correct about the pattern of the resurrection victims, Tim. Heightened empathy connects us all." And as he stared at her, she added, "No, I couldn't observe the moment you said this to Weintraub and Miller, but the conversation is still in your memory, and you've been puzzling over what that connection of empathy means ever since you suggested it to them. You have insight. There is no insight without empathy. Where do you think such a gift comes from?"

"If you're about to tell me it's a gift from Heaven—"

"I don't know anything about Heaven."

"Crystal will be disappointed."

Emily Derosier sat back and smiled, almost as if she had expected this reaction from him all along, as if she had hoped for it and was proud he had come through a modest test. "You're not surprised by my answer. Because you don't believe. Again, this is the kind of unordinary thinking that made you the right person to come to. I must say you're showing remarkable restraint in not asking where I arrived from."

"You told me if I asked, I'd be a bore like others," he reminded her.

"So you would. But that's not the reason, is it? It's because you don't think I'll be truthful with you."

He ignored this, sitting forward and trying to be casual as he took another sip of the Merlot. "You still haven't told me what the immediate problem is."

"Viktor Limonov."

"Limonov... What do you know of him?"

"Things that you need to know."

"He's a war criminal and a sociopath," snapped Tim. "And he's so far demonstrated he's still a regular human. Or are you going to tell me that going through the Booth gave him abilities like the resurrected victims?"

"No," she said tensely, all playfulness from her voice gone. "No, he's the same man—for the moment, as far as I know. But he doesn't want to stay that way. He actually wants to leave this earth."

"If he wants to shuffle off his mortal coil, they gave him a chance in Amsterdam."

She shook her head. "You're missing it. You're missing the point completely. You're assuming Limonov came out of the Booth in Delhi *by choice*."

19

Tim felt his heart quicken. He looked to the two French detectives, needing someone else to share in his disbelief. *What?* Limonov came back because he *couldn't* be executed in the Karma Booth?

"Damn it, enough games! That couple hunting you at the Beaubourg—Ana Tvardovsky and Dmitry Zorich. They're tied in with Limonov—"

"Yes. Very good."

"They were trying to find *you* for Limonov. What the hell is this about? If you really want to help us, then *help us*! I watched Zorich die. *Crystal shot him.* And the bastard grinned at me like it was a joke! What makes Limonov different from him? From any other murderer? And just what are you? Why did you come back and where are you from? What does a psychopathic war criminal want with you? What is that thing you sent me in the picture frame? Miller says it's alive—"

"It's not," she broke in. "And it is."

"The truth!"

"India but not India," she said quickly, making him stop and calm down immediately.

He waited for her to go on.

"You were there, Tim, near the border. And the monks demonstrated to you a horrifying punishment for evil acts committed. You've tried to reconcile that power with what appeared to you to be a lack of compassion, a summary judgment. But you didn't give in to a reflexive impulse of believing in myths. Where others see a divine hand, you felt a vague presence of... colonialism."

"What are you telling me?" he whispered.

"Once upon a time, Viktor Limonov was one of those monks, interfering from another tier of existence," she said, keeping her voice low and confessional.

"From where you came from?"

"I didn't come from the same place as Viktor Limonov," she replied with a note of disgust. "I was born in Kingston-upon-Thames in Surrey, and I lived and died at twenty-nine years old in Paris, France. Viktor Limonov is far older than me—far older than you can imagine. All I can make you understand for now is that there are multiple planes, tiers, levels—whatever you wish to call them. Think of it as..."

She paused for an instant and then, inspired, said, "Think of it in terms of *evolution* if you like. Limonov was one of those monks, Tim, but as much as he's been a monster here on earth, he excelled in cruelty in that form. There was a war, a horrible war that consumed two whole realms of existence near the one where I... where many human beings go. When it was over, they exiled him. They dumped Limonov on the bottom rung of corporeal existence here on earth. No matter where he is, no matter what he is, his consciousness has never forgotten what he *was*, and he has never forgiven his exile. He's slithered and crawled and scuttled and galloped and run his way back up to humanity, and from humanity to a position of influence and corruption. He can't be allowed to cross over."

"Cross over into what?"

"Those other realms of existence."

"But the Booth…"

"He can't find his way back through the Booth. He'll seek other means."

"If you know all this, if you've been sent back by someone," asked Tim impatiently, "why can't *you* stop him yourself?"

"I told you. You over-estimate what the resurrection victims can do. They're still quite human, I assure you, despite having abilities that allow some of them to fight back. So am I right now, in fragile ways you would scarcely believe."

Tim studied her beautiful face, her eyes so tender in their sincerity. "He murdered you. Didn't he?"

"No. By then Limonov had been exiled to this plane of existence, trying to climb back up. I was murdered by one of the monks, actually by one of those you met in India." Before he could interject, she added quickly, "It doesn't matter which one, really. And I've stopped caring. But yes, I remember the stranger in my apartment. I can remember how he spouted self-righteous platitudes after he stabbed me the first time. The first of many. It hurt so much. My killer said that I had gained an understanding of things human beings weren't meant to know in their lifetimes. So he would 'help' me progress. I did."

"These monks are your enemy," said Tim. "The enemy of wherever you come from."

"Enemy is too strong a word," she answered. "Let's just say where I… went, we don't approve of their methods, though sometimes we can understand their verdicts. We'd prefer humanity here figure things out for itself. Like I said before, their approach is *colonial*. Their methods are loud, obnoxious, vulgar. Limonov was once one of their own, but they made a mistake, and they could make everyone everywhere pay for it. And they're not strong enough to stop him on their own."

"I don't understand," said Tim. "You're saying he's mortal—you're mortal. Wouldn't shooting him or—or if he was given a lethal injection, wouldn't that send him back to where he wants to go?"

"It doesn't work like that."

"Damn it! Then how does it work? You talked about evolution. Colonialism. Is that it? We accidentally opened a gate, and now we see our zoo handlers? We're not 'ready' for the true reality of our existence, I suppose? What's the problem? You'll get back to us when we're mature enough? Is that—"

"No! No, it's nothing like that—"

Tim reached across the table and gripped her forearm. "*What are you?* What is Limonov? What's happened to the Karma Booth victims?"

"Let go of me," she said quietly. "Please."

He resisted for a moment. He hadn't known what to expect with her, and she had appeared so suddenly, he was afraid she might blink out of the restaurant like a passing thought the way she had come.

"*You* people, you on Earth—*you* happened to the victims. The Karma Booth interfered with their natural progress. Because of your choices."

"Wait a minute... Progress?"

"Yes, progress. Everything evolves, Timothy. No one is trying to keep the truth from you. Not even Limonov—he's past caring, which is part of what makes him so dangerous." She looked across the restaurant, then back at him warily, as if she were afraid he might physically impose himself on her again and prevent her from leaving. "I can't stay."

"It's not enough," he said, feeling frustration leak out of him from every pore but knowing he couldn't stop her.

"It has to be for now," she answered, lingering by the table. "You have answers. All of you here—even me when I lived here the first time—have access to the answers. You'll figure out more in the days ahead, and when it's safe... I said I would help you. Listen to me closely, my dear. There are natural laws to all things. Even if something fantastic has broken through into what you perceive as reality, it follows and must conform to the natural laws from where it came."

"Even you with your mind tricks?" he demanded.

"I told you. I was born here. I'm a woman here like any other in most ways. Limonov is gathering strength, but he's still trapped in this plane of existence, one where he has limits even if he's partially successful. Whatever extraordinary power he has is because he's stolen it. *Remember* that. I have to go..."

"You've barely told me anything!" he complained. "If humanity is supposed to learn some great truth then you'll have to spell it out plain because—"

She made a high moan of exasperation, gripping the table with her small hands. She seemed to hover on the edge of a swoon from pain. "Tim, *please*. Stop...! Just *stop*. Why can't all of you simply be here? I told you how back when I lived, we gloried in the now, we enjoyed what was here, and it was real enough for us! Maybe because of the Great War. Maybe that was the reason, but the reason doesn't matter—there shouldn't have been a reason. Just the joy! Why does your morality need an outside force or influence to make it true and right and good for you *here*?"

He couldn't say anything. It was the way he had always wanted to live, the way he had tried to live. And now, by her declaration out loud, she was demanding he shed all embarrassment for his private conviction and adopt a new courage, one that didn't abandon curiosity but accepted that the world was as he found it.

She sighed and leaned in close to his face. "Yes—*yes,* you will live and die and go on to a new level, Tim, because everything evolves. And if you kill and rape and torture and steal, you hurt yourself and your own evolution. But it's an evolution that has pertinence *here* just as much as for the next level. There's *no* revelation waiting for your lovely Miss Anyanike or you or anyone else! Or if there is, I haven't climbed to it yet, but I revel in where I am just as I reveled in the life I lived *here.*"

"Then where is it that you came from? After you died? What is that place?"

"It's different. That's all. There are wonders like the painting I gave you. Pleasures sensual and textured in their delights and with intellectual splendors to challenge a contemplative mind. Like *here.* There are vistas to explore and microscopic anomalies and shorelines of infinite beauty! Like *here.* Here, where they're squandered. Why do you think I was at peace after Ceylon? I discovered great things are in store for us, but we already have such wonders here!"

She laughed, a beautiful, self-deprecating laugh, and added, "Don't you see? I was murdered because the monks are as flawed as all of you! As all of us out there! There is more wisdom with knowledge, Tim, but that doesn't mean more discipline over wants and ambitions and fears. They were paranoid I might share a great revelation when the truth is simple: it's just *different.* They didn't want all of you to know we're not gods out there!"

She leaned over and cradled his face in her hand for a moment. "You are so gifted, you have no idea. Haven't you guessed? The others went away and came back with empathy. But you..."

He sat, stunned, not knowing what to say to that.

"Monsieur Cale—"

One of the French detectives at the table nearby was coming out of whatever she had done to them. He and his female colleague sat staring in disbelief that Emily Derosier could suddenly, impossibly be *there*, just as Tim had been amazed only a short while ago.

Tim came back to himself, putting aside her tantalizing compliment and knowing he still needed answers. The detective could wait. "But Limonov..."

"Imagine a Hitler or Stalin gaining abilities like the ones you saw in Mary Ash, in Geoff Shackleton," said Emily. "Remember, Limonov was exiled to a place where such abilities were incompatible with the natural laws. Here: this place, your existence. Now the Karma Booth has upset all that. He has to be extinguished. *He* should be your priority. I have to go now."

From the corner of his eye, Tim saw Crystal rushing into the restaurant. Her eyes were dark, and he could read a mild panic, a protective anger as she hurried to what she must have thought was his rescue.

"What about the Booth?" he asked. "Wait!"

As he stood up, she was suddenly very close, stealing a kiss from him and smiling at his bewilderment. *What are you?* A woman. The answer was a woman. Here. Now.

Crystal hung back, almost as surprised, clearly uncertain what to do. Then Emily Derosier reached out and took her hand. "Sorry, I couldn't resist him, anymore than you could! But he's yours. You'll know what I've told him."

Crystal stood still as their mystery woman let go and walked—in no rush at all—out of the restaurant like any other patron.

"She's leaving," said Crystal.

"But you don't want to stop her either," said Tim.

"No."

"You don't think we can."

"No," said Crystal. "Do you think it's true? That there's no great revelation waiting?"

So she had kept her word, thought Tim. Heightened empathy, sharing of thoughts—the "illusion" of Crystal sitting at the table instead of Emily wasn't such an illusion after all. Crystal must have been present all along in some form, passively listening, retaining all that she heard and awakened at Emily's convenience.

"Tim," Crystal tried again. "Do you think it's true?"

"I... I don't know."

In this moment, it hardly mattered what he believed. His witness sounded credible enough. And Emily Derosier's words were on rewind and playing over and over in his mind: *I discovered great things are in store for us, but we already have such wonders here.*

Thinking over the encounter later, he decided Emily had never intended to be deliberately cryptic. He didn't know why she had rushed off. Perhaps she was still in danger from Limonov's network of accomplices, though she had said nothing about this. Given the power she had demonstrated outside the Beaubourg, it was difficult to imagine. He couldn't help but wonder whether she flitted back and forth between their plane of existence and what now must be the one that was native to her. But if that were so, then coming through the Karma Booth would have been unnecessary, especially when she was so easily detected.

It's different, she had told him. *That's all.*

But there are wonders there, waiting to be explored.

He was convinced—as was Crystal, his witness—that Emily Derosier had mysteriously arrived to help. They certainly needed help. It was possible she could be acting in an interest they couldn't fathom, at least not yet or maybe not ever, but he couldn't see what there was to gain in arranging the meeting and bothering to confide details to Tim at all.

Orlando Braithewaite was "not their immediate problem." Interesting how she had put that. And she had suggested that Limonov craved a power beyond human comprehension. Could it be that simple? That, while he might have existed once in an advanced realm, he was no more than a predator, just as he was in the human life that the world was familiar with now? At least we know what's he done here, thought Tim. His tortures and cruelties had been enough for a sentence of death before.

Hunt Limonov. He should be the priority, she said. He found it strange that Emily should issue no warning over the Karma Booth. Mankind had opened a door to a spot where morality intersected with the physics of actual existence, though she wanted to impress on him that mankind was supposed to live by its own laws as if within a closed system. But if the Booth had upset these natural laws, why wasn't she urging him to get the technology destroyed, banned, kept out of the hands of those who might abuse it?

She said there had been a war. She said that war was over.

He wanted to believe she had come to help, but he wondered if he should accept all that she had told him.

And he found himself wanting to believe the vision she had imparted, that there were multiple realities beyond the stained-glass Sunday school hierarchy, still elusive enough for Man to no longer fear death, but to treat existence beyond lives here as a new ocean waiting for exploration, with fresh and lush continents.

It was far more comforting than Heaven, because she suggested—no, she practically *confirmed*—that life here was not a test. A good person was an end in him or herself, and that even in failure, Nature wasted nothing. There was redemption and a reward past these humble molecules and cells and fluids: knowledge itself, the promise of existence different than before and stimulating enough to last whatever duration of "life" was given the next time.

It occurred him just then why the Booth had rejected Limonov.

I know what you want with the Booth victims, thought Tim.

He didn't know how or why he knew. He just felt the truth of it. The precious insight she had complimented him on was working. He hoped, he almost prayed, he was right this time.

Maria Gigliotti slept. Exhausted after her traumatic return to the dark, stinking closet, her body simply gave up on sobbing, sweating, shaking, *dreading* what was to come. And so another hour must have passed, and then the closet door was rudely yanked open with a creak, and the big man was there. He'd decided it was time to amuse himself with his new toy. His meaty fist grabbed hold of her ankles, and as he dragged her out, Maria yelled through the tape because of the rug burn searing into her back and shoulder.

Oh, God, this is it, she thought. *No, no, no*, and she could understand him now, just as she had understood the strange brunette girl, though she had never taken any lessons in English. Perversely, she wondered in spite of her mounting terror: *How can I understand him?* Talking, muttering crude things to her: "Going to sink into you, mmm, yeah…"

Impossibly, suddenly fluent in English, just as she had understood the brunette girl's words.

And she knew his name was Emmett Nickelbaum, and she knew now what he had done to the girl, Mary Ash, and a box-cutter blade in his hand slit the electrician's tape binding her ankles so that he could pry her legs apart and start doing the same terrible things to her. It made it so much worse, the knowing.

"Yeah, you squirm!" growled Nickelbaum. "Squirm for me, go on!"

And then something happened that Maria didn't understand. It was as if her whole trembling body had become a searchlight, its beam pouring out of her at an impossible wattage. Blinding in its beam, driving Nickelbaum back so that he flung his arms instinctively in front of his face.

"*Ahhhrrrrggghhhh!*"

The light dimmed, fading, and Nickelbaum jumped up in a feral rage, staring at her, then turning and rushing to the doorways leading to other rooms in the decrepit slum apartment. Satisfied that no one else was here, that it was a trick of the light or his imagination, he panted with renewed sadistic lust and dropped to his knees, grabbing Maria's legs again. She screamed through her gag, and he didn't care—

Then there was another volcanic burst of light, forcing him away. Only as the light faded this time, he kept on screaming, now grabbing his temples.

The light has gone into his head, thought Maria Gigliotti. And something else, too. Strangling his consciousness, like so many cluster migraines, piled on top of each other.

The strange brunette girl with the two bloody stumps for fingers sat on the floor in a corner. She wasn't there before but now she was. Mary Ash. Watching him. Watching him suffer.

"Splinters," she said softly.

She stood up and walked carefully over to Nickelbaum.

With a hideous strength, he opened his eyes, staring in terror at his former victim. It was a sensation he hadn't shown since he was pushed into the Karma Booth. "You…"

"Me."

Maria Gigliotti lay on her side, hands still bound behind her back, mouth taped, but her own fear was beginning to subside. Instead, she was captivated by the unfolding spectacle. She couldn't help but watch, but something told her a reckoning was coming for Emmett Nickelbaum as horrific as the tortures he had planned for her.

"Splinters," Mary Ash repeated, her voice still gentle as she spoke to him. "It was, like, so obvious when you think about it. It's how *he's* going to lose, too. I mean I can't predict, but I'm pretty sure." Dreamily, she looked towards Maria Gigliotti cowering on the floor and commented, "Her, yeah… That wasn't me who took her away. I mean it was, but it wasn't. It was something I borrowed."

Emmett Nickelbaum shook on his patch of molding carpet. His eyes rolled up in the back of his head, and then he suddenly, explosively vomited. Sweat poured down his massive skull, drool and specks of leftover vomit on his chin stubble, and he tried to rise. Couldn't. His eyes squeezed tight, and he gritted his teeth in agony. And Maria thought once more: *The light—whatever it is, whatever it means—has gone into his mind.*

She was still talking. Mary Ash. In her singsong, ethereal way. Taking the time and courtesy to explain.

"They moved Geoff Shackleton after you killed the boy," she said. "I knew that wasn't good enough. So I got away from those agent guys and reached out to him today. Little thoughts, but they did the trick. He heard me. He brought me right to him, and I made him understand, and he got it. He's pretty cool... He got right away what had to be done. He didn't loan me the power—he *gave* it to me. 'Here, go ahead.' I mean wow. Isn't that nice? Wish I had a teacher like him in school."

Nickelbaum crawled. If nothing else, he could die with his hands around a throat. It didn't matter if it belonged to Mary Ash or the Italian girl. Maria Gigliotti, staring, gagged, understood this and whimpered a warning, but Mary Ash was serene.

"Don't worry."

Nickelbaum screamed as another psychic bolt made him give up the attempt.

Mary Ash took a step closer to him. "I want you to know 'cause of what we had—I mean, it was so *intimate*—that I think you'll appreciate this. The teacher gave me his ability so I could go and get her—"

She turned slightly, indicating Maria bound on the floor, as if Nickelbaum was paying attention and not clutching his skull, dry-heaving and moaning.

"So that's where that comes from. That's him. He gave it to me. Moving people around like Monopoly pieces. We can do stuff like that, but I guess you already know, huh? I mean that little boy—he made Mr. Cale taste music. That's where I got the idea from... the borrowing." She pursed her lips together, suddenly remembering something and added, "Oh, right, I guess you haven't met him! Well, you get it, I'm sure. So my point is: what you're feeling? *All* of what you're feeling? That's me."

She crouched down and savagely yanked his greasy long hair, pulling his head up, forcing him to look at her.

But her voice was still quiet. "That's all *me*. My idea, all mine. I knew ever since I came back I could be in you, but that wouldn't be good enough. Then I thought, okay, why be selfish?"

Nickelbaum stared. He was still drooling, eyes shining and reflecting and bouncing with the light trapped now behind his pupils, and in every reflection was a scream. He gibbered and shook and stared and stared and *stared* at Mary Ash. Two fingers and a thumb and two bloody stumps gripped a lock of his filthy hair as she grinned wide and asked:

"How is it in there now?"

No answer.

She leaned in even closer and dropped her voice to a whisper. But Maria Gigliotti could still make out the words as she told him: "I found a secret! You'll go on and on and on, thanks to this. Isn't that great? What do you think? Hey, Nickelbaum... Are you *hard*?"

And then Emmett Nickelbaum died. Or at least he seemed to die. It was more as if his body shriveled as a pear or apple would shrivel after days of being left out. When the eyes blinked, Maria Gigliotti burst into fresh sobs of trauma. It was too much to take, far too much to take.

Mary Ash turned around and her eyes brimmed with tears. "I'm sorry," she said.

She sunk down next to the terrified, sobbing girl and gently pulled the electrician's tape off her mouth, but Maria Gigliotti couldn't say anything for a full minute, only crying. She heard Mary Ash take the box-cutters and slit the tape binding her wrists, and it was so good to be free. In spite of the muscle ache from hours in that position, she found herself hugging Mary Ash like a toddler.

And Mary Ash rocked her with a maternal embrace.

"He didn't get to do what he wanted to you yet, but he did enough. Here…"

Maria looked up at her, not comprehending, and Mary Ash repeated *here*. Then Maria felt different. It was like fresh air in her lungs. Warm sun as you emerged from the ocean. She was naked and soiled, but it didn't matter anymore. She felt clean. She felt as if she had woken up from a deep, restful sleep, all of her senses sharpened and honed and eager to be tested. As she stood up with the peculiar brunette girl, she felt something more, and then she understood what this sensation was.

"Yeah," said Mary Ash. "It's good, isn't it? I got to go now, but I think you'll be okay. I'm sorry I used you, but… It's good now, right? We're good?"

Maria Gigliotti slowly nodded, unsure why Mary Ash was still silently crying. It was as if Maria's forgiveness would provide a temporary respite, but whatever this girl still carried with her would forever drag and scrape behind her like chained weights. Whatever Mary Ash had done for her, she couldn't do for herself.

"Good luck," she said, and then she was gone.

Maria Gigliotti found the tattered scraps that were once her clothes, did the best she could to cover herself, and then padded barefoot two floors down to knock on a door where she heard music. A Somali woman holding a six-month-old baby in her arms waved for her to come in, come in, and then she phoned the police, and they arrived soon enough. And Mary Ash proved correct. Maria Gigliotti knew she was okay.

20

"Think of antibiotic resistance."

Tim had suggested he brief the others on his ideas down at the lab where the French allowed Miller to work. Crystal was paying close attention, while their neurologist looked impatient, bristling at Tim daring to use medical terminology.

Noting his sour expression, Tim added, "It's only a metaphor, Andrew. I don't care for now if it's imprecise, I'm trying to make a point. Evil, if we're to accept the word of Emily Derosier, is *real*. I don't know about you guys, but I can't think of it as something outside human experience that's supernatural. It only makes sense to me as a disease."

"You think Limonov is *E. coli* bacteria or something?" asked Miller, unimpressed.

"No," said Tim, arching his eyebrows at the bizarre idea. "I'm saying Limonov was exiled here and dumped on the bottom rung as Emily said. But if we evolve into higher forms with each incarnation—if we earn brownie points as we go, advancing up the line—how could Viktor Limonov *stay* evil? How could he grow in influence and power? Emily said his consciousness has never forgotten what was done to him. He's never forgiven it lifetime after lifetime. So what about all the ones who have followed him? They can't have come from the same realm, at least not all of them. Some must have been born here, and they must have led ordinary human lives once, just as Emily Derosier had."

Crystal nodded, understanding his point. "You're saying over time, Viktor Limonov built up a resistance to the karmic power that would push him back down the evolutionary scale. He can't wind up as a bug or a dog or a shark anymore, he can only bounce back into human incarnation."

"Exactly," said Tim. "There are terrible things that people do—the *regular* terrible—and then there's Pol Pot. Hitler. Stalin."

Miller frowned, still not quite sold. "So you're saying beings like Limonov are the flip side of the karma equation?"

"Exactly. He and others like him don't build up 'merit' if you want to put it in Buddhist or Hindu terms. They grow stronger with each failed attempt to inoculate the universe against them. The Booth couldn't take him elsewhere because all those neighborhoods on the other side don't want him! Or, if you want to keep it in karmic terms, he just plain hasn't earned his graduation. But he's had one clear advantage over regular sadists and psychopaths like Dmitry Zorich and Emmett Nickelbaum. He has the knowledge of what he was and of these extraordinary, imported natural laws Emily talked about, the things the resurrected victims can *do*."

"So what's he trying to do with them?" asked Miller. "He's killing them off so he can, like, collect them or something? I mean, how does that work?"

"I don't know exactly," said Tim, shaking his head. "I don't know if what he's doing works at all, or if he just *thinks* it will. Emily said he has to be stopped. That implies to me he could become successful."

"Shit," muttered Miller. "I think... I know."

Tim and Crystal waited.

"Think of the octopus again," explained Miller, and when the two of them looked at him blankly, he added, "Camouflage? Bait-and-switch. Hiding, you get it? Okay. You guys told me this Derosier chick said the stuff that's fantastic still has to be real and follow rules."

"She said," Crystal corrected him, "that there are natural laws, and even if something fantastic has broken through into our reality, it still has to follow the laws of where it came from."

"Okay, sure, whatever," Miller went on impatiently. "My point is Limonov can't escape *our* reality through the Booth the way he is. He's, like, worked his way up from spider to wildebeest to human but that's as far as he can go, if Tim here has got it right, and I think he has."

"Thanks," said Tim.

"No problem." Miller sat down, propping his sneaker up on a countertop, his hands gesticulating in wide circles. "Okay. The Booth 'reads' a murderer and a victim, and it scans Limonov and kicks him back, right? It spits him out— yech. But the Booth victims all came back human *plus*."

"You're saying," said Crystal, "he's collecting these abilities they have in order to fool the machine or whoever the gatekeepers are on the other side?"

"That makes sense," said Tim, nodding to Miller. "Look who Limonov targeted first. Gudrun Merkel, who may not have known what she was. She was vulnerable. She didn't fight back. He moved on to Edward Brewah. By then he might have suspected we were on to him, so he sent Emmett Nickelbaum to kill the boy. And your theory explains why Limonov has wanted to find Orlando Braithewaite."

"In case he fails with the camouflage effort," said Crystal.

Miller shrugged. "If you can't get the car started, nice to have the mechanic nearby. You guys got to stop him from killing any more resurrected victims."

Tim looked at his watch. "Crystal and I have an appointment. It just might help with that."

Michael Benson, lugging his laptop under his arm, his thumb clicking a reply to a text message on his phone, took his time strolling to the end of the Pont Neuf Bridge where it connected with the Île de la Cité.

It was a pleasant walk to the island that was home to some of the oldest structures in Paris, and if you knew where and how to look, you could find houses that dated back to the sixteenth century. But Benson was busy with his phone and all the work from DC waiting on his laptop, and he hadn't come to Paris to sightsee anyway. He had come to straighten things out with Timothy Cale, who was waiting for him up ahead with his arms folded, a lock of blond hair almost in his eyes and looking uncharacteristically grim.

Next to Cale stood a beautiful young black woman Benson assumed had to be the British police detective, Crystal Anyanike. And there was a second man waiting that Benson didn't know or recognize. Terrible suit, watery eyes, weak flabby face, everything about him saying managerial bureaucrat; the kind of person an airline sends to crash victims to express condolences and make sure nobody sues.

"We participate," said Tim quietly as Benson came up, "because we trust."

"What the hell's that supposed to mean?" asked Benson, mildly annoyed.

"It means sometimes we trust too much."

Timothy Cale had demanded that Benson change the time of their meeting after his flight, and he hadn't bothered to offer an explanation. Benson would normally be miffed and bark that a contractor, no matter how self-important, is the one who gets summoned. But he had received an email from the Department's Deputy Secretary no less; in carefully worded but strict language, it warned: you *will* comply. Not only was he to go, but alarm bells had gone off for Michael Benson that the Deputy knew about this meeting.

"What the hell is this, Tim?"

"You know, that's the funny thing. I don't think I've ever called you 'Michael' once, but you've always been quick to use my first name. You're everybody's pal, aren't you?"

"I'm informal," snapped Benson. "Fuck's sake, I know we're in France, but you call me down here for a lesson in etiquette?"

"No, we dragged you down here because I have a feeling you call Limonov 'Viktor.' You see, we've been asking ourselves how he could trace and kill resurrected victims from the Booth. We don't think he could see people's lives the way Mary Ash can, and I don't think he can move folks in and out of buildings the way Geoff Shackleton does. He got on a *plane* to get to Germany. There's still plenty of human in him. So how is he doing it? How is he finding them? And then Crystal here thought of something. And I remembered you're a holdover from the last administration."

Benson was indignant. "What the hell does that have to do with anything?"

"When you were still with the CIA, you brokered the services of Viktor Limonov for half a dozen ops. That psycho Russian sold weapons to both the Taliban and the Northern Alliance in Afghanistan, but I guess you didn't know that

until that paperback bio on Limonov came out. What was
it called, *Soldier of the Biggest Fortune* or something?"

Now Benson laughed in his face. "Jesus, Tim, you want to
screw over your contract and go back to Poli-Sci classes? Is
that it? What am I hearing? A warm-up for your fall semester
lecture? If you want to post-mortem State Department hypoc-
risy, go work on your blog! I helped draft the executive order
that called for Limonov's extradition! Remember? That was
back when he trained death squads in the Congo."

"Mr. Benson, you're not very tech savvy, are you?" asked
Crystal.

"What are you getting at?"

"In 2012," explained Crystal, "foreign spies left corrupted
memory sticks lying around where defense personnel would
plug them into CENTCOM network computers. A code
was downloaded into these machines that allowed the spies
to follow military traffic. They could view documents and
interfere with steps taken by the Pentagon. Personally, my
money's on Russia behind it. Could be China, I don't know.
Your DOD's not saying, but it was nice enough to warn
our Ministry of Defence in Britain, which, of course, told
MI6—which told me."

"I still don't know what you're—"

"Your office computer was subject to a regular intelligence
security sweep two years ago," she pressed on. "But *you*
personally ignored a direct order to have all personal laptops,
smartphones, BlackBerries and mobiles checked during that
same period."

"That's about the time you were still dealing with Viktor
Limonov," said Tim.

"The code on your notebook, Mr. Benson, is the same code
used to get past the firewalls and security checks at the US

Department of Defense," Crystal went on. "We *know* you met Limonov years ago on more than one occasion, and you probably traded information with him as partial payment. You remember, don't you? Back when you needed his services in places like Libya and Mali. I reckon you two must have been in a café or somewhere, and he pulled out the memory stick himself to make the download faster. Am I close?"

Benson paled, his lips parting to make sounds, but no words came out.

"You called me here in Paris the night Crystal got taken to the hospital," said Tim. "Right after Zorich slashed her with his knife. My mind was distracted, but still, I wondered why you were so pissed at me for going after Limonov. I just assumed it was politics. I mean, any embarrassing 'State Department hypocrisies' as you call them would have come out at his trial in the Hague. Arms sales, dealing with dictators... But you were scared shitless over something else, right?"

"The Pentagon learned about the memory sticks and debugged their system ages ago," said Crystal. "But Viktor Limonov must know you're a creature of habit. Same files, same laptop. After he got all the information on the Booth victims, he could flit around the globe as he pleased. You couldn't very well go to your tech boys and own up to your mistake now, could you?"

Tim shook his head. "You stupid bastard."

Benson leaned on a stone wall as if he had trouble standing up. "Tim, *I* got you this contract! I recommended you! I got *her* in on this—"

"Oh, no, you don't," said Tim. "Crystal got her gig on her own. You only rubber-stamped the recommendation of London. And as for me, that's also a crock! Justice Department brought me in, and my guess is you volunteered to play my babysitter." He pointed to the gray, listless figure who had said nothing up to this point. "This man's name is Schlosser. He's the first person to ever tell me about the Karma Booth. He showed up at my university one day and claimed he was from Justice, but of course, that was a lie—he's from your department. A little dark corner of your department, Benson. They keep him for dirty jobs like this."

"I'm here to take over as liaison, Mr. Benson," said Schlosser. "And to ask you politely to surrender your phone and laptop computer. There are federal officers who will come and *take* them from you, sir, if you don't."

Benson made another appeal to Tim. "You know what you're doing will cost me my job. You know that, don't you? It could have happened to anyone in the department! It could have happened to you, Schloss—whatever the fuck your name is, you basset hound prick!"

Tim watched. He remembered his own rudeness to Schlosser and how the man didn't appear to be fazed. He was unruffled now as well.

"Mr. Benson," said Schlosser quietly. "I will only ask you a second time. After that they send the federal agents to your house. They like to do it around six o'clock when the neighbors are coming home from work and will be interested. You know... for maximum effect."

Benson dug his cell out of his coat pocket and slapped it into the bureaucrat's hand. Then he dropped the notebook computer under his arm onto the cement before walking away. Schlosser picked it up and nodded a silent goodbye to Tim and Crystal.

"Viktor Limonov won't have the names of the newest resurrections, but it won't matter," said Crystal. "He knows where every Booth is located around the globe. If Andrew's right, and Limonov wants to use one to get back..."

"He can go almost anywhere," Tim finished for her. With a gallows smile, he added, "Damn it. Just when Miller stopped being a smug pain in the ass, he turns out to be right about the end of the world."

Later that afternoon, Tim and Crystal drifted back to the hotel and made love, taking their time, treating each other by turns with passionate hunger and affectionate, languorous care. Crystal called it her "celebration" over her belly stitches being removed. They dozed, spooned into each other. Lying together, suspended in their cocoon of all too brief intimacy.

After a long shared shower in Tim's suite, they joined Miller, who gave them a put-on sour expression, pretending to resent the fact that Crystal had made Tim her choice of lover. Dinner for three was a somber affair at Bofinger in the Rue de la Bastille. As they sat at their table in the restaurant's downstairs under the *coupole*, the stained-glass dome, there was little small talk until after the plates were removed.

Then Miller commented, "You know I went into neurology because I wanted to be an explorer. I mean, I was going to be the dude with the answers! I saw Gary Weintraub in his first documentary for PBS, and I thought, 'I want to be him.' I was over the moon when I got on his team."

"You're still the guy with the answers," Tim assured him, reaching for his wine glass.

Miller squinted at him as if he were a specimen under a microscope and asked, "Why did you go into diplomacy?"

"Why shouldn't I?" laughed Tim.

"No, dude, it's fine! You've done great. I just mean it sounds like you could have been one of those CIA guys like Benson—hey, no face! Don't give me that face! I didn't mean like Benson *exactly*. Or you could have gone into politics or hell, just gone into being a prof to start with! You end up with ethics consulting—and that's cool. But all the globetrotting shit, that's... wild."

Tim was conscious that Crystal was paying close attention in her seat next to him. He looked down at the linen tablecloth and then took in the sweep of other diners reflected in the great Art Nouveau mirrors.

"It may surprise you to know, Andrew, I wasn't very confident when I was young. I never felt comfortable in my own skin. I didn't realize I had a different way of seeing until it was pointed out to me. I got it into my head that if this was true, it would help me if I worked somewhere *away* from English, away from American culture."

Crystal reached for his hand under the table. "It seems to have served you well."

"What about you?" Miller asked her. "I'd never pick you out as the bad-ass cop type."

Crystal laughed and arched her eyebrows. "Thanks! I think? There's no big revelation for you, I'm afraid. They came to me. I just thought: Well, this beats working in a Tesco's deli like my cousin or grading painfully stupid undergraduate papers."

"Anything beats that," groaned Tim sympathetically.

Miller downed the last of his wine. "I didn't like you very much at first," he said to Tim.

"Yeah, I picked up on that."

"And you didn't give a shit."

Tim smiled. "Nope."

Miller turned to Crystal. "Hey, I liked you!"

"Yes, you made that very clear," she answered, smiling.

Miller shook his head sorrowfully. "Jesus, you guys are good at this. I can see that. I don't even know what *this* is—part crime investigation, part séance shit. But you got to solve it."

Tim and Crystal both sat still, looking to each other, neither one able to summon a reassuring response.

"We screwed this up," Miller went on, nervously chewing a cuticle. "Gary, me, the team. *We* did this, so the answer's not going to come from us. I'm not going to take us off the hook anymore with any rationalization bullshit. I'm done. I don't care if Braithewaite gave these Booths out. It's on us! But you guys... Sorry, but you got to think of something."

There was another long moment filled only with the whispered chatter of other people in the restaurant and the clinking of silverware.

"Limonov's going through Booth victims," said Crystal at last. "He picked the most vulnerable, Gudrun Merkel, and then he went after others. If he hasn't got what he needs yet, we might still have a chance. Maybe if we knew who he'll finish with."

"But how do we determine that?" asked Tim.

She sighed. She didn't know. None of them knew.

She reached for her cell phone, and her thumb clicked down a series of text messages from London. She held up the display for him to see. "You've heard about this, too, right?"

"Schlosser sent me details, thanks."

Miller was in the dark. "What is it?"

Tim and Crystal both explained about the strange living death of Emmett Nickelbaum, found shriveled and catatonic in a slum apartment in Brindisi, Italy. Between the Italian authorities' interview with Maria Gigliotti and what Gary Weintraub and others back in White Plains could put together, Mary Ash was what happened to Nickelbaum. She had somehow appeared, helped free Maria Gigliotti, and then she was gone.

Tim had already arranged through Schlosser and Weintraub to speak to Geoff Shackleton via a secure Skype connection that afternoon. The resurrected schoolteacher was fine, living under witness protection conditions in New Mexico. He had been downright cheerful when Tim had reached him.

"No, I can't do that crazy stuff anymore, Mr. Cale. It's gone."

"What do you mean it's gone?"

"That girl needed it. You know her—she explained everything. How you folks are over there in France, trying to stop this nasty Russian character. Truth be told, Mr. Cale, I'm glad to give her the ability. I feel like I'm done with all that Booth stuff now."

"But... But Geoff, how did she find you? No, strike that—I have a pretty good idea how she found you, but how did she tell you all this?"

And Shackleton had looked at him as if he were simple, one of his slower students in class. "We're all connected, Mr. Cale. That poor German girl, the African fella, all of us...I can't rightly explain it for you, but she sort of knocked on my door, so to speak, and she *needed* to see me."

And so he had brought the girl to him.

And Mary Ash had taken his ability away to use for Maria Gigliotti.

Tim brought Crystal and Miller up to speed now on his conversation with Shackleton. No, there was no one who knew where Mary Ash was currently. Not the Italian authorities, certainly not the scientists back in New York or the FBI.

Tim was still thinking of the schoolteacher in New Mexico. Shackleton had wished Tim the best of luck in hunting down Viktor Limonov and again, he had seemed the most *normal* of all the resurrected victims. Even more so with the weight of his strange powers lifted, taken away by Mary Ash. He had defied the pattern of the other ones, changed and then trapped in a world they were no longer suited for.

It occurred to Tim that Limonov would have no reason to try to go after Shackleton now. Maybe Mary Ash also knew that.

"Why didn't Limonov go after her?" asked Miller.

"What?" asked Tim.

Miller leaned forward. "He's ticking them off, and let's say he's, like, going from weakest to strongest. That's our working theory for now, right? Gudrun Merkel and so on. Why ignore Mary Ash?"

"But he didn't," argued Crystal. "Nickelbaum was in the States to kill the boy for Limonov, so maybe he was supposed to go after Mary Ash next."

"But hey, that's kind of my point," said Miller. "She's like, across the country, up in New York. Instead of heading there, Nickelbaum hops on a plane to get the hell out of there and lie low in Italy. He picks up this Maria Italian chick to satisfy his own sick urges, right? Why didn't Nickelbaum go after the girl first or after? Why hasn't Limonov tried himself? And it can't be just because US security is so shit-hot."

"It's a good argument," said Tim absently.

Crystal turned to him. "What is it? What's on your mind?"

"I'm still thinking about 'weakest to strongest.' If Limonov needs the abilities of the victims to camouflage himself or whatever before he sneaks through the Booth then maybe we *do* know who his final target is."

Miller and Crystal stared at him, neither of them able to guess.

"Don't you see?" prompted Tim. "It's so simple and obvious that even his target doesn't get it! The strongest person with abilities is Emily Derosier. She called herself a resurrected victim. She told us that she's still very human in ways, but she certainly fits how Andrew's defining them: 'human plus.' And she came back through a Karma Booth of her own free will—she wasn't yanked back like the others. She came to warn us, but Limonov will use her to do the very thing she's trying to prevent!"

"Jesus," whispered Miller.

"But if you're right," said Crystal, "we got to find her all over again. She's got to stop this bloody mysterious act and help us!"

"I know, I know." He sat bolt upright in his chair. "Oh, God, I'm a damn fool."

"Why?" asked Crystal.

Miller was anxious as well. "Dude, come on, give! What is it?"

Tim put a hand on Crystal's arm as he said, "Wait here for me, will you?"

Then he was off, heading for the elevator and back up to his room.

21

He used his key card and flipped on the lights, moving in front of the easel with the hypnotic, otherworldly painting Emily Derosier had left for him. Since they had met in Au Dauphin, he had purchased two more of her original compositions from the small gallery, the ones that hinted at her knowledge back in the 1920s of life beyond their own plane of existence. But this painting, *this* one—with its vivid reds and blues, its shimmering sad nude and its Cubist musicians—held the key. He was sure of it.

"Miller said chromatophores," Tim mumbled aloud. And as the validity of the idea grew in his mind, he was certain he was no longer talking only to himself. "That means organic, and that means you're alive, whatever you are."

He slid two fingers along the faded gilt of the frame, as if touch could bring this alien stranger to waking consciousness. He was startled for a second as there was, indeed, a reaction. He thought for a moment it was a trick of his mind but the colors definitely shifted and the texture thickened. But it was still the same scene, the café with its nude and street musicians.

"Artists paint what they see or what they dream," he said with renewed confidence. "I don't recognize this café but I

322

know she imbued something of herself in you. So you tell me. A dog will find its way home. Even a plant can turn itself towards the sun. So come on! *You* tell me. Because she didn't just leave you here for me to admire, did she?"

The texture thickened. The colors shimmered. They rolled into each other, and Tim was reminded of the cascades in a wave machine. It didn't happen all at once but by subtle, slow degrees so that when he had his answer and had pulled himself away, he saw that half an hour had passed. The picture now had an almost digital clarity, as sharp as a photograph or a 1930s movie still with its Technicolor hues. And he should know this place. He should *know* it...

There was a knock at his door. Insistent. Another knock. He hadn't heard it the first time. He yanked the door open, and of course, it was Crystal on his doorstep, her mouth open and about to complain when he announced feverishly, "I know where she is."

She looked past him to the painting. It didn't make sense to her, but that didn't surprise him, because he had studied the life of Emily Derosier intensely in the last couple of weeks.

"We should hurry," said Tim. "If Zorich could find her once, Limonov must be smart enough to find her again."

Montmartre. Emily Derosier had painted an ethereal Futurist scene based on a narrow little street in Montmartre.

Every night in his hotel room, Tim had stared at the picture for a few minutes before turning in, and now he realized his mistake. He had presumed all this time that Emily Derosier *must* have been painting a scene of a street in the Latin Quarter, near where she lived. Or Montparnasse—likely Montparnasse because it was the hot district for artists, writers, composers and dancers after the Great War. But no, he had superimposed his assumptions over the image, and hadn't she talked in Au Dauphin about *prosopagnosia*? Face blindness. He had looked, but he hadn't *seen*.

The pale moon in the composition was a hovering, upside-down tulip, but when Tim addressed the painting, it gradually showed him it was the dome of the Sacré Coeur basilica.

"Here, make a right here!" Tim urged Crystal, who was driving.

She yanked the steering wheel and grumbled, "We're going to have to get out of the car sooner or later, Tim. I can barely turn down these streets."

"Yeah, okay."

She turned into the relatively wide, cobbled thoroughfare of Rue Gabrielle and parked in front of a set of closed shops, their windows dark or covered by aluminum shutters. The temperature had dipped, and they could see trails of their breath in the chill night air. Crystal looked up and down the street, which was eerie with its emptiness.

"Where now?" she asked him.

Tim wasn't sure. He was trying to conjure the view the painting had given him, but it was difficult. He had to push out the fairytale images of Emily Derosier's composition and see ahead of the 1920s buildings to how the avenue looked today—and how it looked in *this* light. It was so different. This was tourist-trap central during the day, but at this late hour, the artists making spare money with their portrait easels and the street vendors with their knick-knack stalls had long packed up and taken commuter trains home.

"I... I don't know," he said to Crystal, suddenly feeling like a fool.

"This way," she said confidently.

As he wondered how she could be so sure, she explained, "You used the basilica as your reference point, didn't you? But you can't see it at the painting's angle from here. The best possibility is this way. Come on!"

As she broke into a run, he saw she was thumbing the keypad on her phone. He was lucky for her presence of mind in quickly taking a digital snap of the living canvas before they left. Now she used her phone's GPS.

Then as they jogged up the street, a voice called out to them. "*Oh, please, let me save you some time!*"

The voice had a mild accent, and it was loud, being projected from above their heads. Tim looked to Crystal, and they both guessed the reason. They ran back towards the end of the street where the Rue Foyatier began its multiple sets of steps leading up to Sacré Coeur.

Viktor Limonov had his head out a window, looking out over the false wrought-iron balcony to jeer at them.

"*Yes, yes, yes!*" he shouted down. "*You're soooo clever. She's been hiding in an apartment here for weeks. Here you go! Congratulations!*"

There was a shatter of glass that sounded incredibly loud. The noise bounced on every stone and cement surface of the staircase street—

Emily Derosier's limp body fell six feet onto one of the flights of steps.

"Emily!"

Crystal, shouting her name.

She and Tim rushed up the steps, taking three at a time. The young woman from almost a century ago was still, her body wrapped in a dark navy silk dress, her feet barefoot, as if she'd been about to go out for a night on the town.

Interrupted again, the way someone had once cruelly interrupted her decades ago, in another life.

Dead? *No.* She rolled, moaning, and then she gazed up at Tim and Crystal heading towards her.

Limonov jumped out the window and landed not far away. Then he, too, was rushing up steps.

"Limonov!" yelled Tim.

"You all right?" Crystal called to Emily, close enough now to offer her arm for support.

"Yessss... Yes, I think so..."

"It's a wonder he didn't crack your skull," said Crystal, pulling out her weapon.

"Don't," said Emily, meaning the gun.

She stood, swaying a bit as she recovered from the fall, and then she took a step, her strength seeming to return. Her eyes narrowed as she followed the running Limonov, and it was as if her presence projected itself in a blast of sound. But there was no sound. Except the one coming from the Russian, who let out a guttural yell, stumbling, knocked over by... what?

"*Bitch!*" he roared back, gathering himself up.

When he turned, he was different. Tim and Crystal both recoiled as Limonov bared his teeth in a feral expression of white-hot loathing. But it was the *thing* that was on his arm that made them stop in place, the revolting scrotal mass that gnawed on his arm and then vomited up tendons and flesh. And the other slug-like organism that appeared to be pushing itself into a gash in the Russian's skull. Limonov's hair was suddenly blond, his eyes a glacial blue. Tim was overcome by a wave of nausea. Music, he tasted—

"*Bitch!*"

Another concussive blast of invisible, indecipherable power that staggered Limonov, that sent him reeling backward until he reverted to his old self. Tim felt the nausea pass. *She* was doing it. Emily. Keeping Limonov from attacking them.

Limonov deliberated for all of a moment. He bestowed another smug grin on Tim and Crystal running rapidly up the steps, and then turned once more to flee. Tim gave chase, but he no longer heard Crystal's steps alongside his as he kept after the Russian. Had she fallen back to protect Emily? He didn't know.

Can't let Limonov get away.

Stupid to shout as he ran, but he did anyway. "What's the matter? She give you a bigger fight than you expected?"

"You are so funny, Cale!" came the reply from the shadows above him.

"Wonderful. I know you, and you know me."

Tim could just make out Limonov in the darkness above, scratching his chin with the backs of his knuckles. "Benson kept very good notes. He was quite impressed with you."

"Yes, we know about your little IT piggy-back maneuver. You didn't answer my question, Limonov. Was she too tough for you? Or was it you couldn't find what you need and get across town quick enough?"

In the dimness over the staircase street, Limonov stood motionless.

"Le Santé Prison," said Tim, slowing down, moving more carefully now. "The French keep their Booth there. It's where you want to go right afterwards, isn't it? It's the closest, most logical exit for you."

"It's not as if I'm really a Russian," replied Limonov, looming two flights above him. "I presume she has told you, yes?"

"You do speak better English than Zorich."

Limonov chuckled in the darkness. "I'm a citizen of the world. Just not this one."

"You brought Nickelbaum back, didn't you? Or showed him the way back."

"Yes."

"*Why?*"

"Oh, murder loves company."

"Like Zorich and Ana Tvardovsky?"

"They were not my kind."

"But you got them to work for you just the same," replied Tim. "Because you offered them insight into their true nature. Like Nickelbaum. And oh, yeah, let's not forget your bullshit promise about setting them free."

"I don't make empty promises, Cale. You will see that soon enough."

Tim took two more steps. "And Emily? How did you track her down for your goons?"

Limonov laughed again. "Whoever said it was *me* who put them on her trail?"

Tim didn't get it. The bastard was still laughing, thoroughly enjoying himself, denying responsibility, and *why* is he still laughing? All of a sudden, he felt dizzy, disoriented, and neither of them stood anymore on the steps of Rue Foyatier. They were back on Rue Gabrielle, a few yards away from where Crystal had parked the car...

In the distance, he could hear frantic footsteps on stone, two pairs. Crystal was calling his name. What had the bastard done? But Limonov was turning his head, spinning around and on his guard, and Tim knew it wasn't the Russian who had done this.

Then he saw the monks.

But they weren't dressed as monks, not this time. They walked in their patient, shambling way in the same manner they once did years ago in their cheap flip-flops on Indian mud, only now there were no robes—instead, they wore street clothes and suits, neglected dress shoes needing polish and ratty, torn windbreakers. Nondescript clothes. But it was still them. Had to be. Here was a leathery-faced elder, and there, an androgynous young woman with a shaved head, and another teenage boy with alert, brown eyes. And others. There had to be about a dozen of them or so, approaching with that familiar and ominous practiced humility.

Tim realized that if he stared at one individual, the face defied categorization of ethnicity. Blink, and the almond eyes were round; check again, and a tone of skin lightened or grew darker. Perhaps their Asian color more than a decade ago had been another deceit of convenience.

"Is it true what he's saying?" Tim asked them. "Did you sic those maniacs on Emily Derosier? You gave them some... power or something?"

"She does not belong here," said the teenage boy.

"*You* decided she was interfering!" prompted Tim. "*You* come in and take it upon yourselves to decide who lives and who dies! She was right about you! He's one of yours—a fucked-up renegade—and when he crawled and slithered and climbed his way back up to human form and got stronger, *you* got pissed! So you wanted to discipline him for yourselves, is that it? And she had the decency to let us know *we* can get rid of him!"

"You are not supposed to know these things yet," said the elder monk.

"Why?" demanded Tim. "Because *you* say so? *Fuck you.* You put him down here! And then you play chess pieces with his crazy-ass followers? People have died because of your imperious bullshit! Fine, you found him, so take him out of the game now that you're here!"

"What makes you think they can?" taunted Limonov.

"I've seen what they can do," growled Tim.

"Oh, yes, of course," purred Limonov, nodding. "The avenging angels who stood in the rain and slaughtered a whole village to rebalance the scales! Didn't you ever wonder about the logistics, Cale? They killed, but they didn't kill you."

"I wasn't murdering baby girls," Tim reminded him.

"No, you weren't. That's one explanation."

"He was untainted," said a female monk. "Receptive."

"Oh, please!" drawled Limonov. "You cannot see the truth, Cale? This, I think was their warped idea of what you call a recruitment drive. *Your job interview.*"

Tim looked in horror at the female monk. Her face was serene, her eyes on Limonov. And the bastard was still laughing.

"Allow me to give you some knowledge, Cale, from having been in their privileged club. They cannot hurt you. They couldn't then, and they can't now. They've bound their abilities—their force of will, if you like—to their energy of moral certitude. I prefer to call it hubris, but do not worry, Cale, they are mere wind-up toys when they are on this plane of existence. They come in like soldiers with their pointless little missions, and they cannot deviate. You were moved to this street only because you are a few feet away from me. You are, how shall we say…? In the blast zone, so to speak, yes. Oh, I am sure the British woman, Derosier, told you about the war?"

Tim nodded. He hated this man, this being, whatever he was, but the exile was speaking more truth than he would ever get from the monks.

"And who do you think really lost this war?"

"That is not accurate," insisted the female monk.

"Ah, yes," said Limonov. "Your side '*won*' that war the way Britain won World War Two. Does that give you a fuller perspective, Cale? You're a student of history, aren't you? Think rubble in the aftermath. Rations and ruin and empty lingering doubt over what you think you gained!"

"All due to your betrayal," said the teenage boy gently. "There were beautiful places where petalled and crawling things could live and flourish, but did not need to grow in a biological sense. They lie charred and burnt, yet white in their ashes. There are trenches of light made from your destruction, filled with shallow rivers of emotional cess, breeding infections and despair. And yet there can be a rebuilding. You were sent down here not for this world to be a prison, but as a redemptive opportunity. Now you *stain* this place."

Limonov kept the same mocking insolence through the boy's speech and turned again to Tim. "Tell me, Cale. What do you think would happen if you sent one of these sanctimonious frauds through the Karma Booth?"

"I don't have the authority for that," snapped Tim. "Legal or moral."

"Well, when *do* you, Cale? You watched a massacre unfold years ago, didn't you? Yes, you could tell yourself then that you didn't have the power—that you were an impotent witness. You saved an old woman and a child, and good for you. But now! Now you have the luxury of new information! *You could bring those dead villagers back.* Maybe you do not even need the Booth! Have you thought of this? Maybe if you kill one of these fools right now, you'll get... Oh, five, ten illiterate cattle herders in trade?"

"Nice try," answered Tim. "But they're not from here and neither are you. My bet is your former coworkers stroll out of a Booth on the other side of the world just like you did."

"You are so weak?" countered Limonov, feigning surprise. "You are saying you don't really have a choice?"

Maybe he did. Tim looked to the monks, wondering if the bastard was right. He could do nothing back then because he had been overwhelmed, but what if it was within his grasp now? Emily's words came back to him. *There are natural laws to all things. Even if something fantastic has broken through into what you perceive as reality, it follows and must conform to the natural laws from where it came.*

The problem was that he stood between two evils.

"No."

"No?" echoed Limonov, looking offended that his gambit had failed. "Fine. Let's see if they can die without the Booth!"

Then the disgusting mass was back on Limonov's arm, and the hissing, slurping thing returned to the side of his head. His hair had once more changed, and his eyes were no longer his own color, no longer even the dead boy's glacier blue. Worms feasted within the corneas, and Limonov's mouth drooled something viscous that fell and *clung* to the cobbles of the street and allowed crawling centipede things to scuttle down.

All of this ugliness… but nothing compared to the screams of the teenage boy and the female monk a few feet away, their skin blistering and popping with grotesque ruptures, their bodies dropping to the ground and convulsing into fetal balls, then jerking spasmodically as if beyond the air and the concrete and the distant traffic rhythms of any decent life. They were being toyed with and violated by unseen creations of Limonov's hate. There were tearing sounds and more screams. All of the other monks looked ashen and drained, unable to comprehend that this was actually happening to two of their own. And still it went on.

The monk victims became smears against the palette of night air.

Scarred limbs on the ground like portions of dumped meat.

Clothes that were never ripped but now rags.

A torso.

A burned hand.

"Tim! Get away!"

Crystal's voice. At the foot of the steps of Rue Foyatier.

The monks didn't even care anymore that Emily Derosier was within their reach. They backed away. They were turning to retreat and to disappear. Limonov was too strong for them. *No*, thought Tim. *You come back to interfere, and now...*

He snapped. A switch was thrown in his consciousness, a trigger pulled, and it wasn't out of pity over the slain monks. He hated them. But he hated Limonov's senseless, gleeful carnage far more. He was blind in his rage, throwing himself at the phony Russian, this mass murderer and Booth escapee, and it shocked even him to find himself with his hands successfully around the man's throat, rolling on the hard, wet cobbles. Limonov's fist exploded in his jaw, and then the monster ran down the street.

Through his rage, Tim knew it was insane to go after him. If Limonov could kill the monks, if he could kill the Booth victims, why didn't he turn his fury on Tim? Only Emily Derosier seemed able to hold her own against him and while Limonov might have to flee from her, he had plenty of time to kill Tim before he escaped.

They ran. Tim after this man who was more than human and worse.

Tim lost track of where they were.

Limonov turned into a major thoroughfare where the traffic picked up, and he rushed into the intersection with cars honking around him, swerving to avoid hitting him.

"You're useless, Cale!" he railed over the traffic. "Why don't you wish to kill the monks as badly as you want to kill me?"

Tim looked for an opening in the traffic. There was none. A Peugeot bleated a warning and barely missed him as he stepped off the curb.

"You had a trial, Limonov! You *were* found fucking guilty, and you *were* sentenced to die! You stole and cheated and killed for every extra minute you breathe on this earth! You hunted down those resurrected victims all to—"

"Who weren't supposed to be here any more than your flapper girlfriend! Do you *like* what they can do?"

Damn it. The psychopath had made it across the street.

"Do you think all these things are natural, Cale? A man who grows an obscenity on the back of his head, and a Greek boy who can swap his face with those he knows? A girl who can tell you when you brushed your teeth and went to work and when you fucked and when you slept on any day of your life? You do not believe that they will not get *darker*? Like Zorich?"

"You're raving," said Tim. "You're raving because at the end of it, you know you had your verdict! It's not about them."

"Oh, you want to speak of justice!" scoffed Limonov. "Your own government hired me, Cale! Not once but *three* times! When do statesmen become convicts for the Booth?"

There was a break in the traffic. Tim raced forward, but Limonov wasn't moving. He was looking past him, and now Tim saw why. Whatever gifts he had stolen from the resurrection victims, he was using one now, and down the street, a woman was screaming in terror and agony behind the wheel of her car. She didn't understand what was happening to her. She couldn't understand.

Tim dashed to the side of the street where Limonov stood, but his target was running again, and Tim couldn't follow. Emily Derosier must have been protecting him from direct assault, but their enemy had poured all his hate and bile and nightmares into the traumatized woman behind the wheel. Tim was on the pavement, but the car jumped the curb and followed because it had to follow, the woman desperate to kill the nightmare—

He tried to get away but two tons of steel and rubber and glass slammed into him, crushing him against a telephone pole, collapsing his lungs and ribcage, forcing blood to spew from his mouth.

Blood stopped pumping. Oxygen stopped reaching his brain, and then there was nothing.

22

Naked as a babe, he was born, and naked, he emerged back into life, legs weak and giving out under him as his fingers reached through mist and touched the thick index of glass.

The Booth. Oh, my God. Then...

How much time had elapsed? How much had he lost?

Couldn't focus. Couldn't summon words.

His eyes were wet. Feeling. Overwhelming, cathartic feeling over life returned, because he remembered the agony of blood in his lungs, of his smashed-up, impotent body. *No, you're alive. It's real.*

Then Miller and Crystal were staring at him, taking his arm, and why were they staring at him so strangely? He was back, wasn't he?

Sheets. Bed. And then there was nothing again for hours.

He woke up again in a hospital bed. Crystal was curled up in a chair next to him, asleep. Probably exhausted. Distantly, he could hear a doctor being paged in French over the intercom system in the hallway. The place had the usual hospital smells of disinfectant and mop cleanser and anxiety. He hated the foul taste in his mouth, and would have loved to brush his teeth. His eyes felt tired. He idly scanned the room, and Emily Derosier sat on the opposite side of his bed from Crystal, watching him with an affectionate smile.

"Hello," she said pleasantly.

"How… long?"

"Only an hour after he killed you," she answered. "You fell unconscious once you were out of the Booth, and they moved you here. It's been about a day. I've come by every so often, but I don't like to stay too long. Your friend, Miller, would have too many questions. So would she." Meaning Crystal.

"You did this?" he whispered.

"I protected you from Limonov's attacks, but I didn't bring you back, no. If you don't believe me, Crystal will verify I was with her. She assumed I made your body disappear—fade out like the bodies of those slain monks. Well, she thought it was me or Limonov—at the time, she was understandably upset. Scattering pain and outrage everywhere, poor thing. I could feel you were still with us and told her there was a chance."

It came back to him. Le Santé Prison. The Booth there. Before that, there was nothing but the agony of the car against his chest, and the blood stream in a geyser from his mouth with its coppery taste. No memory of whatever was in between.

"I don't understand," he whispered, still feeling drained. "Limonov wasn't executed. Nobody else was executed over me. So how…? I came back like…"

He was about to say *like you*.

"If you weren't responsible, then who?"

"It's an interesting question," she said.

"I don't feel different."

"Because you're not different," said Emily. "And I don't feel any connection with you over the kind of abilities the other victims have." She laughed lightly and asked, "Are you disappointed?"

"Christ, no."

"Good," she said sweetly.

"And Limonov?"

She frowned. "I'm sorry. Gone. Escaped. I think you know where he'll try next."

He followed her meaning. "Help us then. Help us get there first. Please."

"I will when the time comes," she answered. "But... I think *he* prefers you to try to find him yourself. He's waited for you to figure it out."

She rose and leaned down to kiss him on the cheek like a loving sister. Glancing at Crystal still asleep in the corner, she said, "I think she's in love with you. Just my opinion, but I used to be very good at telling such matters. Take it as you please."

He tried to sit up, the stiff white sheets crunching under his effort. "You're not going to clarify things, are you? A million questions over this. A million more over your life, what it was like back then, your time?"

She smiled at him as she took a step towards the door. "As to the first, well, I don't want to be accused of stealing his thunder. As to the second... I've given you a sort of 'welcome home' gift. You can open it any time when you're ready. And she can join you if she likes, if you two decide to move forward together."

He didn't understand at all, but then she was waving goodbye, saying simply, "You should rest now. That can wait. I have a feeling it will be terrible before it's all finished. You'll need your strength, and you'll need to be strong to think clearly."

There was no point in calling after her. He heard her heels click along the hallway tiles. Then he dozed for an hour, and when he stirred again, Crystal was sitting on the edge of his bed, holding his hand.

From the windows of the private jet, the vast green and brown landscape of Tanzania looked eternal. And for all they knew, maybe it was. It was a nice thing to hope for, thought Tim. In the hot and busy airport in the capital of Dar es Salaam, a black man in a white dress shirt and khaki trousers met Tim, Crystal and Andrew Miller as if they had been expected well in advance, and he explained cheerfully that he was to be their new pilot. Pilot, noted Miller. Not driver? The answer was no. Where they were going wasn't easily accessible by road, so they would have to take a small Cessna plane in.

"I thought Mr. Braithewaite owned a complex outside the capital," said Tim.

"Mr. Braithewaite does not own anything here," said the pilot pleasantly. "He is our very honored guest."

"Then where are we going, man?" asked Miller.

"Selous Game Reserve."

While Miller thumbed through his guidebook, looking up *Selous*, Crystal glanced to Tim then back at the man loading their bags into the plane. "Wait a minute, I've been to your country before. The Tanzanian Game Department doesn't allow any permanent human settlement in the Selous Reserve!"

The pilot, unruffled, opened the cabin door for them to get in. "The Tanzanian government is quite willing to make an exception for Mr. Braithewaite."

Tim and Crystal traded another look of mild surprise. All they could do was speculate over whether the rules were bent for Braithewaite because of his enormous wealth—or the enormous power they knew he discreetly wielded.

I don't want to be accused of stealing his thunder, Emily had told him. Orlando Braithewaite.

The billionaire had given the world the Karma Booth, and he was the one with the answers for everyone. But Emily had left it for Tim to learn where the Great Man was, confident that he would.

And in the end, Tim had tracked down the billionaire almost the same way he had divined her location.

Because Emily's words in his hospital room had reminded him of something.

After he had finally convinced Crystal he was all right and had told Andrew Miller to stop being ghoulish, waiting for him to display "victim powers," he had informed them he needed to cross the Channel and take a trip right away to Norfolk. He knew he would have to do this chore in person.

In a rural locale, there was a large biosphere constructed thanks to Braithewaite Sciences Inc. It waited with exhibits that were open to the general public in the summer and autumn seasons. Braithewaite had made news in *Forbes* and *New Scientist* twenty-three ago, and while he refused to pose for any promotional photos, the teams of researchers from the universities of Cambridge and East Anglia were happy to smile over their generous grants.

It was here that Tim had to come. One of the exhibits on display was a project that looked seemingly forgotten by the research teams, but which the brochures assured visitors was monitored twenty-four hours a day via CCTV. Strictly speaking, according to Miller, it was called biomaterial. It looked like an otherworldly collection of green vine and algae and lichen that gradually changed hour after hour. It would turn into a nautilus shell, then gracefully back to plant life. Then to petrifying wood. And back to lichen again. It grew—slowly, steadily. Twenty-three years ago, it had been as modest as a bonsai tree. Now it snaked and twisted its way to half the length of the exhibit room and stood almost eight feet high.

The researchers and scientists assured visitors that it was growing into a structure. It would take almost two centuries to slowly complete its matrix, but Orlando Braithewaite had announced through a media release years ago that it had been developed as another secret project he was bequeathing to the world. Environmentally sound, a possible construction material with limitless potential, etcetera, etcetera. Children on school field trips giggled through this sunny atrium and touched the lichen, smiling and soon losing interest.

Braithewaite had arranged for a brass plaque to be mounted near the biomaterial, and it was a quote from Buckminster Fuller. Tim found the billionaire's selection oddly cryptic, given how he had put up these lines next to the organism without any explanation for context. Fuller had once said: *"Nature is trying very hard to make us succeed, but nature does not depend on us. We are not the only experiment."*

Tim came here, suspecting the organism wasn't a building material at all, not even perhaps a research project. Not really. Braithewaite had arranged for it to be placed here as another canvas, waiting like the one that Emily Derosier had given him. A message that waited for a time when people might discover they could taste music, and when a sad and lonely German girl could escape into the daydreams of those on the other side of the world.

He touched it as the innocent children touched it.

And through his fingers, like Braille read by a blind person, in a chlorophyll language all its own, it delivered its sponsor's location.

He's waited for you to figure it out. Braithewaite.

For years, the biomaterial had been here, a mesh of sentient ivy and stone and preserved memory that the enigmatic billionaire had planted as a legacy for *him*. For Timothy Cale and other protégés and allies. It humbled him. He couldn't understand why he deserved such access, except that the answer might lie in more words from Emily Derosier, what she had said to him back in Au Dauphin when she had cradled his face in her hand.

"You are so gifted, you have no idea. Haven't you guessed? The others went away and came back with empathy. But you..."

Orlando Braithewaite had waited all this time, ever since the seemingly chance meeting in a rainforest in Thailand. As the Cessna roamed lazily over the savannah of the game reserve, approaching a white adobe complex, he wondered if the monks were not the only ones who might have planned to recruit him.

Braithewaite insisted on seeing Tim alone. In the bungalow where they were temporarily housed, Tim listened patiently as Andrew Miller complained about being shut out. The neurologist was having a tantrum. He was a teenager again who couldn't borrow the keys to Dad's car. It had been a goddamn long flight, and this was a fucking clear snub to his credentials, and for Christ's sake, why couldn't he meet one of the greatest entrepreneurial and scientific minds of their age?

It didn't matter how long or loud Miller vented. They needed Braithewaite. They would have to honor his terms.

Crystal, for once, lost patience with Miller and with a surprising edge in her voice, she reminded him, "We wouldn't bloody well *be* here unless the man allowed us this far! It's

Tim he wants to see. He waited for Tim to figure out where he is. And it's always been Tim they wanted in their game."

Tim didn't comment over this. He was mildly embarrassed at the truth of her analysis. She was a crack analyst and his equal and superior in so many ways. She had every right to resent being barred from the audience with Braithewaite as much as Miller.

But she didn't. Instead, she stood on her toes to kiss him and said with concern, "Whatever Braithewaite tells you, whatever role Limonov and the monks *think* you play or ought to play, I believe Emily Derosier told you something useful."

"Which is?" he asked.

"Be here. You're part of this world—it should have your allegiance. Forget all the implications they keep throwing at you over these other planes of reality. She gave you good advice."

"I didn't realize you two had become friends."

"Shut up," she said, kissing him again. "Go see what you can get out of the old man."

He had expected to be ushered into a white and sterile vault of a high-ceilinged room where the billionaire would be sitting behind a desk, monitoring news reports on a widescreen computer. There had always been something about Braithewaite's image that suggested the lab rat was still playing within the corporate giant. And if not a lab, a greenhouse could have been the perfect setting, calling Tim back to the jungle where he had first met his host.

Instead, a spectacled receptionist led him into a vast room of wooden paneling and high teak shelves filled with curios and souvenirs. There was a nineteenth-century hand-cranked pump for surgical operations. An oscilloscope sat lonely on a shelf, as if packed away, only it was switched on, its signal

line jumping and bouncing away. And there was a chromatophoric painting hanging on the wall—similar to the one
Emily Derosier had given Tim. Its scene depicted a market
in ancient Ulan Bator. The figures in it moved, like those in
old silent movie footage hand-tinted with color. The whole
place had the atmosphere of permanence, and yet for so
many years, the rumors went that Braithewaite was constantly
changing locations, seeking out different countries where he
could avoid legal wrangles over his patents and controversial
corporate decisions.

The billionaire sat behind a scratched, wooden table
under a green shade lamp, studying, of all things, a cracked
and yellowed newspaper. His head had the same shock-
white frosting of hair, but the doughy face had more lines
in it, reminding Tim of the fallen soufflé features of the
poet W.H. Auden.

Braithewaite stood up and greeted Tim with avuncular
gusto. "Look at you! Very good for your forties. Lean and
trim. You've done well."

"Thank you," said Tim evenly. "Not bad for someone
who's supposed to be dead. I suppose I have you to thank
for bringing me back. I *would* like to know how you did
that. No one that we know was executed in a Booth."

"No one had to be," replied Braithewaite. "The woman
who crushed you with her car wasn't responsible. It was an
accident. What I did was merely—oh, what shall we call it?
A fancier version of a doctor bringing you back on the oper-
ating table. Your life ended, your sentience moved on, and
I simply turned you around and pushed you back through
a convenient door, the one in Paris." Watching Tim absorb
this, he smiled puckishly and said, "The *hows*. All the *hows*
on your mind, as well as the *whys*. We'll get to those."

"Fair enough," said Tim, trying to relax, knowing questions were bubbling and waiting to pour out of him. "I never did get the chance to thank you for the scholarship."

"I didn't need thanks."

"You come from the same place as she does, don't you? Emily Derosier."

Braithewaite smiled. "It's been many years. I should have anticipated you would be this quick. We're both quite human, Tim. It's just as Emily and even Limonov told you. If the past is a foreign country, so is the future."

"Then you sent her?"

"No, no, no," said Braithewaite, shaking his head and waving him to where a silver tray with port waited. The offer was so quaint in its antique civility that Tim couldn't resist pouring for both of them. "Emily came on her own. I realize that it's a human tendency of *here* to think in terms of alliances, but you have to get past all that. Let's just say what I've done is greatly disapproved of back where…" He laughed as he carefully added, "Where you might say I get my mail."

"But those at home can't mind that much. They didn't come after you, did they? Like the monks?"

"No."

"Even after the mess you've caused? All the ethical tangles and human fallout? You're a genius—at least you're considered one here. How could you not think it through?"

"I did think it through," replied Braithewaite, sipping his port and slumping into a leather chair. "I was *hoping* for the 'ethical tangles and human fallout' as you call them. Call it good returns on my investment."

"My God," said Tim. "You couldn't have built it for profit! You don't need it."

Braithewaite laughed. "No, of course not! I didn't mean it like that. To make the Booth for profit would be ludicrous. I made it simply to push Man to the next step. Period."

"I don't understand."

"No, I suppose you don't—my fault for not explaining. You know, if you study the history of the sciences—go ahead and pick one, biology, astronomy, whatever discipline you choose—there will be religious zealots who will fight the plain facts right before their eyes. Any reasonable, open-minded person, even one who believes in a god, has to be demoralized by the homicidal ignorance and spiteful violence unleashed on the world, all tracing its way back to a fear of the unknown. And death."

"So you built this technology to slay God," said Tim. He perched himself on top of the table, carefully setting his glass down.

"You're missing the point, young man. And by the way, I'm no gleeful atheist. To kill God or anyone else for that matter, you have to acknowledge their existence. I can't disprove he exists, but I've never been persuaded he does."

"Then you're right," said Tim. "I am missing your point."

Braithewaite shrugged. "At least you admit it candidly. As you grew up and I followed your career, I used to wonder if you're a seeker, Tim, but now I'm sure that you're something much more interesting. Most seekers—religious tourists, if you like, all those belief shoppers—they want *certainty*. That means they abdicate their own responsibility to think, to stay curious. I believe you like being curious. But I also think you're searching for scientific and guiding principles. You inherited a few that have let you down."

Tim knew he was defensive, but he couldn't help himself. "Not all."

"Admit it to yourself if you won't be honest with me," said Braithewaite, his wrinkled hand waving away this minor quibble. "But to answer your question, I manufactured the Karma Booth to spread doubt. The world is drowning in certainty, and it needs more doubt—a hell of a lot more! It's the only thing that'll save the human race. And I need your assistance with that."

"What could I possibly do?"

"Oh, just a bit of intellectual vandalism! You can use the old-fashioned kind if that works. But I suspect your profile is too big now, so you'll have to rely on public relations, negotiation and the ever-reliable lubricant of money. You need to take them back, take them away."

"Take what?"

"The Karma Booths, Tim. Tell the world they're defective, say they're dangerous—whatever gets the job done. I can give you the financing and means to have them stolen or sabotaged, but they must be taken away."

"But—but *why*? We have the technology now to—"

"Oh, no, you don't, Tim. You have the technology, but you didn't create it. What I gave the world has turned into a crutch. I expected that to happen, but now I must take the crutch away, and the world can walk on its own two feet, if you please. What's left will be a lasting impression of *potential*, of doubt in every belief system and a hunger to replicate and improve the process. The focus will turn from trying to imitate my machine to moving up to these states of existence without one."

Tim stared at him. "How can you be so naïve? They'll never allow the machines to be destroyed or shut down! They'll save one. Hell, they'll save ten or more! They'll take one apart and maybe they still won't be able to figure it out, but they'll keep at it until they do!"

"And they'll get the same results," laughed Braithewaite. "After all, the power source never emanated from the machines."

Tim was staggered. It took him a moment to fully comprehend what Braithewaite was telling him.

"You control the machines from here…? You control them *all* from *here*. You always did."

"I wouldn't say 'control' them. I control the power source." He chuckled as if over a practical joke, adding, "I'm Con-Ed. The power company. *They* decide what they do with the current I provide. The authorities of each individual nation utilize the Booths as they see fit. I've only ever intervened once, when I felt I absolutely had to."

Tim followed his meaning. "Dieter Wildman and Desmond Leary."

"Correct," said Braithewaite. "Very good. Leary was a despicable human being. One could argue, however, that in a way, I gave him what he wanted."

"And you did it all from here."

"Well, to say I control the power from *here* is incorrect as well."

"But then how… how does it work? Gary Weintraub, all of them—they've searched for a power source, any kind of satellite signal or—"

"I can't explain it to you," said Braithewaite with a shrug. "Well, I could, but it wouldn't help you very much."

"That's not an answer."

"It will have to do for now," answered Braithewaite patiently. "Tim, do you remember when Weintraub was on television, telling the world how the Karma Booth uses about seven times the power that's needed for the Large Hadron Collider near Geneva? Oh, he was full of juice, announcing how they had confirmed the existence of tachyons, slep-tons, photinos, squarks! And yet the lovely fellow completely missed the obvious."

Understanding dawned on Tim. "All those atomic particles winking in and out of existence... Because the power source you're using isn't on our plane of existence at all... We can't trace it because it doesn't come from anywhere in this universe."

"Very good," said Braithewaite. "So you see, if I want to explain the functioning of a Karma Booth to you, I might as well sit you down and explain all the new physics that work on completely different principles somewhere else." He added slyly, "And you'll have plenty of time for that later."

"Why can't you simply shut them all down to serve your purpose then?" asked Tim.

Braithewaite groaned. "Ugh! The world will still want to rely on this crutch after the power is off. You're right—I can make them silent and still, and I intend to do so, but to really get on with the job, the Booths must be destroyed *by Man* so the world can learn to walk again. Their removal will be that big push."

"Braithewaite, you know this isn't right! The lives you've disrupted—outright shattered! The turmoil and chaos! All of that might have had some justification if we learned something, and now you're just going to take it away—"

"So that something *will* be learned! The unfortunate problem with Man is he doesn't like to jump to his next level. He often has to be pushed or dragged, kicking and screaming. Many years ago, before I advanced into... Let's say where I am confident you and Miss Anyanike will go... Way back when I was living one of my old lives, I became disillusioned with things. People told me well, that's reality. Fine, I thought. *I'll change reality.*"

23

From Tanzania, Tim flew to London and then on to Washington, DC, where he had to brief the President and warn her over what was coming. How Orlando Braithewaite planned to turn out the lights of the Karma Booth, hoping Man would eventually stumble out of his ignorant, supernatural darkness. When the cabinet secretaries in the Oval Office grumbled and complained about Braithewaite's imperious attitude, some even wanting a Navy SEAL strike on the game reserve property in Tanzania, it was the President who snapped for them to stop being ridiculous.

"This was never *our* scientific breakthrough," said the President, wagging a finger. "And if you want to think of it as a gift then I'd say we've done a terrible job of using it. I think Braithewaite always expected we would. How can any of you say keeping these things around is a good thing, given all that's happened? He's offering us a chance to put the genie back in the bottle. Let's take it."

Karma Booths stopped working in Iran and China, in Germany and Greece and Australia. Victims no longer came back. Murderers did not disappear in flashes of light. As the news leaked out and received official confirmations, the media took their usual man-on-the-street polls. People reacted with all the expected variations of spiteful disappointment, suspicion of cover-up and tearful exasperation that loved ones could not be returned.

The resurrected victims—ones whom Viktor Limonov had not hunted down because he had no need for them or no interest—were very good at avoiding media attention. When a victim was tracked down, an enterprising reporter and his cameraman found themselves experiencing anxiety attacks. Or simply mistaking an address. Or feeling the weight of a voice in their heads that told them firmly: *Don't. Just don't. We have no answers for you. Leave us alone.*

The President of the United States announced at a media conference in the White House that the Karma Booth in New York State had stopped functioning and would be dismantled. Scientific experts now believed the energy that powered them was proving unstable, and if something went wrong, it would be akin to ten atomic bombs going off on the Eastern Seaboard. Tim didn't think this was too much of a lie.

He heard from Miller that Weintraub refused to stay in White Plains when army personnel showed up to dismantle and confiscate the Booth equipment. Tim at last tracked down his old friend in a cave of a basement jazz bar in New York's Greenwich Village. Jazz had always been a bond between them, and at four o'clock in the afternoon in the empty bar, the famous scientist and documentary host looked less like a Nobel Prize nominee than a portly, spectacled accountant fleeing his family to knock out tunes behind a keyboard. As he peered through his thick glasses at Tim, he went from playing Oscar Peterson's slow and pensive "Hymn to Freedom" to Chopin's Funeral March.

"That's very droll," said Tim, signaling the bartender. He saw Gary was drinking Scotch so he ordered one for himself and another for his friend.

Weintraub was bitter. "It wasn't an attempt at humor, Tim. Single-handed, you've set scientific discovery back maybe thirty years. You and Braithewaite."

"He may have pushed it forward by a hundred."

Weintraub stopped playing and lifted a hand. "Please, spare me the reasons. The White House sent me the briefing notes. Did it ever occur to you that he could have helped humanity by simply coming forward with what he knows and making it available? Let us work through the ramifications *gradually?*"

"He had a plan. I understand it now, and I respect it."

"I see," said Weintraub. He began to play a Miles Davis tune, "So What," clearly knowing Tim would get the reference.

"As much as I enjoy your passive-aggressive sarcasm through music, you have any other points to make?"

Weintraub stopped playing. "Yes, I do. You were always against the Karma Booth, Tim. I could respect your caution. But now you're asking us to abdicate our own emancipated collective will for this... this *individual*, whatever Orlando Braithewaite really is. As if he's a god! You expect us to follow *his* agenda! You're the one who always stood against that sort of thing."

Tim sipped his Scotch, sighing into his glass. "Gary, Braithewaite will shut off the power no matter what we decide. We've always been on his timetable. We simply didn't know it. You may not see it now, but I think he might have done humanity an enormous favor."

"I don't think I'll ever see it."

Tim downed his drink and turned to leave, knowing with sadness that this was quite possible. It frustrated him because science was supposed to be about the long game, and his friend was not prepared to come watch the great experiment that was about to unfold, that *had* to unfold. He walked out of the bar, knowing Gary Weintraub might perhaps never want to see him again and condemn him for a peculiar new breed of convert. And what a bitter irony that would be.

He flew back to Paris, where Miller and Crystal were waiting. In the time that he had spent in New York City, Crystal had flown across the Channel for uncomfortable debriefings with MI6 and with the prime minister in 10 Downing Street. Downing Street had then called Washington, but in the end, the two allies agreed that Orlando Braithewaite should be left alone. So Crystal had gone back to Paris.

Tim had not mentioned to Gary in the bar that there was another timetable for Braithewaite, for them all. All the Booths would be shut down save one.

The one in Le Santé Prison.

The only door left unlocked that Viktor Limonov could still try.

Braithewaite had refused to admit any culpability over Limonov and the Booth. In the billionaire's view, the Russian war criminal had always been a threat and would have kept on being one—constantly recycled through human incarnations—had the Karma Booth not presented him the opportunity for escape back to his former existence. Human authorities were the ones who sentenced Limonov and then put him in one of its chambers. It was on them.

But Braithewaite had agreed to help stop him.

"You're not worried he'll come after you?" Tim had asked back in Tanzania.

Braithewaite had been stoic. "There is no Karma Booth here. And the power source is safely on the other side until a machine is switched on. There is nothing he can do but kill me, and he knows that will get him little. You see I have no ability for him to take. Oh, don't look at me like that, Tim! I have comforts, but I'm quite as ordinary as you here. Limonov gains nothing, no extra strength to help his passage. I don't even think he'll go after Emily Derosier again. He knows that if he did, she could merely step through the Booth on her own and rob him of stealing her talents."

"You're betting he'll just make a run for the border, so to speak."

"Exactly."

"Why not switch off the Paris Booth as well? Then he has no exit at all."

"You can't bluff him that the machine still works when it doesn't. He'll know that. He's extremely powerful now after all that he's collected from the victims. Keeping the Paris Booth on will lure him out and give you a chance to catch him, to stop him. Of course, it's a risk, but he has to be stopped. I believe Emily explained to you why."

"Yes."

"Good," said Braithewaite. "Then you know he cannot be allowed to cross over. Don't allow that to happen."

Now back in Paris, Tim could only cluck his tongue over how Braithewaite acknowledged their task but implied that it was simple enough. *Don't allow it to happen?* What could they do to stop it? The last working Booth was in a French prison with guards, and Crystal had arranged for a crack SAS team, including some familiar faces from their Ireland trip, to provide extra security. No one doubted that bullets could injure Viktor Limonov. Their concern would be the nightmares he could inflict before a soldier got the chance to pull the trigger. And now they knew that even mortal wounds only delayed his coming back stronger in his next human incarnation.

"Capital punishment," said Tim, thinking aloud.

There was a young Algerian man sitting on the Métro train next to him, gently bopping to music. He pulled out one of his ear-buds. "Excuse me?" he asked in accented English.

Tim offered a polite smile. "Sorry."

The young man returned to listening to his music and reading a French university textbook.

Capital punishment, thought Tim. This is how it all started, with Braithewaite changing the rules temporarily for an issue that divided the world.

Only he hadn't changed anything, not really.

The world was still divided over it.

Viktor Limonov had demonstrated he was worthy of a noose, a firing squad, a lethal injection. And yet he had also defiantly proved—just as he'd taunted Tim in the street—that he was beyond such ultimate sentences. You could argue both sides of the issue with a Limonov, he thought. No one could pick a side in the debate and think he was left with clean hands.

So what do we do with you? thought Tim. Or had Orlando Braithewaite, consciously or not, decided that the great push for humanity would start with how they dealt with this monster? And what a terrible thought that was, he decided. You had to wonder on whom a sentence was being passed.

*

When he caught up with Crystal, she was in the Sainte-Geneviève Library, one of the most gorgeous libraries Tim had ever seen. Its reading room felt like a cathedral—fitting for a place associated with a centuries-old abbey. Tim strolled past long and simple wooden tables with quaint lamps, past shelves of rare volumes, but it was the architecture that stunned. There were columns with cast-iron pillars that shot into the ceiling and formed a spidery network of metal arches for barrel vaults of plaster. Gaining knowledge here would feel like taking communion.

He found the disciple he was looking for at a table in the back, poring over a document encased in a protective plastic envelope. It looked to be written in Amharic, and Crystal was checking a translation. Finally, she noticed him.

"Thought I'd hit the books again," she whispered. "More research on those African gods and mythologies."

Half a beat behind her, he suddenly understood. It wasn't so long ago that he had first met her, and she had been reading an antique volume from the University of London's School of Oriental and African Studies.

"You could say I'm having a crisis of faith," she explained, looking mildly embarrassed.

"After all we've seen, who can blame you."

He was surprised to see she looked abruptly offended. "It's so easy for you, isn't it? Damn it, Tim, I watched you *die*. And you came back—Braithewaite sent you *back*. I suppose for you it's no more than having woken up from a bad traffic accident. I don't know what to think anymore, and you tell me *that's* what he wants! He's got one hell of a streak of cruelty!"

People at other tables glanced at them irritably. Crystal whispered an apology in French and motioned to Tim that they should go. He waited as she returned her borrowed materials to the front desk.

"I don't think he's being cruel," said Tim as they stepped out into the busy street. "Braithewaite."

"Well, you wouldn't now, would you?"

"Crystal," he tried again, adopting a soothing tone, "you told me when you first met me that you believed Heaven is somewhere—that you didn't give a tinker's damn where the road signs pointed. No, it's not easy for me, not as much as you'd think. God and Heaven used to be intellectual exercises that were as neutral for me as wondering if there's life on other planets. You know something? My world view has been rocked more than yours, trust me! You can still have God out there. Braithewaite's freed you in a way, all of you. He's told you that death has nothing to do with God, if God exists. You can keep looking for Him in life after life, on level after level. But every atheist, every agnostic, now has to look beyond what's tangible, what's here—and adjust. Here, just *here* and the stars, were all we ever had to make our case—all the ego packed into what we could point to in front of us or through the lens of a telescope. Braithewaite's a new Copernicus. As you Brits like to say, it's 'All Change' for everyone."

She was quiet for a long moment, moving into him. Then she muttered, "Toss."

"What?"

"I believe I said I didn't give a toss how the road signs point to Heaven."

"Right, whatever," he chuckled and kissed her quickly.

Smiling, she took his hand, and they began to walk. "By the by, I have been busy with more than Heaven and Earth. Something Miller said has been bugging me."

357

"Lots of things Miller says bug me. Can you be more specific?"

"Serious now," she said. "You remember when Andrew asked why didn't Limonov go after Mary Ash?"

"Yeah, and you said, if I remember, that Limonov *did*. He probably sent Emmett Nickelbaum after her. Nickelbaum came to the States to kill the boy, the one who was reincarnated from Constable Daniel Chen."

Crystal nodded. "Right, but Andrew had an excellent point—Nickelbaum buggered off to Italy, and Viktor Limonov hasn't made an attempt to kill Mary Ash at all."

"Then I don't understand. What are you saying?"

"What if Andrew's only half-right? Yes, okay, let's say Limonov has gone after the resurrected victims, moving from the weakest to the strongest. We've seen him barely hold his own against Emily Derosier."

"Okay," said Tim slowly, not sure where she was going with this.

Crystal stopped in the street. "Who says Mary Ash is the weakest of our victims? We know she took out Emmett Nickelbaum. I don't think he *wants* to go up against Mary Ash. I think he doesn't want to go near her."

Back in the hotel, she showed Tim on her laptop how she had traced police reports and then checked with MI6 to collate more incidents coming in from across Europe.

In Rhodes City, Greece, a fourteen-year-old boy had come back through a Karma Booth, and he had been able to transform his features into the face of someone else in a friend or relative's mind. You talked casually about this or that person, and the boy would change his face right in front of you and *be* that individual. Tim remembered. The boy had been beaten to death a second time, raped, and his body abandoned in a part of Rhodes City's Old Town.

Last week, police heard disturbing stories of a young girl, college age, who had visited those allegedly behind the attack. Mary Ash had found the suspects and persons of interest whom the police couldn't charge for lack of evidence.

But Mary Ash didn't need evidence. She could recite the events on all the days of their lives, including *that* day.

She did something to these young thugs.

She did something that made one of them rip the flesh from his forearm with his teeth and *gnaw* through to the bone. As if his limb had been caught in a bear-trap, and he had been left with only this last resort to get free. But there were no markings on his limb, except for the impressions of his teeth. He died, insane, from blood loss and infection.

She did something that made another one take the forefingers and thumbs of both hands and *rip*... Tim didn't want to read the rest of the line on the laptop screen. There was a mention of how the suspect could no longer blink, of course, that there was a corresponding lack of ocular lubrication, but more than this, the suspect screamed and kept on screaming even after sedation.

After *days* of sedation and emergency surgery.

He died, too.

She did something to all of them.

She had started with Emmett Nickelbaum and then had moved on to Greece. In Bucharest, a sadistic rapist had been driven to castrate himself. In Prague, a woman in her fifties who ran a private daycare—later discovered to be a monster guilty of the worst kinds of child abuse—was found near death after repeatedly, obsessively bathing in cleansers and bleach in her filthy little bathtub.

They were haunted, all of them, and those who didn't die right away told of the girl with two bloody finger stumps who visited them and who spoke—always fluent in their language—in a distracted, singsong voice. Reminding them of what they had done. Telling them how their victims would forever be changed and could never be what they used to be. Tim recalled how Mary Ash had mentioned she had never seen Paris. Now she was an avenging Greek Fury, on a warped version of a college kid's backpack tour of Europe, scalding the minds of the human monsters she visited.

In Brussels, there was a crooked man named Jacques Binchois, and far from the Grand Palace and Cinquantenaire, on the outskirts of the city in a grim industrial park, he kept girls and women from China in a shipping container. They were all destined to be sold as domestic slaves to rich businessmen and trophy wives in the fashionable parts of town and as far away as Milan and Munich. When you got past the thick smell of rusting metal chains and slid open the vault-like panel door, you picked up the stench of unwashed bodies and excrement left in the only toilet, a bucket.

Jacques Binchois opened the container this evening because he had to pluck one of his charges out and get her cleaned up. She would need his typical splurging of a McDonald's Happy Meal and a shower, and he considered himself merciful to actually grant one of these human commodities a single night's sleep on an office cot before he handed her over to a customer (it didn't help business if a client phoned him back and complained how "listless and dull" the girl was before she started work).

It was, truth be told, a pain in the ass doing this chore, but he preferred to do it himself. When he had given the job to his men, they had occasionally messed around with the product. He didn't give a shit about that either, but one of them gave a girl a dose, which she then passed on to a customer. That was also not good for business.

So he grumbled and spat and smoked his tenth cigarette as he unlocked the chains and prepared himself for the unbelievable stink. The familiar odor hit him as he yanked the panel back, but there were no girls moaning and whimpering and shading their eyes from the sudden fluorescent bulbs.

There was only one girl, and she was white. She was plain and thin and brunette, and she looked up from hugging her knees on the cold cement floor with the most depraved sunny smile, as if Daddy had come home and brought her a present.

She brushed back a lock of hair, and Binchois interrupted his disgusted *what-the-hell-is-going-on* outrage to feel natural sympathetic horror over the two bloody finger stumps of her hand.

"*There* you are," she said cheerfully.

He understood enough English to know what she was saying, but when next she spoke, he heard it in perfect French. Her light, thin voice overrode all his blustering demands of *who are you* and *what do you think you're doing* and *where are my girls* so that all he heard was, "It's going to be very cramped for you."

Jacques Binchois didn't know what this strange girl meant, but he instantly understood it was to be something terrible. He kept a weapon under the seat of his car, but he had grown lazy and hadn't had any trouble with competition for months. He never took it along to the container anymore. She was a girl, just a girl. He shouldn't need a weapon. But she frightened him. And now she got to her feet—

"Mary."

And then Binchois was no longer important.

Timothy Cale stood in the shaft of light pouring into the great cave of rented containers from the parking lot. Belgian police officers would be coming along soon, driving up with no lights and no sirens because that was how Crystal had arranged it. It was understood that Tim had to go in first. Because if he didn't make his case, it wouldn't matter how fast the police arrived.

"Hello, Mr. Cale. It's nice to see you again."

"Mary, please," said Tim softly. "The police can take care of this garbage. You've sent all the girls home, haven't you?"

"Yeah, they're fine," she said absently, her eyes still fixed on Binchois. "That nice schoolteacher let me keep his gift—he doesn't want it back. It's kind of cool. I mean, it's very convenient."

"I imagine it is."

She looked over to Tim at last and smiled. "You surprised me. I mean, like, I knew you were looking for me. Thursday, four o'clock, outside the Centre Pompidou, Crystal Anyanike said to you, 'Do we get her to help us or beg her to stop?' And you said, 'Knowing Mary, she already knows that we've tracked her. The question is whether she'll come to us if we ask nicely.' You don't have to be afraid of me, Mr. Cale."

"I'm not, Mary."

She laughed her tinkling laugh and said, "You *surprised* me. I guess you figured out I know where everyone is every minute but if I turn my attention somewhere else... That's really clever. You waited until the last minute, didn't you?"

"Yes, Mary."

"How did you know I'd pick him?" She meant Binchois.

"I didn't. Crystal and the police are waiting outside a murderer's home—we thought you might have gone there.

362

The Belgian cops have kept their eyes on him for some time. Like this one."

Binchois—confused, pissed off, frightened—turned and ran towards the parking lot. But Tim didn't go after him. He knew he had to appeal to Mary Ash.

"Mary, *don't*! Please don't! The police are right outside, they'll get him and put him away."

"It's not enough," said the girl quietly.

"No, maybe not. But please... With what you can do, all that you can do now, we need your help for a worse evil than him."

"You mean Viktor Limonov."

"Yes."

"I can't read him, Mr. Cale. He's not like Nickelbaum. He's not like anyone else. I don't think I'll be any good to you."

"Please help us, Mary."

He saw her eyes were wet. Her voice cracked with feeling, and she said, "I told you before... It takes every ounce not to *float*, you know? And it gets harder."

He forgot what she was, whatever she might be, and he couldn't identify where the paternal urge came from, but he pulled her into his arms and hugged her tight. Comfortingly. Tethering her, even if briefly, to his world. She sighed a little and let out a small grateful moan.

"In the Musée d'Orsay," he mentioned casually, "you stand in front of the Van Goghs, and the textures pop right out at you. You never get the same impact from photographs. It's amazing."

She let go of him, wiping her eyes. "You'll show me?"

"Of course, I will."

"That's good," she said, her eyes looking away and her voice again drifting. "I've done terrible things. It's good that you still care enough to show me what's beautiful there."

*

They waited in the wheel. In a special room of the hub-and-spoke design of La Santé prison, with French CRS riot police and British SAS officers fanned out and deployed in the various cellblocks. They kept vigil behind Victorian Age brown brick and stone. The Ministry of Justice, briefed by London, had taken the extra precaution of evacuating the other inmates to Fleury-Mérogis and Fresnes Prisons in the Paris suburbs. Some police officers posed as inmates, and they were so convincing that a few of the regular guards even began to verbally abuse them.

It was a prison. It was one of the most famous prisons in Paris, in France itself. They shouldn't expect anyone to be able to get in. But they knew better. For three days and three nights, they held a vigil. Tim, Crystal, Miller and Mary Ash, usually lost within her thoughts, sitting quietly in a corner. Tim trusted Braithewaite's prediction that Viktor Limonov would "make a run for it"—coming for the Paris Karma Booth because all others had been shut off. And even Limonov had to know he was expected. He wouldn't care. There was only one gate left open to him, and they were its keepers.

Miller didn't disappoint, proving as expected to be the most nervous of them all. "Guess it kind of fits the French put the Booth in here."

Crystal didn't turn, still tapping away on her keyboard, checking reports at a desk, but she bothered to ask politely, "How so?"

"Did some reading," answered Miller, fidgeting. "This place was one of the last homes of the guillotine. Hey, bringing you better capital punishment through innovation!"

In the background, the two transposition booths were perfectly still and silent. There was darkness behind their thick indexes of glass, and no lights blinked on the control panel.

"A guillotine, man, that's a creepy thing to use!" Miller babbled on. "There's this guy, right? This doctor who actually *studied* whether the heads were still alive after their necks had been chopped. He saw blinking eyes, and one of the heads even answered his name when the doc called! I mean, it sounds impossible, 'cause there's automatic reflex and you got cerebral blood pressure dropping—"

"Miller," Tim cut in gently. His eyes flicked over in warning to Mary Ash, sitting in her corner again.

"Sorry," muttered the young scientist.

He had, of course, been present when Mary Ash had first been resurrected, but he had steered well clear of her when Tim had brought the girl back to Paris and ushered her into their little control center in the hotel room. He was spooked by all that Crystal had reported the girl could do. And had done.

Nothing showed on the banks of screens for the CCTV cameras scattered throughout the prison.

One of the top corrections officers walked briskly in, his scuffed dress shoes clicking along the cement. He didn't bother to look up from his clipboard as he said idly, "Your man does not show again?"

"Not yet," replied Tim.

They had no way of knowing when he would show. They had come here for three nights, and even expecting Limonov to come at night was a presumption. Tim didn't know at what point they should admit defeat and have the Karma Booth in this room dismantled like the others. Humanity might have to take its choice with merely capturing Limonov or executing him the more pedestrian ways, leaving a debt of his evil for another generation to pay for down the road. He wasn't even sure that Mary Ash could do anything to Limonov that would keep him from coming back.

"Look who's joined the party," said Crystal, her pen tapping a screen.

Emily Derosier. Dressed in a simple blouse and peasant skirt, looking very much like the woman she once was in the 1920s.

"You called it," she added.

Yes. Somehow, Tim had figured that she would show up, that she would lend her own abilities to this final confrontation.

"She hasn't come the other nights," said Tim. "Which means..."

"He's coming," she finished for him.

She got out of her chair and pulled out her gun. Miller stood up nervously. The corrections officer looked from Crystal to Tim and then walked briskly back out, no doubt to tell his men to look sharp. The only one who displayed no reaction was Mary Ash.

24

Limonov appeared on the surveillance screens minutes later, walking in his confident stride through another part of the prison. Then—

Comet trails. Frames cut out of context from the running loop of film. *Akinetopsia*. What Emily had done the first time they had seen her. Damn it, thought Tim.

SAS officers dressed as inmates rushed out of the grimy, dank cells to surprise and tackle the Russian. He simply wasn't there. Gone through the funhouse mirror of consciousness. CRS men—fully decked out in their riot squad helmets and clear faceplates—rushed Limonov, their truncheons ready. He laughed at them. They met with more comet trails. Up ahead, more police fired tranquilizer darts, enough to put down a rhino. They shot Tasers at him. Nothing.

In the room with the Karma Booth, Miller was running through his personal fuse towards panic. "They're not stopping him. That's—that's not good. They're *not* stopping him."

Mary Ash rocked in place, whispering, "Doesn't make a difference—he's already asleep. Gudrun knew. Conscious control over your REM atonia."

"What?" asked Miller.

"Andrew, later!" snapped Crystal, chambering a round in her weapon.

The police and guards in the tiny screens of diffused light and color suddenly screamed. They dropped to their knees and rolled on the floors. Many vomited. Limonov had done something to them. He paused a moment, standing over several of the fallen cops, enjoying his work, nodding in satisfaction as if a framed picture on the wall had now been adjusted correctly.

And on one of the surveillance screens, Limonov suddenly *appeared* down a hallway, where Emily Derosier waited.

This time, there was more than simply seeing the effect on the screens. The shockwave hit them all, even in this room. It was the forced intimacies outside the Beaubourg. It was the agony of a burn victim, every nerve ending and torched skin cell still igniting in *pain pain pain* and the sickly-sweet smell of cooked flesh in your own nostrils in an ICU bed, and Tim yelled in horror, thinking for a moment it was Crystal who was burning in front of him, but he shut his eyes, blinked—no. No, it was in their heads, but they couldn't stop it. Not her flesh, not *your* flesh, no, but it hurt so much. Crystal was physically fine, but on her knees, shutting her own eyes tight against the horror. Miller was in a fetal posture in a corner. And on it went: a shearing of the most private thoughts, taken away and replaced by the darkest impulses and memories of assault. The urge to hit and strike back, an urge fulfilled in a revolting scene playing out of brain matter splattering under a baseball bat and then the vomit-inducing *crack* of wood against skull. Sick urges of razors on skin. Razors peeling back—no, *no, NO, NO!*

She hit him full force. Emily. Like a psychic battering ram, she struck Limonov with the despairs of crushed ambitions from those lying unconscious around them, the drowning, choking sensations of lonely, broken self-esteem. Shame over pitifully squalid, momentary lapses in decent moral judgment and scatological embarrassments, shame that expressed itself in more than one rutting worm squirming along Limonov's head but not enough *and why don't you*

Simply
Fucking
DROP.

Tim felt more than saw. He felt Emily Derosier throw everything she had at him. The nausea was overwhelming, his head bursting with cluster migraines and all the residual loathing and self-loathing and pain of their battle, and he crawled up from the floor and staggered to the bank of screens, seeing Limonov still standing. Emily lay on the floor. Oh, no.

"Tim..."

He ran over to Crystal, helped her sit up, and they hugged each other tight, rocking for a moment in each other's arms. Tim remembered Miller, now slumped against a wall, tears streaking down his cheeks.

"Oh, Jesus..."

"Andrew! Andrew, it's okay. You're all right, you're not hurt—"

"No, but... Oh, fuck, I'm not. Then why...? Oh, Jesus, I'm so sorry, I'm *so* sorry—"

"There's nothing to be sorry about," said Tim, helping him to stand. "It's not you. They did it, they..."

He didn't finish, looking around for Mary Ash. Had she gone out to face Limonov? No.

Still sitting in a chair, staring at nothing, back to the pensive, haunted girl he had first met. No sign of the young

graphic artist who had temporarily returned on Tim's
guided trip to the Paris art museums. She had smiled at the
Impressionist paintings. Her spirit had lifted, and he had
hope for her then. But now—

She hasn't moved, he thought. She said she wasn't sure if
she could fight him, and she's just sitting there.

And she isn't helping us either. Lost within herself.

There was a low hum.

The control panel for the Karma Booth had switched on.
None of them had touched the controls.

It was operational. There was a sizzle and crackle and lights
began to flicker within one of the transposition chambers.

But they *hadn't* turned it on.

Tim ran out of the room to intercept Limonov. He had
nothing on his side. Emily had told him he had come back
through the Booth seemingly unchanged, with no gifts like the
others. Limonov had strangely not bothered to kill him last
time but had tortured an innocent instead, directing her to run
him down and impale him. All he could hope for was that the
bastard still needed others to do his dirty work when it came
to Tim, but that all the policemen were either unconscious
or too ill and traumatized to respond to his mental whims.

"*Limonov!*"

Unless he just plain killed Tim with his mind.

The Russian was walking leisurely down the hall, heading
right his way and towards the room with the Karma Booth.
As he saw Tim, he let out a convulsing laugh that grew to a
wheeze like a cartoon dog. Then to an insane child's giggle
and finally to a Saturday night drunk's wet bellow.

"Well, look who is back! Are we rested?"

"Limonov, there are still ways to stop you. There's a good
sledgehammer back there. I'll take it to the machine."

"Fine, Cale, I shall give you a five-second head start. Right before I give you a few things to think about."

And he filled Tim's mouth with the angry dissonance of noise, sound that tasted like rust and corrosion, and new sounds that made him want to vomit; all the hedonist melodies at his command, stolen from a mute blond child. Limonov blistered his mind with Edward Brewah's Sierra Leone corpses stinking to high heaven and buzzing with flies and maggots, and when he ran out of those, he scorched the inside of Tim's brain with bloody amputated limbs of Rwanda and the sodomies of Myanmar's Insein Prison, the grisly, slow deaths in Syria's civil war rubble. The mental parade of bloodlust and cruelty went on, but Tim clutched at the thought of: *Ignore.*

He didn't know where the strength came from, but he managed to stay on his feet. Still in the monster's way.

Limonov kept walking towards him, and in his human life, the Russian had been a trained mercenary, skilled in hand-to-hand combat, just like Zorich had been. The bastard could kill him with his fists and a well-placed roundhouse kick if he wanted to. Shaking and hating himself for it, Tim knelt down and picked up a fallen truncheon next to an unconscious CRS officer.

"I must say, Cale, you really are proving hopeless. *What* are you protecting? *This place?* This world? I will be gone from this place in a few minutes! And even if I stayed, you'd be on the losing side. You do not see the bigger picture."

"Enlighten me," said Tim, gripping the truncheon tight. *Time.* He needed time. Someone to come help. Emily to recover if she were still alive. Mary Ash, if she could come out of her reverie.

"It's simple enough," said Limonov, pausing a moment, standing in place. "You know all those Discovery Channel items about so many species of animals and insects disappearing every week, every month? They're gone. Wiped out forever. What a tragedy! Now think about endangered species. And reincarnation. And *us*. You know... all the ones that your kind with narrow vision label evil. Well, it means we will not have to work our way back up the food chain to humanity—those irritating ladder rungs of karma. No more slug, dung beetle, fish, badger, chimp, whatever. Human incarnation, no waiting! Thank you, uncaring humanity, for wiping out the other species! And so here is a new toddler setting fire to cats, a wicked gleam in a little girl's eye. And there is another one. And another. *And another*. They wait, and they grow."

Tim didn't answer this. The truth was, he couldn't think of any useful comeback.

"All your life you've heard it, yes?" Limonov went on. "How the world is getting worse: more serial killers, more pedophiles, more genocide... You never put those two facts together. Yes, *we* recycle. Well, I suppose not 'we' to be fully accurate, but those sympathetic to my interests."

"It has to be more than a numbers game," said Tim, but the words sounded weak even in his ears.

He would have to hit him. He would have to try. He had found the strength to fight Zorich, but he had been armed with a gun, and even then he had failed. *Try anyway.*

"Oh, let me guess!" mocked Limonov. "Good inevitably wins? You already know we are beyond such pitiful constructs. You've met the colonial masters. Now *we* are taking back the country."

Tim tensed, sinking a little on his knees, knowing he would have to push forward and swing the club. And then Crystal was standing next to him, breathing hard but steady on her feet and holding up her gun, aiming at Limonov. But before she could fire, she cried out, her eyes shutting tight in pain once more, and her shot going wild. It was impossibly loud in Tim's ears, and he was astonished to see Limonov knocked back, sinking to one knee as his shoulder bloomed crimson.

"You *cunt*!" he roared.

She collapsed to the floor under a new invisible onslaught, and Tim knew Limonov would kill her if he didn't swing now. The Russian was already muttering words to himself that the injury didn't matter, none of it would matter at all in a few seconds, everything would be different. The truncheon in Tim's hand whipped through the air with a *vooom* sound and hit nothing. Limonov's boot lifted and neatly shot to the side of Tim's knee, kicking him down, and then the Russian's fist hammered down on his collarbone. Had Limonov not been hurt, he surely would have broken it.

Get up, you fool, thought Tim. His head hurt. His knee was on fire, but he could limp, nothing broken.

Crystal. Crystal was glancing back to him as she ran after Limonov.

"I'm fine!" he shouted. "Stop him!"

As she disappeared into the room with the Booth, he heard gunfire, Crystal's Glock. But he also heard the familiar noises of the equipment...

He rushed in.

Miller lay on the ground, weeping again, clawing at an unseen thing on the back of his neck. Nothing there, but still he felt the threat. Crystal still held her gun outstretched, but she was no longer firing. She merely stared impotently at her target, and Tim could see why.

Limonov was facing off against a new opponent. No— an old one. Emily Derosier was haloed in the blinding whorls and nebulae of the Karma Booth only she was *outside* a chamber. Tim understood. When the equipment had switched on, it had come from her. And she must have given him the strength, too, to ignore the monster's mental assault in the hallway until she could join them here and hold the line.

Limonov couldn't have done anything with the machine and neither could they until she had come on the scene. Faked out the Russian completely, making him think he had won. *Braithewaite*, thought Tim. The machine's creator had said *he* held the power source, and he must have bequeathed it to her in the same way Geoff Shackleton had given up his abilities to Mary Ash. Mary... Where was...?

The girl had collapsed to the floor. She looked drained and was panting, tears down her cheeks. She had tried after all. She had clearly tried against Limonov. Her smoky eyes looked sadder than Tim had ever seen them, and in those eyes was now an expression of grief that was eternal, universal. A doctor's leukemia verdict. Crinkling, yellowed telegrams of every mother's son blasted to bits on the distant Somme. The mumbled announcement of the well that had gone dry, dooming an entire refugee village.

They were rendered almost silhouettes in the dazzling phantasmagoria of the first Booth chamber and around Emily herself. Limonov, too, changed, his hideous will expressing itself in a dozen alternating faces depicting hate and ugliness, his taut mercenary body at an angle as it struggled against her hurricane. She wouldn't let him past her. The Booth blazed with its light, promising him escape, and she wouldn't allow it.

While in the flickering shadows near the desk and camera screens, Mary Ash radiated grief.

"Nickelbaum," she said, her voice breaking with the admission. "I enjoyed what I did to him too much. I've got to go now..."

Crystal had come over, and now she and Tim traded a look, both sensing what the girl meant.

"Mary!" shouted Crystal over the din of the Booth equipment and the battle raging behind them. "There's no need for sacrifice! Please don't be a martyr!"

Mary Ash offered her a tight, little smile. "It's not about that. I wasted it. I wallowed. You saw how I wallowed, Mr. Cale, didn't you? I could have had my revenge just by *living*." Another laugh that ended this time in a sob. "A clean new life! Fresh and warm as a blanket out of the dryer!"

Neither Tim nor Crystal bothered to answer. Tim wanted to tell the girl that she was being too harsh. He wished he had a brilliant way to articulate the question that needed to be spoken: How could she possibly put it behind her in coming back? Her rape and torture and her own murder. Who had the right to demand of her anything different? She was entitled to mourn the person she once was. She could still live, just as she said, only to her, it was too late. Life insists on constant, expedient re-invention, and she had floated back to this world a glacier, untouched by the relentless changes she could track in her mind for every soul on Earth.

"We didn't fix anything with what we brought back," said the girl. Her voice was soft, but they could still hear her under the noise of Limonov's guttural yells and the Booth equipment humming and getting louder.

"Thank you anyway for the Louvre," she said. "The Louvre and the Musée d'Orsay. And oh, yes, the Rodin Museum."

"But there's more to see, Mary! *Please!*"

"Thank you. But it doesn't matter."

She opened her cupped hands, and Tim and Crystal saw again the shuddering, filthy miniature version of Mary Ash, naked and being raped, growing out of her palm. Of course, thought Tim. That Nickelbaum was now gone made no difference to her carrying it. She would always carry it, forever.

"Let me fix something before I go," she said, and the shrieking, sobbing thing in her hands melted into her skin, and then she was grabbing Tim's arm. Resigned, perfectly calm, she looked towards the Karma Booth, making her intent clear.

"What will that do?" asked Tim.

Mary Ash turned and laughed with abattoir glee. She was leading Tim gradually towards the first chamber, and he halted, shaking away her grip. "How can killing yourself—"

"*Please, trust me!*"

She yanked on his arm to take Tim with her. He knew instinctively that she meant him no harm, but he couldn't understand why she was pulling him along. As he tried to drag her back, he didn't recognize the sudden strength the girl had. She couldn't have weighed more than a hundred and ten pounds, but she was still tugging him with little effort towards the chamber.

Limonov and Emily took no notice of them, locked in their horrifying duel. Mary Ash and Tim were approaching the chamber at an opposite angle, and Limonov was still fixated on Emily as his obstacle.

Tim didn't understand. Yes, Emily had started the equipment, but Mary Ash couldn't know how it worked. Yet the lights in the chamber kept flashing and now they absorbed her into their sunburst stream, carving into Mary Ash's slender frame seconds before she poised herself behind the tinted glass. She let Tim go—

Physically, at least.

He cried out as a storm thundered in his brain. Lives piled up on each other—thoughts and images from millions, no *billions*. The remnants of curried dishes for orphan children and slices of wedding cake for a Boston couple, the smell of hay on a Montana ranch for a girl of thirteen and a young man's first look at the Duomo Cathedral in Milan, the life-light dying for an insurgent in Monsul thanks to a U.S. army sniper. Life and life and life and too many events and he *knew* what Mary Ash had passed on to him before she walked through the curtain of white photons. He wouldn't be able to contain it all for long.

Limonov was still battling Emily—and winning. She sobbed and fell to the cement floor, and Limonov would not be fooled a second time. The nimbus of light around Emily dissipated and faded. The Russian kicked her savagely in the stomach and stepped over her to head to the chamber, still pouring out its display of pulsing colors and flashes.

Tim ran after him.

"Splinters," he muttered.

Mary Ash had said it once, and he knew now what she meant, and now was the time to use her idea.

We're all connected, he thought.

Mary Ash had passed something along to him, and he had only seconds to master it and figure out what to do with it, but he had no choice.

"*Limonov!*"

Perhaps he didn't need to scream at the top of his lungs to get the maniac's attention. Let him think it's bravado, he thought. Let him think it's desperation. He knew what he had to do now.

Limonov laughed, shaking his head in a silent message of "Too late," but he didn't guess the truth. Tim no longer wanted to keep him from the chamber. *He wanted to help him into it.*

Into the nova of a glass capsule. Into the cleansing light, followed by exploding, shooting stars...

At the last second, he didn't know if his plan would work. The chamber's light bounced off Tim's face and his white shirt sleeves, and the whorls and nebulae forced his eyes shut, but not before he caught a final glimpse of Crystal, staring at him with terrified concern and much more... A tender gratitude and devotion for his daring to make it right. Eyes almost slits with the bursting whiteness, he fixed his eyes on her, wanting to *stay*.

All while he passed on Mary Ash's legacy.

Viktor Limonov shrieked in pain. Tim held on, knowing his limbs and extremities were intact, knowing the light would not carve him as it did the dragon he had by the tail. Limonov wasn't flailing and screaming because of the process of the Booth; it was because of the terrible gift he was passing on. And the thing Limonov feared the most *locked* him in a posture of hysterical, frenzied defiance, his skin erupting with boils, pustules—but in each sore and inflammation was a face—

Tim let go and dashed out of the chamber, slamming the door shut. Limonov, trapped inside, quaked in epileptic spasms as his skin grew a mosaic of a billion faces. And a billion more. And another. The light of the Karma Booth opened him at last as it did every executed prisoner, yet the atoms and vortexes kept on shimmering with the features of anonymous souls, until Limonov disappeared in a glistening topographical map of human portraits. The *face-face-face-face-face* of a palm, with so many portraits like the compound eye of an insect, slammed once against the thick index of glass before the vision tore open into the familiar constellations of the Booth procedure, the horse head nebulae and comets and dazzling lights that signaled Viktor Limonov didn't exist anymore. Not here. Perhaps not anywhere.

"What happened to him?"

The question came from Miller, looking haggard but appearing to recover from his ordeal.

"I forced him to take what Mary gave me," answered Tim. "Her ability to know what's happening to every human being around the world."

He looked around now for the girl. Gone. He had expected it, but still... He had hoped. He'd hoped she hadn't given up her life.

Let there be peace for her elsewhere then.

"Son of a bitch put me through the wringer so I'm kind of slow," said Miller. "He *can't* die when he goes through the Booth. We all agreed he can't die in there, right?"

"Doesn't matter," explained Tim. "I didn't kill him. Not technically. I figured the Karma Booth still processes him somehow, and that's where Mary Ash's ability came in. She saw billions of lives, every minute of them—holding them, keeping them safe. You were right all along, Andrew. Limonov never went after her, and that's why. When the Booth processed him this time, he didn't have just his abilities he stole from the other resurrected victims. He had an ocean liner of baggage—all the dreams and aspirations and tragedies and loves of billions of people, plus who knows how many sentient animals and insects. All the reincarnation possibilities."

"He's not dead?" asked Crystal.

"No," said Tim. "But my guess is that he's split into a gazillion sub-atomic particles now, scattered in each one of us and countless others. There is no Limonov consciousness anymore. He was overwhelmed by Mary Ash's power. Evil fueled him every step of the way, and there's no empathy in evil. So he had no empathy to control this mind-blowing omniscience she had."

"You know, man," remarked Miller. "You compared him once to a pathogen. If that fits then, hey, you've just infected the human race with that psycho."

Tim rolled his eyes. He didn't want to argue, not anymore. "Everybody on this planet has been coping with a spark of a bad impulse since time began. I doubt a whiff or a dust cloud of Limonov will make any difference."

"Sub-atomic particles don't travel in 'whiffs' or 'dust—'"

"Let it go," Crystal told Miller, patting his shoulder. "Where's Emily?"

They glanced around, searching the room, and Crystal checked the TV monitors. Miller poked his head out into the hallway. Emily was gone, too. Of course.

"Maybe she went home, wherever home is," said Crystal. "But what about the others? The ones Limonov murdered? Gudrun Merkel, Edward Brewah, the little boy? Do you think they went... back? I mean to their higher planes of existence?"

"Let's hope so," answered Tim. "It's not like we can ever be sure, but I'd like to think they did."

"Faith," murmured Crystal, with a little smile.

"Never," replied Tim. "Guarded optimism. I'm tired. Let's get out of here."

25

He remembered that Emily Derosier had told him while he was in hospital that she had given him a gift. He could "open it" any time he was ready, and Crystal could even join him if she liked. "*If you two decide to move forward together.*"

After a couple of days, he understood. When he explored the Latin Quarter now, there was a palimpsest of memory that could emerge through his consciousness whenever he wanted it to. *Her* memories. Figures of legend in art and writing sat and smoked and drank and quipped *bon mots* in the cafés, and he heard the gossip they offered her and could recall her replies. But it was more than that, more than insights into her celebrity friends. Those with cameo roles, fondly remembered in her life, also breathed again, her local butcher and her confidante in a dress shop. He was aware of every fresh loaf of bread bought in a market and every barometric shift in political mood as her local neighbors listened to the radio. She was gone for good, having returned to whatever higher level she called home today, but she had given him her era, that age that he idolized from behind a barrier of time.

He and Crystal walked hand in hand on an afternoon down Boulevard Raspail past the Café de la Rotonde, and she told him how her mind was flashing on people she didn't know... and yet she did. Conversations were so vivid, and there were faces she recognized, belonging to strangers she felt affection for. Emily's friends—now theirs. Orlando Braithewaite's necessary doubts and the horrors of the Karma Booth had bound her and Tim together, but there was also this gift that they could share.

"I miss her," said Crystal as they walked on. "Not so much the woman we met as... the woman we know."

"I do, too," said Tim.

Maybe that was Emily Derosier's point in leaving them this unique view. Maybe she and Mary Ash were not so very different in some respects.

Tim and Crystal both had debriefings and reports, people to answer to. Tim flew back to Washington for another session with the President and select cabinet secretaries, while Crystal had another appointment with 10 Downing Street.

Two days later, back in his office in New York, Matilda handed Tim a set of interview requests as thick as a pad of Post-it notes. He swept it into his recycling bin. He would have been happy months ago to appear on CNN or even Fox News, which he detested. It was good for business and brought in the clients. No more, at least not for a long time. Thanks to his hefty fees billed to the government, he wouldn't need to work for months, except for his lectures and duties at the university. And he had no desire whatsoever to speculate on karma with armchair pundits.

Andrew Miller had somehow got his direct line and had left him a voice mail. He was being awarded some prestigious science medal next week in Washington, and Tim was invited to the banquet if he cared to come. He could naturally bring a date, and yes, Miller had a good idea of who the consultant would bring if she were in town, always easy on the eyes—

Delete. Tim wouldn't be going. He decided Matilda could send the young genius a congratulatory card.

He managed to dig himself out of his neglected correspondence, including an email to his faculty's dean over a suggested new course curriculum, when his phone rang. Matilda put Crystal through.

"Some old business to cover before the personal stuff," she announced. "MI6 has unconfirmed reports out of Tanzania that Orlando Braithewaite is in a private hospital. Now that we know where he is, he hasn't bothered to hide much. Maybe he doesn't need to anymore."

"Oh?"

"He's dying, apparently. Pneumonia of all things, in the middle of Africa."

"How quaint of him."

"Sorry?"

"We don't know what dying means as far as he's concerned," mused Tim. "Huh, check that. We don't know what it means anymore for any of us."

"You helped me when I had my little crisis of faith. Take some time off and let me help you."

"As long as it doesn't involve any prayers," warned Tim.

"Wouldn't dream of it with you. We did good, Tim. It's over. Someone can try to put one of the Booths back together, but we know they'll never get them to work."

"I know," murmured Tim.

Matilda had left the television on in his study, and he reached for the remote. Some amateur footage caught his eye, and he couldn't explain the impulse to watch, he just knew he had to. But then the blur and jump cuts were gone, and there was a new item on about a garbage workers' strike in Italy. Despite the Booth's revelations over the infinite, the world was getting on with its prosaic material concerns.

"You sound tired," said Crystal.

"I am. About that help you offered... How much leave time they give you at Counter Terrorism, DI Anyanike?"

A brief laugh, and he was grateful that she could keep a light mood, that she could push the concerns of the Karma Booth away now. Yeah. A rest was the answer. You can never escape the world, he thought—well, not in *this* lifetime anyway. But there were places where you might enjoy the view and dream of simply existing, without a thought for what happened after or what deity might be responsible for Creation.

"I get enough," she answered. "And I can certainly file this rubbish under psychological leave. You like Scotland?"

Not particularly, he thought, but he kept that to himself. The news channel on the television was doing the fifteen-minute wheel of top stories, and now it was replaying the amateur video.

"How about Spain?" he asked.

"Turkey. Nice beaches."

"Done. I'll email you my flight details."

She said great and hung up as he turned up the volume on the television. The amateur video was for a story about big cats at a zoo in San Francisco. Greta, a female mountain lion born in captivity that had known the zoo's chief veterinarian all her life, had suddenly lunged from her cage on Tuesday. She had torn out the woman's throat. The mountain lion had to be put down.

As the digital cam zoomed in, Tim saw the flicker of higher sentience in the yellow feline eyes. Then he had to snap the television set off. He didn't want to know any more.

9 780008 120597